WELCOME TO AVERNUS

WELCOME TO AVERNUS

CHAPTER I

GREYSON BLACK

This novel is entirely a work of fiction. The names, characters and incidents portrayed in it are the work of the author's imagination. Any resemblance to actual persons, living or dead, events or localities is entirely coincidental.

Cover Art/Design: E Scott Clevenger

Sainan Books, LLC
Bolingbrook, IL 60440
United States

ISBN: 978-1-972832-00-4 (Trade Paperback) | ISBN: 978-1-972832-01-1 (eBook) | ISBN: 978-1-972832-02-8 (Hardback)
Library of Congress Control Number: 2026908776

AI usage statement - No generative AI was used in this novel. All finished text is the original creation of the author.

For every kid who wished that life came with extra cool factor,
That friends were as easy to find as listening for skateboards,
And that the scary parts were safely tucked away in a book.
--- Greyson

To E. Scott Clevenger. Who not only makes this possible, but worth it.

Content/Trigger Warning(s)

Blood/gore, Kidnapping, Alcohol use/abuse, Gun violence, Homophobia, Action violence, Parental domestic abuse, Death of a parent, Psychological manipulation, Psychological horror, Discussions of sex, Implied sexual situations.

By Greyson Black

Welcome to Avernus

Welcome to Avernus: Chapter I

By Greyson Black & E Scott Clevenger

The Manticore's Shadow

War of Night

Old Bones, Old Ways

WELCOME TO AVERNUS

CHAPTER I

Chapter ONE

Welcome to Avernus

I'd never known someone so in love with the Mob as my dad. As stupid as it sounded, as unbelievable as it was, that's actually why we were driving all the way to northern New York, in a shiny new car. All because of my dad's obsession with the Mob.

My dad had joked all my life that he worked for the Mob. He thought it was hilarious. There was an urban legend claiming the pharmacy chain he worked for only existed as a laundering front for a crime family out of New York City, and he loved to think that being a store manager at one of their locations made him "connected". So, he always joked that he "worked for the Mob" whenever he got the chance.

It was garbage, of course. He was a pathetic manager at a rundown drug store, and he was lousy at it. Of course, Mom wasn't much better. My sweet mother thought she had won the lottery when she got knocked up by an honest to goodness big shot manager, while he thought he was in hog heaven for getting to marry a stripper. For fifteen years they had been unhappily-ever-after, angry at each other for their failures, and the accident that was me. I mean, they were perfect for each other.

But now, all their dreams were coming true. After all those years of being a screw up, drifting from lousy job to lousy job, Dad finally had gotten a real one. And what was he doing, you ask? He was going to be getting paid more than three times his manager's pay, to go be a bookkeeper. Not even a full accountant, just a bookkeeper.

And why was he thrilled, aside from the money? He said he was legitimately going to be working for the Mob. Like the actual, for real, Sicilian Mafia. Or what's left of them in the good ol' US of A. I'm not sure I really believed it, but Dad was thrilled. I mean, why would a New York Mob family pick up some nobody from Alabama? Dad claimed they found him from the drug store he managed.

So here we were, finishing up the second of two long-ass days in our new car, completing our drive from Alabama to northern New York. "Upstate" they call it. It would be bad enough if I could have said we are moving to a place like Albany, but apparently, we weren't even stopping there, but going even further north, to some empty area called "New Russia". Kill me now.

Alen and Lisa were my two best friends from back home. But while Lisa had been cool with my move, Alen had fallen over laughing when I told him where we were moving. He said he just knew I was going to get jumped by a gang, or get mugged, or get run over by a taxicab. When I asked him what the hell he was talking about, he said that kind of stuff happened all over New York City. When I told him I was moving to the state of New York, and not New York City, he asked me, "What's the difference?" I have a moron for a best friend.

Had, I guess.

We finally pulled into the parking lot of the Avernus Inn and Suites around nine at night. I was surprised to see it was a really nice hotel, not some fleabag motel like we'd stayed at the night before. The place was really corporate-looking, something like a Hilton or Marriott, all shiny neon and imposing height. The parking lot was barely half full, but most of the cars were black and expensive looking, and most of them looked alike. Shiny black SUVs with tinted windows. Not what you'd expect at a small-town hotel.

I got out of the car with the parental units, and the moment I climbed out, it was like a weighted blanket pressed down on me. The dark of the night fought against the glaring lights from the building before us. I thought it might have been the shock of the unexpected cold added to the extremely long drive, but it was ominous for sure. Once we got inside, I was even more surprised to see there were several people behind the counter, even this late, two guys and a girl. And they were actually wearing uniforms, in a fairly stylish blue and grey. The older of the two men behind the counter looked up.

"Ah, Mr. Docker and family, I presume. Welcome to the Avernus Inn and Suites. We have been expecting you."

The dude was definitely weird looking. He was bald, with a long, thin face, and was over six feet tall. I couldn't tell his age. He could have been thirty or fifty, and looked like some bad horror movie caricature of a man. I think my parents were surprised at being recognized and greeted without so much as asking for ID. Before they could really react, the man snapped his fingers and the younger two hurried from behind the counter. The girl stopped short of my dad, giving her head a slight bow.

"If you could please give your car keys to Richard, here," she said, "he will take care of parking your car and bringing in your luggage."

My dad looked completely in over his head, but he fished into the pocket of his jeans and surrendered his keys. Satisfied, the girl motioned for us to follow her. The elevator ride was awkward even though we were only going up one floor, mostly because my parents didn't know how to act with such controlling treatment. I found it hilarious, because they were getting a taste of how adults usually treated kids like me.

As we made our way down the second-floor hallway, the girl finally spoke again. "My name is Mina, by the way. We have already been contacted by your company, and the bill is already taken care of. We were instructed to let you know you should enjoy your stay. If you need anything at all, just pick up the phone in your room. Zero will get you the front desk. One will connect you to Room Service. Nine will connect you to an outside line."

Halfway down the hall from the elevator, Mina stopped at room 210.

Popping the door open, she gestured for us to all enter.

I groaned inwardly when we walked in. It was a nice room. Much better than the ratty motel we stayed in the night before. Much cleaner, bigger room. It had a nice king sized bed, a sweet 40-inch or something TV, and even a table with two chairs. But there were no options here for me to sleep. Last night, it had been either the floor or the car. The car hadn't been bad. But that was like eight hours south, and a lot warmer. It was only nine o'clock and already around freezing outside. The car was going to be an impossibly chilly option.

I was debating my choices or lack thereof when Mina started talking again. "I do apologize, but the dining room closed at nine. However, you are free to take advantage of the minibar here in the room, and the kitchen is open for room service twenty-four hours a day. Any charges for either are charged to the room and already taken care of, so please avail yourselves."

She stepped in and laid a pair of electronic key cards on the corner of the dresser below the TV. "Richard should be up in a few minutes with your luggage," Mina added. "Also, I must apologize. We tried to arrange a suite for you, but they are currently all booked. Therefore, Jason, if you will please follow me? Since we were unable to arrange a suite with separate bedrooms, we have you booked in the room next door, in 212."

My father scoffed, "Why bother? A new room's a waste for this punk."

"I understand your concern," said Mina with a small smile. "This was an arrangement by your company, and not an expense you need to worry about, Mr. Docker." She paused, then added, "However, I suppose I do understand your concern. If you would prefer, we can bring up a foldaway cot for your son? We thought you two adults might prefer some privacy after several days on the road together. Gosh! All the way from Alabama?"

Her last line was sarcastic as hell, but Dad didn't catch it. He ate it up. He was being fawned over, and was playing right into her hands. I wanted to laugh, but didn't want to get yelled at. She paused, waiting to see how my dad was going to handle this. Seriously, if he thought I was going to sleep on a goddamned hide-a-bed when I could have an actual room, he was insane. But I knew it wasn't a risk anyway. She'd hooked him with the idea of having me out of their hair, and for free.

"Fine," he said finally. "Take him." Then turning to me, he added, "Jason, if you embarrass me, we will have words."

I didn't even bother answering him. He was basically showing off. Marking his territory. Pissing all over the walls and floor. Mina was completely cool about it, though.

She nodded and said, "Please enjoy your stay. And no need to worry, any alcohol has been removed from the minibar in 212."

Then she smiled and put her hand on my shoulder to motion me out of the room ahead of her. She took me next door, like literally next door. Like there was probably six inches of wall between our doors.

"Relax, Jason, I know what I'm doing," she said with a laugh. I think she felt my shoulders drop slightly at how close to their room I still was. "This way you are sharing a wall with your TVs back to back, instead of your beds."

"Ew," I chuckled. "No way do I want to think about that. I hear it enough as it is."

Mina opened the door to my room and pushed me inside, still steering me with her hand on my shoulder. As we walked into my room, she took things a step further by reaching around me and slipping my key card into the front pocket of my jeans. I have to admit, I blushed at her touch. I mean, I'm fifteen. Teenage guys like me react to a stiff breeze. When I'm forced to label myself I say I'm gay. But I don't think I'm gay-gay. Maybe more like eighty-five percent gay, fifteen percent pan? And the pixie cut hair she had was a look I go for in a lot of my female friends.

"Your parents seem like a real piece of work," she said silently. "Richard should be up any minute with all of your bags. Want me to hang out for a minute to make sure you get your own bags in here okay?"

"Naw, I'll be good," I said.

Her idea was sound. Grab my bags before I had to deal with going into the next room. If I had my way, I wasn't going to see my parents again for the next twenty four hours. Even still, I didn't really want this woman to see my ratty bags. My parents went out with their signing bonus and grabbed two shiny new suitcases for themselves, along with some shiny new clothing to wear the next few days while they met all the new people. I had to deal with using my school backpack and an old duffle bag from soccer.

"Well if you need something to do, the TV has a full cable package," Mina said as she made her way back toward the door. "Watch out though. It does have Pay-Per-View that will get paid for by your dad's new company." She winked at me, then whispered, "but they will probably tell him if you order porn."

Please, just let the floor swallow me whole. I blushed like mad at the idea of her knowing I watched porn. Next, she was going to tell me to keep it down while I jerked it tonight.

"Thanks for the advice," I managed to mutter. Thank God we heard someone out in the hall. Sure enough, it was Richard with the luggage. I slipped past Mina real quick, muttered an inaudible "thanks" to the dude as I grabbed my two bags, and slipped back into my room. She grinned at me as I did so, touching my cheek with her hand as I tried to grab at the door.

Looking conspiratorially behind her to make sure no one could hear her, while Richard organized the suitcases on his cart, Mina said softly, "You know, you're pretty cute. You are going to be popular here."

If I thought I was blushing before, it was nothing to now. But now there was a touch of what, pride? hope? in my thoughts at her compliment this time. But as I was retreating back into my room and getting the door shut, I heard the other guy out in the hall, Richard, muttering something to Mina.

"Damn. August is sick. He put them in 210? I thought we were being nice to these guys!"

CHAPTER TWO

UNUSUAL HOSPITALITY

I slowly walked around the room, running my fingers over the different surfaces surrounding me, kind of losing myself in the moment. It was a mirror image of my parents' room, including a king size bed of my very own. I noticed on the table there was a folder with the hotel's name surrounded by roses. The freaky part was that the flowers were bleeding. Not just drawings of blood. Giant glistening drops of crimson ran down the edges of the cover.

I blinked, and I was no longer seeing splotches of blood, but instead lacy and delicate rose petals drawn fluttering down the page. I must have been more tired than I thought. Nervous but curious, I opened the folder. There were several pages inside, including a channel guide, what looked like a list of some local restaurants, and then the Holy Grail, a room service menu.

Forgetting the imagined images, I felt an almost naughty sense of excitement as I looked through the items on order. I'd never been someplace with room service before. It felt exotic. Thrilling. Forbidden, even. Like I was breaking some unspoken rule by treating myself. My hands were practically shaking as I picked up the phone. What number did Mina say to dial? Duh, it was right there on the front of the menu.

"Room service. What can we get for you this evening?" said a pleasant male voice on the other end of the line.

"Um, do I just tell you what I want to get?" I asked. Real cool. Why did I sound so nervous?

"Absolutely, Master Jason. What can I get for you?"

How did he know who I was? Caller ID, probably. And Master Jason? Must be a New York thing, I guess. "Um, can I get a hamburger?"

"Absolutely, sir. Standard, it comes with lettuce, tomato, onion, mayo, and ketchup. Do you want everything? And would you like to add cheese?"

"Um, sure. I guess load it up. And it says it comes with fries? Sorry, I don't really know how this works."

He laughed, but it didn't sound like it was meant in a bad way, like at me or anything. "Don't worry, I'll hook you up. Are you sure a burger and fries are all you want? I mean, we have many different offerings. We have steaks, seafood, and plenty of other options."

"Wow, um no. A burger should be good. Thanks, dude."

"I'm glad to hear I am worthy of being a 'dude'," he chuckled goodnaturedly. "Well sit back and I hope you enjoy your evening. Your food should be up in approximately twenty minutes. And if you think of something else you would like, please call us back, or dial zero for the front desk."

And with that, the line went dead. I cut the TV on and started flipping channels. Adult Swim was starting an episode of Bob's Burger, so I stopped there and dug into my backpack to find my phone charger. As I started checking my phone for messages and such, a weird shudder went up my spine. You know the feeling when someone is hate-staring at you? From far away, like from across the cafeteria? Yeah, that's what it felt like. I tried to ignore it and went back to my phone. The curtains were closed and I was on the second floor. There was nobody watching me, but it sure felt weird.

I relaxed and in no time there was a knock on my door. When I opened it, I was met by an amazing looking guy. Early twenties probably, dark tanned skin, black eyes flanking a hawk-like nose, and shiny black hair riding down on both shoulders. He was wearing a uniform similar to Mina and the others from the lobby, except he was wearing a long white chef's coat over it. He was also standing behind a rolling server's cart.

"Good evening. My name is Devon. We spoke on the phone. May I come in, please?"

I mumbled something incoherent as I stepped back to let him past me. He immediately made his way to the table, and with a level of efficiency that absolutely intimidated me, set a spread with white linen and everything.

"I apologize, but we neglected to discuss drinks, so I brought you a variety of pop. I've got Coca Cola, Sprite, and Dr. Pepper." As he spoke, he set two cans of each on the table. "Any you don't want, just toss them in your minifridge for later. If you would rather something else, I would be happy to fetch it for you. Tea, milk, coffee? It would have to be non-alcoholic, I'm afraid."

"Darn," I laughed. "There goes my plans for the evening."

Though I was surprised when I saw everything he was laying out. It was not exactly "just a hamburger", for sure.

"Um, dude? I don't think I ordered all this."

I was starting to laugh a bit more by this point. He had a plate with a really nice looking burger sitting on a plate, the top and cold toppings set on a separate side. Two different slices of cheese were melting on top of a burger that I swear was an inch thick. He had set two smaller plates beside the main one, each covered with a white cloth square. He pulled each back to show me one was a plate absolutely loaded with crispy crinkle fries, and the other a healthy portion of giant onion rings. But from his tray he also set out smaller bowls of cottage cheese and another of what looked like peaches, but they were more white. Maybe pears?

Then he set out a final plate with a giant slice of lemon cake with some kind of drizzle all over it. Then he grinned and popped open a lidded box. From inside he pulled out an honest to God banana split in a clear plastic container, that he walked over and put in the freezer portion of the minifridge.

Putting his finger to his lips in a "shushing" motion, Devon said with a conspiratorial grin, "I told you I was going to hook you up. Oh, and don't feel bad if you can't finish it all. Hope you enjoy." For a half a moment, his smile seemed almost predatory. As he made his way to the door with the cart, he stopped abruptly. "Oh, I almost forgot." Then he dipped into the underside of the cart and pulled out a white plastic shopping bag. "For later," he said, handing it to me. I looked inside, and there were like, a half dozen bags of single serving chips in a couple of types, along with a couple of Payday bars, some Skittles, and a few small bags of sour gummy worms. A thousand thoughts went through my mind, but before I could put words to any of them, the door was closing and I was on my own.

The food was amazing. Near orgasmic. And there was enough to feed three of me. I was lucky to eat half the burger, a third of the fries, and totally stuffed myself with like four of the giant, amaze-balls onion rings. Like, I've seen pro cooking shows that couldn't compare to how this food tasted. Seriously. In a hotel? This late? I don't know. Maybe this is normal and I'm just not used to it. I've never been able to eat fancy foods like this. My parents didn't necessarily starve me, but for us, fancy eating out was going to Arby's instead of McDonald's. I felt almost guilty getting treated to food this supernaturally good.

By the time I had stuffed myself I was restless. I dumped out the contents of my sports bag to grab the skateboard laid across the bottom. Remembering how cold it was outside but having nothing better, most of us in Alabama don't even own a real coat, I dug out a second hoodie and put it on. Checking that my room key was still in my pocket, and blushing again as I remembered how it had gotten there, I grabbed my phone and my skateboard and quietly made my way out into the hallway, making sure my door didn't slam shut.

I made my way downstairs nervously, knowing how most "civilized" people reacted to seeing a skateboard. As I exited the elevator, I saw that only Richard was at the front desk. As I crossed the lobby, he looked up, noticing me, and gave a small nod. His stare was unblinking, almost chilling. Like the weird smile of Devon's, it went away as fast as I had noticed it.

As I made it about halfway to the front doors, he said just loud enough for me to hear, "The outer doors lock at midnight, but after that your key card will open the front doors. And I'll be right here all night. Tap on the door if you can't get in, or call this number." He held out a business card and motioned for me to come over to him. As I grabbed the card from his hand, he said, "Turn left out of the parking lot, and go down the road about six hundred yards or so. The lot between us and the old warehouse has some culverts and tunnels that should give you what you need. Are you sure you don't need more than your hoodie?"

"I'll survive. Thanks, dude."

Who knew I could find someone cool around here? It gave me hope. He didn't seem to be hitting me with that disapproving look like most people did. I had to have imagined his creepy stare. When I hit the outside air, I did a double take and almost turned right around. It felt like it had dropped another few degrees since we got here. Still, there was no wind, so that was a blessing.

True to his word, the area out behind the hotel was amazing. It was decently lit so I could see what I was doing, had some awesome surfaces, and was far enough away that I knew guests in the hotel weren't going to be annoyed with any noise I was making. The grass around the road was covered in snow, but it seemed to have melted off the pavement in all but the deepest culverts. That was a shame, because those could have been nice to ride. The biggest downside was that even with the hoodies, I was freezing. But no guts, no glory, right?

I had been grinding for maybe half an hour when I started getting that feeling again.

Goosebumps ran up my arms and I felt a shiver down my spine. My brain screamed at me that I was being stalked, or at least being watched. But seriously, it had to just be the dark and the cold. I mean, I was out here in a bubble of light from the street lamps, surrounded by a sea of darkness and shadows. Anyone would feel a little spooked, right?

I did my best to ignore my paranoia. But it just wouldn't be ignored, like the dread you get when your foot is hanging off the edge of the bed. I stopped at the lip of the culvert I was on, popping my board up into my hand, and looking around. I couldn't see anything at first, but as I looked past the lighted area, I could see movement. Not people. Probably the breeze playing with the grasses. After all, I had seen on the way in that the other side was a field, although I didn't get why the grass would be swaying, since I felt no wind, only blistering cold. I felt uncomfortable. Exposed and vulnerable. Some indefinable feeling, almost a force, washed over me.

I looked around, trying to find what it was I might be feeling. Whether there really was someone out here with me. I looked back to the hotel, seeing that random windows were lit up all along the second floor. As I looked over the building, I first noticed the portions of the first floor that I could see did not seem to have any illuminated windows. Random, but whatever. But I also saw that the central third of the hotel had a third floor. I hadn't realized, but that was why the front of the place had seemed to tower so high. I was going to double check when I went back in, but I was pretty sure the elevator had not had any indication of anything more than two floors.

Then I noticed a group of lights subtly flashing on the roof of that tallest section. But I realized they weren't flashing. There were people walking back and forth in front of them. I was insanely curious, but at the same time, kind of afraid to know. I started walking back to the hotel, ready to get back into the safety of my room.

I rounded the front of the hotel to find a quad of suited men standing outside under the drive-up awning, eyes scanning the parking lot. In their midst stood another man, his shorter height making him stand out as much as his looks. I would have killed for his fashion sense. He was standing right under the lights, which gleamed off his glossy black skin-tight three piece suit. Over that, he was wearing a wide, loose fitting silk trench coat, with long, silky black hair that lost itself in the material. His whole look gave a Neo-Asian vibe that came straight out of an Anime.

As I approached, I was able to see that the dude's trench coat even had a massive hood on the back. As I got closer, I noticed a few last details that made me wish I didn't have to walk past them to get inside. Two of the goons were clearly carrying guns under their suit jackets. But the other two were making my blood go cold, when I saw they had actual machine guns on slings under their jackets. The last jokes I had about this place really being part of the Mob drained out of me, like the piss I almost lost.

The Asian-looking dude openly stared at me as I cautiously approached. The look on his face was really creepy. He wasn't smirking like someone trying to intimidate me. It was more like disbelief. Like he knew me, and was surprised to find I was standing in front of him. He was seriously freaking me out. I actually slowed my walk and pulled out my phone. I was two seconds away from backing away and calling Richard at the desk.

I definitely decided that cowardice was the best policy here, and I started backing away. Then the man gave the smallest of smiles, before opening his mouth and running his tongue across the edges of his lips. I had thought his eyes were black, but he must have had some funky contacts in, because he shifted slightly, and there was an almost metallic orange flash to them.

Then the world went dark.

CHAPTER THREE

EXPLORATION

The next thing I knew, I was waking up groggily. I was in the king size bed up in my hotel room. There was sunlight cutting in around the curtains, and my pants and shoes were gone.

What the hell?

Checking my phone, I saw that it was only a few minutes after seven. I really wanted to roll over and not deal with... whatever happened last night. But that wasn't an option. I was miserable with discomfort. It took me a moment to wake up enough to realize what was wrong. First, I had socks on in bed. Seriously, who the hell sleeps with socks on? I also felt pretty grimy. A full day in the car, and then I hadn't taken a shower before sleeping. Well, that was going to be the first thing to fix.

I stripped off everything else and headed to the bathroom. Standing under the hot water felt divine. Fortunately, the skating time, short as it was, had let me stretch out any stiff muscles from being trapped in the car for hours on end. Well, almost all the "stiff" muscles. Hehe. I thought about taking care of that, but oddly I didn't really feel the need, even though I hadn't taken care of business last night before bed. But no dwelling on that. I don't need to be thinking about last night. Not until I can make sense of it, at least.

I walked back into my room, still kind of drying myself off, and froze. I had only just realized that the table was cleared off. So was the nightstand and the top of the fridge. I hadn't done anything with my extra food before going out skating, planning on having a quick snack before bed. But now there was no food. Running the towel through my hair, I opened the fridge. The extra Cokes were in there, and opening the little flip-up door, I saw the banana split was still in the little freezer section. I shut the fridge and walked over to check the trash can. It was empty as well.

Somebody had obviously been in here and cleaned everything up while I was asleep. Creepy. And they had brought me up here and put me in bed. Creepier. And they had undressed me. It made my skin crawl in a way I wasn't used to. Unless I sleep-walked up from the outside last night?

I jumped when my cell phone rang, jolting me out of my thoughts. I picked it up to see the screen. Ugh, Mom. I swiped up.

"Hi, Mom."

"Mornin', Honey. My, you actually sound awake. I expected to have to drag you kickin' and screamin' out of bed this mornin'," she said. God, what did I do to deserve her being so full of pep this early in the morning?

"Yes, Mom," I said with a deadpan lack of enthusiasm. "The world has come to an end. I'm actually up."

"Now come on, Jason," she reprimanded me. "That's not an attitude I want to hear out of you, even if it is the ass crack o' dawn."

"Sorry, Momma."

"Come on downstairs and have breakfast with me. I'm about to head out of our room now." I could hear her rustling around with something. "After all, Jase, we've got a lot to get done today."

I started to say, "Yes, Ma'am", but was cut off mid word when she hung up. Huh? What was this all about now? What did she mean, "a lot to get done"? I wasn't starting at my new school for another week. Even our house wasn't supposed to be ready for us for another couple of days. What did we really have to do that couldn't have waited until noon? Or tomorrow?

Great, so now I don't know what we are doing today, so how should I dress? Well, business casual it is. A clean pair of jeans, a metal band T-shirt, and a black zip-up hoodie. Oh, and my ever present Cons. I took a few minutes to run some gel through my hair and brush it out. Once I was presentable, I grabbed my phone, wallet, and room key, and made my way down to the elevator.

I made it downstairs and followed some signage to the dining room. I thought I was going to have to really look around to find my mom, but she was nearly alone in a room which could have seated probably thirty or more. The only other person there was an older man, dressed real nice in this tan wool-looking suit. Maybe it's too early for most of the guests? Or maybe it is too late and they have all already started their day? Either way, weird.

"Hey, Mom," I said by way of greeting as I slid into the chair across from her. "Where's Dad?"

"Mornin', Sweety. Your daddy got picked up about thirty minutes ago. Something about a 'power breakfast' or somethin'."

I paused, trying to figure out what the hell that meant. "This whole thing is effed up, isn't it?"

"Language!" she fussed, smacking my hand.

But I could tell she was only trying to mean it, considering she used worse pretty much daily. I think she was just as overwhelmed as I was. Not just this hotel, but this whole damn situation. The job, the employer, obviously, but just, all of it. It was so much bigger than us.

We were poor nobodies from Alabama, the armpit of the country. Just the name of our lousy state is like, the ultimate joke about redneck hillbillies. Up here, even in the wide open nowhere of upstate New York, even this felt more cultured than back home. At least here I doubted I was going to see a Confederate flag on every third pickup truck.

"What are we supposed to be doing? You said we had lots to do today?" I asked her.

Before Mom could answer, a server started toward our table. As we waited in anticipation, the room seemed to stretch, pulling away like one of those long shots in movies. Each of the server's steps seemed to move her away rather than forward. The details of the room blurred, focusing only on her. Then I blinked, everything snapped back to normal, and she was standing right at our table, pen and notepad in hand. She looked down at me with a cruel glint in her eyes before it clicked, and her face was normal, a kind and friendly smile on her face.

Mom gave no reaction at all, seeming to take it all in as normal. She exchanged pleasantries with the girl and gave her order. When they both looked at me, I stammered through what I wanted to eat, while Mom gave no sign anything had happened. "So where were we?" asked Mom once the server walked away.

"Um," I said. What the hell was going on? I really needed things to start making sense. I shook my head, forcing myself back to the conversation. "Oh, um, I was asking what we could possibly be doing today, when we have no house and no school yet."

"Don't be a smartass," she said with a laugh. "Your daddy got a signing bonus, and it would have been silly to do all our shopping back home, just to pack it in the car and bring it along on the drive up here."

"Well there's not exactly going to be a mall or anything around here, is there?" I asked.

She laughed, as if I had said something completely ridiculous. "We haven't moved to Siberia or something, Honey," she said. "There's stores here in Avernus, and there's a big ol' mall up in Plattsburgh, about a half hour from here."

"So," I paused, not even sure myself whether it was out of confusion or for dramatic effect, "you want me along to help... carry bags? Or what?"

Mom kind of looked at me funny, as if I was missing something obvious. "You're gettin' new clothes, too, Sweety. Especially school clothes." Then she uttered the phrase I'm sure every kid hates. "Or if you'd rather not go, I suppose I can pick out all your clothes for you."

Ugh. Now if I didn't go, she was going to pick out, I don't know, 1950s corduroy pants or something equally hideous and embarrassing. I'd seen what kinds of utter crap she'd bought the times we had a little bit of money. She had the style and taste of, well, a former stripper. And I'd seen her idea of what she thought teenagers like me were supposed to think were "cool". Just no.

The food arrived after about fifteen minutes and despite my mood, I had to admit it looked fantastic. I had ordered what they called a fajita omelet, which was stuffed with steak fajita meat, onions, peppers, and cheese, and then topped with salsa and sour cream. It totally worked for me. Since we've never had money to go out, I was quickly getting spoiled by all the fancy food. I could get used to eating like this.

We pretty much dropped the conversation while we ate, and soon enough we were ready to go out. Since Dad hadn't needed to drive himself, we were able to take the car. I was kind of surprised he was letting Mom drive his new baby, but I guess there wasn't much choice. Mom even seemed a little nervous getting behind the wheel. She entered something into the GPS on the dashboard and we started off. It was kind of nice to be able to go out and get a look at the new town we would be calling home.

The hotel was on the southern outskirts of the small town, so we were able to take everything in as we headed deeper in. Everything was set up in a really convenient grid system, two main roads running parallel to each other north and south, and another two running east and west. These main roads had two good sized blocks of houses between them, changing to businesses before leading to a giant town square like you always see in TV shows.

The buildings lining the square had a giant town hall on the north side, a huge church facing it to the south, and strips of old businesses lining the east and west sides. In the center, there was a pretty big park lined with trees, and a big grassy area with four fountains, each with a statue in the middle, at the four corners of a big covered gazebo. I swear, either this place had been built by someone who had watched all those cheesy small town TV shows, or all those shows were modeled after this town square.

We drove around the square slowly, and I spent the time looking out the window, trying to guess what some of the stores were. I saw three in particular I thought I should come back and check out later: a winter gear sports store, what looked to be an old classic record shop, and surprisingly, a comic shop.

"Are we stopping here?" I asked.

"In a bit," said Mom. "We have a couple of stops first. And from what I'm guessing, most places here won't open until nine or ten anyway."

I shook my head at that and checked the clock on the dash. She was right, it was barely 8:30. I was curious where we were headed next, but decided it was easier to be patient and satisfy my curiosity in real time. We turned off the square and I saw that literally the next block was residential houses. Only four blocks from the square, we turned off onto a side street and then into the driveway of the third house.

"Is this..." I slowly began.

"Yep, this is it. Day after tomorrow, this will be home," Mom said.

"It's big," I said in awe, taking it all in. It was two stories, wood siding painted this weird blue. Kind of halfway between a primary blue and a baby blue. Maybe a turquoise, but without a hint of green? I couldn't tell if the trim was a pale grey, or if it just looked grey against the blue paint. "Can we go in?"

"Unfortunately not, Honey," she answered. "They are supposed to be finishing something with the walls and floors today. But don't worry, there's a nice, big ol' room in there, just for you!" She finished her response with a laugh.

We pulled out of the tiny, narrow driveway after Mom put something else into the GPS and we headed to our next mystery destination. It was only a five or six minute drive, and I should have guessed where we were going. It was someplace I was both dreading, and morbidly curious about. My new school. Let's see, a five minute drive meant about a fifteen minute walk at these residential speeds. Guess who would be walking their ass to school?

The visit to the school was surprisingly short. Mom thought there was a whole process to finish the registration that had been started over the phone last week, but apparently everything had already been done, except to tell them I was actually here. They had even received my records from back home already.

It was otherworldly, being inside the school building with those quiet halls, knowing all the classrooms were packed and I wasn't in one. It felt alien, surreal. It was worked out that I wouldn't be able to start until the next Monday, but they did arrange for me to come by on Friday to pick up my school issued laptop, schedule, and examples of where my classes were in their progress. This was supposedly so I could use the weekend to be caught up by Monday. As if.

Going back to the shops on the square turned out to not be as fun as I thought it would be. The winter store was more gear than sports, and we quickly agreed we needed to wait and learn what was actually required for the kind of weather we were going to get up here. Sure, we knew I needed a better coat, but what kind, right? The "record shop" turned out to be a very run down general electronics store. Now that all the music could be gotten online, they kept all the record decorations around, but didn't really sell any. The comic store, though, turned out to be real, and looked cool from what I could see through the windows. Because they weren't open until noon, I had to follow my mom from store to store while she checked out the clothing and other garbage.

Finally, we got on the road and headed to the mall. She had said it was thirty minutes away, but it was more like forty, and felt like two hours, as slow as she was driving. I read somewhere that at one time right after the automobile was invented, people were concerned that if the human body went faster than twenty miles an hour or something like that, it would have a catastrophic breakdown and have, like, a heart attack or something. I swear my mom was driving under that assumption.

When she was driving around Avernus, Mom was nervous and stressed, driving Daddy's new car. But it seemed like the moment we got out on the highway, she really opened up and relaxed behind the wheel. She still fretted over every lane change and crossroad, but it was like the mood totally lightened. She started driving here in New York the way she used to drive the old car back in Alabama. Still slow as molasses, but more in control of where the car was going.

I was surprised when the trip turned out to be more fun than I expected. Maybe it was being able to get out and explore the area a bit, but Mom and I both seemed to be in a pretty good mood. It was weird, too, since the "mall" turned out to be a dozen lousy stores that in the south would have been on a strip. I could tell Mom was just as disappointed with the place as I was, and we joked about it a good bit. We finally got on the road back to Avernus a bit before two, and I could tell Mom was beat.

"What's got you so worn out?" I asked, then joked, "Want me to drive?"

"Quit bein' a smartass," she snapped at me. Then, realizing she had overreacted, she said softer, "I'm sorry, Baby. Your daddy and I didn't get much sleep."

"Ew! TMI," I said with a grin.

"No, not like that, silly," she said. "No, we both had some bad dreams is all. We talked about it for a minute while we were getting' up, 'cause we were in each other's dreams."

"Sorry to hear that. Nightmares suck," I said.

"What about you, Honey? Did you sleep good?"

"Yeah, Momma," I answered. No way was I going to tell all the weird crap, so evasively I said, "I crashed early, and don't remember if I dreamed."

"Well once we get back to Avernus," Mom said, "maybe we can take a nap before dinner."

Yay. Back to 'Ass-ver-nope'."

The rest of the drive back was quiet. We listened to the radio, since the new car came with Sirius XM and there were some cool channels we both liked. That had been a godsend on the long trip up from Alabama. Getting back near Avernus, I got hit with a feeling of "being back to the boring and mundane". It was weird, because I don't think we had been here long enough to have that feeling. But the creep factor from the night before seemed to ooze into the car with us, sucking the fun of the last few hours out of our moods. Even the sunlight felt more muted, even though it wasn't overcast or anything.

Once we made it back to the hotel, Mom said she was going to take a nap. I told her I was going to go out exploring, and reminded her I had my cell phone if she needed me. She told me when to be back for dinner and I grabbed my board from my room and headed out.

CHAPTER FOUR

THE NEW CREW

My intention was to check out the comic store, but that interest only lasted until I reached the square. The store fronts had barely come into view when I heard the song of my people. The hissing and clack-clacks of a group of skateboards nearby. It was certainly a sound I could not ignore, so I popped my board to the ground, snapped it around with my feet, and headed across the street to a group of boarders riding the sidewalks in the park in the center square.

One of the guys hopped his board up to grind about a foot of the front edge of one of the benches lining the sidewalk. As I got closer, I noticed the benches were green weathered paint, but they had newer metal strips lining the front edge of the seat. I had a funny feeling they had been ridden so much that someone had been forced to reinforce them with metal strips to keep the benches from falling apart.

I had to be careful how to approach this. Skaters are funny about interlopers. Often a good fellow skater can drop right in, and they will give him a chance to prove he's not a poser. Unless they are a crew, a team, a clique. If they have rivals or enemies, they can often be extremely territorial. I needed to pull a trick that would be decent enough to show I could handle my board, but simple enough I was guaranteed to not screw up. I decided the safest bet was to emulate what I had seen a couple of them do.

I stayed about twenty or so feet away, but easily within hailing distance, and built up a bit of speed. As I approached one of the benches, I ollied up. It was a bit taller than I was used to, but I eyed it pretty well, and managed to hit the edge pretty smoothly. I ground the lip of the bench, and as I approached the end, I had to make a split-second decision. Do I ollie back off and hit the ground, or do I try a flip kick? In the end I took too long, pussied out, and just ollied off the edge. Still, I hadn't busted out, so I was fairly satisfied.

Two of the guys stopped their skating to watch me approach, kicking up their boards. I decided I needed to do my signature move to impress them a bit, and once I got a few feet away, I did an impossible pick up, rolling the board over my foot to bring it up to grab with my hand. I'd practiced this move enough times that I could pull it off smoothly, and I knew it impressed.

"Do that again!" barked out the taller of the two guys. "I want to see if that wasn't just an accident."

"What, this?" I dropped the board, stopping it under my foot. Then I popped it up, rolled it over my foot again, and caught it. "It's just a basic impossible, but you catch it partway."

His buddy dropped his board and walked himself through the trick. He had his impossible down, but it took him a half dozen tries to get where he could intercept the board properly before it hit the ground again. The first guy watched him for a minute, then hopped on his board, and... just did it. Do or do not, there is no try, I guess. I was impressed and said so.

"It's flashy," he said, "But once you wrap your head around it, not really difficult." He said it as though it were fact, not ego. He stuck his hand out. "I'm Taki."

"I'm Jason," I responded, shaking his hand. "Taki?"

"It's his favorite food," laughed the shorter guy as Taki flipped him off. "Liam," he said, offering his hand as well. "Where you from?"

I winced, knowing what was coming. "Alabama."

"Alabama?" laughed Taki, imitating an exaggerated southern drawl. I know I have a southern accent and hate it. Did he have to mimic it right to my face? To add insult to injury, he added, "Isn't that right around the belt buckle of the Bible Belt?"

I absolutely hate the south. I hate the attitudes all the RepubliKKKans down there have, and I hated everyone else's opinions on finding out where I was from. But I've dealt with it online for years. No reason the same tricks shouldn't work here in person.

So I responded, "No, it's pretty much the asshole of the south. You can't make fun of it more effectively than I can." I made sure to keep my demeanor joking, and Taki and Liam both chuckled. By now their three friends had come over to see what was up. Now I had a real audience, so I continued.

"What has twelve heads, twelve peckers, and twelve teeth? An Alabama jury." A few chuckles, but also some excitement as to what was coming next.

"Speaking of juries, why is it so hard to solve a murder in Alabama?" I looked around, seeing that everyone was grinning in anticipation. "Because there's no dental records and everyone's DNA all matches," I said with a laugh. They all laughed right along with me, so I kept it going.

"And you know why there's so much incest in Alabama? After all, if you can't keep it in your pants, at least keep it in the family!" They all burst out laughing at that one and almost missed the last line. "I mean, why go across town, when you can go across the hall!"

Success. Situation diffused. I didn't know if Taki, Liam and their friends were going to be buddies, but they certainly weren't going to be enemies. I was in. While the mood was still jovial, I was introduced to the others. Scott, Boots, a nickname, and Wheeler, going by his last name. They all seemed to be roughly my age, and only Boots was shorter than my five-and-a-half-foot height. Taki and Wheeler were both tall and lanky, easily topping six foot, and towering over me. Taki looked to be Hispanic, and Wheeler was a well-dressed black guy. So now it was time to take advantage of my new friendly status and gather some intel.

"So, what do I need to know about this place, since I'm new in town and all?" The group settled down a bit now that a new discussion was getting started. "And by new, I mean we literally drove into town last night after dark."

It was like a blast of cold air hit the group. All five guys shivered and looked around at one another. After a moment, Taki looked back at me. "After dark? Why do you say it like that?"

I was a bit taken aback by everyone's reaction. "Nothin', man. I only meant that we got into town super late, so you guys are literally the only residents I have had time to talk to, other than some hotel staff."

"Staff, huh?" asked Liam. "You're staying at the Avernus Inn?" When I nodded, he added, "You aren't staying there long, are you?" He glanced around at the others while he asked this.

"Yeah, we don't even get our house 'til Thursday, and our stuff won't arrive until Friday. So I think we are staying there the whole week."

"Better you than me," muttered one of the ones in the back. I didn't catch who said it, but it was such a weird thing to say.

"What," I asked with a shaky laugh, "is it haunted or something?"

"Probably safer if it was," replied Taki. "You get used to seeing weird BS happen around here."

"I've definitely seen some Mob type crap around," I said, not sure if I was trying to say it as a joke or seriously. But either way, I was fishing for information, and I think it was pretty obvious. "Any gangs, bullies, or rival crews I need to avoid?"

All five started swiveling around, as if each were daring someone else to be the first to speak. Finally, Boots spoke. The moment he did, all four of the others looked away, not making eye contact with either him or me.

"Ravens," said Boots quietly.

"Huh?" I asked, not sure I heard right.

"The Ravens," said Wheeler. He had a high, squeaky voice that didn't fit with his towering height. He had to be well over six foot two, and I was expecting a baritone, if not a good bass. "Watch out for the Ravens. They're nothing but trouble." Everyone nodded as he said this.

"This another skate crew? A gang, or something?"

Liam looked up at Taki, then at me. "Kind of a gang, I guess? You make your crack about the Mafia. But picture what their kids would be like, and you have the Ravens. Just stay away. They're trouble with a capital T."

"Or don't!" laughed Taki. "We're not your mother. Let's skate."

The mood now broken, we all split and rode in different directions. I think everyone needed to get the tension out of our muscles. I felt less need now to show off, so I started making riskier tricks. Some landed, drawing comments. A few landed me on my ass. I got some laughs, but they were good natured and encouraging. These were good guys. Like all good skaters, we pushed one another. We dared, we showed off, we succeeded, and we wiped out, all in equal measure.

The sun was starting to dip to the horizon when Wheeler was the first to leave, saying he was expected home.

"He's latchkey and needs to fix dinner for his little sister," commented Boots. "But you watch. Now that he's leaving, everyone else is going to disappear in the next ten minutes. Liam's not even going to say anything. He'll just slip off."

Sure enough, it happened exactly as he said. It wasn't even five minutes before Scott announced he needed to head home. Taki almost immediately stated he should really head out as well. And just as Boots had said, I hadn't even noticed that Liam had vanished at some point. I was starting to agree as I noticed how much the temperature was dipping as the sun lowered behind the surrounding buildings. The carefree mood started to drop away like a blanket smothering our fun.

I looked over at Boots, who shrugged his shoulders as if to say, "See?".

"You headed out as well?" I asked.

"Naw," he said. "I can walk you back to the hotel, if you want."

"Sure," I said, pulling out my phone to check the time. I had about forty-five minutes before I needed to meet my parents for dinner. I told Boots my deadline and headed out. He grabbed a ratty coat out from under one of the benches and caught up with me. We skated partway, but then snatched up our boards so we could talk. He filled me in on some of the drama of my new school. Liam was the oldest and a sophomore, but Taki was the group's unofficial leader, being the most assertive and outspoken. The other four were freshmen, like me. Wheeler was from one of the few black families in town, but Boots told me that nobody gave him grief about it.

It was really too early to be thinking such things, but I was having to admit that Boots was kinda cute. Most people would probably worry he was a bit on the skinny side, but he was obviously athletic and had a killer smile, so I didn't see it as a problem. He had brown hair like me, but I liked how his was a decent bit lighter than mine and easily caught the light. He had a nice sharp jawline as well. I couldn't tell which way he swung, but I realized I wouldn't mind finding out.

We got within eyesight of the hotel and Boots' whole demeanor changed. He went from friendly, outgoing and charming, to cold and closed off.

Immediately after, I felt the same feeling from before. Someone, something, was watching me. Staring at me. It was the same feeling from the night before. It was like my soul was being x-rayed. It was almost like I kept catching movement in my peripheral vision, but could never catch whoever it was. It was very creepy.

"I… I gotta go," muttered Boots. I looked over at him, and one thought went through my head when looking at him.

Prey. Victim. Target.

"What the hell is that?" I whispered to him. "Do you feel it, too?"

Boots backed away from the hotel. I reached out and grabbed his arm, and he jumped as if he hadn't even known I was there. I could see real fear in his eyes.

"What is it?" I asked.

He shook his head, as if trying to deny what he was experiencing. Boots pulled away from me, nearly pulling the sleeve of his coat off his arm. I let go and he backed away, wrapping his coat tighter around himself, as much against the… whatever… we were both obviously feeling, as to ward off the oncoming chill of the night settling firmly around us. Neither of us said another word as Boots bolted off at a run. He was barely out of range when I heard the snap-hiss of his wheels hitting the pavement.

Chapter Five

MEETING THE NEIGHBORS

"There the hell you are," my dad called down the hallway. He was being loud because he was trying to embarrass me. It made me mad that it was working. "Been out terrorizing the streets, I see. Why aren't you ready for dinner?" He strode down the hallway toward me by this point, my mother hurrying to shut their hotel room door and catch up to him.

I pulled out my phone to double check the time. "I'm ten minutes early, dad," I said.

"Don't you talk back to me, boy," Dad said. I could tell he wanted to raise his hand for a backhand, but he held back. Maybe because of the unfamiliar location, maybe something else. "Get your ass in your room and clean up. Then get downstairs." He slammed my shoulder with his as he passed me, knocking me into the wall like a damn high school bully. "I'm not waiting on your ass."

I rubbed my shoulder and let myself into my room. After putting on a clean shirt I hoped neither of my parents could find offensive, I headed downstairs. It was only six o'clock, and yet the dining room was almost as dead as it had been that morning. There were two couples sitting at different tables, and the same old man from this morning.

When I got to their table, my parents were in the middle of an argument. The only thing making this one different from any of the thousands I had sat through at home was that they were both whisper-shouting at each other. It wasn't because they were in public. They'd screamed at each other, and me, in public plenty of times. So I guess being in such a swanky place had them acting more polite than normal. When Devon turned out to be our server, I did my best to hide any interest I had in him. My mom didn't care, but there was no need to remind dear old dad his boy was queer.

That being said, I still wanted to take an opportunity to both tease our oh-so-hot server, and also test out whatever weirdness was going on with how the people in this hotel were treating me. So when I was asked what I wanted to eat, I looked him in the eye and with a smile said, "Surprise me."

Devon smiled and nodded at my request, giving me a wink. As soon as he had walked a few feet away from the table, however, I was caught by surprise by a backhand across my face. There wasn't a tremendous deal of force behind it, more of a sting, enough to make me flinch and get my attention. The lack of force was because Daddy was trying to be subtle. But it got my attention, all right. I caught myself glancing around, trying to see who noticed my embarrassment.

"Why do you wanna be such a brat, huh?" said Dad, barely keeping his voice down. "You trying to screw around with what these people think about us?" He raised his hand, as if to threaten another backhand. "Grow the hell up, Jason."

Sure, Pops. I'll grow the hell up. You'd better hope I don't grow up and turn into you. Also, Devon had gotten it, so it wasn't the problem Dad was making it out to be.

Trying to calm myself down a bit, I looked around the dining room, focusing on who I saw and trying to figure out who they were. The dining room was practically empty, with only three other tables occupied, out of probably two dozen. There was an air of silence in the room, as if we were sitting in a library and someone was going to swoop down on us if we spoke too loudly. Even Devon had kept his voice low when he had taken our order.

At one table, the old man in the suit from breakfast sat in his same seat, seemingly lost in his own thoughts as he ignored the dining room. Not knowing who he was, I tried to imagine what his deal was. Probably old enough to be retired and wear a nice suit, but not a fancy one. Retired Mob? Maybe an advisor to somebody? Or maybe his nephew is someone important, and the old guy is here to ride his nephew's coat tails. Seeing him here again made me figure I'd be seeing him the next morning, too. The way he acted, sitting there sipping on a dainty cup of coffee, he looked like he lived at his table.

One couple was a bit older than my parents, dressed real casual, nothing fancy. Everything about their look and demeanor told me real easy they were traveling, just passing through. They gave off the same kind of vibes I imagine my parents would, if I wasn't too close to see them properly. Real comfortable with each other, but out of place with their environment. Plus they were each doing the kind of sore and stretching thing everyone does when they've been stuck sitting in one position for way too long.

The third table consisted of a guy and a girl probably in their early twenties. I did a double take when my impression of them shifted on a dime, and I realized I had been wrong about them. They weren't adults at all, but teens like me. They might have been a bit older, I couldn't tell for sure, but they were definitely high school age. I could have sworn they looked older a second ago. It felt odd that my initial impression had been so wrong.

They were sitting, so it was hard to confirm, but they both gave the impression of being tall. Maybe it was both of them having Jack Skellington-style arms and legs, their limbs being so impossibly thin you assumed they were long. The boy was kind of cute, but merely the kind of cute you see in every Netflix teen drama. A very "social media influencer" type of attractiveness.

The girl with him made me question my little gay-boy vibes, the way Mina had done. She had long, fine hair that was an unnatural perfect white. I swear, I had never seen a Santa outfit with hair this white. It had a sheen to it that almost made it look to have a glint of silver to it. Her hair was long, too. Like crazy long, past her waist. It was like all of her features went for vertical, nothing trying for depth. The two of them combined, from their stiff, disdainful attitudes to their too-perfect appearances, made them look like the worst kind of influencers. So again, no appearance of depth.

My attention was pulled back to the table when I realized I was being discussed. My name hadn't been dropped, yet, but a subject near and dear had been mentioned.

"... hasn't even been here two seconds and he's already managed to hook up with a crew of degenerate skateboarders," my dad was saying.

"Well if he has, at least he's making friends," said Mom, reaching across the table to grab my hand and give it a maternal squeeze.

"As if those are the kind of friends he needs," scoffed Dad. "That was you, right?" he asked, looking at me. "Tearing up the benches at the town square?"

I glanced over and saw that, unlike my mother's glass of soda, his glass had beer, and was already empty.

"Well, boy? Answer me," he yelled. Then remembering where he was, he lowered his volume, but not his tone. "Tell me that wasn't you out there with those hoodlums."

I pulled back, releasing my mother's hand in order to make sure I was out of his immediate reach.

"Yes, Dad. I met some guys. Most of them are in my grade, and are going to help me out with getting used to the new school."

Devon showed up before my dad could get in another verbal shot at me. He had my drink and everyone's appetizers, a salad for my mom, and for me and my dad, matching shrimp cocktails bigger than one of my fingers. To my dismay, Devon also swapped out Dad's glass for a fresh beer. Mom's soda was also swapped out for a beer.

With more alcohol and something to stuff in his mouth, my dad forgot about badmouthing me for the moment, and Mom started into a lengthy monologue about the shops and other places she had spotted that she hoped to explore in the coming weeks.

"Christ, we just got here," griped my dad. "I haven't even got my first paycheck and you're already spending it."

While I started in on my shrimp, I went back to looking around the room. I caught the old man looking our way, but as soon as he saw me notice, he quickly averted his eyes. I got the weird feeling that he hadn't just been looking at our family, but at me specifically. It was odd, and made me feel a bit uncomfortable.

Then I looked back over at the influencer couple. The girl had turned slightly so they were both facing my direction, rather than the side view I had been presented before. I felt like a spotlight was on me, as I realized both of them were unabashedly watching me. It was unnerving, and the fact they weren't eating anything, just staring, made me kind of self conscious about eating my own food. They were kind of pissing me off, so I started staring back. I even craned my neck forward, just to be obvious and obnoxious.

Seeing my antics, she smiled coyly, almost knowingly, as if I had shown a meme she had understood. It made me curious, and I'm sure it showed on my face. For a fraction of a moment they both stared at me in a way that reminded me of a shark, as if they were about to flash sharpened teeth. Then just as suddenly their faces were normal, giving a cross of both bored and mildly entertained. Confused and not a small bit unsettled, I relaxed my more aggressive staring and took another bite of the shrimp still in my hand. Seriously, these shrimp were tastier than any shrimp I had ever had before. And the cocktail sauce was to die for. For a half a second I almost asked my dad if his were this good, but then I came to my senses with a wry chuckle. No conversation with him was ever worth it.

Whatever look crossed my face got the girl's attention, and she actually gave a softer, more friendly smile. I suddenly realized she was much younger than I had originally assumed, maybe even as young as me. It was the way she had carried herself, the same way the guy with her was still acting, that made her first appear so old. It was like she had been jaded and world weary, and only when she relaxed did her true age reveal itself. I know the whole "women should smile more" thing is crap, but in her case, it gave her a complete makeover.

She gave a subtle nod toward me and turned back to the guy with her, raising her dainty little coffee cup to her lips. I started to turn away, but caught the angle just right, and I'm pretty sure her cup was empty. I only saw it for the briefest of moments, but seriously, all I saw inside was white. Maybe she was drinking milk out of a coffee cup? Maybe she was just taking the last swallow from the cup. Or maybe I just wasn't seeing it right, and I was making something of nothing.

It was only a few minutes longer before Devon showed up with a serving tray. He had hooked me up with a breaded and fried boneless pork chop, and more of those amazing onion rings. To the side, he set down a separate bowl of cottage cheese. Somehow that seemed funny, since it had been brought up last night but I hadn't gotten to eat any of it.

The food was amazing, better than anything I had ever eaten back home, and maybe better than the burger the night before. I wish I could have said the same about the company. Both of the parental units were kept well lubricated with beers, and with the increase in alcohol came an increase in both volume and attitude.

Somehow I managed to keep my head down and stay off their radar as their tempers flared. Thank God for that. The traveling couple finished and left a short time after we started eating, and I caught them throwing some disgusted looks our way. I wanted to sink into the floor over how white trash my parents were acting. After a particularly loud bit of name calling, I glanced over and saw the influencer couple getting up to leave. The guy had an amused, condescending smirk on his face as he glanced at my parents, but the white haired girl actually gave me a more friendly, more pitying smile. Something that said, "It sucks, but I get it". I flushed with embarrassment. The knowing smile over a situation I was trapped in was almost worse than her friend's condescension.

Finally, Dad pushed back and stood up to leave, and I was able to get away from the table. I knew better than to have been an "ungrateful little punk" by asking to leave the table before he was finished. I didn't run and I didn't make it obvious, but I was ready to bolt. I did make it a point to walk close to the girl's table and get a good look at her cup, just out of morbid curiosity.

Sure enough, it was bone dry. So was his, actually. I wouldn't have thought anything of it, except so many other weird things were happening around here that I had started cataloging them. Just one more thing to add to the list, a pair of impossibly pretty influencers who like to sit in a hotel restaurant and pretend to drink coffee from empty cups. It reminded me of the line from that old movie, where Tom Cruise says something about "eating from empty plates, and drinking from empty glasses".

CHAPTER SIX

ROGUE ENCOUNTER

I wasn't about to sit in my room if there was even a chance I would have to listen to my parents on the other side of the wall, so I grabbed my board and both hoodies, and bolted. The tall, bald guy was at the desk this time. Rather than giving me a greeting, he just kind of stared as I crossed the lobby, as if I was a mildly interesting TV program rolling past him. I didn't even think he blinked the whole time.

It was a lot colder out than it had been when I skated the back lot the night before, and I definitely wished I had picked up a heavier coat that morning when I had the chance. Still, skating was skating, skating was life, and nothing was going to keep me from it.

I'd barely gotten started when that feeling crept over me again. Somebody was watching me. I was getting tired of this, especially the part about not knowing what the hell it was. It wasn't that vague yet easily identified feeling you get after watching a good horror movie and it feels like something is creeping around in another room. No, this was something more tangible, yet harder to describe. It was like, if you could get goosebumps inside your brain. Or an itch in your attention span. I stopped and kicked up my board, looking around at the dark around me.

That field on the other side of the road kept drawing my attention. Maybe it was the waving of the tall grasses in the darkness beyond the street light. It was breezier tonight than last night, which was definitely adding to the cold. I strained to see past the light, trying to make out anything moving contrary to the grass.

"Good evening, Jason."

I either jumped out of my skin, pissed myself, or both. I did jump to some extent, dropping my board. The voice had come from behind me to the left, back in the direction of the hotel. It also hadn't been shouted, but spoken at a calm volume. Even so, I had heard it as if the person were standing right beside me. I jerked my head around in the direction of the voice and saw... him. It was the boss guy from the night before. Same shiny suit, his hair and coat flicking around in the wind. Realizing who he was, I glanced around to see if his henchmen were around, but he seemed to be alone.

"Damn, man. Where'd you come from?," I responded. My heart was in my throat, but the words came out a lot calmer than I expected to be able to pull off. "If my skating's bugging someone, I'll leave."

He chuckled at that. "There is no issue. I am no threat, Jason." His voice was soft, cultured. Definitely fancy. Money and breeding dripped off every syllable. "I am Dominic Tsui. Currently your host," he waved a hand vaguely toward the hotel behind himself, "and hopefully soon, your friend."

"My friend?" I asked with no small amount of confusion. "Why do you care about a kid?"

"Let's just say, you have positive attributes."

"Sounds sus, to be honest," I said. I didn't trust this guy, and had no idea of either what his intentions were, or what he was capable of. No way was I playing his game.

"What's this about you being our host?" I asked. "What, do you own the hotel?"

"Among other things," he replied with a smirking smile. "But I am also the one who hired your father, and I am footing the bill for both your move and your stay in this hotel."

"Um, thanks, I guess," I deadpanned.

His smile became wider. "How about this? Why don't you join me for dinner? Tomorrow, eight pm." His attitude became more serious. "I'll ensure it is cleared with your parents."

My skin crawled. No way was I going to do anything like dinner with this creep. The list of reasons was as long as my arm. I started speaking, planning to tell him he was a creep and to get lost. "Sure," I heard myself say instead. "I'd be happy to join you."

What the hell was that? Did I just say that? I opened my mouth again to tell him to get lost, but nothing came out. And I don't mean like, "I spazzed and couldn't think of what to say". No, I mean, I literally could not talk. Then before I could give any other kind of reaction, the world spun and I nearly fell over. I dropped to my knees before the feeling passed, and Mr. Tsui was gone. Not like he walked off. He just... wasn't there.

What the absolute... What was going on? Was I going crazy? That must be it. My brain only made up this idea of getting the hell out of Alabama, and I was actually sitting in a loony bin down in Birmingham. I knew it had to be too good to be true. But as my friend Lisa always joked, if everything's screwed up, you may as well go with it.

Staying out there in the dark and the cold after that was not an option, skating or not. So I headed back to the hotel, eyes peeled at every shadow all the way. I goofed off on my phone for a bit before I remembered the ice cream in the freezer and pulled it out. I only got through a couple of bites though, before I started remembering that creepy meeting and all the weirdness last night, and tossed it in the trash can in disgust.

I decided to take my friend Lisa's philosophy as appropriate to the situation. If I'm experiencing this weirdness, I may as well act on the assumption that it is real, in case it is. After all, if I'm sitting in a padded room, pissing a diaper and drooling, then nothing I do here can impact that. Whereas if it is real, then not acting can absolutely have an influence. So in that case, what's most likely going on, and how should I respond?

I tried to go back to playing around on my phone, but my mind was too distracted. I needed my own room, with my own stuff. I needed friends to hang out with, and to talk things out with. I thought about Devon, or maybe Mina. Both had been nice enough, and had seemed normal. But they were both employed here at the hotel. They could be part of the problem. No, for now it was just me.

Thinking of my old friends though, got me thinking about these new guys, Taki and his crew. It was interesting that Boots had walked me back to the hotel. He was kind of cute, even if he gave off a kind of "little brother" vibe. And of course, thinking about them made me wonder about these Ravens they had said to avoid. At first they had made it sound like some kind of a street gang. But the air they gave them, the fear, the... respect, made them sound dangerous. Not just some rivals who happened to be bullies. More like the crap my friend Alen had been babbling about, when he was confusing New York State with New York City.

I needed someone to talk to, and I didn't have anyone, at least not yet. I texted Alen and Lisa back home, but neither returned my messages, not even leaving me on read. Eventually, even though it was only around 9:30, I decided to call it an early night. I figured maybe a shower would help me clear my head. In the end, I only managed to clear my "little head", as it were, and went to bed.

CHAPTER SEVEN

REFLECTIONS

I had a stark, vivid dream that night.

I was dancing with the influencer girl I saw at dinner. She was at least a foot taller than me in the dream, and I kept having to work hard to keep my face out of her boobs, which were right at eye level, except I remembered from the dining room that she was very flat chested. Probably to do with how insanely skinny she was.

She moved in a very jerky, stop motion kind of way, really playing up the Jack Skellington similarities I had noticed at dinner. She was wearing slacks and kind of a jacket-looking blouse, both in a blinding, pristine white. It was very similar to the crisp white top she had worn in the restaurant, and even in the dream, I realized I had not actually noticed whether she had been wearing slacks or a skirt before.

We danced around the room in some old-fashioned waltz.. I couldn't really define what kind of room we were in. It started small and intimate, just me and her. The longer we danced though, the more the walls and ceiling stretched away from us until the room was massive. The room changed even further as one entire wall was suddenly.a giant mirror. However, while she was dancing I was not visible in the mirror's reflection with her. In fact, in the way you absolutely know something in a dream, I knew she was dancing alone, and not only that, but she was glad I wasn't there. The version of her here with me, I just knew, was happy I was dancing with her, but the reflected version was not.

A new feature introduced itself.

The reflected person was wearing exactly the same top, but instead of pants, she was wearing a white skirt that ended just above the knees, with knee length boots of the same brilliant white. She smiled at me and nodded, and at the same time the version of her I was dancing with reached up and cupped my chin to look up at her. She smiled as well, giving me the same look of satisfaction that I was here, instead of with her reflection.

As much as this girl was capturing my attention, I spied Mr. Tsui, the creep from earlier, in the shadows of the corner. He had this absolutely wicked grin on his face as he watched us, as if this scene was all part of some master plan he was watching unfold. Then I realized he wasn't just in one corner, but was standing in all four corners of the room at once. In absolute dream-confidence, I knew all four copies of him were still the same man. His stare was hungry, arrogant, and predatory. It made me feel like I was the most delectable piece of steak he had ever smelled, and I was cooked to perfection.

Behind all the copies of Mr. Tsui, the shadows coalesced into a strange red mist. The mist didn't flow out into the rest of the room. Instead, it stayed densely packed in the corners. Occasionally, it would expand, attempting to flow past the crime boss before pulling back. Almost like it was afraid to touch him. It pulsed, back and forth, almost as if the mist itself was breathing.

Instantly, the girl I was dancing with was more my height, and I realized it was my friend Lisa. She was laughing at me, not to embarrass me, but because she always flirted with me, just teasing her queer friend. Why was I thinking of her, though?

I realized it was because of the hair, shaved up the right side, then parted to the left in a wave that became longer the further out to the side it went. She had never been able to get her hair right, because it was always fried from bad dye jobs and cheap styling products. In the dream it looked awesome though, and it occurred to me the connection was that she and Mina wore the same style cut. And the second I thought of the hotel employee, the girl I was dancing with switched to her, and once again, I was dancing with a girl a foot taller than me.

Mina swayed against me, moving her hands from my shoulders down to my butt, sliding her hands into pockets I hadn't even realized were on the seat of my pants. I looked away from her, embarrassed even in the dream at her audacity, and Mr. Tsui was there again. His eyes seethed with jealousy. The red mist behind him pulsated, sparkling like glitter, active in opposition to his anger. He looked like he was ready to rend someone in two with his bare hands. Hopefully not me!

As Mina and I spun once more, I caught our reflection in the wall mirror. I was in the reflection this time. I was dancing away with Mina, who's reflective version looked scared to death and on the verge of panic. I looked at her there in my arms, and suddenly it wasn't her at all, but instead I was dancing with Boots.

This shocked me even knowing it was a dream. Even though I thought he was cute, I didn't know him like that. I looked at him, eye level with me, and his face showed... nothing. Just a calm blank stare. No emotion, no recognition of who I was or what we were doing. He may as well have been a puppet, a placeholder there in my dream. I looked over at the mirror, and saw that in the reflection, I was dancing with the girl in white again, the one in the white pants, not the skirt. She looked out of the mirror at me with a sad look, a look of loss and defeat. The look somehow seemed to make her even more beautiful.

It felt like my life was about to get a lot more complicated.

CHAPTER EIGHT

LAZY DAYS

The next morning, I woke up with a weird cloud hanging over my head. The full dream played over and over, leaving me in a bit of a daze as I hopped in the shower. Unlike normal dreams, the details didn't fade away. Instead, each moment stayed crisp in my thoughts. My mind had cleared a bit by the time I walked out of the steamy bathroom into the main hotel room, running the towel through my hair.

I had actually gone to sleep crazily early, so it didn't surprise me at all when I picked up my phone off the nightstand and, yes, it was barely 7:30, even without an alarm. I also saw a missed call from my mother, and a text stating I had better be up, and if I wasn't downstairs by eight, she was going to "tan my hide". I wanted to laugh because I knew she would never try to give me swats. But I wouldn't put it past her to get Daddy to go after me, and he already hated my existence as it was. No need to give him extra ammunition.

I wasn't exactly thrilled to have to go see my parents again this early, but I was hungry, so I got dressed and headed downstairs. It turned out to be an eerie duplicate of the day before. Mom was sitting at one table, alone with no Dad, and the old guy in the tweed suit was sitting off in a corner by himself, sipping his coffee and reading a newspaper.

"Another power breakfast for Dad?" I asked as I sat down opposite Mom.

"I suppose," she sighed. "I didn't ask, considering the mood he was in. But he left the car again, so there is that."

"It's almost like we got two cars," I laughed. "Yours, and whatever it is he is doing."

"Oh shush, you," Mom said playfully, slapping me on the arm. "Besides, I'm mad at you,"

"What did I do?" I exclaimed, returning her smile. I really hoped she was teasing, but both my parents could be nuts sometimes.

"Why didn't you tell me and your daddy you got invited to join this youth club? Why did I have to hear it from one of their adult chaperons when he came to ask permission?"

"Huh?" I asked, really confused.

"The nice man said it was some kind of community service youth club?" She looked at me like she was stunned I didn't know what the hell she was talking about. "He said they were the Ravens, I think?"

My stomach felt icy. Taki and the guys said the Ravens were dangerous, and implied they were the kids of all the Mob guys. Did I tell my mom all this, or shut up and keep it to myself? It was probably better I keep quiet for now. Find out what the hell was going on. Then I found out, all right. Found out the bad way.

"Anyway," she continued on, not even noticing my reaction. "Yes, you can go."

"Can... go?" I asked confusedly. "Go where?"

"To the meeting tonight, silly," she said, laying her hand on my arm. "He said it was at eight, right? And they would be feeding y'all?"

Damn, so that was his way of getting permission. Just lie to my parents for me.

"Silly name though. Right out of Arkansas," Mom said, lost in her own little entertaining world. "Mister Sou-ee," she said with a loud laugh.

"Haha, yeah," I muttered.

My head was swimming. I had been positive I was going to be able to avoid his dinner invitation. Hell, I still probably would. But now it came with the trouble of my parents, or at least my mom, not only knowing about it, but being excited for it and convinced it was a good thing.

For all I knew, not going could cause problems for Dad's new job, since Mr. Tsui said he was the one responsible for hiring Dad. Wouldn't that be just my luck, to screw everything up by ignoring this creep's dinner invite. I'd talk to the guys and I'd fight to come up with an excuse, but for the moment it looked like I had dinner plans.

"Momma, I need a favor," I said midway through my plate of waffles and bacon. "I think I need a coat sooner, rather than later. My hoodie's just not enough once the sun goes down in this place."

"I see," she said. "Are you going out today? Maybe meeting up with those skateboarding friends again?" she asked with a bit of a smirk. I could tell she was daring me to deny it.

"Maybe," I hedged.

"Well if I recall," she drawled thoughtfully, "there's a Mom 'n Pop style diner on the square." I nodded vaguely, not quite sure if I remembered something like that or not. "Why don'cha meet me there around noon for lunch and we'll walk over to the sporting goods store to get something for you."

"I can do that, sure."

"And if you want to make it real easy on your Momma, you can go on in there on your own before lunch, and see what they might have you like."

"Yes, ma'am, I can do that, sure."

"Only one thing that's gonna get in your way, Son," she said, looking off into the distance to hide her grin. I looked up at her. "If you do get to hang out with a single one of those boys before I meet you for lunch, that's the last you're gonna see of any of 'em!"

"Why, Momma? You've never had a problem with me skating."

"It's 'cause those boys had best be in school!" she said with a laugh.

"Oh, yeah," I said with a sheepish grin. "I didn't think about that."

CHAPTER NINE

KINDNESS AND UNKINDNESS

I headed pretty much straight to the square anyway, figuring if I couldn't hang out with my new friends, maybe I could at least get in some solo skating. I wasted most of the morning riding my board and watching the traffic around the place, both car and foot traffic. It didn't take me long to learn that while the streets and sidewalk might be pretty much clear of snow, there were occasional patches of ice in some shady spots I had to watch out for. I met my mom for lunch, and yes, I had gone into the sports store and checked out a few coats. I even talked to the lady working there, to get some idea of what was going to be practical and durable, rather than cheap or flashy.

I had a good lunch with Mom, and even though afterward she dragged me around a few other stores like I feared, we did end up getting me a good heavy coat, as well as a medium jacket. It was about the heaviest I would have needed back home, but would just be a more mild job here. By around two o'clock we were ready to go our separate ways, and that was when she totally floored me.

"Baby, I think you need to go and be able to enjoy a bit of this good luck we're havin'," she said, putting her hand in mine. I started to say, "huh", when I realized there were some soft paper edges in between our hands. She pulled her hand back, and I saw a bunch of curled up twenties in my hand.

"Whoa," I breathed. "Momma, you sure? Daddy's not going to come looking for this, is he?"

Mom laughed and said, "No, baby. That's yours. Just don't go crazy with it. Don't expect this all the time."

Flipping through the bills, I was able to count them out. "There's like two hundred dollars here! Are you sure?"

"Yes," she laughed louder. "I'm sure!"

"Thanks, Mom," I said, hugging her. As I pulled back, I looked her in the eyes, really looked at her. In a more serious tone, I said, "This is really a thing, isn't it. We finally made it to something good, didn't we?"

"Your Daddy's done good with this," she answered with a softer smile. "We wouldn't have moved to the 'Great White North' if we weren't sure."

Once we split ways, I hung out for a bit, but having looked up the GPS route earlier on my phone, started heading in the direction of the school, assuming the high school would let out around three. When we drove here the other day, I hadn't had a good chance to really take in the building. But approaching by foot this time, I was able to get a better vibe of the place.

It was bigger than I expected for the size of what the town seemed like. Shiny steel letters stood out against the red brick above the carport lining the front, spelling out "Theodore Roosevelt High School". But then I noticed, off on the right side of the building, another sign announcing "Theodore Roosevelt Middle School". So I guess they shared a building.

Some resource officer wanted to harass me for not being in class, but once I explained I had just moved and hadn't started attending yet, he grudgingly left me alone. At 2:50 the middle school let out, and then at 3:10 the high school joined them. I was surprised there weren't more kids being picked up by car, but even in the middle school it seemed most of the kids were walking home in pretty much every direction.

I was keeping a good lookout, so I spotted Wheeler when he came out the front of the high school. His towering height and dark skin made him easy to stand out. I waved him over, and found out Scott was already with him. We all bumped fists as we said 'hey'.

"So how does this usually work?" I asked. "Are you guys not allowed to bring your boards to school or something?"

"No way," laughed Wheeler. "That's the best way to get suspended. The principal here is a demon when it comes to skateboards. Taki's house is like two minutes from here, so we all ditch them there."

"Are you guys meeting up today?"

"Hell yeah!" exclaimed Scott.

Texts were exchanged, and we all met up in another area they enjoyed skating. After about an hour, I called a halt to the fun and told them I needed more info.

"I need to know more about these 'Ravens'," I said.

"Ugh, don't tell me you're looking for them," said Taki.

"More like the other way around," I said. "I got invited to meet this guy named Tsui tonight, and he told my parents the Ravens were some kind of community service youth group."

"Oh, you're screwed!" exclaimed Taki.

"So help me out," I pleaded. "Who are they, for real?"

"More like, what are they," said Taki. "They're not an official organization, that's for sure. Like we said, they are more like a gang, or a club."

They looked around themselves, seeing I was still confused, as if trying to decide who was going to fill me in. Like yesterday, Boots was the one who finally spoke up.

"They are like a club," he said. "But not one you can walk up and join. More like," he paused, searching for the right words. "More like a secret society, like something you would see at a fancy private school or a university. They're elitist, and like we said yesterday, mostly the kids of the people who own this town."

"So if they are wanting to meet me—"

"Then either you have something they want, they think you are worth hanging out with, or they want to mess with you."

"Well, I'm a poor nobody from Alabama, so that rules out the first two," I said glumly.

"Like I said," interjected Taki. "You're screwed."

"Guys, where's Liam?" asked Scott suddenly.

We all looked around, but he seemed to have taken the opportunity of the conversation to bail. The talk seemed to have busted everyone's mood, so Wheeler said he was going to go ahead and head home early to see his sister. Scott said he was going to do the same. We only had an hour of daylight left by that point, so I mentioned I wanted to head to the square and finally check out the comic shop. Boots decided to come with me.

Taki checked his watch, then looked up at the sun. "Yeah, there's enough time."

CHAPTER TEN

ENVIRONMENTAL IMPACT

It was surprisingly crowded when I got there, and the place turned out to be a lot bigger than I was expecting. There were a half dozen guys in the store already, along with a pair of girls, even. The shelves weren't limited to just comics, either. The store had a bunch of card games, board games, and even miniatures. I was impressed, but then, I wasn't in backwards Alabama anymore.

In the back of the shop there was a large open area with dining room-sized tables. At first I couldn't make out what was scattered all over them, but as I got closer I realized there were hills, trees, and all sorts of cool little buildings like you would see on a train set. But instead of trains, the tables were full of science-fiction army men.

Three of the boys and a girl had all these cool science fiction miniature army men and tanks and stuff littered over two of the tables. They had books and dice scattered all over the place, and were using tape measures to move the army men around. I had heard about games like this, but had never actually watched one before.

Me and the guys walked over to check out what they were doing. One of the guys nodded at us in greeting, and I nodded back. I did my best to watch for a while, without getting close enough to get in their way or anything. Taki nudged my shoulder and muttered, "I think this is that game Liam plays."

I watched long enough that Taki and Boots said something about catching me another time and took off. I walked them to the exit, then immediately went back to watching the games being played. I was pretty fascinated by what I was seeing. The four players were soon joined by another half dozen players and the room was rapidly filling up with army games.

One of the new arrivals saw me watching and invited me over to their table. He and the guy across from him were older, but more like twenty and forty-something. They admitted to being a father and son and I thought it was cool they had an activity they did together. Deep down I was a little jealous.

They told me a bunch of stuff about the story line and intricacy of this game, Hammers & Hordes. Before I realized what was going on, my skate buddies had abandoned me, leaving me to hang out and watch the game. The players were really cool about my interest, backtracking and explaining what they were doing in their particular match.

Eventually, I let them get back to their game, and I went over to the merchandise section to look through the various model kits for sale.

I was fascinated by both the hobby side and the lore side of the game. Something like this had never been an option for someone like me. Financially there was no way I could have ever played something like this, but even if I had found the money, I had never known any friends who would have had any interest. But now I had some money, and they both said I would never have any problems finding people to play around here.

From what the dad had said, this was a science fiction game set way in the future. Even though there were Humans, most of them were the bad guys, living under a dictatorship and trying to conquer the galaxy, killing anyone standing in their way. There were also two other Human factions that acted as rebellions against the Empire, plus a dozen or so alien races.

I was told this game had been being played here for a long time. The dad had said he had played an earlier version back when he wasn't much older than his son, and they did painting nights together as father and son. No way did I ever expect that to ever happen with my old man, but it was exciting to know I wouldn't be wasting my effort if I turned out to like the game.

At least half the boxes were from one or more of the Human armies. That alone turned me off, since a giant selection meant everyone played them. I'd be completely lost in the crowd, especially being so new to the area. That left all the aliens. I knocked off a good chunk of those from consideration because they looked straight out of the military industrial complex with spiky guys and space suits. This left me picking through some of the others that drew my curiosity.

I was musing back and forth between unit boxes from two different alien armies. One was a lizard-like race called the Starhost, the other looked like a cross between Mad Max and Anubis, creatively called The Jackals.

A door in the back of the store opened and pulled me away from my musings. I watched a group of ten or so teenagers enter the main store. You know when you are watching a movie or show and the really hot, popular clique walks into the room? They always go to a slow motion shot, with lots of perfect outfits, wind out of nowhere that waves their hair gently while a popular rock song plays like a WWE intro? Yeah, I had never seen that in real life until now.

No, music didn't start playing, and the world didn't stop rotating, but man, these guys walked in like it had. Most were older teens, but there were a couple that looked a little younger than me. The way they moved, it was graceful, feline, casually slinky. I had never seen anyone move like that. And here was a whole group walking in like they had choreographed the whole thing.

I recognized one of them. It was the guy with the sandy brown perfect hair from the hotel restaurant the night before. The one that had been with... her. There she was, the girl with the long, white hair. I had only seen her sitting down, and with her impossibly thin limbs she had seemed tall, the way she was in my dream. Seeing her now, I saw she was a very average height, only a couple of inches taller than my five and a half feet. The group had entered the store as if they were a flock of birds, moving in coordination with one another. They barely seemed to look around. But as they entered the store proper, they moved in different directions. Four of them headed out the front door, a few headed into the gaming area, and a few approached the checkout counter.

The girl in white approached the section where I stood, transfixed.

CHAPTER ELEVEN

HOBBIES ENGAGED

She wasn't wearing white today. Instead, she had on a track suit-like outfit made of soft, slightly fuzzy material in a pale sky blue. Her pristine, straight hair poured behind her shoulders and down her back like a fine curtain. It looked more like cloth than hair. I couldn't pull my eyes away from her. Sure, like I said, I was mostly gay. Much as what had occurred with Mina at the hotel, there were certain types of girls that absolutely hit my buttons.

"So you're him?" she said casually, seeming to address me. It took a moment for me to clear my head enough to register what she said, and that it was said to me.

"I'm *a* him, I suppose," I quipped. "Good to see you again."

She looked over at me when I said that. "Again? Oh, of course."

"You know, dinner last night?"

"Right," she said, giving a noncommittal half-smile. Picking up a box of the Human soldiers, she tapped them in my direction. "So, you play?"

Don't blow this, moron. Her voice was silky, dusky, almost deep for a girl. There was a slightly inflected accent, but it was subtle and I had no way of identifying it. It suited her perfectly. But now I was desperate to hide my southern drawl.

"I just got introduced to it. I'm interested though."

She pointed at the boxes in my hand. "Are those the two you are debating between playing?"

"Maybe," I answered in the most cringe-worthy drawl. "Any advice?"

"Well," she said, delicately setting her box back on the rack and taking the Jackals from my hand. The skin of her fingers just barely brushed mine, and I felt how cold they were. I guess because of how skinny she was, she had some circulation issues. Or maybe she had been outside in the last few minutes.

"If you are going purely for 'rule of cool' then that's all on you," she said. "Pick the shiniest plastic. The Starhost are religious fanatics and the Jackals have no high tech, so they steal and scavenge everything. However, if you want a good introductory army, both of these suck."

I was kind of surprised. Hearing her say even such a mild cuss word just seemed, I don't know, beneath her. It wasn't really a cuss word, just that she just didn't strike me as someone crass, or I don't know, uncultured. Maybe I was showing my Southern upbringing, where girls were either cussing, spitting, and rolling around in the dirt, or they floated above everyone else.

I guess that just goes to show I should quit prejudging other people. Hell, I fuss when they do it to me. "Skater trash" and all that. My opinion of her from dinner the night before was that she was going to be arrogant and stuck up, like so many clique girls I've known from school. Instead, in opposition to how she dressed, she was down to earth and totally cool helping out a noob antihero like me.

"The Starhost have some fairly complex rules compared to some of the others, and the abilities of the Jackals are positively bottom tier. Both of them mean you have no chance of winning a game unless you become an expert."

"Thanks," I said, gingerly placing the Starhost box back. Then gesturing in the direction of the display wall, I asked, "So give me some options that are more, as you say, beginner friendly."

"Oh, that's easy." She pointed out a box of Humans dressed in oversized

Mech armor.

She noticed the look of distaste I gave and changed tack. "Since you instinctively went for these two, it seems you are looking for 'weird'?" she teased, "Or is it more about liking something wild and dangerous?"

I had to think about that for a moment. Was I just trying to rebel against the status quo? "Cool, dangerous, and unusual," I challenged. "I want the underdog with a freaky side."

"Ah, so you need something fairly straightforward, deadly, and likely to be the only one playing them."

"Sounds perfect," I laughed.

She looked sideways at me with something of a smirk. "Are you okay playing the bad guys?"

"As long as they have, what did you call it? The rule of cool?"

She knelt and grabbed a pair of boxes from the bottom shelf, then stood back up and handed them to me. One was a team of five soldiers that looked cool as hell, seeming to be some kind of cyborgs carrying rifles and draped in cloaks. They were painted a collection of blacks and greys. The other box were a pair of exoskeleton walkers with these near naked guys strapped into their middles, stretched out like they were being tortured. Both boxes claimed to be part of the Archeo Legion.

"So these guys are kind of the Spanish Inquisition of the Cosmos Emptor," she said. I recognized that as the name of the Human fascist empire. "They are fairly straightforward to play, mainly dealing with snipers, hunt squads," she pointed to the first box, "and big, tough war engines like these," she gestured to the second box.

"Alright, that's one option," I said. "Just curious, why don't people play them?"

"It's kind of a niche section of the story line. They are a decent army, but they don't get as much model support as some of the other armies. The Jackals have the same problem, but at least the Archeos have decent rules."

"Anything else you might recommend?"

"There are other armies I could recommend, sure. But this is the best option if you want both rarely played and easier to learn."

"What if I just wanted easy to play?"

"Then that's easy, go with Cosmos Emptor or the Scion Rebellion."

"Both Humans," I said. I think she heard the subtle disappointment in my voice.

"Are you buying today, or just looking?" she asked.

"I mean, I *can* buy, if I decide on which one I really want to start with."

A voice called out over the store. "Erin, we need to go." She looked up at the call. It was the boy she had been sitting with at dinner.

"He your boyfriend?" I asked. She scoffed, making it obvious that was, to her mind, a dumb thing for me to say. "Sorry," I muttered. "Not my business."

"No, Garrett is decidedly not my boyfriend. He's barely a friend."

Confusing, but alright. They had seemed chummy enough last night, and had arrived here together.

"Do you want my advice, for real?" she looked over at Garrett, just as he was calling for her again. When I nodded, she said, "Do more research. Why spend twenty-five dollars on a box of models that you end up regretting when you see something better two days later?"

"Fair," I answered. Sure, I definitely wanted the 'new shiny stuff', as Mom would say, but she was right. Plus, maybe buying these now wasn't the best idea. They would probably get lost or trashed somewhere in the unpacking and getting my new bedroom set up.

"Well, I really must be going, Jason. Perhaps I'll see you soon."

And before I could get in a reply or even ask how the hell she knew my name, she was gone, along with several of the others she had entered with, through the back door into the back of the shop. I went over to that side of the store, and saw there was a sign on the door, labeled "Employees Only – No Exceptions". What the hell ever. By this point, it was just one more stupid weirdness I was forced to experience.

In fact, too many weird things were going on.

All the stuff at the hotel. Master Jason, really? And I may not be familiar with room service, but no business, nowhere, deliberately loads you up with triple the food you paid for, even if you're not the one paying for it. And then first Mina, and then Richard, go out of their way to try and be cool to teenage skater trash in ratty clothes. They would suck up to my dad, sure. The new guy coming to work for the people they just have to know are the Mob. That all makes sense. But you don't bother with his kid.

Not to mention everyone behaving like they knew everything about me. Devon hooks me up with a bag of snacks, including candy bars, and somehow knows I don't like chocolate? Yes, I noticed the banana split had caramel sauce subbed out for the traditional chocolate. And how did they know I actually like cottage cheese? What was going on? Who were these people?

Why were Taki and the other guys so afraid of talking about stuff in Avernus? Most skaters I knew tossed out a dominant and cocky attitude, whether they really felt it or not. These guys straight up admitted their fears. Not to mention, why was there such a big school, when I only saw enough students to half-fill the place?

Add to that, the crazy nightmares Mom talked about having. Then the psycho dream I had. It made no sense, but it was so vivid. Even now, I could remember every detail with surprising clarity. And now getting to talk to Erin, the girl from my dream. The girl who drinks from empty cups.

That was even without Mr. Tsui and the Ravens. I couldn't seem to get a straight answer out of anyone about that. It was definitely something I was going to push at this dinner, and it gave me a solid reason to actually want to go. I was not one to ever be satisfied with secrets and answers being withheld.

CHAPTER TWELVE

ALL MEN MUST EAT

The visit to the comic store had been so interesting that it felt like it had lasted forever, but I was still back at the hotel in plenty of time. Decisions, decisions. Dinner where I get attitude from Dad, or dinner with Dad's creepy boss? I sighed, knowing I didn't exactly have a choice. At least I could avoid getting yelled at.

At 7:45 I headed downstairs in the nicest clothes I had. Fortunately, Mom had made me pack a nice shirt in case it was needed for some school reason before the movers got here at the end of the week. I would have to mention it to her tomorrow. She would love the brownie points. Once I got off the elevator, I waved to Mina and took a seat in one of the chairs off to the side.

Deciding to kill some time and some curiosity at once, I pulled out my phone and Googled a list of all the different Hammers & Hordes armies available. There were several I had not noticed before, when looking up at the store. I was starting to realize just how vast the game's model collection really was. I started glancing through the catalog, realizing how expensive the game could be, as some of the bigger units and vehicles were upwards of thirty to forty dollars. Even if I spent the whole wad of cash Mom gave me, it might not be enough to get into this game. I had no idea how many boxes I would need. Even more research, I guess. Maybe I could con Mom into an allowance?

"Sir, if you would please accompany us?"

The voice made me jump.

I looked up to see two of those bodyguard FBI looking guys standing over me. Both were white guys around thirty or so, built like they obviously worked out on the regular, and both wearing carbon copy dark blue suits with white dress shirts and dark ties. I half expected sunglasses, even indoors at night. As I slipped my phone in my pocket and stood, I saw one of the guys adjust his suit jacket and was rewarded with a flash of a gun in a shoulder holster.

I wanted to ask where we were going, but knew there was really no point. One of the men started walking back toward the elevator, while the other gestured for me to follow, then fell into step behind me in turn. We passed by the elevator, however, and rounded the corner into the hallway of ground floor rooms. Almost immediately around the corner was another elevator. Why it wasn't faced next to the main one I didn't know, but I did realize the shafts had to be adjacent to one another. The man I was following had to swipe an employee badge to call the elevator, whose doors opened immediately.

This elevator looked fancier than the one around the front. The inside was a darker color, with trim that looked gold or brass. I took a sidelong glance at the buttons, and instead of floor numbers, saw letters labeled B, G, and L. My escort had to enter a key and turn it, before pressing the third option. A voice came out of a speaker, saying something in a language I didn't understand. The guy next to me replied something back that sounded like "sing-co", and the elevator began to move.

I was seriously apprehensive about what was waiting for me, considering how difficult it seemed to be getting to what I assumed was the section of the third floor I had seen from outside. After the ride up, the elevator door opened.

The elevator opened onto the kind of lobby I had seen on TV used for high end businesses or law firms or something. The walls were chrome edging around this creamy off white. The floors were carpeted in a pale grey that looked expensive. There was a semicircular reception desk with no one sitting there, lending an air of abandonment to the place. I supposed it made sense though, since it was after hours.

Big glass doors led into a conference room behind the reception desk, which held a table that looked like it could probably seat twenty or more people. There were two men in there, currently hunched over something at the table, their backs to us. To the left was a set of heavy, industrial doors leading off the lobby. I was led to the right, to a more simple door which was held open for me by one of my scary armed escorts. From there, I was led down a plush hallway, our footsteps swallowed by the carpeting.

It was a long hallway, with plain fluorescent light panels in the ceiling and nothing on the walls to draw my interest at all. Some ways down, I could make out four doors, two on each side, near each other, and another door at the far end, way, way down the hallway. The gorilla leading me went to the first door on the right and knocked twice. He didn't wait for a reply, but instead opened it and gestured for me to go inside.

I had no idea what to expect, so I wasn't disappointed. It was, I don't know, a fancy dining room. It could have been in any fancy house I've seen on TV. A big oak table dominated the room, with chairs at each end and five more chairs lined up on each side. There was a long, thin serving cabinet of some kind along the outer wall, where I would have thought there would have been windows. Sitting at the other end of the table was Mr. Dominic Tsui. A woman was standing beside him, leaning in and murmuring something in his ear. Seeing me enter the room, he nodded and waved her off casually.

"Jason Docker," he said grandly, standing and raising both his arms, palms open in greeting. "At last, a proper conversation between us."

He was slender, but seemed still well muscled. His Asian looks made me wonder if he did some kind of martial arts. Or maybe I was just being a racist moron. Either way, he looked cool. Dangerous and intimidating. His long black hair was shiny and flowed past his shoulders. He was wearing black slacks, a pale grey shirt of some kind of shiny material and a black fitted vest that accentuated his upper frame and made his shoulders look wider than with the trench coat I had seen him in before.

The woman walked toward me around the table. She had a sharp look on her face toward me, almost a look of hate, her mouth puckered up like she'd just sucked on a lemon. My attention was mostly on her as she approached, but then she passed me and exited the room. As she left, I looked back to Mr. Tsui. He was still smiling, and gestured for me to take a seat. Considering the only places that were made up for use were the two end chairs, that is where I sat down. Once I had pulled out my chair and was sitting, he sat as well.

"It's much better seeing you in this light," Mr. Tsui said.

I wasn't sure what to say to that, so rather than being sarcastic or rude, for once I bit my tongue. It was tough, because I don't deal well with power trips, and this guy was coming off like a more smiling version of my dad.

"I am surprised. I was unsure what I might find, once you arrived." His accent was crisp, practiced, cultured. Rather than making him seem friendly, it only added to his intimidating nature. I was so far out of my element with this guy that it wasn't even funny. But I always found that the best defense was a good offense, so I spoke up.

"Surprised in a good way? Or a bad way?"

He smiled, looking amused. His grin was oily, like just beneath the surface hid the over the top toothy grin of a Disney animated villain. "Oh, I am pleased, my boy. Very pleased."

"I'm glad I can please," I said, still trying to suppress any sarcasm or annoyance. "Can I ask, what is all this about? Why are you even talking to me?"

"Why wouldn't I, Jason?"

"It just seems kind of weird. You hired my dad, sure, then you keep creeping on his teenage kid?"

Mr. Tsui did not seem upset by this, but instead was still amused. "I suppose it does seem, as you say, 'sus', when look at that way."

Just then the door opened, and a pair of men wearing white chef's coats walked in. An entire platter of food was brought in and laid out before me. Everything looked amazing. Over the top really. I was starting to feel less like the hotel served everyone ten star meals, and more like this guy and his staff were trying to fatten me up and impress me. Still, my stomach was wanting to make it work. Some kind of stuffed chicken, a half dozen sides, and three different drink options were provided. Neither of us spoke as all of this was set in front of me.

Only a single opaque wine glass was set in front of my host.

Mr. Tsui spoke into the silence. "Please, eat."

"Are you not gonna eat?" I asked. It felt weird with all this food in front of me, and him having nothing.

"All men must eat."

"Ohh-kay."

I looked over the food. It did smell amazing. I tentatively cut into the chicken and it was juicy, practically falling apart as it oozed a stuffing of cheese and asparagus. But as good as it looked, as good as it smelled, I wasn't exactly interested in food at the moment.

"So back to what you were saying. Why are you bothering to talk to me? You hired my dad, not me."

Mr. Tsui laughed when I said that. You would have thought I told him an award-winning joke.

"My boy," said Mr. Tsui, waving his hands almost as if he was drunk. "I gave your father that wastrel posting as an excuse to bring you here."

As I struggled to understand why he would say something like that, my head spun. I continued to hear his voice, but it was muted, as if my head was underwater. I noticed a warmth on the side of my face, as right along my ear I felt a ring of cold.

I tried to make sense of what was going on, I thought I heard Mr. Tsui as he muttered in almost a stage whisper to me, "*Taai ging jan liu!* The power I feel coming off of you. How I have craved that."

My vision weaved in and out of focus, and I began to wonder why my plate of chicken was sideways and only inches from my eyes. Was I laying with my head on the table? Oh damn, was my face sitting in a plate of food?

Then I heard him yell, "Bah! This isn't wor—"

CHAPTER THIRTEEN

POISON IN YOUR COFFEE

The early morning sun was streaming in between the edges of the drawn curtains, forcing me awake. I was warm and cozy, but there were oddities that made me uncomfortable. It had happened again. I was sleeping in socks, I wasn't showered, and someone had put me to bed.

I was getting sick of this, but I was also scared. Scared that I was so easily being manipulated. Scared that I had so little control over where I had been and what was being done to me. Scared of being so vulnerable. Scared I might get used to wearing socks to bed.

After grabbing a shower and getting dressed, I headed downstairs for breakfast. Only once in the elevator did I think to check my phone, and realized it was only 6:30. I was worried the reason I woke up like I did was that I had been drugged, but I had never gotten around to even drinking anything, much less tasting the food. I couldn't wait to get out of this damned hotel and into some privacy.

But that was twice I woke up in bed in clothes I would never sleep in, after not remembering how I went to sleep. And both times that creepy guy was nearby. It really seemed like I was either in real danger, or going insane. I didn't know which outcome scared me more. The reason I couldn't tell which was happening was the reason I couldn't tell anyone. I had no proof either way.

It sucked.

I got to the dining room and there were actually a few more people taking advantage of the place. Maybe this is just a really early rising area? Who knows. Maybe the guy in the tweed jacket is the mascot of the place? Or maybe he is a statue, and I only thought I saw him moving. I laughed to myself at that thought.

I took a seat at a table that gave me some distance from anyone else, and the food I had ordered was just as good as anything else I had tried at this place. If they wanted to keep bribing me with the food, I wasn't going to stop them. I was just tucking into my first few bites of cream cheese stuffed french toast when the shouting voice I hated above all others pulled out of my relaxing breakfast.

"What the hell do you think you are doing?"

A lady with two children a couple of tables away looked up and scowled as my father stormed across the dining room. She wasn't the only one to be annoyed at the scene he was making, he was drawing the attention of everyone in the dining room. Even the old-man-mascot shook his head in disgust as he went back to his newspaper.

He ignored them all as he hurled obscenities at me while storming across the room like a thundercloud. My mother was walking a few steps behind him, looking with a cross between embarrassment, and the desire to grab his arm and hold him back.

Reaching the table, Dad slammed himself into a seat, grabbing my arm and spattering the forkful of food across the tablecloth.

"You too good to call us and let us know you were up?" He practically threw my arm away from himself, causing me to drop my fork and sending it clattering against my plate. "Didn't want to bother waiting for your mother and me?"

I was in no mood for him this morning. There was already too much weird stuff going on. I didn't need his bullying as well. So of course, I showed what a genius I was and opened my mouth.

"Yeah, if I had called, you'd be yelling at me for bothering you too early!" I was trying to keep my voice down. I kept the volume out of it, but not the venom.

"I was planning on calling mamma in a little bit, but I assumed you were off for another of your super breakfasts."

I didn't even know what happened, but the next thing I knew, I was laying on the floor, my mother was scolding out my father's name, "Jeremy, no!" My father rubbed the back of his hand like he hit it on something, acting for all the world like the pain in the side of my face didn't matter.. I was burning with shame and embarrassment as I picked myself up off the floor and got back into my chair. My father had scooted so close, that getting back in my seat put my face inches from his, even as I tried to lean away.

"Remember your goddamned place, Jason. Don't you dare talk back to me like that."

My mother said nothing, so I backed down meekly. If she wasn't going to jump in, I had no chance. Fortunately, my supplication seemed to be working, and the animosity at the table seemed to be dissipating. Within a few moments, a server approached the table. "Is there a problem here?"

I didn't look up.

"Yeah, there's a problem," said my dad. "Me and my wife don't have no menus. When's breakfast?"

"My apologies," the woman said. Layers of sarcasm tinted her tone, but, as always, my oblivious father didn't catch it. At least it wasn't pity for me. "I'll be right back with those menus. Coffee to drink?"

"Yes, thank you," said my mother soothingly.

I kept my head down and my mouth shut for the rest of breakfast. I did overhear my parents talking that, joy of all joys, Dad was taking today and tomorrow off to deal with moving into the house. My phone dinged with a text alert, but I knew better than to take out my phone when Dad was in this kind of mood. Breakfast dragged on, and I couldn't wait to get away from the table. The food that had seemed amazing when I started eating had lost all its taste.

I was still pissed when we finished eating, so when Dad got up from the table, I held back. Not only did I not want to ride up to our rooms together, my goal was going to be to avoid him the rest of the day. Maybe the weekend if I could figure out how. Maybe the rest of the school year?

My mother burst my bubble by sticking around to give me a quick word. She needed me to meet them back in the lobby in a bit to go over to the house with them, and to "bring a book". Great. That meant we were going to be sitting around a bunch. I asked if I could bring my board, and she shook her head, nodding my Dad's direction.

There went my day.

CHAPTER FOURTEEN

HOME SOUR HOME

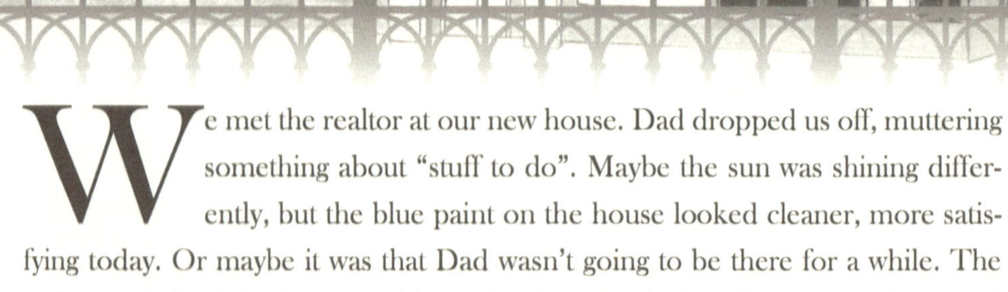

We met the realtor at our new house. Dad dropped us off, muttering something about "stuff to do". Maybe the sun was shining differently, but the blue paint on the house looked cleaner, more satisfying today. Or maybe it was that Dad wasn't going to be there for a while. The realtor unlocked the house and let us in. I was excited and curious as I entered the house.

The downstairs was divided into two main areas, with the larger being a big area that had the living room, dining room, and kitchen all in one space. It looked nice, but it was all open and I could already see there was going to be no privacy down here. I would need to figure out where I could hang out to avoid Dad.

The rest of the downstairs was the master bedroom and bathroom. It had a standing shower with glass walls that was huge, probably enough room for three or four people at once. There were even multiple shower heads built into the sides. Next to it, with big bay windows looking out over the snow covered back yard, there was a giant tub with jacuzzi jets.

Then I got to go upstairs.

The stairs opened onto a wide space, almost like a second living room. One wall was a pair of five foot tall windows overlooking the street out front, while the back wall had a door to a bathroom. At the end of the area closer to the stairs was a bedroom with a decent closet. Nice, but nothing special. The other end, though, had the prize.

There were two bedrooms side by side, with one being almost the size of the master bedroom downstairs. Even better, both bedrooms shared a bathroom, meaning I wouldn't have to go out in the hallway anymore. It also boasted a shower as big as the one my parents had downstairs as well. Between this and the living space outside the bedroom, it was going to feel like I had my own house up here!

"Oh, this is nice!" came my mother's voice from behind me. I jumped, but turned to her with a grin.

"So that's your bedroom over on the other end, right?" she teased.

"No, ma'am. I assumed it was the closet off the kitchen!"

"So what do you think of the place?"

"Have you seen in here?" I asked.

She came over and looked around the corner into the bathroom. "Just keep in mind that it is going to be your responsibility to keep this place clean. Next door is going to be a guest bedroom, and I don't want to have to keep on you about making it presentable."

"Yes, ma'am."

"This just doesn't seem real," I said, still with a bit of awe in my voice. "We can really afford this place? It's like twice what we had in Alabama."

"Only twice?" she said with mock insult. "You obviously haven't seen the whole place."

"What do you mean?"

Mom put her arm around my shoulders, dragging me toward the bedroom door and over to the stairs. "Oh, poor deluded child o'mine. You missed somethin'."

She took me downstairs and took me over to the double glass doors leading out to the back yard. The yard wasn't huge, but it was nicely kept up, and even had a pair of trees out there, to match the big one out front. Beside them was a kind of cubby room, not very big. With two doors.

She pointed straight ahead, saying, "That there's the garage."

Looking at the door on the left, with my voice tinged with curiosity and apprehension, I asked, "And that door?"

"Open it and find out."

I opened the door and was met with the scene from half the horror movies I'd ever watched behind my mom's back. A set of stairs led down into deep, suffocating darkness. A deep, dark basement.

The lack of light meant there was no way to tell the condition of the stairs, or what might be awaiting us down there. The ceiling in front of me sloped down just as steeply as the stairs, blocking my view. The space seemed to absorb sound just as well as it stole the light. These stairs were narrow, claustrophobic. Perhaps because of the bright and open nature of the rest of the house, this space felt menacing and dangerous.

Then it did more than feel dangerous, as I heard whispers coming from down below. The dark shadows seemed to ripple, as if things were moving. I froze, unable to sense what was real and what was impossible. Then out of nowhere...

I jumped about a mile, nearly toppling forward down the stairway, as Mom's hand landed on my shoulder from behind.

"Well go on down!" my mother said cheerfully. I think she enjoyed making me jump.

"Meanie!" I laughed, trying to slow my racing heart. It was just my imagination, clearly. There was nothing moving down below. Nothing whispering up at me from the darkness.

"Seriously, where are the lights?"

"Are they not down there on the wall?" she asked. "Oh, wait." I heard a switch behind me, and a small light came on over my head, just inside the stairwell. It was enough to let me see where I was going. The stairs went straight, all the way down. Once I got about halfway down the room opened up, as I got low enough to be below the ceiling level. There was a small amount of vague light, and although I couldn't make out the full room, I was able to get the impression that it felt cavernous. Once I got to the bottom, I found a bank of light switches and cut them on.

Sure enough, there was nothing out of place down there. I was not wrong when I felt like the place was massive. It was probably the same footprint of the house above us. It had a full height ceiling, and only at the far end was any of it divided off, with two doors in the far wall. There were two spots in each of the long walls, the front and back of the house, where there were narrow windows maybe six or eight inches tall and a foot and a half long, set right up at the very top against the ceiling. Otherwise, the room was open, except for six round metal poles set at regular intervals, maybe a foot off the wall, obviously there as a support system for the upper house.

"Oh, yeah," Mom said as she joined me. "Get some carpeting down here, maybe something on the walls. This could be a nice man cave, don't ya think?"

"So Dad's man cave, huh?" I said, the magic of the room draining right out of me.

"We'll see," she said. She patted my shoulder understandingly. "Come on back upstairs. The delivery people should be here soon enough, and we need ta' make sure we know where they're puttin' stuff."

As we headed back upstairs, I asked, "What's being delivered? I thought the movers weren't getting here 'til tomorrow?"

"Well," said Mom conspiratorially, "On top of a sign-on bonus, we were given some money to furnish the house with." She put her hands on my shoulders and walked me in front of her.

"This is a lot of money getting thrown at us," I muttered.

I was thinking about some of the vague phrases from the night before. I couldn't remember most of the conversation, and I had the impression that the few words and phrases I could recall were only the tip of the iceberg. But one line that stuck out in my head was where Mr. Tsui mentioned hiring Dad to bring me here. I didn't get it.

Who was I?

I'm nobody. And yet, everyone knew what foods I did and didn't like. I was given my own hotel room. The desk staff were going out of their way to be cool with me. And here we were, getting a house that was big enough that I got my own bathroom, and was only a short walk from school.

The day turned out to be a lot of "sit and wait", interspersed with bouts of frenzied activity whenever a truck showed up. Dad showed up a few hours into it. Nearly every room in the house got new furniture, while I was told that what I had for my bedroom was "good enough".

Dad started into a loud rant about the place being too big, and how much the electricity was going to be, not to mention the taxes, the cost to get furniture for the place, and who knows what else, so I slipped out and sat on the front steps. The paved steps were cold, but at least they were dry and free of snow.

I decided to pull out my phone to look over some more of the Hammers & Hordes armies, when I saw the notification for the text message I had received at breakfast. I had forgotten all about it. It was from an unknown number. No other way to find out, right? I texted them back.

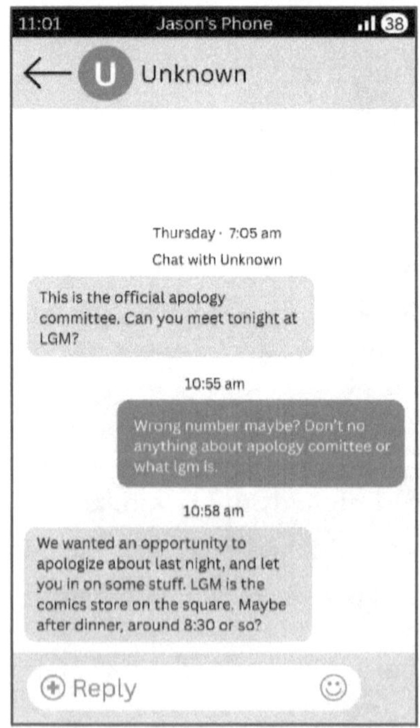

Huh? "Apology committee"? If, and that was a big "if", this was meant for me, it explained nothing. The response was quick, considering it had been a few hours since the original text.. I decided it was too weird and didn't bother responding. Maybe my curiosity later on would be enough for me to go check it out. Right now my curiosity was just enough to make me a little paranoid, and honestly, to piss me off quite a bit.

I was being messed with. Whether it was an elaborate prank or some kind of scheme, I didn't care. I was sick of being blind. I tried looking around at models, but I was too distracted by the frustrating message. As far as I was concerned, Mr. Tsui could kiss my ass.

Even though I wasn't allowed to help the delivery guys, I still wasn't allowed to leave the house. At dinner that evening, Dad managed to behave, and the mood was actually tolerable.

After dinner I was not interested in hanging out in the hotel room the whole night, so I decided to go meet the mystery texter after all.

Just as I was stepping into the elevator, I heard a door down the hall slam open and my father's voice yell out, "Hey, Jason! Get back here!"

"Oh, no," I muttered under my breath as I lazily pressed the Door Close button. "Look at that. The door is closing and I can't do anything about it." I kept pressing the button over and over, trying to hurry the doors to close, all while muttering, "Sorry, Dad. Nothing I can do."

CHAPTER FIFTEEN

THE APOLOGY COMMITTEE

When I got to the square, I took a closer look at the front signs all around the comic store. The text message said it was supposed to be called "Little Green Men," but I hadn't seen it. The words "Comics & Games" were written in large letters, much bigger than any other signage. Above that was the name of the town, Avernus. But in between that was what I had taken for doodling and some random signage. That's what I get for not paying attention.

The line in between, the one I had missed, said "Little Green Men", with the letters being climbed around on by some green space aliens, some fantasy Goblins, and a few of the plastic green army men, like they had in Toy Story. So there you go, the actual name of the store was Little Green Men, aka LGM. Finally, one of the hundreds of mysteries had an answer.

I pulled the door open and walked in. Even at eight o'clock on a Thursday, there were easily a dozen people in here. I ducked my head back out of the door and checked the posted hours. Sure enough, they were open until one am, and three am Friday and Saturday nights. I was starting to get why this place had weird hours. There were a bunch of night owls around here, though it was the only place on the square with anyone around.

The door was barely closed behind me when I heard a voice call out, "You're early."

A guy was approaching me, smiling widely and waving casually in my direction. I couldn't tell if his complexion was more Hispanic or a pale African descent, but it was working for him. He was an average height, meaning several inches taller than me, and maybe twenty or so. He was decently attractive, but I did not recognize him in any way.

"Do I know you?" I asked.

He laughed, stuck out his hand, and said, "Sorry, I'm Montgomery. I'm part of your apology committee."

I tentatively shook his hand, and Montgomery instantly pulled me in so that the next thing I knew, his arm was around my shoulder and I was squeezed against his body. Any concept of personal space was gone as he guided me across the shop, giving me very little control. The best I could do was not stumble and fall. He was strong enough that I had no say.

"Anyway, me and a couple of others were sent here by Dom to straighten things out. He felt bad about how things went last night."

"He sent you? Why not come himself?"

Montgomery laughed, and I honestly couldn't tell if he was laughing at me, or what I said. "We dance to his tune. If you don't already know how it is, you will soon enough."

I definitely got the impression I was a chore he had been assigned. He was talking *at* me, not *to* me. He led me over toward the gaming tables with the buildings and trees all over them. Once I saw who he was taking me to, and I instantly had no problem with where we were headed.

My girl with the white hair, was moving a line of miniatures along one side of a table, facing across from "definitely not my boyfriend" Garrett. It occurred to me that while we had discussed options about what I might play, I had not asked what she played. As we got to the table, I pulled away from Montgomery and he let me go without a fight. I took a look at her miniatures, and saw they were the boxy, armored models of Cosmos Emptor, the big evil Human empire. Since she had said they were easily the most popular to play, I wouldn't have expected her to be playing them.

She looked up and I said, "Hello, again."

"Hello, again, I suppose." Rather than the casual warmth I had seen yesterday, I saw a look of disdain, or something similar. Maybe she was just annoyed at being interrupted. She glanced past me. "This is the kid we were sent?" When Montgomery nodded, she looked at me. "Welcome to Avernus. What do you think of our humble home so far?"

Before I could even answer, Montgomery scoffed, "Are we really going to go through the small talk? Don't we have real things to discuss?"

She continued studying me, even while addressing him. "We are supposed to be the welcoming committee, so you could at least *try* being welcoming. But if you would rather be your charming self, I've got this, Montgomery." She made a shoo-ing motion with her hand. "You can go."

"Yes, your queenliness." To me he said, "Welcome to the Ravens. Don't get pecked to death by these two, little boy."

Erin went back to moving her models around.

"Please sit," she said to me. And just like that, she was softer and more friendly. It was obviously Montgomery she disliked. "This jackass across from me is my good friend, Garrett."

"Don't even start," Garrett said with a playful smirk.

"I remember," I said. "Curious... Yesterday you barely wanted to acknowledge his existence."

"Did I now?" she said with a grin. Garrett laughed, obviously in on a joke I didn't get.

I tried to move past my awkwardness and confusion. "Anyway, I did what you said, and did some more research. I think I found an army that you overlooked."

"Is that so?" Erin was looking at me like I was some amusing puppy doing tricks for her. It was the weirdest, most awkward feeling, and it was starting to piss me off.

"Do I need to go or something?"

"No, please," she said. "Please stay, Jason. I should quit being catty. You don't deserve it, and I'm just accidentally taking my frustration with that inflated walking ego out on you"

"Yeah," said Garrett. "You're going to get yourself censured over the town's newest toy. Neither of them are worth it."

Erin glared at him, and for a moment, I thought she was going to leap across the table. Then just like that, she was calm, and that friendly warmth filled her eyes.

"I apologize for being rude." She held out her hand for me to shake. "I haven't introduced myself. I'm Wren."

I took her hand, and she held it limp. It was as cold as it had been yesterday. I let it go, not bothering to shake it. My face went dead and I looked straight at her, going for my best "resting bitch face". It was difficult, because she was the kind of "hot" that fought to keep my attention despite the attitude.

"So which is it? Erin or Wren?"

With the most playful, Cheshire grin, she asked, "It depends on when I saw you last. Was it in here, last night? Or was it two nights ago, at the hotel?"

"Alright, I'm done." I was pretty tired of the twists and turns, and didn't want to play the games anymore. I turned to leave. Screw this noise. It was bad enough that something or someone was messing around with me behind my back. I wasn't going to have it done to my face.

"Wren, cut it out," I heard Garrett say. "I get being pissed at Dom, but this kid didn't ask for this."

I was a full table away when she called out to me. "Jason."

I was still pissed, but her soft brown eyes filled my mind and I stopped walking. I knew if I turned around now, there would be a softer look in them. There was something tugging me back, some compulsion I couldn't understand. As much as I wanted to storm off in anger, I suddenly wanted to make her happy. Not just that, but I wanted her to be happy with me, specifically. I took another step and just knew I was going to upset her if I continued going. I desperately didn't want that. Not only did she have answers I needed, but I wanted to be on her good side. I wanted her to like me.

"Please, Jason," she said. "I apologize. Come back."

I slumped my shoulders and turned back. I tried to stay mad, but the look of relief and friendliness on her face meant I just couldn't. I walked back over to their table. I wanted to let her know I was still upset though, so I walked over to Garrett's side of the table. It was the best way I could think of to punish her back. Childish, and yet petty. Nice.

Looking down at the models on his side of the board, I said, well. "These are the Rebellion guys, right? The Scions, or something like that?"

Garrett's eyes flicked up at Wren, then back at me. "Remnant, actually."

"Cool."

"Yeah, the Scion Rebellion are the traitors from the Cosmos Emptor. They get power suits and tanks like them. These are the Remnant. They are the other rebellion group. More grassroots." He picked up one of his men, a Human wearing a more normal conventional military uniform. "These guys are about throwing meat grinders at the enemy. More of a horde army."

"Oh, cool." I said.

"What was the other army you found?" Garrett asked. "You mentioned 'Rin overlooked an army, and you did some research?"

"Oh, yeah," I said. "The Collective."

"Interesting."

"Yeah," I said. "They looked really cool. Looked unique."

"It sounds like you are just getting started," said Garrett. "Do you have any experience with tabletop games? Can you even handle anything more than a starter army?"

So much for being welcoming. This guy was proving to be just as arrogant as I originally thought. He seemed a perfect example of judging a book by its cover.

"If you are just starting," our friend on the other side of the table interjected. "Why not try out Cosmos Emptor? It's pretty much everyone's starting army. The easiest to play and easiest to collect."

Sighing and shaking my head, I moved away from Garrett's side of the table and answered, "Like I said yesterday, Humans are boring." Looking back at

Garrett, I asked, "Just clarify that I'm not going crazy," He grinned at me, "but you saw me talking to her, right?" I gestured to the girl. "Last night, right over there?"

"We are not trying to mess with you," said Garrett. "I promise. *Wren* and I were watching you eat dinner two nights ago, and you had a conversation with *Erin* yesterday."

"Multiple personality much?" I smirked.

"You tell me," Erin-Wren said, nodding to indicate the store behind me.

There she was again. In addition to sitting across the table, there she was walking across the store toward us as well. She was dressed exactly the same as the girl across from me and Garrett, in acid washed skinny jeans and a rose colored skin tight hoodie. The white hair was the same, as were the eyes.

"I'm so damn slow," I muttered. "Twins. Of course." I glanced across the table. "So you're Wren, and she's Erin."

Wren nodded. "Correct. My sister and I are twins. We have cultivated a look."

CHAPTER SIXTEEN

REFLECTED GLANCES

"Jason," called out Erin, smiling as she approached. She was carrying something like a small suitcase. "It's good to see you again."

"At least this is finally cleared up," I said. Even I couldn't decide if I was annoyed or relieved. "So were you two messing with me on purpose?"

"No, babe," Erin, the real one, said as she leaned into Wren for a side hug. "It was just a coincidence that we were running into you at different times."

"Any more secrets I need to know? Anything else you guys aren't telling me?"

The two sisters glanced at each other, practically touching foreheads, they were so close, then looked at Garrett. "There are a few," said Wren, the seated one, "although we can't tell you everything right now. Public, and all that."

"I'm seriously not going to put up with this garbage for much longer," I said. "What can you tell me then?"

The twins looked at me in a duplicate eye stare that was really creeping me out. Wren gave me the impression he was enjoying it, but it didn't seem like Erin's vibe. Wren spoke up, saying, "There's unfortunately some things we can't get into right now. I'll make you a promise, Jason. These two will witness it." Both of the others nodded, as if this were something more official. "I'll ask for permission. You are kind of a special case, after all. Everything I can get permission for, I will share with you."

"They were effin' right," I muttered. "You Ravens are a secret society of something."

"Something like that," Wren said without a trace of humor.

"I'll give you something to chew on," said Garrett with a laugh, changing the mood, "since I can practically smell the pheromones coming off you, kid." I looked at him, trying to decide how much he was messing with me. "These two, over here?" he said, gesturing at the two across the table from us. In a sing-song voice he added, "They-'re no-ot si-sters!"

"What?" I was completely confused. I looked at the two girls. They had to be twins. If not, they looked remarkably alike. But then, Wren had mentioned they had cultivated the look and all. "Seriously, you're tellin' me you two aren't twins? You're messin' with me, right?"

"Oh, they're twins, alright," said Garrett. Erin and Wren smiled at me in a "we've got you" kind of way. Then Garrett added, "Just not identical. Wren here... is Erin's brother."

"The hell you say!" I laughed.

"Nope," said Wren with a seductive smile. She, or rather he, slid Erin off his knee and leaned forward, resting his elbows on the table, practically laying across the terrain. "I'm one hundred percent, all natural, home grown boy."

"Well screw me sideways."

"If that's an offer," grinned Wren, in a stage whisper loud enough for just our table to hear.

I gulped and blushed, unable to keep my interest hidden. I was normally better than this, but at this moment, I was a hundred and ten percent horned up, and shamefully would have done anything he asked. Out of nowhere, I found myself lost in his cocoa brown eyes. Nobody else in the room existed. Hell, nobody else in the world existed. I was so unworthy of this man's attention, and yet I had to be with him. I had never felt this way, ever.

And then something snapped in my head and the... whatever that was, passed. I felt like people describe how being drunk is supposed to feel like, light-headed and wobbly on my feet. I felt foolish over the thoughts I had just had flash through my head. Sure, I'd found him unbelievably cute when I thought he was a girl. And he was flat out hot, knowing he was a guy. But whatever had just happened was way harsher than the deepest lust I've ever felt. It was wrong, and it scared me.

I really needed to get the topic off this *whatever* I was feeling. "Back to the point. You say you called me here, yet you can't tell me anything. What happened to this apology committee?" I said, sarcastically.

Garrett laughed while looking at Wren. "That's all you."

Wren sighed, clearly annoyed. "I've been sent, well, I and Montgomery over there, were asked to apologize for Dominic Tsui being unable to meet with you last night as planned. He will reschedule-"

"But we did!" I interrupted.

Silence hung over the four of us. Finally, Wren asked, "You did, what?"

"We met," I insisted. "For dinner."

"You did?" asked Garrett.

"Yeah. Third floor, long hallway with a dining room instead of a hotel room?" When the other three looked at me like I had a third head, I continued, trying to convince them. "One of his armed goons took me up through a second elevator around the corner from the first. Takes you up to a lobby with a reception desk and a glass conference room?"

"Mother–," muttered Garrett.

"Hey," said Erin. "Hey potty mouth. No need for that."

"Drop it, Erin. This is serious."

"Fill me in, guys," I said.

They glanced at each other, their eyes questioning.

"Seriously. Fill me in or I walk. Was I drugged or some crap? 'Cause I passed out in my food, and woke up in bed."

Erin had her face in her palm by this point. Garrett was looking at me like I was crazy. Wren started laughing.

"Dom's lost it," Wren exclaimed. "I love this. Maybe he'll fail here, finally!"

"Guys? Hello?"

Wren looked up at me with a serious look. "Let's just say that Dominic... overstepped. He's done a few things he had the power to do, but not the authority."

"What's the difference?" I asked.

Erin answered, saying, "You have the power, the ability, to walk over there and punch the store owner." Instinctively I glanced over at the guy behind the counter reading a magazine, then looked back at Erin. "However, you don't have the authority to do so, and would be arrested."

"So what you're sayin' is, Mr. Tsui has done something he shouldn't be?" All three nodded. "Like bringin' me here, maybe?"

"Bringing your family here, yes," said Wren.

"Naw uh. Bringin' *me* here. Me." I was getting frustrated and a bit scared. My Alabama accent was coming out, which of course frustrated me even more. Still, I had to get everything out and try to get some answers. "He said so, last night. Mr. Tsui said my dad only got this job to get me up here."

Wren looked over at Garrett. "And you were worried about *me* getting censured? If he plays this wrong, this could bury him."

"Ugh," I yelled in frustration. A few people from other tables looked over at my outburst. "I'm not going to get any answers from you people, am I? And here I thought you guys were gonna be nice."

Wren looked at me in genuine surprise, a smile on his face. "Oh, I think I'm going to like this kid," he said to the other two.

I was shaken, really thrown off my guard, and I think the others knew it. "Jason," Wren said, leaning over to lay his hand on my arm. I hated that I liked his touch. "I know this is frustrating. We really want to tell you more, and hopefully we can really soon. I promise, the Ravens aren't your enemy. In fact, we are the opposite. I fully intend to get the necessary permission to prove it. All I can ask for is a little patience."

I appreciated his attempt at reassurance. Then Garrett had to stick in his own two cents. "Assuming you decide to be worth the effort."

Both of the twins glared daggers at him, but it seemed the business was concluded. Wren went back to rearranging his models with Garrett. Trying to defuse the tension, Erin grabbed the case she had walked in with and guided me over to the next table. From her case she pulled out trays of miniatures, talking me through what she played, and asking me about my research.

I told her about finding a new army called the Collective, and that they seemed interesting. They were an insectoid species, something like the Zerg from Starcraft. But instead of being monsters, they were a psychic race of scientists, using other non-sentient creatures bio-engineered as weapons in order to protect their planets from the Cosmos Emptor. So they looked like cool monsters, yet they were intelligent and crafty, and just as "human" as the Humans.

We spent about an hour where Erin used her models to teach me a bunch of the basic rules of the game. Meanwhile, I kept trying to ask questions and dig for more information, even telling her things about me to get the ball rolling. She did her part in teaching me just how good she was at dodging questions and deflecting away from answers.

"What am I supposed to tell my parents about all this?" I finally asked.

Erin grinned at me. "Do you always tell your folks everything going on with you?"

"Heck no, but I usually don't have people like Mr. Tsui walking up to my mother and telling her I am being invited to join a social club for teens," I responded. "She's going to ask how it went and what we did."

"No, she won't," Erin said confidently.

"Yes," I insisted, "she will. You don't know my mother."

"I'll let it go," she said cryptically. "How about this? Don't bring it up first. If she *does* bring it up, tell her... you met a few friends that will help you out with some socially acceptable hobbies." She gestured at the game room as she said this.

Eventually we ended up back at the merchandise wall, where Erin pointed out the few boxed units they had for the Collective army. I ended up picking up a specialist unit and a leadership character, but they had no basic troops. I felt like I was being led around by the hand as she pulled me over to the counter and explained to the employee three different boxes for him to order, that she just insisted I needed. He explained that orders were placed on Mondays, and arrived on Thursday, meaning it would be a week before I would have the models I needed to play. Then, as I was paying for my two boxes I had, I got hit with more disconcerting news.

With Erin on my left, her voice spoke from behind my right shoulder. "So what colors were you thinking about painting them?"

I whipped around, confused, only to realize Wren had joined us at the counter. "What do you mean, what color?" I pointed to the box artwork. "They're grey and brown, right?"

For some reason I shuddered as he placed a hand on my shoulder. It wasn't dread or horror or anything. More like anticipation, or desire. I couldn't quite identify it. Then Wren leaned into me, reaching to point at a small line of text printed in the lower corner. "All miniatures supplied unassembled and unpainted."

"Damn it guys," I muttered in embarrassment. "These are gonna look like crap. I've never done anything like this before."

As Wren pulled his hand back, there was a "click" sound, like someone was using one of those little clickers used for animal training, and he bumped into me, shoving me slightly against the counter.

"I apologize," he said, placing his hand back on my shoulder. I hadn't realized he had removed it. Then he set another box on the counter. "Roger, put this on my tab."

I looked at what Wren had set down. It was labeled as a beginner paint set, and seemed to come with about a dozen choices of paints, plus a pair of brushes. In addition, he added a hobby knife and what looked like a pair of oversized nail clippers. Finally, from a counter display, he grabbed a little bottle of glue.

As the employee started bagging Wren's supplies with my two boxes, I protested, "My guy, I've got money."

"Call it my apology. I did say I was with the apology committee, did I not?" He picked up my bag, swinging it around to pop into my chest. Not enough to hurt, but hard enough to engage my reflexes and make me catch it. "When do you need to be back?" he asked.

I pulled out my phone and checked. It was just after nine. "Hrm. I probably need to be back by ten. So maybe another twenty minutes?"

"Good enough," he said.

With Erin in tow, Wren casually tossed his arm over my shoulder, much as Montgomery had done earlier, and walked me back into the gaming area. But Wren was only a couple of inches taller than me, rather than towering over me like Montgomery. Plus, I really didn't mind his closeness, in a way that stirred up my stomach. Garrett joined us at an empty table that was not set up for gaming, and the three of them spent some time showing me how to use my tools, as well as the basics of using my paints. Erin ended up pulling out some partially done models, letting me practice with the tools. The modeling knife kind of scared me at first, with how much it looked like a scalpel. But they went over safety and tips for using the tools and assembling the models. We didn't open my own boxes due to time, but at least I had some idea of what to expect when I did.

Both of the twins offered to meet me the next evening, but I told them I wasn't sure if I would be available, with the unpacking and all. I thought it was kind of cool they respected me enough to not ask for my new address, but then again, maybe they weren't interested enough. Eventually I felt like I needed to break away and say my goodbyes. I've never seen another group of people manage to walk such a fine line between being disappointed, and yet not seeming to give a crap. It was truly weird.

Chapter Seventeen

Life Is Moving Fast

Leaving the shop with my bag of new hobby materials, I carried my board and began walking back to the hotel. It was starting to snow and I had no clue how slick it might be yet. Besides, my mind was too distracted, and I knew I would hit a rock and go flying.

Garrett was exactly what he had been in my first impression. He was handsome, well put together, and gave off the impression of wearing designer everything, from his scent to his clothing. He also had a designer attitude, meaning he had seemed to only have time for me once it was apparent that Wren, and then Erin, had an interest in me.

Speaking of the twins, they fascinated me in a way I hadn't felt before. Erin was funny and entertaining, with a kind streak that stood out whenever I was around her. In comparison, Wren stood out as, not arrogant, not quite, but more... confident. There was a sureness to him, almost like I imagined someone with authority and power would act. It's like he knew the world around him was going to bend to his will, so he didn't feel like he needed to stress *how* it would happen. It wasn't condescending, even though it felt like it should be. Because once he spoke, his confidence didn't come off as arrogance. That was Garrett, not Wren.

And this whole thing with the twins looking *exactly* alike, like they were the hottest girls I had ever seen, and yet one was a boy. What was up with that? And I didn't mean that in a judgmental way. Rather, I was fascinated. Wren obviously used "he/him" pronouns, yet the way all three of them had discussed him, it didn't seem like they were saying Wren was trans. No, it was made clear that they were decidedly *not* identical twins, and instead had cultivated their looks to be identical, and definitely on the feminine spectrum.

Speaking of feminine. Ho-ly hell-in-a-handbasket. I've always self-identified as, like, 98% gay, but the closer a person can get to the line between boy and girl, the more it tickles my fancy, if you get my drift.

Androgynous, they call it. Hot, I call it.

Erin had already been getting my attention, in the same way that someone with a lot of those Goth and Emo looks did. But then to get the same girlish body, skinny waist and long hair, while knowing the right equipment was waiting down below? I was one hundred percent interested. Not that I stood a chance, but I was definitely interested.

I could have predicted exactly how the next day was going to go. I kept my head down through breakfast, but all that did was frustrate my father, since he didn't have anything to yell at me about. Even still, he took every opportunity to tell me I somehow took too long in exiting my hotel room, even though I was packed and out by the car well before either of my parents. Mina and the old, tall guy were there to check us out.

But the real problems started when we got to the house. While waiting for the moving truck to arrive, I was both "in the way" and yet also "being lazy and not helping". Not helping with what? All they were doing was sorting their suitcases from the trip. They had new furniture to put their stuff in. I had nothing until my furniture from the old house arrived. I doubt they wanted me helping out in their bedroom.

Then the movers arrived. Dad shouted at me to help the three massive guys begin unloading the truck, but the guys were cool and told me, politely, that their insurance didn't allow me to help. All the boxes were marked where they belonged, so I figured the best thing I could do was head up to my new room, and as my stuff was brought up, figure out where it went. I mean hell, I knew what furniture there was and how big it all was, so I had already decided what would go where.

Barely an hour into the truck being unloaded I heard Dad yelling at me to come downstairs. I figured it was for lunch, given the time. It was a little earlier than I expected, but whatever. Instead I was met by him being pissed off. What a surprise.

"Why am I just hearing from your mother that you have to go to your school today?" he yelled.

"I don't know," I said. "Yeah, I have to pick up my laptop and schedule and stuff. But, I mean, I wasn't given a time."

"And it didn't occur to you to get it done *before* all this," he gestured his arms around us, "got so busy?"

"Jeremy," yelled my mom from the kitchen, "leave the boy alone! He's got plenty of time and not much to do!"

"Stay the hell out of this, Renee!" he yelled back. "His punk ass needs to be here to help out."

"God damn it, you bastard!" came her reply. "You will not talk to me like that!" She came storming out of the kitchen, a skillet in one hand, a saucepan in the other. "I put up with your attitude the entire time we were in the hotel." I was glad I wasn't on the receiving end of her screwed up face this time. "But this is my house we are in now! And I won't have it!"

"The hell it's your house, woman! You'll take whatever the hell I give you!"

A pair of the moving guys slunk down the stairs during this exchange, clearly uncomfortable at being witness to all this, and I shrunk in embarrassment, knowing how screwed up both my parents were acting. The dudes were staring, unsure what they were witnessing and how bad it might turn. When Dad yelled, "The hell you looking at?" toward the guys, one of them put up his hands in a "We're not part of this" gesture, and then hurried outside.

Using the movers' interruption as an opportunity to de-escalate, Mom looked in my direction and in a more normal volume said, "Baby, why don't you run up to the school now. We'll eat lunch when you get back."

"The hell he will," yelled Dad. He wasn't about to take the hint about calming down. "He'll stay here and get back to work."

"Jeremy, you know now's as good a time as any. He's in the way of the guys unloading right now anyway."

Like turning on a dime, Dad looked in my direction and yelled, "You heard your mother! Get your ass to the school and get your crap!"

He was yelling as if it had been his idea the whole time. I was done with this and ready to get out of the house. I didn't even bother going upstairs for a jacket. I just took the opportunity and slipped out the front door. This turned out to be a mistake, because not only had it dropped a couple of inches of snow overnight, but it was also snowing now. And here I was with nothing but my ever-present hoodie.

Finding the school from this side of town wasn't difficult, especially with GPS on my phone, and taking care of everything there was pretty harmless. It didn't take nearly as long as I hoped. So, I guess I had to go back.

I made it to the house, only to find out Dad had run out and picked up fast food without anyone bothering to ask me what I might want. It brought me back down to earth and made me realise how spoiled I was getting with the hotel's food. It made me wish I could befriend the cook up there, Devon.

A couple of hours after lunch I was upstairs in my new room, staying out of the way and reading over the instruction booklet that had come with the painting kit, when I heard my dad's voice.

"Oh, hell no!" he yelled, all the way downstairs. It was the type of call I always dreaded. Closer and clearer, I heard him yell, "Jason, get your damn ass down here!"

Seriously? No idea what that could be, but the longer it took for me to answer, the worse he was going to make it. I got to the stairs as quickly as I could without running, and looking down, there he was at the bottom.

"There you are! Get your ass down here."

He kept staring and motioning for me as I made my way down the steps. I kept expecting him to say something, since he looked like he was ready to explode, but it was obvious he wanted me down there. I had two stairs left when he lunged forward and grabbed a handful of my hoodie, yanking me off my feet and down to the ground.

Before I could even comprehend what was happening, he was already tearing into the back pocket of my jeans, ripping the fabric and grabbing my wallet. Dropping me to the floor, I looked up to see him going through it.

"You goddamn thief," he growled. Taking out the money I had, he threw the wallet at my face and stuffed the bills into his front pants pocket.

"What the hell-" I said, catching my wallet reflexively.

"Your mother told me you had a bunch of my money!" he yelled. He reached down and grabbed my hoodie again, lifting me up as if I weighed nothing. It had been a while since I had seen him this pissed. "Where's the rest of it?"

"She said it was—" I was lifted up higher by his grip on my chest as his downward fist found my face. My neck snapped to the side with the force of the blow, and then I dropped to the floor as he let go of me.

"Don't lie to me, you little punk!" He growled down at me. "Get out of my sight."

I stumbled back to my feet and bolted up the stairs, slamming my bedroom door. I went into the bathroom, needing to see how bad it was in the mirror. And it was bad. I was going to have a shiner. Not my first, and probably not my last. But definitely enough to piss me off.

Thank God nobody was here watching me lose it.

I didn't even realize that my emotions and the adrenaline were catching up to me, and I found myself crying. Not hard, but unable to hold it in. Of course, that just frustrated and humiliated me more. My throat started locking up and cramping from trying to stop the sobs, and my knees kept giving out. I sat on the edge of the bed, flinching at a scratching sound at the door. I stared in confusion and fear as the door warped in the frame like a balloon. I heard a "woop, woop" from the street and in a flash the door was back to normal.

I saw flashing lights reflect off the ceiling, coming from down below my window outside. Minutes later, I heard shouting from downstairs. I heard my mom's shrill voice, and of course Dad's yelling. But also other voices. First one, then more. I thought it might be the moving guys. I was a bit in shock and wasn't putting two and two together.

Whatever was going on, if Dad was downstairs, I was staying up here. The yelling continued for a couple of minutes, then sounded like maybe it had moved outside. I did my best to ignore it, calming myself down and wiping my face. I was too caught up in my own head to pay attention, but at some point the shouting stopped. Well, the people yelling back at my father stopped. Dad, I could still hear yelling at Mom and occasionally yelling my name as well.

The dumbest thing occurred to me. That I had a bit of an advantage with this setup, due to the shared bathroom. If it really came down to it, whichever bedroom he entered, I could always run out the other. I don't know how long it was, whether it was three minutes or fifteen, but I heard a few other voices. I heard my dad yelling, but the talkers weren't yelling back. I was curious, but unsure whether I wanted to ignore it or investigate. Someone knocked on my bedroom door and I jumped, ready to bolt. It opened before I could answer. In my head I saw my father, but instead I saw a uniformed police officer standing in the doorway.

Chapter Eighteen

Petty Significance

A few hours later, I found myself kind of wandering around in a bit of a daze. The police station I had slipped out of was right off the square and I didn't know many areas of Avernus yet, so my feet kind of took me where I knew. The sun was just setting as I came out of the side street onto the square. The town had already cleared the sidewalks and I happened to run into Liam there, skating solo, and went over to say hey. He stopped when I approached, but seemed wary of me.

"Hey man, nobody else around?" I asked.

"Yeah. It's just me. Why? Is that a problem?"

"Naw, my guy," I said, hands up in surrender. Liam's eyes glanced up at my eye and for a moment his face softened. I tried to use that as an opening. "Everything okay? You seem like you've got a problem with me now or something."

Just as quickly it went back to sullenness and he asked, "Did you go hook up with the Ravens?"

The question shook me for a second. "Well, I mean, I talked to a couple of people, mostly Erin and Wren. Do you know them? They seemed nice, but I was watching my back with them." I saw that I was losing him as I ended weakly with, "They didn't seem bad?"

"Figured," Liam muttered. "I thought you were cool. But you want to side with the Ravens, don't say we didn't warn you." Then he dropped his board, hopped on, and took off.

I just stood there. His attitude was the last thing I needed. But considering the day I'd had so far, it fit right in. Well, nothing else seemed to be going my way, so I crossed the road and went to the only other place I really knew, Little Green Men.

Dark settled in, and all I had was the hoodie I had been wearing all day in the house. It would be warm in the game store and I had my phone on me. Mom could call me any time. She was still back at the police station. Honestly, I was supposed to be back there, too. For all I know, there were going to be squad cars out looking for me any time.

I grabbed one of the rulebooks for Hammers & Hordes off the shelf and took it over to one of the hobby tables. At this point I didn't care that I hadn't paid for it. I was only going to flip through it, not ruin it. In the mood I was in, I was daring someone to mess with me about it. I just wanted to block out the stuff going through my brain.

"Whew," someone whistled a few minutes later. I looked up to see Garrett and one of the twins standing over me. Even in my funk, I couldn't help but admire the, I don't know, almost an aura around them. Something that pulled my view to them and tried to give me butterflies.

"That looks painful," said the twin sympathetically, reaching out to gently touch my bruised eye. It hurt being touched, but their cool fingers felt soothing. I closed my eyes for a moment, enjoying the cool touch on my bruised face."You're with Garrett here, so..." I gestured to the twin. "Wren?"

He nodded. "What happened? Did you get in a fight?" The look on his face told me he didn't really believe that. I went ahead and confirmed his suspicions.

"Not exactly," I muttered. "Don't worry about it."

Garrett jumped in. "You forget, we were there in the restaurant that first night. Your dad slapped you then. Was this more of the same?"

I flushed and glared at him. Why did he have to call me out like that? It pissed me off. "So basically I can't take care of myself, is that what you think?" I rounded it off with a few extra choice words.

"Nobody is saying you can't stand up for yourself," Wren said calmly.

I backed down a bit. I wanted to back down. I didn't want Wren annoyed with me, but I also didn't want him thinking I was just some kid. I mean, he didn't seem that much older than me, but he was calm, collected. He was cool. I wanted Wren to like me.

Flicking my eyes to the side, I smirked a bit inside. I kind of agreed with Erin's opinion of Garrett. First, the crack yesterday about my gaming experience, and now his pity about my dad... Garrett could go hang, for all I cared.

Garrett chuckled at something, maybe some thought that crossed his mind. Then Wren reached over and tapped him on the arm. Something, some look, passed between them. Garrett nodded, looking a bit serious, and stood up. He walked across the store, back over around the counter. Wren and I both watched him go.

"What's that all about?" I asked.

"It's alright. He'll be right back," said Wren. He had a look of genuine concern on his face when he asked, "Will you tell me what happened? Please?"

I explained the argument over going to get the school laptop and about the movers not wanting me to help out, and how it seemed to annoy my dad. Then I explained about him finding out about the money my mother had given me.

"He didn't like you having money?" asked Wren in surprise.

"He accused me of stealing it," I said. "He damn near tore my jeans off trying to dig my wallet out of my pocket, grabbed the money out of it, and then slugged me for having spent some of it."

"So, what happened?"

I got distracted when I saw Garrett coming back over. However, he wasn't alone. Mr. Tsui strode before him.

Now I was absolutely confused.

The look on Mr. Tsui's face and the way he carried himself seemed to emanate waves of energy. All around the shop, players seemed to notice him and get out of his way.

When he reached our corner, he walked around the end of the table to stand over me. I almost felt like I should stand to meet him, and then because of how aggressive he was entering my personal space, I did. My initial impression was correct. He was only a couple of inches taller than me.

His eyes were a deep black, to the point that there was no noticeable difference between his iris and pupil. His long, black hair was a mirror of Wren's pure white hair, both fine and straight, flowing down their backs. His clothes were very fancy as usual, but his expression was as blank as I had ever seen.

Mr. Tsui studied my face. I couldn't tell if he was paying more attention to my facial expression or my black eye. "Where is your father?"

"I guess Garrett over there said something?"

"He did," said Mr. Tsui in a calm, quiet voice. His face contorted into a violent rage. Then, as suddenly as if a switch flipped, his expression went back to a relaxed, non-threatening stance. It was creepy, almost like there had been a frame-jump in a film. "May I please have my answer?"

"He's in jail," I spat out. "My mom, too. They are trying to decide whether to charge her with child endangerment." I blushed a bit, at having to refer to myself as a child.

"I see," he said quietly. "And does anyone know you are here?"

"I got sick of being ignored and walked out of the police station," I said. Even now, I knew it sounded like a stupid thing to have done. Maybe even something that should have been impossible. However, I was in a mood to be stubborn. "I've got my phone on me. I'm not hard to find."

"Indeed." He then took a further step back and seemed to waiver slightly, as if he were lightheaded. Then in an almost jovial tone, he said, "Well, it seems I have work to do. Wren, please see to our young Jason. It may be that company would do him good."

And without waiting for a reply, he strode off across the store, walking out the front door. I slumped into my seat, completely confused and more than a little scared. Wren watched him go, his fists balled at his side. His shoulders were tensed in anger, and as he turned to face me, I was sure that anger was going to be turned at me. But when he pulled out his chair, his face was already showing his concern. In some ways, that made me even more embarrassed.

“What even is my life?” I muttered.

Chapter NINETEEN

MELTING HIS SMILE

"You alright?" asked Garrett.

"I've been here four goddamned days!' I exclaimed. Then I snapped at Garrett, "No, I'm not alright. That's my dad's damn boss. We just moved here, and now it's absolutely gone."

"I doubt it's as bad as you think," said Wren.

"Yeah," I scoffed. "I guess the Mob doesn't care too much about domestic violence." I laughed a mirthless laugh. "Maybe they'll give him a raise."

"You misunderstand your situation here," said Wren. "You yourself told us Dom brought you here. That your father's job was an excuse to meet you. So don't you think he might want to protect his investment?"

I had to stop and think about that one. I really hadn't put two and two together. Maybe this guy might keep us around anyway. He did say I was the important part. The situation was confusing, and definitely screwed six ways from Sunday. What was this thing with Mr. Tsui? I went ahead and asked that one out loud. Even if they didn't answer the question, how they avoided it could still give me something.

"What's his deal with me? Why is Mr. Tsui so interested in me?"

The two teens looked at one another. After staring at each other for a moment, Garrett shrugged and looked back at me. Wren sighed and, looking me in the eye, said, "I wish we could say exactly. You have something he wants. When you will be told what that is... Well, that is still being worked on."

"Yeah, right," I scoffed. "I've got nothing but me. And there's nothing about me that's different from anyone else."

"And yet you're here. So when you are told what he wants," asked Garrett, "are you going to let him have it?"

"Oh, I'll let him have it," I said, slamming my fist on the table in frustration.

"Oh, I like you," Wren said with a smile. "You're a fighter."

"You've seen the splendid role models I've had," I said. "I've had no choice but to be a fighter."

"You don't think there might be a reason why he is going through all this trouble, just for you?" Garrett seemed pissed, and it was coming out of nowhere. "You're going to hold out, just because it's uncomfortable?"

"Hold out from what? Nobody's told me anything yet!"

My words got no reaction. Wren wouldn't look at me, and Garrett looked off in either anger or frustration. The silence stretched on, telling me in no uncertain terms this topic was over for now. In that case, it was time for something else that was bugging me about these guys.

"I want a straight answer about something. What exactly are the Ravens? I know y'all aren't a 'community service' club."

The three looked at each other, seemingly studying the others' reactions. After a moment, Garrett shrugged. Wren sighed and they turned their attention back to me.

"The Ravens are... complicated. We may not be the civic group you are thinking of. We don't go around picking up litter or hosting bake sales. But we do perform a significant service for Avernus.I suppose you could think of us..." he paused here, looking to his friend for help.

"In a way," Garrett said, "we provide kind of a bridge between the city council and the general populace of the town."

"But you're a bunch of teenagers!"

Wren jumped back in. "Just trust us when we say it works."

"Is this why you're not in school? Let me guess," I scoffed. "This is just one of those things I have to take on blind faith? Just one more mystery I have to just deal with. Have you tried to get the permission you promised you were going to ask about?"

"I'm working on it," Wren said quietly.

I crossed my arms in defiance. "If you guys are so noble and useful, why are all my friends afraid of you guys? They're convinced I'm going to be eaten alive or something. Hell, my friend, Liam, nearly ripped my head off when I mentioned I was coming to see you tonight."

Wren's face fell. "Liam Anderson?" When I shrugged, he elaborated. "Blond, medium build, sixteen or so?"

"Skater, plays Hammers?" I added, worried I might have just messed up and already wishing I could roll back the conversation.

"That would be the one," Wren said with a touch of sadness. "He lost his younger sister, maybe a year ago. It was an accident, but he blames us. And no, I won't go into the details right now."

I was hit with warring feelings of sadness for Liam's loss, and anger at Wren's deflection. But Wren was here, not Liam, so guess which side won.

"That's convenient," I said. "His sister died and you say you got blamed, but you won't say why you are all innocent?"

"It's decidedly *inconvenient*," said Wren, emphasizing the last word. "I would much rather give you less reason not to like me."

"You want me to like you?" I scoffed.

He nodded, the hint of a smile in the corners of his mouth. "You're interesting. I would rather get to know you better."

"And what about you—" I started to ask Garrett, but I was addressing an empty seat. "Huh? When did Garrett leave?"

"Oh," said Wren. "I'm not sure."

"Fine," I sighed. "Whatever. So if it's just you and me, maybe I can get some straight answers out of you??"

"About what?"

"Anything!" I said in frustration. "You duck questions better than a ninja playing dodgeball!"

Wren laughed. It was a high, tinkling laugh. Very feminine, matching his looks. I think it was the first time I had heard him laugh in a way that was genuine. I kind of got lost in its sound for a moment. Finally, he quieted, but the mirth stayed with his features. It softened his face, breaking up its chiseled perfection. Before he could speak, I jumped in.

"You should use your real smile more," I said quietly. "I like this look better." The smile shifted. Sadly, it went back to his more practiced, plastic smile. "Not that one," I said, with a hint of sadness. "Now you're wearing your fake smile. It makes you look too perfect, like someone's dress up doll."

He genuinely looked surprised. Fearing I had insulted him, I scrambled to walk back my words. "I mean, you look amazing! Really. It's just that, the smile you had after you laughed just now, it looked more real. The smile you changed to, it looks, I don't know, fake."

"Interesting," said Wren, and his face changed again. It was like something relaxed. That genuine smile returned, if only slightly.

"That!" I exclaimed. "That right there! I like it better." My embarrassment caught up to me mid phrase as I said, "I like that smile a... lot better."

"You are intriguing," said Wren, keeping his softer, real smile. "I wonder what other secrets Dom is hiding about you."

"About that," I said, glad at the change of topic. "What's the thing with you and Mr. Tsui? All three of you talk about him like you don't like him. And yet, you do what he says like he's your boss or something."

"Or something," Wren said carefully. "He and I are... well, rivals, I suppose."

"Rivals? Even though he's older than you? Can I ask how old you are?"

"How old do you think I am?" he said slyly, the fake, devilish smile returning.

"There it is again. That fake smile," I muttered, not sure if I was teasing or annoyed. "But I guess you look maybe sixteen or seventeen right now." He got a curious look on his face, so I elaborated. "But sometimes you have this way of looking, like the way you carry yourself, and the look on your face, where you look more adult, like you're in your twenties or something. It's weird."

Then an idea hit me. "Have you been to some kind of boarding school where they taught fancy manners? Or maybe worked in modeling or something? It's like sometimes you just look, I don't know, professional."

"And by 'professional', you mean..."

"Fake," I laughed with a bit of embarrassment. The longer this went on, the more likely I was to piss him off. I really didn't want that.

"You really are intriguing," said Wren, and I was pretty sure there was a level of fascination in there. Some kind of interest. Regardless, his face went back to looking genuine. I was getting whiplash from the expression changes.

I jumped as my phone rang. I dug it out of my pocket and saw it was my Mom calling. Or at least, a call from her phone. Dreading what I might hear, I answered it.

"He-ello?"

I heard my mom's voice. She sounded tired, but a little panicky. "Jason, where are you? I'm leaving the police station, but I don't see you."

"I'm sorry, Mom. I had to get out of there. I'm at the comic store over on the square."

She sighed. From frustration or relief, I didn't know. "Stay there. I'll come get you."

"I can come meet you," I offered. There was a lot going on. I wanted to try to be helpful, after all the problems I caused with Dad.

"No, it's dark out. I'll be over there in just a few minutes." She was silent for a minute, then said, "Are you hungry?"

I realized it had been several hours since my lousy lunch of cold fries and bad burger. "Yeah, but the way I'm feeling I'm not sure if I could eat."

"Yeah," she sighed. "Anyway, I'll be over there in a few minutes. Watch for me out front."

"Yes, ma'am."

"Don't make me come in there after you." The sharpness in her voice made me worried she agreed this was my fault. It definitely did not help my mood. I was not looking forward to what our conversation tonight might look like.

"Yes, ma'am," I started to say, but the call went dead. I slipped the phone back in my pocket and looked across the table at Wren. "Welp, I guess it's time for me to go. I guess they decided not to hold her for now."

"That sounds like good news," said Wren. "Does this mean you can go home now?"

"Home," I scoffed. "We haven't even spent the night there yet, and we are probably going to lose the house." Then the details caught up with me. "They didn't even unload all our shi- I mean, stuff. I don't even know if the moving truck is still there."

He reached across the table, laying his cold hand on mine. I wanted to pull away, but his cold fingers were soothing. I looked up and met his eyes. They were deep pools of a warm chestnut brown. How could I ever think his expression was plastic and fake? But then there was another one of those shifts, a frame of reality skipped over, and the smile was practiced and cold.

Wren withdrew his hand and leaned back in his chair. The look on his face was more subtle, more a smile of sadness as he said, "Take the rulebook with you. You don't have one yet, do you?"

I shook my head and said, "No, but I also don't have any money anymore, remember?"

"I'll take care of it. Get outside so your mother isn't having to wait on you."

I stood up, picking up the book. "Thanks," I mumbled. Two days in a row Wren had bought me something. If this kept up, I was going to owe half my army to him. "Will I see you again anytime soon?"

"Text me when you find out what your weekend looks like. I'll teach you some more about playing Hammers & Hordes."

"What's your number, then?"

"Check the number that texted you before. Make the last digit a nine instead of five. Easiest time to play would be Sunday night, about this time."

"Alright, goodbye then," I said hesitantly. "I'll message you." I blushed a little as I added, "Thanks for the book."

But his voice was warm and laced with concern as he said, "Jason, I'm sure it is going to work out."

I stared back, trying to decide if he was giving a tired platitude, or actually gave a damn. "You're sure, huh?" I said skeptically.

"I can all but guarantee it."

Wren stood to watch me go. In the front glass windows, there were posters plastered everywhere. But in a spot between posters, I was able to see a bright reflection of the store's interior. I looked in the glass to catch one last glimpse of that beautiful boy, but I couldn't see him. As I made it to the door, I looked back to the gaming area, and saw he and Garrett pulling out bags. I guess he had just moved, and I hadn't seen him in the glass.

Chapter Twenty

A Nightmare Weekend

When we got back to the house, we found the movers had simply dumped the rest of our possessions just inside the front door. But at least it was here. They had called the cops during the fight, smartly stayed out of it, then locked up after leaving the rest of our stuff.

I spent Saturday moving boxes, while Mom unpacked the kitchen. On our way back from lunch, I had to ask the question that had been simmering in the back of my mind all day.

"Why did Dad get so pissed over the money? You said you were givin' it to me. You said Daddy wasn't going to be comin' after it."

"Oh, baby, that was my fault," she said. She wasn't looking at me as she talked. "We were goin' at it, and I told him I gave you that two hundred dollars."

"So? You said it was mine."

"I was mad," she said. The way she was talking, I knew what was coming next, and I was already getting pissed. Sure enough, she said, "I... kind of said it in a way that was not... nice."

"In other words," I snapped, "you said it in a way you knew would get under his skin! You said it to piss him off!"

"Baby, I–"

"You didn't give a damn that he was gonna come take it out on me!" My shouts filled the room. "You knew he'd come after me, but you didn't care! All you cared about was winning whatever the hell you were arguin' about!"

How much more of this could I take? This was getting old.

Your mom should be defending you, not setting you up. At least Dad was in jail for the weekend. Mom had said they couldn't do anything about bail until Monday at the earliest. Apparently, that was up to a judge. I'd carry every single box we owned, in exchange for this peace and quiet.

Which was pretty much what I did for most of the day. I was so caught up in my own head and all the work, that I forgot about texting Wren. It was after a dinner straight out of our old, poor, Alabama trailer-trash kitchen, that I finally pulled out my phone and tried texting the new number he told me.

I was tempted to try and duck out of the house, but it had been a really long day, and I was wiped both physically and emotionally. I composed myself and sent my message.

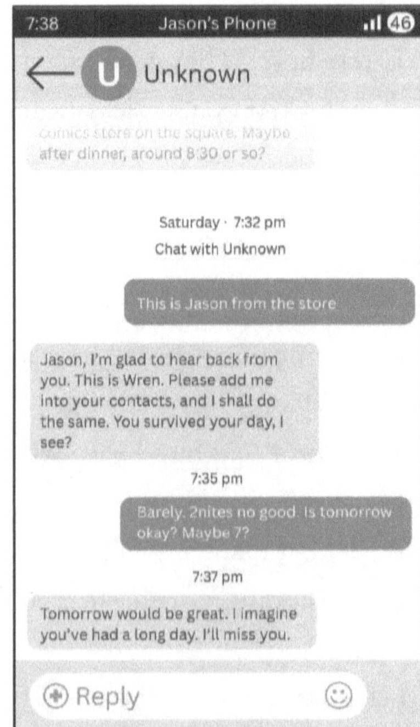

Huh? What did that mean, he'll miss me? Maybe it'll get added to all the other mysteries I was still working on solving. Maybe I should start a journal of everything I had to figure out the answer to. Maybe I needed to take notes of all the clues or something.

Maybe pigs will fly.

However, before calling it a night, I told Mom I was going to be going back over to meet Wren the next evening after dinner. I wanted to explain who he was, but the simplest explanation I could give was that he was a friend I had met. I almost said he was one of the Ravens from the meeting, but then remembered what Erin had said. So far she hadn't asked about the aborted dinner, so as Erin had suggested, I hadn't brought it up either. So I laid on my bed planning out the next day.

Some time later I found myself wandering from room to room in the house, bored. I couldn't quite figure out what was going on, because halfway up the stairs I stumbled across this hidden door that had never been there before. It was tiny, maybe the size of a pet flap. It felt important I figure out where it led. I barely had to touch the frame to get the door to open, then, despite its minuscule size, I was able to cartoonishly squeeze myself through the opening. It was dark inside, but I knew that was only because I hadn't made it into the unknown room yet.

I squeezed through the space and dropped down into the other side of the living room. I was disappointed for a minute, before I realized that now the ceiling had these deep grooves, several inches thick, running parallel to one another, threading and swirling around the ceiling like a maze or a labyrinth. A spot in the center of the room's ceiling lit up by this crimson mist. Sparks of pink lightning flashed within the mist as it began spreading through the maze of grooves, reaching out but never falling out of the paths made by the grooves.

It was searching, I knew. As if alive, I could see where the mist would come to a fork in its path, moving down both sides before one would stop, retreating from its pathway and pulling back, as if to add its volume to the remaining cloud. And while at first the mist was spreading to all sides of the living room ceiling, more and more, the avenues it retreated from were the ones leading to the opposite side of the room. It was searching for me.

I took a step back, prepared to run. At my motion, the mist froze. The pink lightning flashes quadrupled in intensity, lighting up the room with red strobes. Then without warning, the flashing stopped, as the mist launched itself like an ooze, like a liquid being poured at me from a massive pitcher. I flinched, then turned and ran in terror.

The next moment, I was laying in bed. It was that weird part of the dream where you can't tell if you are awake yet, or still dreaming. It feels like you might be waking up, but you also know impossible things are still happening. I was filled with unspeakable terror. A fear so deep, so pervasive, that moving was impossible. Screaming wasn't an option.

I was laying there, but the room was still filled with the weird red mist. Flashes of pink lightning zapped around here and there, and something was silhouetted by the flashes. Even in my dream I became confused, because although I don't remember having ever smelled something in a dream, I was catching an odor this time. It was a cross between vanilla mixed with something floral, but with this undertone of vomit. It was like sweet, with a bad aftertaste.

Some kind of being, some half-formed entity, seemed to float at the foot of my bed. I wanted to yell out, but something, some instinct, made me think that making any noise would increase the danger. Even if I could have screamed, of course. I tried to scramble away from it, when things went slack, my vision suddenly went black

CHAPTER TWENTY-ONE

A REFRESHINGLY EMPTY VISIT

Before I could register what was going on, I was waking up for real. The Sunday morning sunlight drifted in through my half-hung curtains. My brain was already trying to drive the weird nightmares from my mind, particularly since I still had that phantom of feeling something had been touching my foot. The sense of fear lingered. Like a bad taste in my mouth.

My fear wasn't the only bad taste, either. That smell, the "floral peach mixed with puke", was lingering, like a memory of a bad meal, or a bad attempt at an air freshener that hangs there for days.

The day started out as more unpacking, but a bit after lunch I called it a day and took some time for myself. I was tired of thinking about Dad and the fight, and the mindlessness of moving and opening boxes wasn't enough of a distraction to keep the whole thing out of my head. As bad as he normally was, a weekend behind bars, which he was naturally going to blame on me, meant when he came home he was going to be a nightmare worse than my dream the night before. And what would happen if he didn't come home? Would me and Mom even survive?

So enough of that. I needed a distraction, and I had some shiny new pieces of plastic to occupy my attention for a while. Since I finally had my desk again, I opened up the modeling and paint supplies and opened the box with the Collective character. It had a little instruction pamphlet on how to assemble him, but I was so scared I would mess up my first model that I ended up paralyzed.

I decided to wait and see if Erin could help me get started. She would likely be at the store with Wren anyway. I would ask him, but his sister seemed more patient with teaching the hobby stuff. I had been anxious to go see him since the texts the night before, so all my waiting was just an excuse.

I ended up putting all the supplies, rulebook, and both miniature boxes in my backpack, and took them with me up to the store that evening. Mom wasn't crazy about me going out, especially considering the next day was my first day at the new school.

I assured her I had gone over the stuff they had sent me home with, and knew the room numbers for my first few classes. I even reminded her I already had a few friends that were in my grade, and promised to go to the school early to make sure everything would be good. She wanted to go with me to get settled in, which if I had a say wasn't happening, no way, no how, but she had to go to the courthouse to find out about bail.

When I arrived at the store, I immediately saw Wren sitting at one of the work tables. The models on the table weren't his Cosmos Emptor though. I guess the confusion showed on my face.

"Hi there, Jason. Wren says sorry, but he couldn't make it tonight. My brother and Garrett were both called away at the last minute to deal with something." It was Erin instead.

"Oh." I was surprised at my disappointment. I knew Wren had made an impression on me, but yeah. And it wasn't just missing out on some eye candy, either. He had seemed, not nice. Erin was the sweet and nice one. But he had seemed interesting. Friendly, but deeper than I was expecting. As if there were all kinds of personal secrets hidden underneath I really wanted to learn. He had seemed like he wanted to meet up. I mean, come on. "I'll miss you?" I tried my best to let it go.

Erin took me through the basics of the rules while she showed me how to assemble my character and get him ready for painting. She was nice, and gave me a lot of confidence for when I would need to assemble my other models on my own. She even assured me not to worry about painting them in an expert way. I had been looking forward to seeing Wren again, but it still turned out to be a relaxing and fun end to my weekend. I needed it, considering it started with an arrest and continued with a seriously twisted nightmare. I was even home by eleven.

CHAPTER TWENTY-TWO

LEARNING CURVE

My first day of school started out better than I expected. I received a text about an hour before school with Taki's address, telling me to meet them there so I could ditch my board. When we met up, Taki, Wheeler, Scott, and Boots all kind of took charge, grabbed my schedule and divided up my day, swearing they would make sure I found all my classes and would have a table to sit at for lunch. Really, the guys were amazing. They had looked over my shiner but hadn't commented.

The morning was decent, and I seemed to fit into the classes fairly well. I hadn't bothered looking over the schoolwork they had given me in advance , but seeing what was covered in my first two classes, it didn't seem to be too far off from what I was used to. And if it was off, I'd either pass or fail, whichever happened.

Lunch had probably been the time I had been most worried about, considering what a cultural struggle it can be. Fortunately, the gang took care of that for me as well. I had no problem being instantly identified as one of the rebel skaters, since that was exactly what I was, but being in a group of skaters, I was left alone except for some stares.

The guys led me to what was obviously their regular table, and we started cutting up and messing around. Liam had joined us but was staying quiet. He still hadn't expressed whether he was going to stay pissed at me, and I wasn't ready yet to ask. Maybe after some time skating together. Ripping up some concrete together usually smoothed most things out, if there was any friendship there worth having.

Regardless of Liam's attitude, the others were thrilled having a new friend in their group. Wheeler got the ball rolling, filling me in on everyone's family situation.

"You're just jealous," Wheeler said to Scott, knocking him on the shoulder. "The only black family in Avernus, and we're balling harder than anyone!"

"Yeah, yeah," said Scott. "Richie Rich and all that." He looked over at me. "This bum's slumming it with us, when his dad's a super-lawyer who practically lives down in the capital."

"Yeah, but my mom works, too. Which is why I hang out as much as you guys."

"Except when you gotta watch your little sister," interjected Taki.

"Someone's got to be the responsible one!" Wheeler laughed.

I laughed as well. "Is that why you go by your last name? Trying to show off?"

"Naw," said Boots. "It's because his first name is Alfonse!"

"Punk, I will end you!" He smacked Boots in the back of the head, but it was obviously light and they were both laughing. People at neighboring tables kept glancing over, but nobody seemed too bothered by us.

"So Scott, what's your story?" I asked.

"Nada. I'm the boring one. Average parents, average house, average life. I'm the one all these losers measure themselves by!"

I looked over at Boots. "And what about you—"

"My family's the fun one," Taki cut in. "While Wheeler here is the token black family, everyone assumes we are the token Latino family. Of course we're not though! Our blood is from Spain, not Mexico."

"Same thing, right?" But I gave him a wink so he would know I was joking.

"So that leaves everyone's older brother," said Wheeler, tossing his arm around Liam's shoulder.

"Can it," said Liam.

"Are you alright, dude?" Taki asked. "Who pissed in your Cheerios?"

"I don't know," Liam said coldly. "*Somebody* keeps hanging out with the Ravens, even when his friends warn him off."

He looked down, his fists balled in anger. The guys stared at me in a mixture of shock and confusion.

"Dude, do you have a death wish?"

"Hey, they haven't knocked me out and kidnapped me yet," I said defensively. "Besides, they're just teaching me how to play that game. From what I've seen, you pretty much have to be in the same room with them to do anything at the store." I looked straight at Liam. "Don't you play up there, also?"

"Not at night. Not with them."

Boots jumped in. "Guys, chill. Let Jason make his own decisions. I'm sure he's keeping our advice in mind."

Wheeler and Taki gave Boots an odd look, like they were trying to figure out his angle. But they both had a bit of a knowing smile, as well. The conversation jumped over to a couple of events in morning classes, and quickly went back to more entertaining topics. Taki was just telling us about some new website he had found when we noticed one of the teachers on lunchroom monitor duty making a beeline straight at us.

I looked around, trying to figure out if one of us had done something wrong, while also tapping Boots and Scott, the two on either side of me, on their arms. By the time the teacher reached us, we had all stopped talking and were watching her approach. She didn't seem angry, but instead worried.

"Jason? Jason Docker?" she said, looking us over.

"Yes, ma'am, that's me," I responded.

"Can you please come with me?"

"What'd he do?" piped up Boots. He looked like he was ready to jump in a fight for me.

"Please come with me, Jason. You are needed in the office." She stood and watched me, until I finally started gathering up my trash. "Your friends can take care of that for you, right boys? Jason, please come with me."

I was confused and frustrated. I looked around at the rest of the guys and told them I'd check back with them in a bit. Then I got up, grabbed my backpack, and followed her out of the cafeteria. She led me through the school, down the empty halls. Her shoes clacked on the linoleum floors as I struggled to catch up.

"What's going on? Why was I pulled out of lunch?"

"It's not my place to say." She didn't sound pissed or offended. If anything, it sounded like pity.

"Did I already do something to piss off the principal?"

"Why?" she asked with a half smile. "Is there something you're feeling guilty about?"

"Naw, I just wanna know what I'm in for."

Once we reached the front office, I was ready for a fight. It was the third time I had been in here, first with my mother to register, and then Friday to pick up my laptop. And now because I assumed somebody had a problem with some random thing I might have done. I was surprised to see that my mom was there, speaking with the principal. It must have been worse than I thought, if Mom had already been called in. She led me and my mom into a small conference room.

"I'll give you a few minutes alone," she said quietly, closing the door as she left.

"Mom, what the hell? What's going on?" I could tell she was upset, and it was scaring me.

"Baby, there's somethin' I need to tell you," she said, holding back tears. "Your daddy's dead."

CHAPTER TWENTY-THREE

COOLING THE HOT HEAD

My mother and I went home. We didn't even pretend like I was going to finish out the day.

Mom didn't know exactly what had happened, but apparently, he got in a fight with another guy in the jail. A drunk, ironically. I struggled to figure out how I felt about all of this. I got a funny feeling I wouldn't be going back to school. In fact, we were probably going to go back to Alabama.

Pacing around the house was doing nothing for my mood. I tried to read but couldn't concentrate. No way did I want to try my new modeling hobby while I was this distracted. I wanted to skate. I grabbed my new jacket and slipped out of the house, walking to Taki's to pick up my skateboard.

Mom was going to have her own way of dealing with what had happened, and I had mine. I texted Taki and Wheeler, the only two numbers I had so far, to let them know I was out of school for a couple of days, and I'd explain later. I debated bringing them along, but I needed to clear my head on my own.

I hit the pavement, just kind of riding random streets while I thought about my dad. Yeah, he was a piece of crap, a drunk, and could be pretty damn mean.

We never saw eye to eye. He preferred the "good ol' boy" atmosphere back home, while I had a much more urban, skater mentality. Much more laid back on ethics and morals.

Things really came to a head when I came out of the closet. Because I blew that damn door off its hinges, no apologies. I pretty much dared him to kick me out. He threatened it a couple of times, especially when he was drunk and pissed off. But my aunt, my mom's sister, works for CPS up in Huntsville, so she is pretty up to date on a parent's legal responsibilities toward their kid.

Honestly, he wasn't usually as bad as he had been this past week. I couldn't help but wonder if he had been in over his head with the people at this new job. I mean, Mr. Tsui seemed like he absolutely had a scary side, and that was just one guy I had met. Dad was probably working with scarier guys.

Plus, Mom had mentioned she and Dad were both having weird nightmares every night at the hotel, so it sounded like they were experiencing as much weird garbage in this town as me.

Did this mean I was trying to make excuses for Dad hitting me? Hell no. Or at least, I didn't think so. But for all his faults, Jeremy Docker was my father, and was no longer here.

As much of a piece of human shaped refuse as he tended to be, Dad had kept a roof over our heads and food on our table. Sure, he may have had problems with his "screwed up faggot of an unplanned son", but he had never walked away. And as much as they had fought, I know, I mean, I *know*, he loved my mom. And now that was gone.

Every single piece of my life was completely up in the air.

The biggest thing that stood out in my mind was how Mr. Tsui stood before me the other night. When he had seen my black eye, he had smiled and said he had work to do. And here I was, his self proclaimed investment. Had he done this? Could he have arranged to have a man killed?

Everything, about almost everything, since we had arrived had come off as weird and dangerous. All the guys' doom talk about the Ravens came flooding back into my head. Wren had said he and Tsui were "coworkers", so I guess that meant he was also with the Ravens in some respect. Well you know what? Screw it. I had to know what Mr. Tsui's involvement was, both with the Ravens, and with what happened to my dad.

Racing to the hotel, I kick-snapped my board up to my hand at the last second before bursting into the lobby, not exactly being quiet or subtle. Mina and Richard were both at the desk, the latter on the phone, as I marched straight at them. Mina moved around the end of the counter to intercept me.

"Hi there," I said curtly. "I need a favor."

"Sure, Jason," she said in a concerned voice. "Are you okay? You look upset."

"I need you to unlock the third floor for me," I snapped, then added as an afterthought, "Please."

"I don't– I mean–" she stammered, trying to figure out how to answer. "There isn't a third floor." she paused, her eyes searching for Richard. She asked, "Did you forget something in your room? Nothing was turned in to the lost and found, but I can check with housekeeping." It was a distraction.

"Mina, you've been nice, but third floor. Now." I wasn't falling for her confused act. "The elevator around the corner. Call whoever you need to for a key card, or an access password, or whatever it takes." I stared her down. "Or I go to the cops with what I know about this place."

"Look, Jason. I'm not sure what you think is going on, but let me get somebody for you."

She went over to Richard, who just managed to stammer something about calling them back, before Mina hit the lever to hang up the call. She took the handset from him, and he looked over at me in confusion while she pressed three buttons on the phone keypad.

"I need an escort at the front desk," she muttered into the phone. It was obvious she was trying to speak as quietly as possible. She listened to something, said, "Yes," listened again, and then hung up. Addressing me again, she said, "Jason, I've really tried to be a friend."

The emotions on her face were unclear. She was concerned, possibly afraid.

"I don't blame you for anything," I said. "Either of you," taking in Richard as well. "But someone just killed my father, and I'm pretty sure he's in this building.

I'm not leaving until I find out."

"That's a dangerous mood, Jason," whispered Richard.

"Don't even care."

Before anything more could be said, Mr Tsui's secretary came around the corner from the first floor hallway. She was carrying the same leather bound folder with her she had been showing Mr. Tsui before, and was dressed in a very sharp business outfit. I was pretty sure she had just come from the other elevator.

Good. Maybe now I could find something out. Then, when she was about halfway across the lobby to us, I noticed two of the bodyguard thugs that had taken me upstairs turn the corner and stop, watching us all in the lobby.

The woman had the same lemon-sucking hateful look on her face, until she got a dozen feet away, at which point she switched instantaneously to the fakest, most hate-filled smile I have ever seen someone wear. It was the kind of face monkeys show when they bare their teeth. I did not feel any better about her now, than I did when she was scowling.

"Jason," she said in a voice that was too loud, too friendly, too full of letting you know exactly how much she hated dealing with me. "How nice to meet you. My name is Joyce Flanagan, Mr. Tsui's Personal Assistant. If you will please follow me?"

And just as quickly, she did a quick-turn on the toe of her shoe and began walking away. I guarantee her smile disappeared the second her back was turned. She didn't even look to see if I was following. We joined the two men in suits and went around to get into the second elevator. Same paranoid procedure as before, including keycard and foreign pass phrases.

I was in a mood to push my luck, so I asked what was on my mind. "I see buttons for B, G, and L," I said. "I'm guessing G is for the ground floor, since we are going to L on the third floor. Otherwise I would have guessed L was for lobby."

I looked around at the other three in the elevator with me. One of the goons kept a bored face, but the other guy and Ms. Flannagan shared a look like they were questioning my real motivation.

"So what's the L for?" I continued. "I'm already guessing there is a basement, so that's the B."

There was silence, then finally the more animated goon muttered, "Loft."

"Makes sense," I said, with overly fake cheerfulness.

"Now then," Ms. Flanagan said with an impatient scowl as we all exited the elevator. "If you will please follow me?"

I was led by her and one of the goons down to the second door on the right this time, and we all three entered the room. It was a sitting room. Two couches, two overstuffed chairs, a few end tables. One wall was floor to ceiling glass, looking out toward the town of Avernus. Another had a dark bookcase.

"Excuse me, kid," said the guard. "Nothing personal."

Before I could register what was going on, I was spun around and had to drop my skateboard and slap my hands against the wall to keep from smacking it with my face. Now, I've never been patted down before this so I don't know, but dude was thorough. His fingers dug into my armpits, pinched my shoulder blades, slid down my ribs, and squeezed all over my coat.

"Hey, that seems real goddamned personal!" I squealed as he patted my back pockets and then slid his hands around the front of my hips to check my front pockets, before sliding his hands into my inner thighs. I'm pretty sure I didn't have an inch of skin this guy didn't run his hands over.

In the end, he had my phone out of my pocket, as well as my wallet and he even took my pen. I didn't have house keys yet, so he had it all. He kept my stuff, and picked up my board from the floor. All he said was, "Sorry, kid."

Ms. Flanagan, the shrew, addressed me with all the personality as a wet towel. "Please remain here, Jason. Mr. Tsui will be along when he is able."

Chapter Twenty-Four

More Questions Than Answers

They both retreated from the room, closing the door behind them, I heard the locks click in place before I could even react. They had taken all my stuff, including my phone. I wanted to throw something, kick something, anything- something. But I was trapped.

Trying to calm down, I walked around the room. I was kind of intimidated by the decor. It seemed fancy. Nice art on the wall, good carpeting, nice furniture. The room smelled like that kind of clean you get in really fancy places, where it almost smells like nothing. The glass wall at the side opposite the door looked over the entire town. It was impressive.

I thought I could make out the school, but I wasn't sure. I also thought I could identify the courthouse on the square. I could easily see the steeples from the two churches in town though. I wasn't sure what kind they were, since church really wasn't my thing. It made me think of my mom though. She used to love going to church. Maybe she would like one of the churches here. But that just brought me back to how we probably weren't going to be here long enough for her to find out.

Thinking about Mom reminded me that if she texted or called, I wouldn't be able to answer. Man, why did they have to take my phone?

Maybe I shouldn't have made the threat about calling the cops. After all, if Mr. Tsui really were who I thought they were, well, don't the Mob usually buy off the local cops? I mean, he would pretty much have to, if he really did have my dad killed. Now that I had time to calm down, I was realizing how stupid I had been. This was the Mob. They probably controlled everything. I was pretty sure they had killed my father. And I just casually let them take my phone and lock me away.

But stupid or not, I wanted answers more than I wanted to stay alive in my current blindness. I was willing to test just how much Mr. Tsui really wanted to have me here. I had no idea how long I was going to be in here. I tried to remember what time I had come to the hotel.

One wall had a few pictures and a few framed documents. Above them was a wicked-looking sword, with a thin, sharp blade. The narrow crossguard was a curved line of five circles, each with the vague impression of a side-profiled head. It looked kind of cool.

I continued walking around the room, going over to the only other interesting thing to look at, the bookcase on the far wall. All of the books were in perfect condition, most of them with fancy leather covers. And well over half of them were in a language I didn't know. They were embossed with lots of symbols. Korean? Chinese? Japanese? I felt so ignorant for not even being able to recognize what language the symbols were, even if I couldn't read them.

I looked at the ones that did have English on their spines, and saw they all seemed to be mostly philosophy, law, business, or economics books. Boo-riiing. I barely recognized any of them, but there wasn't anything else to do. Of the two I had heard of, The Iliad and the Odyssey sounded too much like homework, but The Art of War sounded cool, and it was short.

I tried to stay interested in the book, just so I would have something to do. I think I even dozed off at some point.

Anyway, I was sitting on one of the couches, one foot curled up under me, watching the sun lazily setting and wondering how much longer I was going to be locked away in here, when there was a knock on the door. I started to get up, but it opened, and the goon from earlier poked his head in.

"I'm passing on a message," he said in a bored voice. "Mr. Tsui should get here in around twenty minutes."

Before I could even ask for my phone, he shut the door. Feeling a bit frustrated, I sat there and watched as the window did that transition you get as it goes dark, where it becomes harder and harder to see anything but reflections in the glass, as the light in the room becomes brighter than the light outside, turning the window into a mirror.

As the minutes passed, I built my anger back up as my frustration grew. I shoved the book back into the shelf, not even sure if it was where I had gotten it from, and not caring. At last, the door opened and Ms. Flanagan entered the room, leather ledger tucked in her arms, sour look on her face.

"Mr. Tsui will be here momentarily. Can I get you—"

"Christ! Will you people quit telling me that he'll be here *eventually*?" I yelled. "Is he here or not? Is this why you people took my phone? So I couldn't call for help?"

She backed out of the room without bothering to say anything else, clearly angry. She probably thought I was a problem beneath her or something. Completely pissed off now, I ran over and banged on the door. I even kicked it a few times, for good measure. Once again, I wanted to start grabbing items and throwing them, but I managed to calm myself down and avoid worsening my situation.

Instead, I went over to one of the chairs and tugged it around, then plopped my ass down, staring at the closed door. I was tempted to decide on an object to have ready to throw it at the next person to open the door that wasn't Mr. Tsui. Fortunately, the need was taken away from me when, a few minutes later, the bigshot himself opened the door.

"I understand you wanted to see me," Mr. Tsui said calmly. He closed the door softly, leaning against it. "A call would not have sufficed?"

I was in no mood to be polite or pussyfoot around. "Did you do it? Friday you said you had work to do when you saw my black eye. Did you kill my dad?"

"Right to the point, I see," he said with a dark chuckle. "Is it going to bother you if I say yes?"

"Hell yeah!" I hopped from the chair, ready for a fight, an argument, whatever he wanted.

"Interesting," he said. "I would have thought you would be happier with your assailant out of your life."

"He was my dad!"

"He was your bully," he replied, his frustration apparent. "Are you such a child that you need your parents to hold your hand?"

"Really dude?" I was shocked, which added to being pissed. "I don't know about being a child, but yes, I still have to have the parents around. But I guess this is what counts as 'family planning' in the Mob? You plan for what part of the family gets to stick around?"

"Very cute." Mr. Tsui stood there, arms crossed, seemingly amused by my outburst. "It is a curious thing, that you do not feel yourself capable of surviving without adults in your life."

"Dude! I'm still in school. I don't *get* a say in my life! My mom's already talking about having his funeral in Alabama, and us just *staying* there."

"Well, Jason. We shall have to do something about this, won't we?"

"You're the one who just killed your excuse for bringing me here, so I guess you screwed the pooch on that one. And even if we could fix that, why would I want to?" I asked. I wasn't agreeing to anything without some answers. "You said you brought me here, and my dad's job was just an excuse. But you haven't told me why you want me here."

"Are you sure you are ready to learn that? It should be enough to know that time and effort have been expended to bring you here, and to keep you here safely."

I stubbornly crossed my arms over my chest. It was as clear as any words I could say.

"Very well. It is a bit ahead of schedule, but I will show you now. Come with me."

I turned to pick up my jacket off the couch, and as I did, I glanced up at the room in the window's reflection. I could see the room décor, the book shelf, couches, and myself. Through the open door, I could see the shoulder of one of the goons out in the hallway. What I couldn't see was Mr. Tsui. I looked back around, and sure enough, he was standing right there in the doorway, his right hand casually resting on the door handle. I did a double take back at the window. Sure enough, no Tsui.

"What the hell?" I managed to mutter, before a wave of dizziness washed over me. I vaguely felt myself fall to the couch.

CHAPTER TWENTY-FIVE

MYSTERIES OF THE MIND

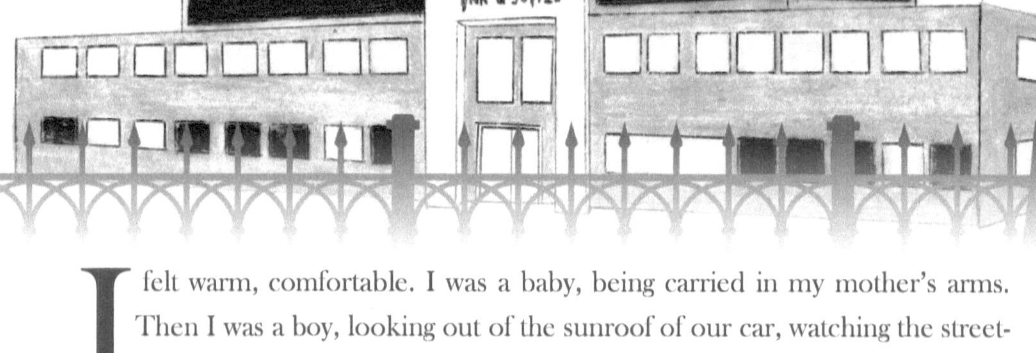

I felt warm, comfortable. I was a baby, being carried in my mother's arms. Then I was a boy, looking out of the sunroof of our car, watching the streetlights pass over us against the night sky. Then the streetlights morphed into fields of stars. I was swimming on my back, looking up at the night sky, and the full moon passed me by, directly overhead, flying across the stars from my head down to my feet, as if on a time lapse. The moon must have passed a dozen times over my head as I floated in the water. But then something had hold of my arms, holding them to my sides.

I struggled. I was going to drown! Then, in my struggles, I saw Tsui's goon, the one who had been standing outside my door, looking upside down over my face. Suddenly I was no longer drowning, and in my adrenaline-fueled panic I realized I was strapped to a gurney. The stars overhead were pinpricks in the ceiling tiles, the moon, fluorescent lights we were rhythmically passing under.

"Sir, the boy seems to be waking."

I heard the goon's voice from far off. Some inner voice was telling me to ignore it, and to go back to sleep. Bad things would happen if I tried to wake.

Nothing but restful goodness awaited me if only I would sleep. Sleep was good. Sleep was preferable. I should sleep *now.*

"Diu nei lao mo," Mr. Tsui muttered at the guard. "How is this possible? This *diu* child should be out."

I fought the voice telling me to sleep. I fought hard. I strained my eyes, forcing them open. I tugged against the straps holding my arms to the gurney. I kicked at the belts holding my ankles. I stopped moving, as they both struggled to deal with me. Mr. Tsui was suddenly at my side. His eyes were no longer black, but instead gleamed a deep golden orange. I fought to stare at him, and then with the pain of getting hit in the forehead with a sledgehammer, I passed out.

Once more I floated. This time, however, I heard the voice and identified it as somehow "not me". I searched for a way to grasp at it, to peel back an edge and fight it. I finally isolated the voice, realizing it was simultaneously Mr. Tsui's voice, and yet somehow different, somehow "off". But now that I knew it, I started working out how to avoid it. How to fight it.

Opening my eyes, I found myself in what could only be described as a hospital lab. An operating room. All the stereotypical equipment was around. The monitors, the overhead lights, even the pair of technicians with scrubs and masks. But also in the room was Mr. Tsui and another man.

However, as I became clearer about my situation and my surroundings, I started to realize maybe I wasn't coming out of it like I thought. I must still be in some kind of dream state. Because the other guy with Mr. Tsui wasn't... human. At least not in any sense of the word that I knew.

He was certainly shaped like a man. But his arms, long and lanky, reached nearly to his knees. He had long, stringy grey hair, tall, pointed ears, and somehow, no nose. Just a blank stretch of skin where his nose should be. When the... man?... saw I was awake, he hissed at me. Hissed, like a damned cat or something!

I've heard people talk about "seeing red" when they get angry. I'm not sure this was what they mean when people say that. When the thing hissed at me like that, his eyes went from black, to some kind of black with a red sheen to it, almost like red dye had poured over two black marbles.

Then out of nowhere, it was like someone had put a red lens over my eyes, like red glasses. Everything became red, with shades of black. I knew it had to be still a dream, because I sat up in the gurney without even feeling the straps. They felt like no more than cotton candy, or whipped cream. The creepy guy jumped at me, while Mr. Tsui leapt away. Both of the orderlies were thrown against the walls by the struggle. We tore at each other, me and the creature, bashing each other and throwing ourselves against everything in the room. It was Mr. Tsui I was mad at, but here in my dream, it was this creature, this thing, that focused my attention. Mostly because I seemed to be the focus of his attention.

He tore at me, slashing at my face and chest with these long claws on his hands, claws that were longer than the fingers they were attached to. I exchanged blows with him, somehow punching hard enough to snap his head back and send him spinning. Whenever he opened his mouth to give another hiss, I saw all his teeth were a darker red than his skin, and every one of them were needle thin, and just as sharp. I don't know how he could even clear his throat without slicing up the inside of his own mouth.

In my dream, I didn't have claws or a weapon, but I seemed to be fast, and crazy strong. As I dodged him, I was able to grab equipment and throw it at him, as if I was picking up blocks of foam. Unlike foam, the stuff I threw cracked concrete walls and dented steel furniture. At one point I grabbed the steel table they apparently were going to put me on, swung it over my head, and brought it crashing down on the damned monster. I cocked back my fist, the room bathed in red, ready for him to get up. And then...

Chapter Twenty-Six

Friendly Enemies

Once more I felt warm, comfortable. My head was laying in my mother's lap this time, and she was stroking my hair as I lay in a bed, or maybe on a couch. It felt so nice. I was relaxed, at ease. The fear and immediacy of the nightmare was long fading, although the details seemed crisp and fresh. Now, however, I was protected from them as if by a sheet of glass, by the knowledge they were merely a dream. As I came more awake, I realized the lap where I was laying my head was not my mother's. It was firmer. Less padding, as it were. Also, although I was warm under the blanket laid across me, I noted that the hand stroking my hair was cool to the touch. Cold, and vaguely familiar.

I opened my eyes to see Wren staring down at me. At least I thought it was Wren.

"How do you feel?"

"Wren?" I mumbled, trying to confirm. He nodded.

"See, you're getting it. Soon you will have no issues telling us, one from the other."

"It's your smile," I said sleepily. "You smile different from your sister."

I tried to sit up, but he gently pushed me back down. "Easy," he said. "Give it a minute. You've been through some stuff."

"I'm dizzy. I need to sit up." He let me, and that was when I realized I was shirtless. "Where the hell's my clothes?" I asked. Then, not recognizing the room, more panic set in. "Where the hell am I?"

"Calm, Jason," said Wren. "Nobody's going to hurt you. As for your shirt, we'll find you something to wear." He pulled up the blanket and wrapped it back around my shoulders as he helped me to a sitting position. Now that I was awake, he seemed more reluctant, or perhaps more careful, about touching me.

"Tell me what the hell is going on?" I asked, my voice rising. I could hear it getting louder, but it was like I had no control over my volume.

"Calm, Jason." And this time as he said it, a similar and familiar voice sounded in my head, repeating the words over and over, subtly and quietly. "Calm... calm, Jason. Calm..."

I relaxed again as my panic waned. Then as if something in me snapped, I shook my head and looked at Wren in anger.

"What are you doing? What the hell are you?" I started scrambling down the couch, trying to get distance from him, as if that might give the voice in my head less power.

"Amazing," Wren said in quiet astonishment. "Simply amazing." Just as suddenly, the pressure in my head that was fighting against my anger vanished, along with the repeating words. My anger flared back into being, twice as strong. Twice as pissed off.

"What. The. Hell?" I said, pronouncing each word in slow, cold rage. I had to be angry. The only other option was scared, and I couldn't let myself be scared right now.

"Truce," said Wren, holding up his hands. "I know telling someone to calm down usually just upsets them more, but I am happy to have a conversation with you. No more tricks."

"What do you mean, tricks?" I asked, still pissed, but trying to listen.

"I mean that I wish only to talk," he said. "To tell you the truth about some of the things you asked about."

I backed down, relaxing a bit. Then I realized I was backing down when I had no business letting my guard down. Something seemed to be going on, and if Wren was here, he was in on it. Right now, nobody was getting a pass.

"You scared Dom quite badly," Wren said with a small grin. "You certainly seem to have the blood of a true Assecla."

My confusion managed to pull me out of my anger. "A what?"

"An Assecla is a familiar, someone into whom a Vampyre has poured some of his power."

"A Vampire?" I scoffed. Next, he was going to tell me there were Smurfs and aliens. Or that that freak man-monster was real. "What, are you a Vampire, too?"

"No," Wren said, his face serious. "We are Vampyre." He pronounced it oddly, like 'vamp-ear'. Then he continued, "There are Vampires, mostly from Europe, who feed off blood. But there are different species of Vampyre from all around the world, such as the Bhoot from India, the Bacloo from Central America, and the Jiangshi from China."

"You said 'we', so you're including yourself in this garbage. Either you're faking it, trying to get me to believe some practical joke." I balled up a fist. "And since I hate those damned prank channels, if I see a camera I will absolutely break something." He gave a small snort of amusement but stifled his reaction when he saw my serious face. "Or you're for real, in which case you are about to pull some 'join us or die' crap on me."

Wren smiled. "You truly are fascinating," he said.

"Be fascinated all you want, but I *will* go down fighting."

"I have no plans to give you a reason to fight, and there is no need to give you some kind of ultimatum. You have already proven you are also a part of the Vampyre. You are an Assecla. Specifically, you are Dominic's Assecla."

"I'm already--- I'm a--- What?" I had to stop and calm down so I could catch my breath. "Is there any part of this that you can describe as if you are talking to a dumb fifteen year old? What do you mean I've 'proven' myself to be this... whatever?"

"Jason, I've watched you the last several days. More than once, I've seen you throw off the effects of powers used around you. Yesterday you kept mentioning my smile, I believe you described it as, 'turning fake'. And tonight, Dom had you completely under his power, but you managed to throw him off in the hallway and wake up. And then you did it again in the lab."

"That place was real?" I yelled, sitting up straighter. "That freakin' monster with the claws and bat ears?"

"That was Solomon, a type of Vampyre called a Kawtcho," said Wren with a serious expression. "And Dom was quite fearfully impressed when you not only held your own in a fight against Solomon..." He paused for a beat. "But also killed him."

Chapter Twenty-Seven

More Answers, Then Questions

I sat on the couch feeling a bit numb. It was too much, coming at me too fast. It was all too stupid to be real. I mean, I'm all for horror stories, but the only ones that are real are where the humans are the monsters. The cool monsters don't exist in real life.

Nevertheless, even if I'm really sitting in a padded cell somewhere drooling into my drugs, it costs me nothing extra to pretend this was all real for the moment. I took a minute to collect myself and re-engage with reality, or whatever passed for it right now. I had a choice, where I could either get angry again, or I could go cold. Earlier, it had taken being pissed in order to get in to see Mr. Tsui. But with Wren here, it might be better to swallow my hotheadedness and try to stay calm. Once again, I needed answers.

"Alright," I said to Wren. "Let's say all this is real, and not some drug-induced side effect. Why has Mr. Tsui been so hot and cold to me? One minute he's trying to have dinner, then the next he kills my dad? He says he's going to tell me what is going on, then the next thing I know he is trying to knock me out and feed me to, what's his name, Solomon? Especially if I'm supposed to be *his* ass-licker, or whatever you said."

Wren laughed. Not a condescending laugh. And not his fake, influencer laugh. No, this was genuine surprise and amusement over what I had said. I couldn't tell if I should be proud I had taken him off guard, or pissed that he found me humorous.

"Assecla," he said, still amused. "It is Latin, and means 'minion', or 'bonded follower'."

"Now I'm a gibbering yellow jellybean?" I asked with a laugh, thinking of those kids' movies. "So how am I his..."

"Assecla," Wren nodded.

"Assecla... if we've never done anything but talk? Shouldn't he have to do something, if I have some kind of power?" Considering how many times I had met him and then woke up the next morning having passed out, a terrible idea hit me. "Wait a minute. Has Mr. Tsui drank my blood or something? Do Vampyre or whatever actually drink blood?"

Wren sighed. I couldn't tell if he was annoyed at my ignorance, or if I was asking questions he didn't want to answer yet. "I need to impress upon you that everything we have been discussing is dangerous information. Don't go spreading this around."

"Fine." I mimed running a zipper across my lips.

"Well, there are many types of Vampyre," Wren explained. "Dom is actually a Vampire, so yes, he does feed on the blood of humans. But no, he has not fed on yours. It would be..." He seemed to be searching for the right words. "It would be, taboo, I suppose? Almost like incest, I guess is the best way to compare it."

"Ugh, alright, we're going to skip right over that for now, and pretend that doesn't exist. How am I Mr. Tsui's Assecla," he nodded when I said it right, "if he hasn't actually done anything to me?"

"For that we have to go back a few years," he said. "Some time in the 1640s."

"Isn't that like the Middle Ages or something?" I asked, unable to help being a smartass.

"Not quite," said Wren with a grin. "The Americas had been discovered by Europe, but the American colonies were not yet looking for freedom from

England. Dominic Tsui was touring the Americas, helping others establish new feeding territories for Vampires from China, alongside those from Europe. At the time, he was still learning to play politics among his European brethren, and was not quite as skilled. He was forced to leave the Americas and retreat back to China. Dom was locked away in China due to a treaty barring the Chinese Jiangshi and their compatriots from leaving the Old Kingdom.

"Worse still," Wren emphasized. "He was separated from his Assecla, who was left behind in what would become the Charleston Colony. What we would soon call South Carolina."

"Wait, so he already had an Assecla?" I asked. "Then what does he need me for?"

Wren paused, but I could tell he was trying to gather his thoughts before explaining.

"An Assecla is more than just a human follower or companion or anything. It is a gamble, in living form. Not all types of Vampyre can make one. But basically, through a ritual I am not entirely familiar with, they pour a portion of their power into a trusted human. That human gains many abilities from this, including greater health and expanded life. And while the Vampyre is weakened, having given away a portion of their power, when they are near their Assecla, this power is returned to them exponentially."

"Again...what does this have to do with me?"

"The Jiangshi treaty ended in 1997, when Hong Kong was surrendered by Britain back to China. Dom immediately came back here to the Americas, now the United States. He had already done a ton of research from his time there in China, but he has spent the last twenty-five years here in the U.S., looking for the descendant bloodline of his original Assecla.

"His last information put their descendants somewhere around central Tennessee. So he began several shell companies, and started flooding money into the region, spreading out hundreds of miles in every direction. He didn't know where the descendants may have migrated to, but he was hoping they hadn't relocated to an entirely different area of the US.

"Fortunate or not, the millions he poured into the project paid off," Wren smiled. "I think if you will remember back to sixth grade, you took part in a genealogy study? You took one of those genetic testing kits for the school?"

I thought back and did remember that. At the time I thought it was kind of cool because it gave all these percentages of what areas of the world your ancestors were from. And while most of my DNA was from various places around Europe, I did remember my mom finding it funny I was thirteen percent from China. Weird, huh?

"Well, that test was part of the vast money Dom was throwing around. And here you are, three years later, and your test proved true. You are the descendant of Dom's original Assecla."

"Ugh, alright, I guess. Why are you telling me all this, and not him?"

"Because you are his Assecla but are not fully claimed. You have too much of his power within you, but it is uncontrolled. So whenever Dom is near you, it feeds back on him, rendering him in a state that is close to intoxication." He looked to see if I was following what he was saying, then added, "And he has been foolish about the way he has been proceeding. Thus, your failed dinner, his failed meeting with you this evening, and all the times you have blacked out whenever you have gotten near him. He has acted inappropriately and had to wipe your mind of the botched attempts to speak with you."

"So, you're saying he can't seem to stay in a room with me without getting magically trashed?"

"Something like that. And so I, having already made friendly contact with you, was tasked with explaining things to you."

"So I'm a task to you?" I wasn't sure how I felt about that. Wren was all over the place. One minute he was friendly. The next, he looked at me almost like I was some kind of science experiment. The whiplash was low-key pissing me off.

"A pleasant one. I could have easily declined," Wren said with a smile. "But I feel like we are becoming friendly, if not yet friends. We thought it might be easier if someone you knew tried to explain your place here."

"Wow," I said with the perfect level of sarcasm. "I'm so glad we're 'friendly'."

Wren seemed surprised. "I'm not using anything with your mind, so I can't tell for sure. But I thought you wanted us to be friends? Am I wrong?" He seemed to ponder something for a moment. "Perhaps you are merely attracted, and nothing more?"

"You think I've got the hots for you, or something?"

Wren smiled, and this time, it was absolutely condescending, the arrogant ass. "Oh, I know you are attracted to me. I haven't told you what form of Vampyre I am yet."

Now I was curious and not just confused. Even if the smugness really annoyed me. "You mean you're not a Vampire?"

"I told you there are many forms of Vampyre, from all corners of the globe. Vampyre is an umbrella term, a 'catch-all', if you will. But no, I do not drink blood. I am a Succubus, and feed upon attraction and sexual energy."

"Wait, a Succubus? So you *are* a girl, like your sister?"

"No, my sister and I are both Succubi. The term refers not to the gender of the Vampyre, but that of the victim. I, and my sister, both feed from men. An Incubus, of either gender, feeds from women."

"How does that work with trans guys and girls?"

"Men are men, women are women. It has to do with the energy they project. Trans men *are* men, and will feed me the same as any man, regardless of the genitals they were born with, or any surgeries they have had."

"What about nonbinary people? Are they like universal donors?"

Wren shook his head slightly. "I don't have all the answers, Jason. I don't bother trying to figure out why some people don't feed me. I spend more attention on those which do."

"Cool," I said. "And how much effort does it take for you to tell?"

"It's not something I have to work on. I can sense attraction and sexual energy as easily as you see color. But feeding is all about the energy given off. Sensing a man's attraction merely helps a Succubus calculate options for approaching someone." He grinned and leaned in, as if sharing a secret. "And while you give off very male energy, I can also tell you are attracted to both me and my sister. You may think yourself gay, but you aren't *all* gay. And Jason?" He smiled with a very teasing grin, "Erin knows all this about you as well."

God, talk about embarrassing! I needed to get Wren off this topic before I just melted into the couch. After all, all I could picture right then was having Wren sit on one side of me, with Erin on the other.

"Wow, huh," I said. All of this was really scary, but also kind of cool. "So it sounds like right now, if I understand what you are saying, right now this power from being his..."

"Assecla," Wren prompted.

"Right, that. This Assecla power is there, but it's somehow uncontrolled? That's why it's messing him up?"

"Exactly," said Wren.

"So, what's his plan now? Why did he bring me up here? What, he wants his power back?"

"That is exactly what he has been planning. To take his power back." He repeated himself, this time stressing the seriousness of his message, "He was planning to forcibly *take* his power back. But now you have scared him a bit, and woken up something of a power lust in him. He was debating between two rituals. One that would renew you as a new, controllable Assecla. One like what he had before. The other would simply strip his power from you, renewing what power he once had."

"He can have it!" I exclaimed. "Take it, wipe me, and let me go be a regular person."

Wren looked at me with a knowing expression. "Jason, you would not survive the experience. This power is part of what you are."

"Then he can stay drunk! The hell with that!" I said with a nervous laugh. Wren smiled at my outburst in understanding.

"Well first off, you've changed his mind about killing you to take back his power."

My whole body went cold. The way Wren mentioned me being killed, just so casually like that, made me freeze. He wasn't teasing. He wasn't being metaphorical. My death had been discussed and planned. Every treat since I'd gotten here, every person who had been nice to me, it had all been with the possibility that I was going to be some sacrificial lamb. Did that include Wren and his sister? At this point, I was all in, and might as well ask the hard questions.

He gave me the moments I needed to collect my thoughts. I asked, "What's your deal with Mr. Tsui? Sometimes you act like you hate him, other times like he's your boss. Or is he a boss you hate?Are you part of the 'Committee to Bleed Jason Dry'?"

He laughed. "No, I find you too interesting. Besides, I'm not too thrilled with the idea of killing people. Especially when there are other, less fatal, options."

"Good thing I'm not boring," I muttered. "So, you? Mr. Tsui? What's your thing?"

Wren looked at me cockeyed. "I'll answer, but first I want to know. What's with the 'Mr. Tsui' business? Why not 'Dom', or at the very least, 'Dominic'?"

"It's just how I was raised," I shrugged. "Where I grew up, adults are mister and missus, or you get smacked."

"Smacked? You mean your father?"

"Well, no," I started, "Well, yes, with *my* dad. But I meant more figuratively. Even adults talking to another adult, unless you know 'em, it's Mr. Whatever. You don't use their first name unless they've offered it."

"Fine, I suppose that is a cultural thing," said Wren. "To answer your question, we are both members of Si-Jing-Fu." He looked at my puzzled eyes and quickly added, "Si-Jing-Fu is the governing council for the Vampyre here in Avernus."

"Si-Jing-Fu? Is that like kung fu?" I asked with a smirk.

"Not in the slightest," laughed Wren. "However, since we are both council members, I don't answer to him exactly, but we are instead coworkers of a sort. And as different species of Vampyre, we tend to have opposing viewpoints on several issues."

"Like me?" I grinned.

"Yes and no. We are both interested in you," he said with his own grin. "But I'm not scared of you."

"No, you just use your 'powers' on me."

"My powers?" Wren tried to hide what he was thinking, but I could spot a bit of nervousness.

"Yeah. Earlier you mentioned your 'fake smile', and when we first started talking a minute ago, you said something about 'no more tricks' after I had heard your voice in my head telling me to be calm. And it really tried to get me to be fake-calm!"

His face went blank again, which pissed me off. Again.

"That! That right there! And when you were talking about that Assecla crap, you also said Mr. Tsui was using powers on me. So, what? You guys can all mind control or something?"

Wren sighed and his face normalized. "You're right. As much as I shouldn't be doing anything with you, it's just habit. Especially with hiding emotions. All Vampyre can do it, and we hide our feelings from one another as much as we do from humans. It is called Mesmir. It's not so much mind control as, I guess, influencing the senses. We can make you see what we want you to see, hear what we want you to hear. It's usually subtle, and only the absolutely weakest Vampyre can be seen through. The fact that you can break through Mesmir is extraordinary."

"Mesmir?" I was trying not to freak out hearing all this. "And this whole 'knocking me out' thing Mr. Tsui keeps doing to me. Everybody can do that, too?"

"No, thank goodness. Dom was able to do that by pushing feedback at you through your uncontrolled Assecla power."

"Alright," I said. I had a ton of questions, but this topic was really too freaky, so I'd save them. "Since you are being a bit open, what exactly are the Ravens? How do they fit into all this?"

"I'm sure you have seen there are quite a number of us younger looking Vampyre here in Avenus. Putting a name on us seems to placate the human population. I suppose the whole idea of a clique or a secret society helps them explain away our more unusual manner."

"Alright, I guess. Then why the rivalry with the high school guys in town?"

"Rivalry?" Wren asked.

"Yeah, I keep hearing 'the Ravens' this, 'the Ravens' that. People talk about you guys like you are million-dollar hoodlums. There seems to be this rumor that the Mob runs the town, and the Ravens are their spoiled kids."

"I have heard that one," Wren said with a laugh. "I assure you, we are not all that. Why don't we table that discussion and see about getting you out of here."

CHAPTER TWENTY-EIGHT

COLD EMBRACE

Wren ended up walking me home. We chatted a bit more, but he kept it lighter. I think he could tell I was “info’ed out“. It was pretty cold, but I was able to deal with it. He had also been able to locate my stuff before we left, so I had my wallet and phone, as well as my jacket and board. My shirt had been shredded in the lab fight, but he was able to find anotherT-shirt.

When I checked my phone, I was disappointed to see that my mom hadn’t even bothered to message me. I’m pretty sure Wren saw that I was a bit upset, but he graciously didn’t say anything. Finally we got to my house. As we approached the door, halfway up the front walk, Wren put his hand on my shoulder and turned me to face him.

“There is something I need to do, and I hope you don’t object,” he said.

Then Wren leaned in and kissed me. His lips were barely warmer than the icy air around us, and yet it wasn’t unpleasant. It was more like the cold of a good spearmint, and as we kissed, his mouth warmed against mine. I was surprised for just a moment, and tensed up, but within seconds I relaxed into it, closing my eyes.

I felt his hand on my back, not exploring, not being lewd, just holding me. His other hand reached up and cupped the back of my head, and it was warm. As his lips continued to warm against mine, his tongue pushed gently against my lips, and I was powerless to deny him.

Nothing about his actions or movements were necessarily erotic, outside of the kiss. And yet, my mind was swimming blissfully, and I couldn't remember ever being this turned on. The other night in my dream was close, but this was even more. I melted. I lost all sense of time. And I was so aroused that I hurt.

Finally, he leaned back, releasing the kiss. I probably would have lost my balance if he hadn't been still holding me. It took a minute, but my head cleared and I opened my eyes. Wren was smiling at me, his brown eyes warm and friendly. He seemed flushed, and less pale than normal.

"You're safe," he said. "And you're not going to have to go anywhere. If you don't trust Dom, trust me. But I mean it when I say Dominic has overstepped, and he owes you." Wren kept both hands on my shoulders, supporting me both physically and emotionally. "Take care of your mother. Take care of yourself." He squeezed my shoulders. "Deal with your father's funeral. Si-Jing-Fu will take care of everything else."

I nodded, not knowing if I could speak at the moment. Between the new information, the kiss, and the reminder about my dad, I was quickly shutting down. Wren guided me up to the front door and asked if I was going to be okay. I assured him I was fine, that I just needed some alone time and some sleep. Saying good night and leaving him on the porch, I let myself into the house. I looked back before closing the door and saw Wren wave as he walked off into the night.

Chapter Twenty-Nine

Reconciliation and Reversals

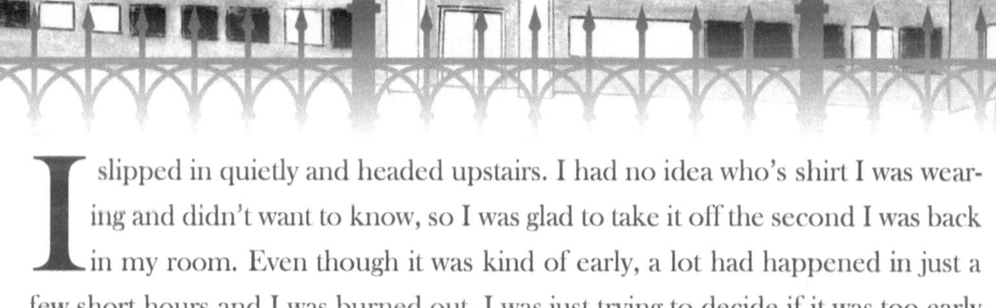

I slipped in quietly and headed upstairs. I had no idea who's shirt I was wearing and didn't want to know, so I was glad to take it off the second I was back in my room. Even though it was kind of early, a lot had happened in just a few short hours and I was burned out. I was just trying to decide if it was too early for bed when I heard a light tap on my bedroom door. I sighed and told Mom to come on in.

"Hey, baby," she said, peeking around the door frame. "Did you get in some thinkin' time?"

"A bit." I shrugged. "What about you?" She nodded, but didn't say anything, so I asked, "Are you and me gonna be alright? You're not gonna shut me out, right?"

She pulled me into a hug. "No, baby. We're gonna be right here for each other."

"I hope so. I was gone all afternoon and I didn't hear from you."

"You seemed like you needed space. And besides, communication goes both ways, mister." She came in and pulled me over for us to sit on the edge of the bed together. "But you're right. We got to make sure we're supporting each other." She threw her arm across my shoulder. "You and me are all we've got up here, right?"

"Yes, ma'am. I'm sorry if I snapped at you. Today's been... a lot."

"Oh, honey, don't I know it."

I heard a hitch in her voice, and it took me a second to remember she was at least as upset as I was. I mean, I was upset over how much my life was just turned upside down, even if I was confused about how I felt that Dad was gone. But Mom was probably upset about both. I mean, she was married to the bastard. She had to have loved him.

"Mom, what's gonna happen to us now? Are we even gonna stay here?"

"I don't know, baby. Do you think we should talk to Aunt Susan about maybe just staying down there?"

I stared at the wall for a minute, confused about why she was asking me. Then I said what I was really thinking. "We're kind of 'damned if we do, damned if we don't', aren't we? I mean, we've got this big ass house that we only got 'cause of Daddy's job, and we can't keep it, right? But we also moved out of that crap house we were renting back home."

She squeezed my shoulder. "I don't have any answers yet. But we'll figure something out. We've got time 'til they kick us out of this mansion here, and maybe... maybe I'll get a job or somethin'."

We both had a giggle at that, and I knew she was picturing the same thing I was. Imagining what kind of job she could get that would make enough money to afford this place.

"Can you just see me learning electronics and computers and all that?" she asked. When I looked confused, she added, "Honey, half the damn town works out at the Revamp plant south o' town. Somebody said they make computer parts or somethin'."

Then she pulled away, saying, "Oh, I got somethin' for you."

She pulled out a white envelope and handed it to me. I took it and looked inside and saw the remaining money Dad had taken from me. I looked up at her with kind of a sad grin.

"This feels cursed," I said, thinking of the fight this money caused, and the subsequent fallout.

"Well, if it is too cursed, I'll take it back," Mom said with a laugh, grasping for the envelope.

I laughed as well, holding the envelope out of her reach. She took advantage of the opportunity and started tickling my exposed side. It didn't last long though, and we ended up in a hug, before I finally said good night and she left, closing the bedroom door and leaving me to my thoughts.

It sucked, but I had to go back to school the next day. As I expected, this was definitely a small town with small town habits.

It seemed like everyone was whispering about me, since I guess everyone had heard the new kid's dad was killed on his first day at school. All that was no surprise. No, the real surprise was at lunch. Liam joined us, same as Monday, but this time he was polite and friendly. He was acting a lot more like he had the first day we all met, not the asshole who was pissed I'd met the Ravens. I didn't dare bring it up, so I wouldn't break the spell. And yeah, I was really thinking it might be a spell. Or a Mesmir, or whatever Wren had called it.

The crew all shared how much it sucked about losing my dad, though nobody really knew how to act about it. We moved past it as best we could, dealing with more weighty subjects, like how much school sucked. We worked on building a "new normal".

That afternoon after school, Mom told me I would be skipping school Friday, and we would be going back to Alabama for Daddy's funeral on Saturday. When I asked her how we were going to get down there in only one day this time, she told me we were flying!

Flying? I've never even been *near* a plane in my life! I didn't even know enough to know if I was going to be more scared or excited.

I told Mom I needed some time to work stuff out in my head, and so after scarfing down a quick early dinner, I grabbed my stuff and headed over to the square. I was beginning to think I was going to like being a fifteen-minute walk from everywhere. Unless it rained, of course. But tonight it wasn't raining. Just a light snow that was trying to dust the landscape.

Anyway, I went up to the store, and saw there were plenty of people around. Since it was after dark, there were a few of Wren's friends around as well, although none I had talked to. Just a few I had seen them with. I grabbed the back table and pulled out all my stuff, then started working on my models.

I jumped when a big, blue case was slammed down on the table right next to me. "Hey, Asshat!" exclaimed Liam with a laugh. "Whatcha doing up here?" I barely pulled myself together enough to register what was going on, before he reached out and took the model out of my hand. "Not bad, not bad," he said. "Is this your first time painting?"

"Yeah," I said, reaching for my model. He leaned away to keep out of my reach.

"Not too shabby for a first timer. Collective, huh? Do you have enough for an army yet?"

"Nope," I said, reaching into my bag for the other box. "I've just got him," pointing at the model Liam was holding, "and these. I'm supposed to have some normal soldiers on order, so who knows."

"Are you sure there's nothing over there you can use?" asked Liam excitedly. "Let's go see!"

Even knowing Wren and the other Vampyre had that spooky Mesmir mind control power, it was freaky to see the one-eighty Liam had taken today. He had been friendly enough in school, but now he was practically best friends. Very unnerving.

I felt crappy about it, too, because I was pretty sure I could trace back to when his personality shift happened. I may not have been the one to actually do the voodoo on him, but I *was* the one to accidentally let the Ravens know Liam was pissed off at them. So, it was probably my fault they put him back under their power. As if I didn't already have enough to stress about.

Liam was particularly hyper to help me with my army, but I could see his respect, because even in his enthusiasm, he was delicate in how he set my miniature back on the table. He gestured for me to follow and rushed over to the display wall with all the boxes of models. Of course there was nothing new, since the cashier had said the next new stuff didn't come in for two more days. It took a while, but I finally got Liam's excited self-calmed down and back over to my table. I let him ramble on about game lore and rules while I tried to paint my character.

Eventually someone asked him to play a game, and he said his goodbyes. He wasn't even gone ten minutes before Erin, Wren, and Garrett sat down across from me. I set my brush down and gave a dramatic sigh.

"Don't you guys ever do anything else?" I asked. "Or do you all pretty much live here, playing games?"

"Wouldn't you?" replied Garrett, "if you had nothing but free time?"

Erin brushed him aside. "We have plenty of other things we do, including real work," she said. "But this is a side hobby several of us enjoy." She gestured to my half-painted character. "Now, let's see what you have so far."

Before I left that night, I had the first model painted and the five-man squad assembled. By Wednesday night, they were painted as well. However, I needed to have another real talk with one of them, and it ended up being Erin. Wren seemed to have pulled back a bit after our kiss Monday night. I was starting to worry it was just a fluke. He had fed in a moment of weakness and moved on.

"Hey, Erin. Can I ask you something?" I made sure we were far enough away from others that we wouldn't be overheard. "I was going to talk to Liam Anderson about his sister and whatever happened, but before I could, he flipped and is now acting crazy nice."

"We had to reassert the Mesmir over him," she said quietly but way too casually. "What's your question?"

"Wow, okay," I said with surprise. "A bit harsh. No free thinkers allowed, I guess?"

She looked at me with a look of surprise. "You think I like this? It isn't a matter of subjugation or anything. It's about survival. And not just our's, either. Liam is probably a perfect example. Do you think he is better off being angry and hurting all the time?"

"It's not healthy, and it's not right," I insisted. Then I sighed, my shoulders slumping. "But I guess it's what it is."

"I'm sorry, Jason. I really am." Her voice was softer, filled with sincerity. "Some things just are, and are out of our control. But now, what was your question?"

I let it go for now, knowing it wasn't an argument I was going to be able to do anything about right now. "Is it ever going to be safe to talk to him about what happened to his sister?" She looked over at me, but could only give a noncommittal shrug. "So how do I talk to him about that? If I bring up his sister, is he just gonna go off again?"

"It's probably best that you don't."

I thought I had dropped it, but I couldn't let it go. "This can't be good for anybody," I said. "Is this what you do? Somebody makes you uncomfortable, so you either mess with their mind or kill 'em?"

"Whether we like it or not, it's worked so far." She said it like it was so practical, but I could tell she was uncomfortable with the conversation.

"Sounds like somethin' I'm not gonna get an answer about," I said in frustration.

"Why does this matter to you?"

"Because his sister died, but everybody acts like nothin' happened. Now even him, apparently," I said. "Is that what's gonna happen to me, about my dad? Or is my mom gonna start actin' weird about him bein' gone?"

CHAPTER THIRTY

LIFE IN PLASTIC

The day before we were set to head back I brought the topic back up with Mom. "I think I've decided. If we're goin' back home tomorrow, can't we just stay there?"

"What do you mean, honey?" she asked. "Home is here now."

"But if we don't like it here, why can't we just stay there? Maybe stay with Aunt Susan or something until we find something down there?"

She looked at me like I'd grown a second head. "Why on earth would we do that, when we've got a perfectly good job here? With a new house, and all?" She swatted a towel at me playfully. "Goofball!" she teased.

"Job?" I asked, confused. "What job do you mean, Momma? You found a job already?"

"What?" She looked at me confusedly. "The whole reason for moving up here, silly! My new bookkeeping job for Mr. Tsui?" She turned back to the dishes she was washing, shaking her head. "I swear, boy. You get sillier every day. Now git out of here! Go play with your friends or something. You aren't going to school tomorrow, since we need to leave about ten to get to the airport. But don't think you can stay out all night!"

Job for Mr. Tsui? I guess that answered how Mr. Tsui planned on keeping me here, without the excuse of Dad's job. He was just handing it off to Mom. Unfortunately, that also meant Mom was now under their Mesmir. Can I officially hate it here now?

I dragged my ass back up to the Little Green Men, and sure enough, my models had come in. I felt weird being able to shell out seventy dollars for my three boxes of troopers. It was weird paying so much money for some plastic models. It was even weirder *having* the money.

The twins weren't around that night, and neither was Liam. Considering my mood and how much I wanted someone to blame, that was probably a good thing. I took it as a sign and headed back home. Since Mom's door was open, I poked my head in and saw her packing a suitcase.

"You're back home early."

"Yeah, nobody was up there, so I just came on back." I felt like I needed to approach this again. "Hey Mom, are you sure we shouldn't just move back? Wouldn't things just be a bit simpler there?"

Regardless of what Mr. Tsui wanted from me, I didn't have to give it to him. We'd already paid a pretty big cost coming up here, losing Dad and all. I had a pretty strong feeling I wasn't done being asked to deal with even bigger problems. And this mind control stuff, this Mesmir, well that was just plain creepy. Sure, Liam was being nice now, but I would have rather earned it, you know? And now Mom was starting to act weird?

Mom sat down on the bed and looked at me, her fingers playing with the hem of the shirt she was folding. "Hun, I get it. I really do. This move can't have been easy for you. And now with what happened to Daddy?"

She sighed, her shoulders slumping, for all the world like she was about to give one of her "keep your head up" speeches. Then in an instant she perked up, her shoulders popping up and her eyes twinkling.

"But things are going great now, right?" The smile on her face was downright creepy. "You've got your new friends, this new hobby of yours." She pointed at the bag in my hand from the game store. "You've even got your new social club.

What are they called? The Ravens?"

She stood up and laid the shirt she had finished folding in the open suitcase.

"Besides, Baby, we have new responsibilities here. *I* have new responsibilities here. The money... This house..." She swept her hands to indicate the walls around us. "I kinda owe it to them to follow through with the new job, right?"

I sighed in frustration. "Mom, this makes no sense. Who do you work for? What's the name of the company?" She looked at me with a blank smile. I tried again. "What's the name of your boss?"

"Silly, you know that! It's Mr. Tsui and his company." She looked me over with a bit of concern. "Are you sure you're alright? Look, go finish packing. And since you're back home, why don't you take a minute to jot down some ideas for what we should do with this big 'ol place to make it a bit more lived in, huh?"

When she playfully closed the bedroom door in my face, I got really frustrated. Or maybe a bit down. That wasn't her.

It was the Mesmir.

I had already packed and didn't feel like going upstairs, so I ended up walking around the rest of the house, kind of just taking it all in. The basement still felt as odd and creepy as it had that first day. But this was the first time I had started realizing I wasn't going to be banished from the space.

Before, it had really felt like it was going to become my dad's "man cave". Now it was occurring to me that I could make it something of mine if I really wanted to. We had our couch from our old house down here already, plus Dad's old recliner. Get a nice TV down here, maybe a video game system? This could be a great hangout for Liam, Taki, and the guys.

Then I started imagining being able to have Wren hang out. Although really, he seemed too cool, too... sophisticated, for the basement. He would probably be more comfortable upstairs in the lounge area. I walked back up to the ground floor. Mom was already in her bedroom, so the lights down here were off. I could still see most of it with the lights coming in from the curtained windows. I could just make out all the new furniture. The living room set, the new dining room table, all of it. In the dim light it all felt fake, plastic.

Like Mom.

CHAPTER THIRTY-ONE

HOME AFTER HOME

Flying was not what I had expected. First, we had to drive over an hour to get to the closest airport. That involved a ferry across Lake Champlain. I'd seen them in movies, but somehow thought they had been phased out for bridges or something. It was kind of cool, and was the first time I'd ever been on a boat. I got to stand right up on the railing and watch the water rush up on the front of the boat. Even though it was freezing, it was still fun.

The airport was crazy!

It was packed, with everyone running in eighty different directions. We had to check in, then go through security. They made me pour out my water bottle, but told me I could keep the bottle and fill it up at a water fountain on the other side? So stupid. I wanted to flip the lady off, but Mom was so stressed about figuring out where we were supposed to go that I didn't want to upset her. She had mentioned this was her first time flying as well.

The plane wasn't what I expected, either.

In the movies, you always see the giant jumbo jets, with three rows of seats, two aisles, and lots of room to stand. Turns out those are only used for the really long flights, like going overseas. Instead, we were in this little jet that only held around sixty people. There was just one aisle, with two seats on each side. We sat around on the plane for about half an hour, before we started taxiing to the runway where we would be taking off. It felt like we were driving there, as far as we had to taxi.

Then the actual takeoff.

Mom reached over and took my hand. I didn't mind the bit of reassurance that she was there. Neither of us knew what to expect. But for real? It wasn't bad at all. I felt a bit of vibration as we started speeding up on the runway, then the plane tilted and the vibration disappeared as the wheels left the ground. It was actually a pretty cool experience.

Finally, finally, finally, after a connecting flight we had to run to catch, we made it off the plane in Alabama.

Aunt Susan picked us up and we went back to her place to shower and change clothes. We relaxed for a bit and I hung out with my cousins. Three brats, leaning more to the "spoiled" side. All girls, ages seventeen, fourteen, and nine, not a one of them worth hanging out with. I played nice though, and ended up chatting more with Alen on my phone than paying attention to them.

Since we'd had such an early lunch right before the airport, we all went out for an early dinner. I waited for the fireworks and was not disappointed. Considering Mom's change in story, I knew things were going to be uncomfortable. I'd already heard Mom and Aunt Susan get into it in the kitchen, about whether we were going to move back now. Mom had told my aunt about "her" new job, which caused all sorts of confusion. Then at dinner, Uncle Stewart went into basically the same thing.

"I know what I heard, Renee. Jeremy was all excited about that job up in New York," said Uncle Stewart. "Now suddenly we all heard wrong, and it's your job?"

"I don't know what to tell you guys," said Mom. "I report back to work on Monday."

I had known this was coming, but I did my best to keep my mouth shut and stayed out of it. I had foolishly hoped the Mesmir might have just been local to Avernus and would have gone away once we were away from the town. No such luck, I guess. Of course it was possible it might be one of those things that have to wear off over time. Maybe if we staying away longer?

"Job or not," said Aunt Susan, "Losing Jeremy can't be easy for you. You have no support up there. No family. Jason is probably struggling and if you're busy with this new job...." She paused and shared a troubled look with my uncle. "Well, wouldn't it be easier back here, with family and friends to help out?"

Mom was about to say something, but I jumped in. "I'm right here, Aunt Susan. I'm sorry if that's rude, but instead of assuming I'm struggling or something, can you please ask? Doesn't Mom have enough on her plate without more pressure from you guys?"

My cousins were all three looking at me like I'd grown a second *and* a third head. You just don't do that. You do not interrupt an adult. And questioning an adult without practically bowing may as well be talking back.

Uncle Stewart looked like he wanted to give me a piece of his mind, but Aunt Susan, with patience honed from years working in Child Services, gave a plastic smile that could have given Wren a run for his money and said, "I apologize, Jason. You are correct that I should have asked you directly. How are you doing with all of this?"

This was my own fault for acting before I think. Now I needed to figure out what was best here, especially since I could say any of my real reasons out loud.

I couldn't mention the Vampyre in Avernus or the thought there could be other unknown Vampyre somewhere close down here. Could Mom's Mesmir fade with time if we stayed here, or did we need to be up there to have it removed? And perhaps the biggest concern, what would Mr. Tsui do if we, specifically I, didn't come back? Considering the millions everyone claims he spent finding me and getting me up there?

I screwed on my most apologetic face. "I really appreciate you asking me, Aunt Susan, and I'm really sorry I was rude. I know you care about us and only want the best. It sucks that Dad died, but this is a really good job for Mom and I love how she looks when she talks about it. And up there I've got my own room with my own bathroom." Yeah, it was a stretch since I had my own bedroom down here as well.

"Do I miss Alen and Lisa? Sure. But I've already made friends up there, as well as a cool community service club Mom approves of. And I *may*... have found someone interested in dating me."

All three adults at the table perked up at that. Mom looked over at me in surprise, which quickly morphed into pride.

"I'm glad things are going well so quickly for Jason," Aunt Susan said to Mom. "And I'm thrilled for this new job." She shared another fast look at Uncle Stewart. "But don't you think it would be easier on everyone if you were back here? We can get you set up here in Huntsville instead of that little town you were stuck in. Stewart can help you get another job at least as good, and Jason could be back in familiar surroundings."

"Susan, please—"

Aunt Susan cut Mom off. "You really should think more about this, Renee."

Mom sighed and rested her face in the palms of her hands. After a moment, she looked back up at my aunt. "Look, it's been a really long and stressful week. Let's just eat, and please just help me get through tomorrow."

My aunt and uncle both shook their heads at one another in frank disbelief. Finally, my Aunt Susan reached over and patted my mom's hand. "Of course, Renee. We'll help out any way we can."

CHAPTER THIRTY-TWO

LETTING GO

I was basically on lock down that night. I was sleeping on the couch in their living room, but my mom and aunt sat in the dining room, right off the living room, for most of the evening. It was nearly midnight before they quit their gossiping and went to bed. I spent most of the evening texting Alen and Lisa, trying to ignore my mom and aunt dance around the topic of where we might live. At one point I even messaged Wren. He jokingly asked me about sexting at one point, but I laughed and blew him off.

Everybody was grumpy the next morning, me included. After a hurried breakfast and stuffing ourselves into suits and ties, we then had to cram all of us into a minivan for an hour's drive back to our old town. Nobody wanted to go that far, and since we weren't exactly churchgoers, we could have done this anywhere. But this was where Daddy's family was.

Considering we hadn't stepped in that church since last Easter, it was weird when the pastor was acting like we were the church's best family ever. He pulled us all into a side room, and prayed with us, or I guess I should say he prayed *at* us for about an hour. Dad had been cremated, so there was no casket, no cemetery, and no graveside service.

The memorial service started at eleven. Other than like, six church people, mostly deacons, there were two of Dad's old coworkers. We'd driven all the way down here, and Dad's family hadn't even shown up. Then 11:20 hit, and for the next ten minutes, all of Daddy's family came pouring into the church. Only a handful of them were dressed up worth a damn, and half of them were hung over, drunk, or both. All told, there were probably twenty adults, and about as many kids. They brought the whole clan out for this one. It was utter chaos. Several of them were fussing that there was no casket and no body, since Dad had been cremated. Half were yelling that Mom was the reason Dad was dead. And a few were very loudly screaming at all the others to calm down and be respectful in the church.

The pastor stood there confused and angry, trying to get everyone to calm down. Mom was yelling at most of them, Aunt Susan was crying in frustration, and Uncle Stewart was laughing, along with a couple of the deacons. I was completely embarrassed, seeing the white trash I came from. I started recording some of it on my phone, because I knew nobody would believe me.

What should have been over with in half an hour, took until way past noon and by the time we were finally able to leave, we were all shaken and on our last nerves. I begged mom to let me stay with Alen overnight, to catch up and, I mentioned in a whisper, to get away from my cousins. His mom had already offered to drive me up to Huntsville in the morning, so she agreed.

It was great to catch up with Lisa, Alen, and some other friends. I spent a good bit of time filling them all in on Taki and the gang. I probably spent a little too much time talking about Liam and Boots. Lisa started ragging on me about which one I was hooking up with. A couple of the others chimed in when one of them made a comment about me "knocking Boots". I did not bring up Wren. I let them get their digs in because I knew none of them meant anything by it. In fairness, I think they were impressed I had found some other skaters so quickly.

I showed Lisa some of the stuff I was learning about Hammers & Hordes, because it seemed kind of her thing. She was into all sorts of nerdy games already.

She thought it was interesting and promised to take a look. To my surprise, Alen showed some interest as well. It was rare that he was interested in any games that didn't require a controller.

It was nice being able to reconnect with my old friends, but even now, what, two weeks later? I was already looking to get back to Avernus. That surprised me, but maybe the weirdness was rubbing off on me. It was just, everything there was so big, so overpowered, so, I don't know, important. Avernus was probably the same size as our old town here. But somehow it seemed more vibrant, less dirty, less... boring. Seriously, if we moved back here, what was here for me? Knowing now that Vampyre existed? Giving up contact with that world?

I mean, even if their world is dangerous and horrible, at least there I know *where* it is. I know its borders, how to get answers if something weird happens. Here? For all I know, there are Vampyre up in Huntsville, and I would have no way of knowing. What if someone there, or over in Atlanta, or Birmingham, decided to try and take Mr. Tsui's power from me? He or Wren wouldn't be around to help me, or warn me, or protect me, or anything.

It's not like I really had a choice but to go back anyway. It probably wouldn't take a week for Mr. Tsui to send a pair of those black-suited goons of his to grab me by the arms and march me all the way back home.

Home? Wait, really? Was Avernus already "home"?

Yes, I think it was. It was only a couple of weeks, but the old house was already out of my thoughts. I was already spoiled by the new place and we'd only been moved in a week. I missed how it was reliably cold up there. As much as I really liked Alen and Lisa, I was surprised to realize how much I missed the new crew.

And anyway, there was this thing, whatever it was, with Wren. I know he hit all my buttons in what I liked. But what about me? Did he just like me because of what he was? Or did he like me, you know, for me? That was something I needed to find out. Especially after the kiss we had shared outside of my house. It had been so cold. So cold that it matched the chill of his touch. But as we kissed, as I flushed, so did he. Wren had been cold, but by the end of the kiss, he had been so warm. So...

Wait, why had Wren been warm? Because he had been warm by the time the kiss ended. It was strange, too. Wren wasn't a Vampire. He didn't feed off blood. He said he was a Succubus and fed off sexual attraction.

Did Wren feed off me?

Chapter Thirty-Three

Disappointments and Determination

The next morning couldn't come quick enough. I was up and anxious for Alen's mom to drive me up to Huntsville. Soon enough I was out of my suit and back in normal clothes, ready to run through the reverse process of Friday. This time our layover was in Washington, DC, which was cool in concept, but meant the airport we were rushing through was probably three times as big.

We got to the new gate, and that's when it all started to go wrong. First there was a delay in boarding our plane. Then that turned into mechanical issues, and the whole flight was delayed. We sat around for nearly two hours, waiting for them to find another flight, before they finally told us there was not going to be another flight in our direction that night. "In our direction?" That's how they wanted to word it? Mom was about ready to lose it.

Something about how our tickets were purchased, and the fact that the flight issue was their problem, meant we were put up in a hotel room. I was frustrated, but Mom was *pissed.* Usually, she saved these tantrums for fights with Dad, but she was going *off* on whoever was on the people at the airport. I had to step in to remind her to calm down. I was afraid they were going to throw us out or something. Then like every other time, she ran out of steam and just like that, she was fine.

The hotel was nice though and was attached to the airport. We were in the room barely an hour, when Mom's cell phone rang. She covered the mic long enough to whisper that it was the airline. I went back to texting with Wren.

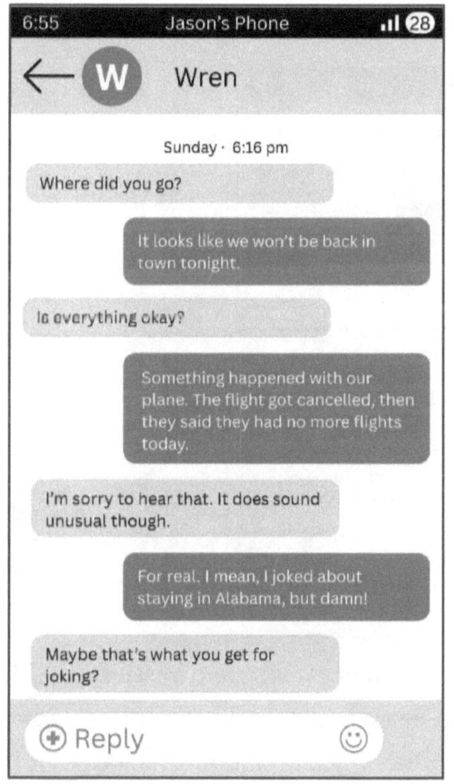

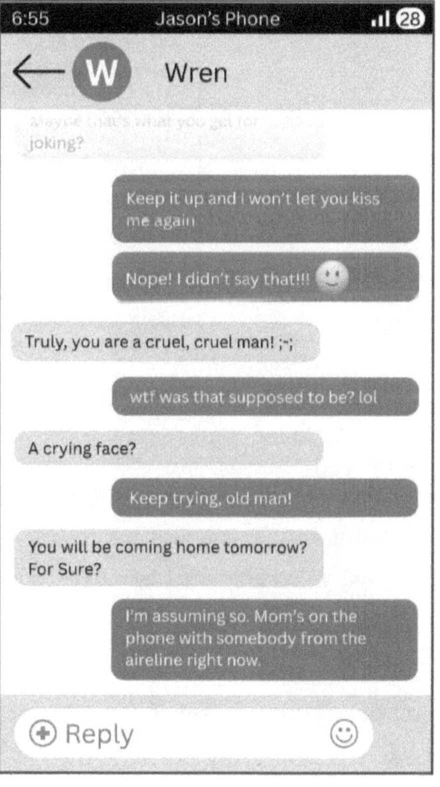

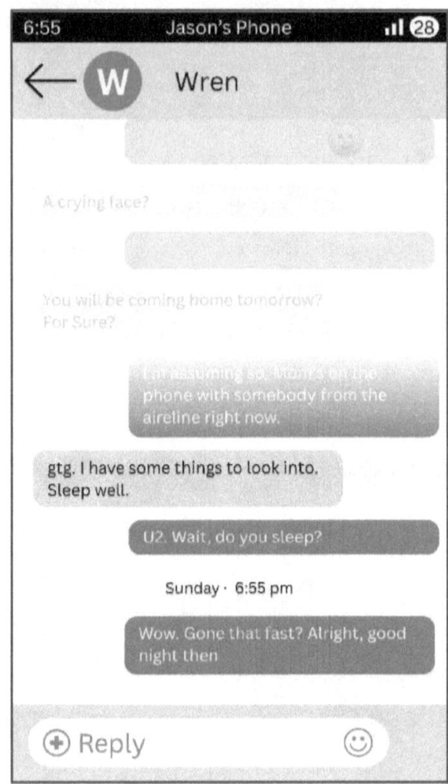

Mom got all excited and mouthed that they had a flight for us! Have you ever seen someone get excited and angry at the same time? She started tossing items back into her carry-on bag. The carry-ons were all we had, because who knew where our suitcase was?

Out of nowhere, she shrieked into the phone, yelling and cussing like I haven't heard her in forever. Next thing I knew, she had thrown her phone against the wall, followed by her bag, the TV remote, *my* bag, and anything else in her reach.

"What the hell, Momma?" I yelled, jumping for cover.

"Oh, they had a damn *flight* for us all right," she yelled right back. "They were trying to put us on a flight *back* to Alabama!"

"What? That makes no sense." I really wanted to help my mom calm down, so I walked over and gave her a hug. I made sure she saw me coming first though! "What did they say the problem was?"

It took her a second to respond. At first I thought she was too upset to hear my question. But then I realized she wasn't still pissed, she was embarrassed. She started laughing softly, hiding her face in my shoulder.

"I, um.. I threw the phone before I could hear why they thought we wanted to go back to Huntsville."

I chuckled a little, which caused Mom to lean away, swatting my arm for laughing.

"Ohhh," she sighed out, wiping her eyes and still laughing at the ridiculousness of the situation. "Baby, get me my phone," she said, one hand on her hip, the other extended as if her phone was going to float over to her.

I laughed, then went and picked it up off the floor. She has thrown it enough times I was not at all surprised that it lit right up when she turned it on. I swear, she should be a tester for phone cases. She looked down at the phone in her hand and uttered something between a growl and a sigh.

"I'm not going to deal with this through a phone," she exclaimed. "I want to look somebody in the eye when they lie to me."

"Please don't go taking a swing at somebody and getting yourself in trouble. You can't just leave me here, you know."

"Don't worry, Baby. I'll only give them a tongue lashing!"

It was a while before she came back, but she said she finally got it sorted. They were claiming there was something with our tickets that got the system turned around between our destination and departure point. But it was now squared away, and we had a flight scheduled for 10am the next morning.

Next morning, we were up exactly as early as Mom wanted us. Why is her argument always that I should be used to it since I always have to be at school at eight anyways? Do I look like I'm going to school today?

If I had thought the TSA lady in the first airport on Friday had been annoying, the guy we had to deal with Monday was seriously terrible. What an ogre! He nitpicked a dozen items in our carry-on bags, stupid stuff. At one point he threatened to hold Mom because she had *keys,* of all things. There's no way car keys are contraband. We were almost through security, and suddenly a supervisor came over. Just as we were getting pulled into their back offices, we were all stopped by a pair of scary guys in dark suits. Somehow even scarier than Mr. Tsui's goons.

One of them eyeballed the TSA guys while the other one looked at me. "Jason Docker?" When I nodded, he said, "My apologies for your delay. If you will, follow me, I will get you and your mother on your plane."

I was confused about why he would be talking to me and not Mom. The TSA people didn't seem to have any intention of contradicting the guy, so we moved to follow him. But first, I had to get in a parting shot.

"Sorry, ma'am," I said to the supervisor with a smirk. "It just wouldn't work out between us. Don't worry. You'll find someone eventually!" Then I scratched the bridge of my nose with my middle finger as we passed her into the hallway.

They walked us right past the entire security checkpoint area and next thing we knew, we were being shown to this open topped golf cart. Me and one of the guys were sitting in these backward-facing seats. I looked over, studying the guy next to me, and realized he was wearing an earpiece like you see in the movies, with a curly chord that disappeared under his collar. At one point he adjusted his jacket, and I saw he was wearing a gun in a shoulder holster. Who were these guys? FBI? Secret Service?

We got to the gate, and our flight was already boarding, so we nearly missed it. One of the guys went up and leaned in to speak quietly to the flight attendant at the gate. After a moment she nodded and started asking everyone to be patient while we were literally, personally, escorted onto the plane. It was another tiny one like last time, maybe even smaller. Again, another quiet conversation with the flight attendant on the plane, a really cute guy in his twenties, and we were seated in some of the first seats right there in the front of the plane. It was only after we were seated that they started letting the rest of the passengers onto the plane. Then the two government type guys stayed right there on the plane, staring down anyone who seemed to have any questions, until they exited right before they closed the plane's outer door.

It wasn't a completely separate section, but the front seats were I guess first class? There was a bit more room, and even though there were only like eight of us in the cushier seats, we had our own flight attendant, while the entire back section of thirty or so people had one more for all of them. We were barely in the air before we were offered drinks, a soda for me, and Mom got a glass and two little bottles of scotch. Finally we were left alone, and I was able to turn around to try and talk to her.

"What the hell happened?" I asked quietly.

"I seriously don't know, baby," she said. She was still shook up, and was practically whispering to me. "They didn't have a reason they were telling me for why they were hastlin' us. It was almost like they were fishin' for something to hold us on. It was like they were stallin', holding us just to hold us."

"Who were the guys that pulled us out?"

"I don't know whether I believe him or not, but the guy driving called himself a 'Special Agent'."

"I'm just glad we got out of there. That was scary."

"Creepy, more like," she muttered. She patted my hand. "Let's just get home."

Mom and I were moody on the drive home from the airport, but for some reason became downright sullen once we got closer to home. It was like a weight hit us, coming back to Avernus.

As if our new house, hell, the whole town, was cursed.

CHAPTER THIRTY-FOUR

MIRRORED RESPONSES

Mom kept me busy until after dinner before she would let me try to get out. Half an hour and two texts from Wren later, I snapped up my board and entered LGM. I was caught completely off guard when I saw that Garrett was in the middle of a game, not with Wren, but with Liam. Damn, his mind must have been as screwed with as Mom's was.

At the table behind them, Wren and Erin were both in the process of unpacking some models, probably to start a game. They were both in matching outfits, charcoal grey ankle-length skirts that were light enough to still be in the grey spectrum and not mistaken for black, with this pale grey sweater that had been knitted so you could see the black long sleeve shirt underneath through all the holes. I went over to say hi to everyone, then went over to one of the hobby tables. I had new troops I hadn't been able to mess with yet!

Wren came over and sat next to me. And yes, I was sure it was Wren. I have slowly been able to figure out subtle differences between them. For one, no matter how much he might fight it, Wren is about an inch taller, and still has a slight Adam's apple. And as I had noticed already, there were differences in their smiles.

"So you had a busy weekend?" He asked, playfully punched my arm.

"More crazy than busy. Definitely weird. Wanna see why I'm so embarrassed of where I come from?" I asked, holding up my phone.

Smiling, Wren said, "Other than everything you see in the news about the South?"

I laughed and groaned all at once, then I showed him the video from the memorial service. "What's this?" he asked.

"My dad's family," I said. "My family."

"Damn," he said breathlessly. "I'm sorry you had to deal with such a circus."

"You should see them at the holidays," I muttered. "But enough about them. I have questions for you." I stared him down, locking his eyes to see what his reactions were going to be.

"So serious," he said, glancing over to his sister, and then back at me. "Alright, what's on your mind?"

"Something that's been bugging me for the last couple of days. Am I being taken advantage of? Did you feed on me that night we kissed?"

It's not that I was violently opposed to the idea or anything. And I definitely didn't mind the kissing part. But I didn't know what I was getting into with all this supernatural stuff. Vampyre, Mesmir, Asseclas? Throw in Succubi, and it was just kind of too much, too fast, you know? Besides, everything had a cost, and I needed to know what kind of price tag I might be dealing with.

"I would say more like I took an opportunity, not that I took advantage. Does that bother you? Or scare you?"

I nodded slightly and said, "Thanks for being honest."

"Hey, if you're going to start with the big guns, I suppose I should be helpful."

"Well, bother or scare? That depends. Is there a downside or some kind of damage to me from being your midnight snack?"

"No, not at all."

"Not even some kind of extra hold? No extra mental manipulation that makes me want you to come back for more or anything?"

"No, nothing like that. If you really want to call it a side effect, you will always get really, really turned on any time it happens."

I stared at him hard. "If I asked Erin, would she give me the same answer?"

Wren chuckled, then seeing I wasn't playing, he sobered up and said, "Let's ask her." He gave a whistle and as she looked up, Wren waved her over.

"What's up with you two?" she asked when she approached. "Staying out of trouble?"

"Have a seat, sis," said Wren, and she came over to sit on his knee. "Would you please tell Jason here, in detail, the different abilities we Succubi have when we feed off a man like him?"

Her eyes had widened when he mentioned Succubi, but I was able to see she took it as the cue to the level of conversation we were having.

"Well, since we feed off male attraction, our feeding kind of 'enhances' that," she said hesitantly. "So you're probably going to get hard, and stay hard. You might even have a little accident in your pants, if you know what I mean," she added with a nervous smile.

I had to mentally downplay my reaction to that. Wren can be a shameless flirt, but somehow it felt "wrong" to hear Erin talk so blatantly about stuff like that. But it did open up an opportunity, and I wanted to take advantage of it.

"That's all fine... well, it's not *fine*-fine, but Wren was talking about it also softening me up for Mesmir attempts, to bring me back for more. What about that?"

She looked curiously between the two of us, particularly confused when Wren grinned slightly, nodding. "What are you talking about? Sure, we can Mesmir, but our feeding doesn't make it easier somehow. There aren't any side effects from feeding, other than the heightened arousal, that I've ever heard of."

"No shortened lifespan, loss of vitality, obsession over the feeder, anything like that?" I asked.

Erin looked at Wren in surprise. "What kind of fairy tales are you trying to scare this poor boy with!?"

"Thanks for telling me the truth," I said. "Wren didn't say any of that. He said the same things you just did. I just had to be sure you all weren't lying."

She looked at me with a twisted smile. "You little bugger! Good work." She laughed, then asked, "But Jason, what if he used our telepathy to tell me the answers he wanted you to hear?"

I groaned inwardly, trying to keep a blank face. Then realizing they could probably both tell my reaction anyway, I relaxed and let my surprise show. Wren had said his sister could tell what I thought of the both of them, so mind reading could be a possibility for all I knew.

"I didn't think about that. Is that really something you two can do?"

They both laughed, sharing a look of amusement between them. Then they looked back at me and Wren said, "No, that isn't an ability Succubi have. That's Garrett's department."

He gave a wider grin at the look of surprise and worry on my face. Then he gave this completely casual look and, as if it was the most boring thing in the world, dropped a bombshell.

"Check your email tomorrow. Dom wants a chat."

CHAPTER THIRTY-FIVE

OFFERS AND ACCOUNTABILITY

I sat waiting in the virtual lobby of the Zoom call and jumped slightly when the screen went black, then came up with the image of Mr. Tsui. He was looking pretty intimidating, dressed all in black and sitting behind a big fancy desk.

"Good evening, Jason. Thank you for meeting with me."

"Hi there," I said. "Before you say anything, I have a couple of ground rules you need to agree to."

"How forward," he said with a grin. "Very well. What are your ground rules?"

"First, no Mesmir," I said. "I don't know if you can even do it over a video call like this, but just in case, don't do it."

His grin widened. "Very well. It had not been planned, but it is good to know your opinion. What else?"

"Wren told me what you were doing when you knocked me out and took me to that lab. No more *trying* to kill me. Either do it, or stop."

He paused, the smile dropping from his face. I tried to read his expression, but it was so neutral as to be blank. The best I could get was he was thinking of how to respond. Finally, his face went from blank to serious.

"My attempt at retaking my power in that manner was a mistake," he said. "And a costly one at that. I'm sure he also told you I now very much want to keep you around. You have my apologies, and my word that nothing else for the foreseeable future will be done without your knowledge and approval."

Frowning, I said, "I doubt that, but I suppose that's good enough for now. So why did you want to talk?"

"As we both know, you hold some of my power, but you are not my Assecla. It is about this issue that I wish to speak with you."

"Yeah, Wren told me you can't just take your power back without killing me."

"That is correct. And I no longer think that is the option we should pursue. I would like to offer to make you my Assecla in truth."

"What is this going to do to me? Is this going to make me your servant or something? Like, are you going to be able to order me around or anything? If so, I won't be an ass-licker. Sorry, Assecla."

His eyes widened momentarily before he responded. Whether in surprise, humor, or annoyance, I couldn't tell. "Rather the opposite, I'm afraid. Having access to some of my power paradoxically gives you resistance to many of my other abilities, as you have already discovered."

Mr. Tsui steepled his fingers and said, "There are other benefits as well, if you would allow this. As my Assecla, you would age more slowly, living perhaps a few centuries or longer. And the sooner you begin, the more years you will have. In addition, you would gain a greater resistance to both disease and injury."

"Yeah, but do you really want me trying to go to college, still looking fifteen?" I asked with a smirk. Then I realized the look on his face. "Wait, you do want me to go to college, don't you?"

"It would be difficult, considering there is no college here in Avernus."

"But what about—"

"And if I did allow you to attend a university somewhere else, it would be difficult for me to protect you."

"Okay, but what about onli—"

"I doubt it will be necessary."

"Then no! The hell with that," I exclaimed. "I may be a dumbass, but I'm still good enough for college. Otherwise I'll be under your thumb my entire life."

"Perhaps there are options we can explore."

"Like online, maybe? Like I was trying to say?"

Mr. Tsui paused. "Perhaps," he answered vaguely.

"Fine. Then tell me, what am I looking to be giving up if I say yes and do this? I get the slow aging, and how I'm not going to be able to buy my own drinks for the next fifty years. But what else, really?"

"Hmm." Mr. Tsui looked thoughtful. "If you are referring to physical side effects, there are few. And even the items you see as problems, have historically been considered benefits. In addition to the slowed aging, I suppose you could find yourself in an unfortunate position if you were, say, to forget your enhanced strength and assault a mortal. Or to be assaulted yourself, and be exposed when you near-instantly heal from a stab or gunshot wound."

"You mean I get super strength and healing?"

"The ability to call upon supernatural strength is known as Potentia, and yes, these two abilities are quite common among the Vampyre."

"So you're saying I won't be normal."

"My dear Jason, you are already no longer normal. You are an Assecla, though an uncontrolled one. I am offering additional capabilities, and the power to control them."

I blew out my breath in frustration. He was hiding things, I just couldn't prove it. I couldn't even say why I was convinced of that. "Fine, but there's something else!" I yelled. "Drop this Mesmir garbage on my mom. It's creepy, and she deserves better."

"I do not think that is a wise idea, Jason. She could easily cause problems."

"It's a deal breaker," I said. "You took my dad. Give me back my mom."

Mr. Tsui paused for a moment. "You are full of demands today."

"Is she really going to do any bookkeeping for you? Or are you just stuffing her in a closet for forty hours a week?"

He chuckled. "She doesn't exactly have the accounting skills we would need.

Your father was barely of a level to be of any use. As you know, the job was a ploy."

"So then release her. You want to keep me here? Go backdate an insurance policy on my dad or something. And give me time to think about this. Maybe not years, but definitely more than a goddamned week."

He sighed. "I understand. I should have taken your age into consideration."

"My age has nothing to do with it. Even if I was thirty, any sane person would want more time to think about this."

"I was thinking more of your points on growth and education, but I understand. I hope your delay does not become a decision you regret. And make no mistake, inaction *is* a decision."

"And my mom?"

"She will be released when she comes home shortly. I hope you are prepared for the difficulty this will cause you. She is certain to notice the inconsistencies in your life and your actions. Most teenagers would relish a parent who gave them whatever they wanted."

"Yeah, well, right now I don't have a parent. I've got a robot. Give her back."

"As you wish, Jason."

"Mr. Tsui?" I hesitated to ask, but I needed to hear his answer, even if it was a lie. "What are you going to do if I decide I can't be your Assecla?"

He appeared surprised at the question, or perhaps at my daring in asking it. Finally he smiled. "Eventually I will have my power back, in one form or another. My very survival may require it, as well as the survival of Avernus. If you are to say no, that may be an answer neither of us can live with."

I thought for a minute, and Mr. Tsui seemed to be waiting patiently. This was crazy. I'm only fifteen. Isn't this kind of a life changing decision? Not to mention an insane amount of pressure he was putting on me. It's like, I don't know, asking me to pick a career while we're still in high school. Or to make plans for college or something. Wait, no, they make us do that, too. Still, I'd known about all this for only a week. No way did I want to make a snap decision that was going to lock me in for the rest of my life.

Eventually I figured out what I wanted to say. "It would seem like we are at an impasse." Impasse, I always liked that word. 'Impasse- a situation in which no progress is possible, especially because of a disagreement.'

"Why is that, Jason?"

"Because I'm not ready to make a huge decision like this," I said a bit too loudly. "I've only been in this creepy-ass town for a couple of weeks! And I've only known about all this for barely a week. You know, when you tried to *kill me*?"

"I see. What do you suggest?" asked Mr. Tsui.

"I don't know. You guys know all the voodoo magic. Isn't there something temporary you can do, that will keep you from going crazy around me for a while?"

"Hmm. If you insist, I will look into it."

CHAPTER THIRTY-SIX

NEW FRIENDS AND PLANS

I slumped into my chair as the Zoom call abruptly disconnected, emotionally spent. We had barely talked for twenty minutes, but I felt like I had been negotiating for my life. I suppose in a way I had been. I closed out the call and headed downstairs, verifying Mom's dinner was still good and warm, and preparing for the worst.

When Mom arrived home, she seemed distracted, confused even. I suppose it was better than the creepy-fake happiness she'd had lately. I gave her a bit to collect herself, then I called her into the kitchen to come eat. She still seemed lost in her thoughts while she sat down to eat.

"Mom, are you feeling alright?"

"Hm?" She looked over as if just realizing I was at the counter with her, even though I had just put her dinner in front of her. "Oh, sorry, Baby. I've just got a lot on my mind and I'm tryin' to figure out what to do about it."

Normally I would leave it alone. Her business is hers and I usually wouldn't care about whether jobs and bills and stuff were bugging her. But this was a little more than regular grownup garbage. This was my own Vampyre garbage.

"What's going on? You keep telling me I should talk it out sometimes. So maybe take your own advice."

She smirked at me, even if it only lasted a moment. "I don't know. Right before I came into the house, I just got hit with this wave of weirdness. Like I'd been missing something and didn't even know what it was."

I knew exactly what had caused that "wave of weirdness", because I'd watched out the window when she'd come home. She had gotten out of the car, then another woman got out of the passenger side. She met my mother at the front of the car, before reaching out and cupping Mom's face with both hands. They had stood there for a moment, before the woman turned and walked off down the street. Mom froze for a moment, not moving at all, before drifting inside.

"Maybe I'm coming down with something. The last few days feels almost like a dream. Maybe your ol' mom's getting scatterbrained. I barely remember anything from your daddy's funeral."

I took a chance to lead her on. "Maybe you're still in shock from Daddy dying, Mom. You've been running flat out since then. Maybe give yourself a chance to rest up?"

It wasn't lying to her, right? Maybe a little omission at worst? I mean, her brainwashing did start after Dad's death. Better to blame it on stress and shock, instead of monsters and mind control.

The next day went a lot better at school. Liam was more mellow. Less "over the top" in how he was acting. He asked me if we could get together to work on our models, since we both had new stuff to assemble and paint. We talked about meeting up at LGM that evening. Taki and Boots gave me a hard time about not getting to skate the day before, especially since it was lightly snowing today and we wouldn't get to make up for it. We decided to hang out a bit that afternoon, even if the streets would be too slick for skating.

I ended up inviting Boots back with me for dinner. I was starting to pick up hints he didn't have a great home life. He seemed to roam the streets solo a bit more often than I first thought.

Mom's car was in the drive, but I didn't see her downstairs. I was surprised when I found her upstairs. She had arranged the open lounge area with a long desk running against the wall under the windows. It looked like it was set for two workstations, and Mom was sitting at one. She waved when we cleared the stairs and she saw it was me.

"How was school, baby?" she asked with a smile. "Oh! Who's your friend?"

"Hi, Mom," I said, with a bit of confusion. "Uh, this is Boots, one of my friends. Is it okay if he eats with us and we do some homework together?"

"Of course," she said. "Nice to meet you, um, Boots?"

"Yes, ma'am. It's Josh, but everyone calls me Boots."

"I'll bet there's a story there," she said with a laugh.

He blushed a bit, but didn't really say anything. Meanwhile, my curiosity was getting the better of me, so I was maneuvering around to get a better view of what Mom was up to. Then I realized she had set up a whole station with tons of supplies, and was in the middle of assembling some Cosmos Emptor models.

"Whatcha doing over there, Mom?" I said with a grin.

"Oh, this?" she laughed. "I thought maybe it could be something we could do together. Do you like?"

"Weird flex, but cool. Want me to make some dinner?"

"No, you boys go get started on homework," she said, putting down her tools and the model she was working on. "I head downstairs and throw something together. How do sliders sound?"

"Cool! Thanks mom."

"Thanks, Mrs., um," stammered Boots. "Um, Jason's mom." he finished lamely.

"Call me Renee," she said with a smile. "Or if you absolutely have to, Mrs. Docker."

I shook my head and led Boots into my room. I grabbed my bag from the corner and let him take the desk while I took my laptop to lay on the bed. Honestly, we goofed off more than we actually worked. After maybe an hour, we were called downstairs to eat. Mom and Boots got along great, and she seemed to be in a good mood. I was worried, after how she seemed when she went to bed. She caught me by surprise though, when she told me about her plans for the next day.

"I may not be home for dinner tomorrow. I have to drive down to Albany to meet with some lawyers," she said casually.

"How come?" I asked. "How far's Albany?"

"About two hours," piped up Boots. Then he covered his mouth with his hand. "Oops, sorry," he mumbled.

He seemed surprised when Mom laughed. "It's alright, sweety. But yes, it's a couple a' hours south, and will probably take all afternoon. So can you figure out dinner for yourself, baby?"

"Yeah, Mom. No problem. What's the lawyers about?"

"Something about some insurance your daddy's company had on him. Bless him, he was only hired a few days, and they managed to not fire him before he up and died. Can you believe it?"

My mood flipped a one-eighty inside. I did my best not to show it. No idea if I was successful or not. Not sure how seriously I cared. We finished eating and went back upstairs. Twenty minutes later, Mom came up and sat back at the painting desk outside my bedroom door. I could already see this was going to be a problem. I sighed and looked over to Boots.

"Hey, man. I need to go up to the game store to meet Liam. You want to come with me?"

He looked back at me, seeming a little surprised. "Yeah, sure," he said apprehensively.

I started packing up my bag with my models and supplies. I guess Mom heard me getting my stuff together, because she got up and came over to lean on the door frame and see what was going on.

"Oh, baby. We've gotta get you somethin' to carry your stuff in better than that bag. Somethin's gonna get broken or messed up."

"Yeah, Mom. We'll figure it out." I really didn't want to talk to her right then. "I'm going up to the store to go meet my friend Liam. I'll be back by eleven."

"Alright, baby. You want me to drive you up?"

"No thanks. It's only a short way to walk, and I'll wear my coat."

Then she looked over to my guest. "Hey Boots? Can you give me just a sec with Jason here before you go? Go on downstairs and he'll be right behind ya."

"Y-yes, ma'am," he mumbled, looking from her to me. I could tell he was trying to figure out the family dynamic here, and if I was in trouble or something. She stepped aside out of the door frame so he could get past, then swung back into the doorway. I could see Boots behind her at the top of the stairs. He stopped for a moment, catching my eye and shrugging his shoulders, seemingly asking what was going on. Then he started down the stairs.

"So baby, this weekend," Mom said. "Why don't you invite your friends over? We'll spend some time the next couple of days settin' the basement up, get some more furniture down there, a TV, and you guys can tear up the place. Whada' ya say? They can spend the night and we'll order pizzas."

"What's goin' on, Momma?"

"Just thought it would be nice. We've finally got the space for you to have friends over. I thought you might like it for once."

"Okay," I said hesitantly. "Thanks."

"And speaking of friends, how are things with that social club you joined? The Ravens or whatever? I never hear you talking about them."

I shifted uncomfortably. "Yeah, that's... going alright, I suppose."

She studied me for a minute, staring into my brain in that way that only mothers seem capable of. Finally she let it go. "Go have fun with your friend." She pulled me into a hug when I tried to squeeze past her to leave my room. Then before I could get away, she whispered, "He's cute. Is he a keeper?"

"Mo-om!" I moaned with a half laugh.

CHAPTER THIRTY-SEVEN

THE INVITATION

At lunch the next day, I gave everyone the invitation about staying over Saturday night. I warned them it would probably be lame, but they all got excited when Boots started bragging about how nice my house was. I didn't know how I felt. I cringed a bit, but I think it was more because I was used to what I always had before, no house, and nothing to show off except a drunk ass dad that was guaranteed for a few traumatic memories.

I was also thinking about some of the things with Mom last night, and how I felt about them. The first and biggest was that she was obviously right back under the Mesmir. That pissed me off. I had told Mr. Tsui I wanted her free, and I meant it. It was creepy living with an "always happy" zombie. Sure, a lot of guys my age would kill for the freedom to do whatever they wanted. But it was too much, too fast. Besides, I loved my mom. Yeah, yeah, gross. I lost my "teen card" and all that. Dad was a complete piece of work, but I still loved him, to some extent. Miss him, no. But I loved him, I guess. I was supposed to, right? But Mom was cool. Sure, she was a forty-plus ex-stripper. But she had usually been cool to me. So yeah, I was okay saying I loved her.

But speaking of love, what was this stuff she had said last night about Boots? Did I like him? I mean, he was cute, sure. Could I see myself making out with him? Yeah, I had to admit that playing tonsil hockey with him could be pretty fun. I still hadn't figured out if he swung that way, but I thought maybe I should test the waters with him. Maybe even this weekend.

But that made me think about Wren. Was he interested in me? Or was I just a tasty snack who was, what had he called me? Intriguing. Of course I was interested in him. I would be all over him if I could be. I wonder what would happen if I could get Wren over to my house, offer to let him feed, and then see how far he might let me take things? He'd dodged my questions so far on how old he was, and that just made me curious in very naughty ways about what kind of experience he might have.

Down, boy. Hehe.

Even so, the second school let out I texted Wren, telling him to let me know when we could talk. I hung out with the crew for a bit, then said I was heading home for dinner and homework. Once again, I invited Boots over with me to eat dinner. He jumped on the opportunity. I was starting to realize he was kind of like I had been back down south. Either he didn't like his home, or he wasn't very welcome there.

We tried to work on homework. We really did. It was a good thing Mom wasn't looking over our shoulders, or I might have been getting fussed at instead. But the whole time we were working, I was also trying to get to know him a bit. What was he like? What hobbies and interests did he have?

Was he gay?

Not exactly something you can just come out and ask, right? Especially since I wasn't really in with the guys enough yet to get a read on how they would all react. No, definitely better to give it some more time before opening that particular can of worms.

Still, Boots was particularly friendly. He shared jokes easily. He seemed to be pretty close to my personal space. He even had this cute thing where he would lean over and gently bump shoulders with me when he found something amusing.

We also found time to talk about weekend details. What time we should get together Saturday, what we might want to do, what snacks and drinks everybody liked, stuff like that. I decided to give him a quick "sniff test" as well. At one point, I went over and put my arm around his shoulders, with the intention of leading him over to check out the basement. But I paid attention to how he reacted. At first he stiffened up slightly, but he immediately relaxed into it. But right after, probably about the time he realized he was giving in, he stiffened up again. Bingo. Gaydar alert!

If only I had the guts to do something about it. I just didn't know him and the guys well enough to make a move. Yet. Either way, I was planning on inviting him around more often, whenever I could. No way was I going to leave him the way I was left.

Boots was equally impressed with the basement, commenting on how much fun it would be to hang out with the whole crew here Saturday night. We already had the couch and coffee table from our old living room down here, along with Dad's recliner. I told him we were also going to see what else we could get down here. The room was really long, so there was plenty of space. I told him I was going to try to get Mom to let me bring the TV from the living room down here for the weekend as well, which Boots thought was awesome.

I told him we needed to figure out sleeping arrangements, and he quickly let me know that all the guys had sleeping bags, plus Taki and Wheeler both had air mattresses they could bring. Since the furniture was only taking up a tiny portion of the basement, that was all set. He would take care of letting all the guys know tomorrow. Then, before I saw him to the front door, I dropped the bombshell. I asked him if he wanted to meet up early and spend Friday night as well.

He got adorably nervous and said yes.

Chapter Thirty-Eight

A Hot Visit

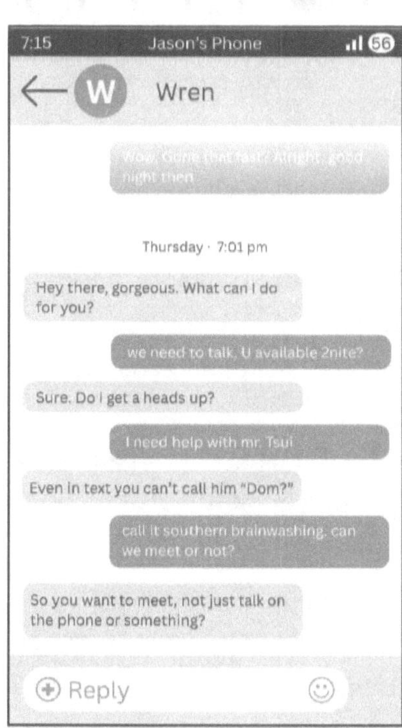

I was glad he texted because I intended to have it out with him.

Wren arrived right on time. He looked as hot as ever, wearing a pale shiny grey calf-length skirt over knee-length, light tan boots, and a white, tight-fitting knit sweater. I know I was doing a poor job of hiding my infatuation, so I decided for once not to try.

"Come on in. That outfit is nice," I said. "Did you wear it to distract me?"

He laughed, with no Mesmir to make it feel fake. "No, I did not take your preferences to heart when my sister and I chose what to wear today."

"Do you two always wear matching outfits?" I asked out of curiosity. "Do you ever wake up and decide to have personal days? Or maybe disagree on what to wear, so do your own thing?"

"Hmm," he said thoughtfully. "I can't recall the last time we have chosen to wear separate outfits. It's just a thing we have always done." Then he smiled and directed us over to the couch in the living room. We sat, and he said, "Surely my fashion is not why you so desperately called me over. The sun had barely set before you sent your text."

"I need advice, or maybe even help," I said. "Tsui is screwing with me, and I don't know what to do about it."

"You dropped the 'Mister'. What happened to that 'southern brainwashing' you were raised with?"

"Maybe I'm trying to be less brainwashed," I deadpanned. "Besides, he's moved more into the realm of a personal enemy,"

Wren's eyebrows raised. "Do tell. I was under the impression the meeting went well."

"Oh, the meeting went fine," I said, and I was unable to keep the anger out of my voice. "But the bastard didn't keep his word. He promised to get the Mesmir off my mom."

"Did he not? I heard about that, and Dom said he did as you asked."

"Yeah, she was back to normal when she came home. I even got to watch some woman supposedly remove the Mesmir. She was a bit confused, but at least I had her back."

"Alright, it sounds all good so far. The confusion is coming from her having to readjust back to reality. It will take a minute, but it will happen, for better or worse."

"That's fine and all, but the next morning, she was right back to being a happy-freak! Controlled by the Mesmir, just believing a new cover story!"

"Damn." Wren sat and looked at me for a moment as I fumed. Apparently I was more pissed than I realized. Finally, he said softly, "That wasn't Dom."

"What the hell do you mean? What, did someone randomly go behind everyone's back and put her back under? Or did he break some law by freeing her, and some 'Vampyre police' put it back on her?"

Smiling sadly, Wren said, "No, babe, she chose it."

"What do you mean?" I asked angrily, scooting away from him. "What, did she go find some Vampyre and beg to forget everything? That's crap."

"She did not need to do something so drastic. And she wouldn't have done it consciously," he said, speaking softly to try and calm me down. I didn't think he was trying to use Mesmir on me, but I went on my guard just in case.

"It's really rare, but it can happen. It's rare enough that Dom likely saw no point in mentioning it. There is a very mild Mesmir over the entire town. Not enough to fully control anyone. Just enough to make our attempts at Mesmir easier, and to ensure they hold better. I cannot say for certain, of course, but likely her subconscious retreated, and she effectively surrendered herself to the Mesmir that had already been there."

I scoffed, skeptical about the whole thing. "So what, once someone has been Mesmirized or whatever, it's there forever?"

"No, like I said, what happened with your mother is very rare. It's complicated. The bottom line, however, is that your mother was released, and no Vampyre has done anything to her since then. Consciously or not, she chose this. Lifting it again may do very little, if she chooses to retreat back to its mental safety again."

"Oh," I sulked.

Wren perked up, his attempts to distract me obvious. "Care to show me the house?"

He complimented the basement, noting the possibilities such a space could provide. When we got upstairs and he saw the work area, he noticed Mom's models. "Cosmos Emptor?" he said with a grin. "Have we changed our mind on our chosen army?"

"Definitely not," I said in mock defiance. "Those are Mom's. It's probably thanks to your Mesmir, but she's decided she's interested in the game."

"Does that surprise you?" Wren said with some surprise of his own. "It's not exactly a kids game. Plenty of adults play, and plenty of women play, as well."

"Yeah, I know," I muttered. "It just doesn't seem like something my mom would be into."

"What, she is only allowed to like sewing and gardening?" he said with a grin.

"Shut up," I laughed.

"And what do we have here?" he asked as he opened my bedroom door. "Aha! The scene of the crime!"

"No crime's been committed in here," I said as I tried sliding past him in some weak effort to block access to the room.

"Not yet, maybe," Wren said as he pulled me in for a kiss.

I let myself be pulled in. He was only a couple of inches taller, so it wasn't much of a reach for either of us. My own warm lips met his cold ones, and the sensation was electrifying. My knees melted but it didn't matter, as he easily held me up. I had thought about this. Hell, I'd dreamed about it. Now it was here, real, and even better than the first time we kissed. As before, the longer we kissed, the warmer he became. He glowed, and it was like I glowed in his presence. I couldn't think straight, or think gay, or... think. I had his attention, and that was all that mattered. All I could think about.

The back of my knees bumped against the edge of my bed, and it woke something up in me. "Wait, wait," I said, shaking my head slightly and trying to regain my senses. "Stop, Wren. Please stop."

"What's wrong, babe?" He asked.

I could tell it frustrated him, or maybe disappointed him. But still, he let go and took a step back. The perfect gentleman.

"I need to ask you something first," I said. He looked at me curiously, so I took a deep breath, steeling myself to ask the question, even through my embarrassment.

"Do you actually like me? Or is this just feeding?"

He looked at me curiously, almost with amusement. Before he could answer, I jumped back in, trying to explain. I spoke quickly, almost tumbling over my own words. "I mean, if it's feeding, that's cool I guess. It's still hot. But like you said, you know I like you. I just want to know if you like me, too."

Wren looked at me, an amused look on his face. I started feeling really embarrassed at my admission, and collapsed to sit on the edge of the bed. He stood there, studying me for a minute. I couldn't take the scrutiny and looked down, away, anywhere that wasn't at him.

Finally, he said softly, "You really are so adorable." I winced, ready for anything from condescension to laughter. "Yes, I really do find you fascinating. Do I like you in a romantic way? Yes, but it is Ludus, not Eros."

"Huh? What does that mean?"

"It means I find you to be cute and sexy. You are interesting, and I want to tease you mercilessly. But it's not something that makes me want to exchange rings and devote my heart for a lifetime."

"Oh." I wasn't sure what all that really meant. Or maybe I did. "So basically, you want to boink my brains out and don't want me hurt, but we're never gonna be boyfriends?"

He laughed. "Something like that. Or at least, that's the way it is now. Are you disappointed with what we have now? Do we really need to put labels and obligations on it right now? Maybe something more intimate could grow. Who can tell what the future may hold?" He looked at me, then moved over and sat down next to me. "So is this a problem?"

"No, I don't think so. I just needed to know where I stand."

"So is it okay if I do... this?" He laid his hand on my leg, barely above my knee. Slowly, he started sliding it up my thigh.

"N-n-no," I managed to get out. "It's fine."

I tensed up as his hand moved further north. I needed to adjust, but with Wren's hand on my leg, I was frozen in place and couldn't move. As he reached to mid thigh and began sliding his fingers to the inside of my leg, a shudder went through me.

Wren chuckled, then turned to me and placed his other hand on my chest, pushing me onto my back. I let myself lay back, but definitely did not relax. I tensed further as he ran his hand, fingers splayed wide, slowly down my chest to my belly. Meanwhile his other hand was moving up my thigh, grazing the inseam of my jeans, then sliding up to meet his other hand at my belt buckle.

It was too much, too fast. Sure, I'd shared a few kisses here and there. Three, to be exact, before Wren. One was even with a girl. And once I did some feeling up with another guy I thought was super hot. We both got super embarrassed about it before we could do anything more. But now Wren was going all the way. Then, Oh My God! The next twenty minutes were like nothing I had ever thought I could ever experience.

CHAPTER THIRTY-NINE

PREPARATION AND REVELATION

I asked Mom about Boots spending the night Friday, before the rest of the guys came over Saturday. Her response was to have him come home with me after school Friday. We ended up driving out of town to hit up a Walmart there for snacks, groceries, and all sorts of other shopping. We found this awesome TV up there that was a 65-inch screen for dirt cheap.

"Oh em gee, this would be so awesome for the basement," I said with a silly grin on my face. "Or in my bedroom!"

She gave a good laugh. "And how exactly would we get it home, young man?"

"Would it fit in the back seat?" I asked.

"Maybe," she said with a grin. "But where would Boots here sit?" she asked, throwing her arm around his shoulder.

I looked over at Boots. "He can sit in my lap!"

Boots blushed and froze. I could tell he wanted to pull away from my mom's arm on his shoulder, but was afraid to. Fortunately she pulled away, and he was able to move back.

"Save it for the bedroom," laughed Mom.

Now it was my turn to blush, while Boots looked away in confusion. It's the difference between your mom knowing you're gay and having her just lay out all your business. And was she also implying she assumed we were already "doing the dirty deed"?

"Besides," Mom added, drawing me back out of my head, "I thought you trusted your ol' Momma?" She pulled me into a side hug, much like she had just released Boots from. "We should have a box sittin' on the front porch when we get home."

I looked up at her with excited disbelief. "A big box?"

She laughed, stretching out the word as she said, "A bi-i-ig box! You boys are gonna have your work cut out for ya tonight."

We ended up picking up some extra bedding she didn't explain, and got me a new sleeping bag, something that would help if I decided to go camping during the cooler months. She said it would also help with the concrete floor in the basement.

When we got home, there was certainly a big box sitting on the porch, but it wasn't all that was there. I don't know how the hell it all wasn't stolen. The giant box was a whole ass futon, a couch that folds out into a bed. Turns out that's what the bedding was for. But behind that box, sitting right out on the porch, was a 40-inch TV, and another, that was a 70-inch. Both of the TVs were just sitting there in their regular boxes, with a shipping label slapped on them. There was no attempt to cover them up or hide what they were or anything.

As we were bringing the stuff in, Mom kissed my cheek and told me the smaller TV was for my bedroom, while the big one was for the basement. I was kind of in awe. I mean, yeah, they were an off brand, but still, how could we afford all this? I had to ask.

"It's all okay, baby. You let me worry about our finances," she said with a smirk, as if I had asked something silly. "Let's just say, everythin' with the lawyers yesterday went real well!"

It took a lot of work, but me and Boots had a blast putting everything together, assembling the futon, and getting the TVs set up. I kept my new TV down in the basement for now, figuring we might like having a second screen for something.

Boots figured we could hook up a laptop to the big one and play movies on it and use the second one for video games. He said Liam had a Nintendo Switch, and Wheeler had a Playstation. We texted them, and both agreed to bring their systems over the next day, with a selection of multiplayer games.

The evening got pretty awkward later on. As we were cleaning up from dinner, Mom pulled me aside for just a quick second and whispered to me, where Boots wouldn't notice.

"You guys try to keep it down tonight, alright? I don't want to know anything about it, but there's an extra bag on your desk upstairs. Make sure you're the one who opens it, and not your new friend, yeah?"

"Mo-om, what did you do?" I moaned, looking nervously over at Boots.

"Just lookin' out for my boy!" she whispered with a grin while also wiggling her eyes in Boots' direction. Ugh, yeah. Sure enough, it was a bag of supplies for doing the horizontal mambo.

Eventually we crashed in the basement. I had brought my laptop down and we were hanging out on the couch watching a movie. The new TV was crazy huge. It was bigger than the one in the living room even.

"You've been like a kid in a candy store today," Boots said with a laugh. "You'd think you'd be used to this stuff."

"Me? Hell no," I said, laughing with him. "All of this is completely out of nowhere!"

I told him a bit about what it had been like living back in Alabama, about how we lived in a house older than my parents, with absolutely no space for anything.

"I would say the whole house was smaller than this basement, but this basement is *huge*! But yeah, between how crappy the house was, and Dad... my dad was, I could never have friends over. I think that's probably why Mom's going so overboard, because we finally have the room to have friends over. I used to spend more time at my friend Alen's house, than I did at home. Or that's what it felt like sometimes."

Boots was quiet for a second, then said, "Yeah, I'm kind of the same way. I'm always trying to hang out at Taki's house, or sometimes at Scott's place." Then he tried to laugh it off when he added, "Sometimes in the summer I'll just camp out, because it's better than being at home. But it sounds like you know about that. I remember the shiner you had when you came to school."

"Dad was a real prick, that's for sure. Is yours the same? That's why you're trying not to stay at home?"

"Yeah, it sucks, but what can you do?"

In a quieter voice, I asked, "When you were out of school the other day, was it something to do with that? The other guys were acting kind of sus about you being gone."

"Yeah, but you probably know how it is. You just kind of get used to it, you know?"

"Man, don't I know it! Dad had a sick sense of humor when he wanted to be mean. Christmas three years ago, he thought it was the funniest crap to give me a Barbie doll."

Then I realized what I had said as Boots looked at me funny. "A Barbie? What was the joke?"

"Oh, um...." I gave Boots a bit of a side-eye, gauging his reaction when I admitted, "I sort of, kind of... came out earlier that year?"

"Ah, then I guess it was definitely a screwed-up joke. Well screw him, then. I guess he wasn't thrilled with your news?"

No negative reaction. Not even a pause to decide how to take it. I took it as a good sign, which pretty much confirmed what I had guessed the day before.

"Mom's been totally chill about it. Dad... yeah, he was not happy to find out he had a faggot, his word, for a son."

"I'm sure it's too soon to say what I really think of his son," Boots said with a smile. Then his cheeks got a bit of a blush as he added, "Guess it's a good thing he isn't here to find out his son is hanging out with another queer boy."

CHAPTER FORTY

BREAKING IN THE BASEMENT

We got up the next morning and started what turned into twenty-four hours of pure chaos. Everybody was there by noon and dumped their stuff, then we all grabbed our boards and roared around most of the day. We hung out, pulled tricks, and scared one or two drivers when we got too near the street for their comfort. Finally, I got a text from Mom around five, asking what kinds of pizzas we all liked. Nobody had any real complaints on toppings, and we headed back to my place in time for dinner to show up. I'd gotten a few compliments earlier when gear was dumped, but now that we were really sitting down and getting settled, everyone was excited about the place.

"What's down there?" Taki asked, gesturing at the two doors at the other end of the basement.

I looked where he was pointing. "Left is the laundry room. The right one is the bathroom. But there's also a toilet upstairs by the kitchen, and another bathroom at the top of the stairs on the second floor."

"So no pissing in the bushes!" yelled out Wheeler, pointing around at everyone.

"Is there a story there?" I said with a laugh.

"There's always a story there," laughed Liam.

Looking around at all the empty space, Taki said, "Dude, you're not even using half the room down here. What are you gonna do with the rest of it?"

"No idea," I said. "I'm sure my mom will make that decision."

We ended up swapping ideas, and the Switch was hooked up to the big TV. There were six of us, and he had several four-player party games. The smaller TV ended up with the Playstation, and a selection of one-v-one fighter games. The pizza was gone within an hour, and around ten, Mom came down with a giant tray of sandwiches, pizza rolls, and tater tots. We'd already been making runs upstairs to get drinks out of the fridge, and had bags of candy and chips laying around.

Wheeler and Liam ended up crashing fairly early, a bit after midnight, and the rest of us called it a bit after two. We pulled the coffee table out of the way, and pulled out the futon. Scott called the couch, and I let Boots have the futon. Me and Taki unrolled our sleeping bags and joined the other two on the floor. Me and Taki spent probably another hour chatting quietly about all sorts of nonsense, before I finally fell asleep mid sentence.

The next two weeks went by without any new tricks. I was finally able to settle into more of a routine. I was figuring out my teachers, finding out what nights were best to go to the game store, and finding times to meet with Wren. We kissed a few more times, but didn't fool around again.

I couldn't get a read on Boots. We started hanging out more, especially after the rest of the crew went home once the temperature dropped after sunset. I wasn't feeling pity for him. It was more like I was proud I could do for him, what Alen had been doing for me back home. He even spent the night a few more times, and I gave him a few opportunities to open up and maybe make a move on me. Either he wasn't interested, or I was being too subtle with my hints. But just in case he wasn't interested, I didn't want to make the first move. Especially if he thought he owed me or something.

Then, just as I was walking out of my last class, I received an email.

YOU HAVE AN APPOINTMENT AT 7
THIS EVENING WITH DOMINIC TSUI

Chapter Forty-One

Threatening Reassurance

At 6:55 I loaded up the Zoom link. No way would I ever give him a reason to accuse me of avoiding him or making him late. I wondered what he could want. Was he going to try and push me for an answer on the whole Assecla thing? I didn't mean I needed weeks to decide. I needed years! Was it going to be about Mom? He could have brought that up any time and not waited so long. Or was it going to be something new?

As much as I wanted to think otherwise, I had a feeling this guy had a one-track mind.

The screen loaded before I was ready. I wanted more time to think. More time to stress over what was coming, maybe. He looked good tonight. The shirt he was wearing was black and glossy, with this bright Christmas red piping which really stood out. His hair was loose and smooth, like it was recently brushed. It made it more obvious how long and shiny it was.

"Good evening, Jason," He said in a pleasant voice.

His looks were distracting tonight somehow. I almost missed that he had spoken to me. "Huh? Oh, um, hi."

"Is everything alright? You look a little flushed."

"Yeah, I'm good," I said, getting hold of myself. "What's going on?"

"I have been experiencing... issues," Mr. Tsui said. He spoke lightly, but he added an edge to his voice when he asked, "Have you thought any more about our situation?"

Yup. One-track mind. "Seriously, dude? You're like, ancient. What's another couple of years to you? Let me finish high school or something, at least."

He sighed. "There is a timetable on this. You say I should wait a few years. I say that even now, you may be a few years too late."

"Alright, then..." I said. "No."

Even I froze at the brazenness of what I had just said. I didn't even know if I meant it. But I would die and go to hell before I'd let somebody push me around. He wasn't my dad.

There was silence as I waited for his reaction. He seemed to be deciding how to answer. I thought he would be fighting against anger, but he didn't seem upset. He didn't seem to be having any emotion. Finally, he took a breath and spoke.

"You need to understand that this is as much for your benefit and safety as it is for mine." Mr. Tsui got a look on his face. It might have been concern or pity, but it seemed genuine. "I have enemies, and they know about you."

"Excellent," I said sarcastically. "So, by trying to use me for your own plans, you sicced your enemies on me? Thanks."

"Sadly, this is the life we live."

I didn't have an answer for that. "That's just cold, my guy. I was hoping maybe you were just calling to see if I was having a good week, instead of more of this Assecla business. Hell, at this point, I would rather have you threaten to take back all the money you've been throwing our way."

"Jason," he sighed, shaking his head. "I have money. Do you need more? Is that what it would take to make you say yes? Would you like a million dollars? Two million? How about ten? You can send your mother to live happily and safely with family."

"Send her away? Why?"

Mr. Tsui looked surprised. "You seemed upset with her being under the influence of the Mesmir. I genuinely want you to be a happy Assecla. I can ensure you are taken care of. That your mother is safe and comfortable. I will give you whatever promise you wish that I will allow you the freedom to explore your higher education through online programs or even private tutors, if this is your wish."

"Money's fine," I said. "Not only is money really cool, but I guess I'm going to need it if I can't get a job for the next fifty years. And I kind of understand what you are saying about Mom, but I just don't know. It sounds weird. But this seriously can't wait til after high school? I don't want to get to graduation and I'm still a skinny shrimp compared to my friends."

"If I thought it could wait, it would of course be preferable. But even now it could be too little, too late."

"Well in that case, why do it at all?"

"Because I refuse to go down without a fight!" he said enthusiastically. "And from what I have seen of you thus far, you wouldn't either."

"Hell no. Scorched earth, baby."

"So then we are in agreement. This needs to happen now."

"No," I said. "I want to know what the rush is all about. What are these enemies I'd be taking on. I'm assuming your enemies would become mine?"

"Sadly there is no way around that. They would become, as you say, your enemies as well." He looked at me through the screen. He may as well have been staring me down in the same room. "However, I would ensure you were well armed, and well protected."

I thought about that, then said, "Right now I'd rather be well informed."

Mr. Tsui sighed, sitting back in his chair. He paused, and I got the impression that whatever he was about to say went against his preferences. Nevertheless, he did finally speak.

"When the Vampyre treaty that held me within China ended in the late '90s, I was not the only Vampyre released to come back to the West. There were few Vampires in China, and I did not dare make things more difficult for myself by making any progeny. However, I had to make... allies. Not allies of convenience. In fact, they were decidedly inconvenient."

"Who were these allies?"

"The Jiangshi," he said, as if uttering a curse word.

I ignored his attempt at being spooky. "I'm lost, and you can ask Wren or Garrett. I don't react well when I'm lost. Who are the Geo-whatever?"

"The Jiangshi are China's answer to the Vampyre. They aren't created from a living human like the Vampires of Europe, or the Asanbosam of West Africa. Instead, they are souls pulled back from the immaterial and forced back into their corpses. In general, they fear and hate the living."

"Sounds like they are great entertainment at parties," I chuckled.

"They feed on fear and nightmares. And the easiest way for them to find those nightmares for them to feed from, is to generate those nightmares themselves."

Is that what has been going on the last couple of weeks? That creepy as all hell dream about the mist on the ceiling? The half dream about that damned floating head hanging out at the end of my bed? And then the first one, where I realized now I was dancing with Wren, and Mr. Tsui was standing in the corners, watching it all. Because now I remembered that once again, there had been that red mist hanging in the air behind Mr. Tsui. It seemed to be what linked all these nightmares together.

"Definitely not fun," I muttered

"They rampaged across the frontier of this land before this new country was founded. There was one in particular who was the most feared, the most... problematic, among his kind. He was the cause of the treaty, along with his fellow Jiangshi, which locked me inside the borders of China, for it locked them there, as well."

"And what, they're here now?"

He looked down, and whether his look of shame was real or acting, it was convincing. Then he looked back up and said, "For my own survival, I had to make alliances. Promises. They are here, now. Collecting on those promises and more, no matter the casualties. And the chief problem among them is one Vampyre in particular."

He locked eyes with me through the screen. "Jason, I need your assistance. He must be stopped."

CHAPTER FORTY-TWO

TERROR LEVEL ONE

Boots was staying over at my place a couple of nights a week now. Usually it was planned in advance, but there had been a couple of nights when he just kind of showed up. I always offered to let him stay over so he didn't have to lower himself by asking. Mom was really good about it. Whether it was because Boots was always so polite and quiet, whether she remembered how often I stayed over at Alen's to avoid Dad, or just because the Mesmir made her more agreeable, I didn't know. I just rolled with it.

Whenever Boots stayed over, he never slept in a consistent spot. Mom tried being overly nice and set him up in the guest bedroom, but he admitted later that he felt totally weird sleeping in there. The next couple of times he was over, if he didn't spend the night in my room, he crashed in the basement. He genuinely didn't seem to mind whether I joined him downstairs or left him alone to retreat to my own bed.

So, Boots was welcome to spend the night whenever he needed. We always kept any noise to a minimum, were in bed at a decent time, and got ourselves up and ready for school without any real fuss. Mom joked that at least Boots didn't eat much.

It was a Wednesday and, since we had school in the morning, we were just having a chill evening, watching a movie in the basement. I was sprawled out on the couch, while Boots had already pulled the futon out into a bed. It wasn't late at all, not even nine, so I was surprised when I looked over and saw Boots asleep already.

Out of nowhere I felt a breeze play across my neck and arms, as if a crosswind had hit me from an open door. I glanced around looking for the source. Scrambling to the far end of the couch, I cried out as I saw... something, floating in the air at the bottom of the stairs.

Regaining my focus, I stared in awe at the mysterious vision. It was a head. Literally a man's head, floating in the air. It had what looked like his spinal cord hanging down below the neck, swishing back and forth like a cat's tail or something. It had long, stringy hair hanging from a bunch of patchy bald spots. But in front, he had a foot long wispy beard and mustache, like a bad movie version of an old Chinese man. The face itself looked ancient and half decayed, with chunks of flesh missing from the cheeks and forehead. From the neck, intermixed with the swaying spinal cord, was this sickening pinkish-red smoky or mist. It looked almost like blood, turned into a gas.

"Ja-ssss-on," it moaned in a high-pitched voice, though its jaw did not move.

I realized I was screaming. Flat out, uncontrolled shrieking. My mind was pressed down with a fear so extreme that it held weight. When I became conscious that I was screaming, I stopped, though it felt like it required every ounce of strength and courage I could find. At first, I was worried I would provoke the thing. I was especially worried about Mom afraid she would come down here and see it as well. To my surprise, Boots was still asleep, with no appearance of waking. Another wisp of sound came from it, like words lost in the hiss of boiling water, the air coming out of a whistle without anything to make the high-pitched part.

"I can feel his power... within you.... Weak in presence yet... strong in potential...."

The voice was hard to follow. It sounded like it was made out of wind instruments, with long stretches of trying to inflate its... whatever. However he was doing it, I was definitely hearing his words with my ears, not just in my head. It was at this moment I knew, from the top of my head down to my pinkie toes, that Dominic Tsui was one day going to get me killed. Probably by this thing right here, or something like it. But as always, I can't take anything sitting down, so to speak.

"What the hell are you? And what are you doing in my house?" I whispered. I couldn't get much volume in my terrified voice, but I could definitely pour in the attitude. Almost as if in response, the red mist around it, the head, whatever, began to sparkle. I was reminded of the nightmare from weeks before, as little sparks of pink lightning began dancing around within the mist. And just like then, my nose was touched by that combination of flowers and vomit. Boots whimpered, but he didn't wake up. That was good because I couldn't afford the distraction.

"I go... where I need to go..." the thing said. "Above the ground... I feel an energy... an emotion... a fear I have fed from before...."

"Above the ground?" I repeated. "You mean upstairs?" Then I realized what it was saying. "You mean my mom! You gave her nightmares at the hotel, didn't you?"

"Her taste... it is familiar.... As is the child... here beside you...."

Boots tossed his head and whimpered again. Oh, hell no. "Touch either one of them, and I'll find a way to mess you up!"

It laughed. Or at least, I think it laughed. It sounded like the hissing of escaping gas, or maybe like a cartoon snake trying to talk.

"Ja-ss-on... Tell Tsui.... you have met... *Beishang de Wenyi*.... Tell him I will have... what he promised...."

I started feeling lightheaded. Like I was going to pass out. Or maybe like I was going to go to sleep, but a drugged sleep. I fought it, fought it like hell. The head-thing was wavy, mostly because my vision was so screwed up, going in and out of focus. The red mist coming out of the bottom of the neck spread, filling my vision. Somehow the thing started floating through the wall, though I wasn't sure, between my blurred vision and all the red smoke.

I collapsed to the couch, and I don't know how long I sat there, staring off and trying to stay conscious. My mind floated, my attention being caught by everything and nothing, all at once. Eventually the feeling, or effects, or whatever it was, started to wear off and I became more aware of my surroundings. Boots started to stir, wiping some drool from his mouth with the back of a hand.

"Um, wow, sorry," he muttered. "I must've dozed off."

"It's all good," I sighed distractedly. "You didn't miss much."

I grabbed my phone, and saw it was nearly ten pm. Whatever it was had felt like fifteen minutes at most, but it had been an hour and a half. How long had I been sitting on the couch trying to recover? Or had I fallen asleep as well, and dreamed the whole damned thing?

I told Boots I wasn't feeling well and I wanted to lay down in my room. He said all was good, so I said goodnight and headed upstairs. I didn't go up to my room yet though, instead sitting down in the living room where I shot off a text to Wren.

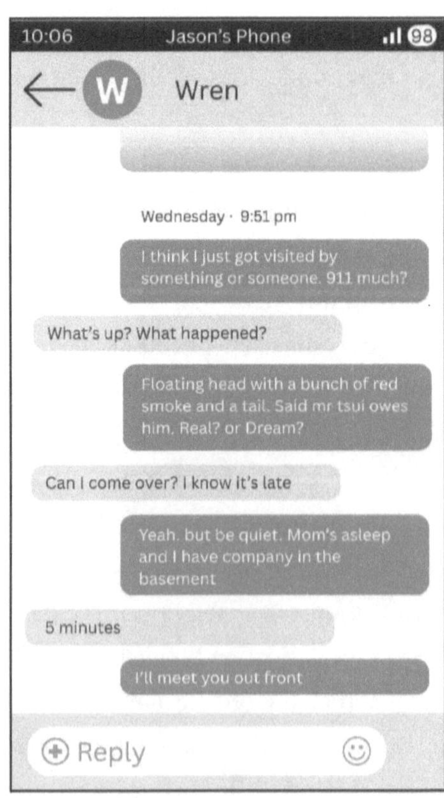

I waited just a couple of minutes, then quietly grabbed my coat from the closet. It was late, and every night seemed to be getting colder. Good thing about being in a nice house, all the doors and windows work right, so they don't make a ton of noise. I slipped outside and walked down to sit on the curb. I don't think I was out there a full minute before Wren came walking up the street.

"Too bad you can't turn into a bat and fly over, or something.," I said quietly.

I stood when he held out his arms, and he took me into a hug. I told him what happened. "It didn't feel like a dream, except for losing an hour somehow."

"I wish it was a dream, babe," he said as he sat me back down on the curb and joined me. "I hate those things, but what you are describing is a Jiangshi, one of the Chinese Vampyre. They are not pleasant."

"Yeah, Mr. Tsui was telling me a little about them. Something about having to make allies with them and promising them stuff. Now this screwed up thing was over here saying something about 'feeling Mr. Tsui's power' or whatever. He also said some creepy crap about my mom's energy or whatever."

Wren sighed and pulled me against him, and I rested my head on his shoulder. "I heard about that when your family first arrived. Many of the Jiangshi visit the first floor of the hotel, feeding on the guests in the rooms above them. I understand your family were put in room 210."

I nodded my head. "Yeah, and I was in 212."

"Your parents were given over to a particularly nasty individual named *Beishang de Wenyi.* It means 'the Plague of Sorrows', and yes, he gave himself the name. I think Dom was hoping to make a deal as part of bringing you here, or to placate him. Something like that. But yes, that particular Jiangshi often stays in 110, right below where your parents slept their first week."

"Great," I muttered. "So this was all planned." I looked over at Wren. "I'll bet this is the guy Mr. Tsui said was the big problem. The one who got everyone kicked back to China? Do you know about this? Is he setting this up to make me feel like I don't have a choice but to tell him yes?"

Wren chuckled dryly. "Dom's subtle, but no. He really is in this much trouble. He had a lot of difficulty convincing any of us to come to Avernus because of the friends he brought with him."

I shivered and he noticed. Honestly it was cold, especially the freezing concrete curb we were sitting on. But I really think the shiver came from the memory of that creature in the basement, and what it made me feel.

"Are you cold, babe?" Wren asked me. "Why don't we go up to your room for a while?"

"Dude, I have company over."

"So? Didn't you say he was staying in the basement tonight?"

"Yeah, but I've also got school in the morning." I was smiling by this point. Sure, I was putting up a fight, but I really wanted him to talk me into it. He didn't disappoint.

"Don't worry, babe. I won't stay long. I'll just tuck you in and make sure there aren't any monsters under your bed."

I sat up a little straighter. "Hey now. With all the weird stuff going on around here, don't give my paranoia any ideas!" I said it with a laugh, but I think he knew I also kind of meant it.

"Sorry about that," he said, then kissed me on the forehead. His lips were as cold as the air around us.

"Fine, fine," I said, standing up and pulling Wren with me. "Let's go get you fed. You're all ice cubes right now."

He laughed and held me as we walked up to the front door.

Chapter Forty-Three

The Consequences of Delay

Wren promised to pass on my message to Mr. Tsui. I had to trust that, though, since I never heard back on it. I didn't hear anything from him for several days, either. It left me feeling a bit cut off and frustrated. Then Saturday evening I was kicking back, watching Liam and Erin play a game up at the store.

I was just starting to really wrap my head around the way the game operated. It kind of reminded me of my Vampyre problem, how it felt like I was just barely starting to get an understanding, but was still sitting on the outside and not really able to participate yet. I'd watched a half dozen games, and twice Erin had walked me through the basics of the rules. But like so much around me, both this game and the Vampyre had a lot of moving parts to keep track of.

I had tried to be subtle and asked where her brother was tonight. "Wren," she said with a knowing look, "is busy with something but will be by later this evening."

Suddenly Garrett came rushing over from the table he was at. "Jason, buddy, huge favor!" he said, all in a rush. "Please, I beg. Go move my models to one of the hobby tables along with my bag, then take over for Erin here!"

He didn't even wait for a response. He grabbed Erin's arm, and the two of them left with four other guys who were in the store. Model collections were abandoned all over the room. I was caught flatfooted, working out what had just happened, what needed to be done, and why was it my responsibility to fix it.

It was obvious something had happened, and it involved the Vampyre. But since I was the only one here straddling both worlds, and I was friends with Erin, I sighed and screwed on my game face.

"Hey Liam, help me out?"

"Why?" asked Liam halfheartedly. "Garrett's an ass."

"Yeah, but he's friends with my friends," I replied lamely. "Just, please? For me?"

Liam paused for only a moment, his face screwed up in concentration. Then just as quickly, he perked right up as happy as Mom tended to act these days. Creepy and concerning, but I didn't have time to deal with it at the moment. We spent about twenty minutes apologizing to people and sorting out which armies got left, and moving them all over to a side table. Not just Garrett's models, but all the abandoned armies. I don't know why I was the one apologizing, except I was the one cleaning up their tables.

Liam and I went back over to his table, and I got him to start explaining what had been going on in their fight. I had been following along, but I was still pretty raw on the specialized rules of each army. Liam was oblivious, but I heard people at other tables still muttering about what had just happened. That was going to be up to the Vampyre to sort out whether they needed to come up and mind-wipe people.

I tried to have fun, I really did. But I kept thinking about what might be going on right then, wherever all the Ravens had run off to. I got the impression they had been pretty even in their game before the interruption, maybe with Erin having a slight edge. But under my stellar leadership, Liam handily crushed the forces under my command.

I promised him a better matchup soon enough, with my own Collective army. I had one more unit and a tank coming in the next week, and then I should be ready for a small game with my own miniatures. We trash talked a bit while we cleaned up, then he decided to take off for the night.

I added Erin's models to the other table, and then sat down there myself, playing around on my phone for a bit while waiting to see when they would come back for their stuff. It was quite a while, nearly ten, before they all came back to the store. All the people who had run out came in at once, including my own "unholy trinity" of Wren, Erin, and Garrett. Once all the miniatures were sorted among their owners, they each made a point of thanking me for grabbing up their models for safekeeping.

"What was that?" I asked. "What just happened, you guys?"

The three of them shared a look. Then Erin reached across the table and took my hand in her cold hands. Damn it. If she was going in for the sympathy play right off, something bad must have happened. Looking across the table at me, she asked, "Jason, what are your thoughts on the offer Dominic made?"

"I think it sucks, and he's putting me in a real crappy position," I said.

"Don't you understand what is being offered here? And what you're risking by stalling?"

The looks they were giving me made me feel like I needed to explain myself. "Look, the offer itself sounds like it could be fun enough. Triple the lifespan, powerful friends, and constant excitement? But like I told him, bad timing! I don't want to still be a fifteen-year-old shrimp when I'm graduating high school."

"So, the timing? Is that your biggest concern?" Erin asked.

"Well, I mean, there are others. Especially about Mr. Tsui's enemies and this power struggle of his. What's going on, guys? What happened tonight?"

Erin looked at Wren, a sense of dread in their eyes. Wren turned to me, his voice deadpan. "Dom was... attacked."

I had to pause and register what she said. It was the difference between being told cars are dangerous and seeing a car accident. Mr. Tsui had said there was danger. Wren said there was danger. But now here was fully fleshed out, real in-your-face danger. He was also right when he said inaction was still a decision. But right then, I didn't know if I wanted to make the jump to Assecla, or cut and run.

"Was it that ghost-head thing?" I asked.

Garrett and Erin looked surprised, both looking over at Wren. He ignored the looks of the other two, nodding to me. "Yes. It was Plague of Sorrows."

"Was it just Mr. Tsui who was attacked?" I asked. "And do we know it was this particular butt?"

"Yes, we know it was him. Beishang de Wenyi," said Erin. "And no." She glared over at Wren, clearly annoyed. "He wasn't alone."

"You were there?" I asked Wren, surprised.

He pulled back his pink sparkled jacket and lifted his shirt. It was the first time I had seen the soft white skin of his torso. Unfortunately, there was a pair of nasty gashes across the ribs high up on his left side. It wasn't quite closed but nearly sealed over with what looked like pink skin within the wound. I jumped up and ran around the end of the table, sliding into a chair next to him. He held his shirt up as I ran my fingers across the wounds. The edges of the gashes were jagged, like claws, not blades. They were torn, not cut. His skin was as cold as always, except at the wounds themselves. Those were hot to the touch, like feverishly hot.

"And this happened just a few hours ago?" I asked. "You are already healing up this fast?"

"The benefits of being Vampyre," Wren said, lowering his shirt and pulling his jacket back in place. I could tell it still hurt though. "You should see Garrett though," he laughed. "What I can heal in hours, a Vampire like him can heal in minutes."

"Sick," I said. I looked around at all three of them. "That's why you asked about Mr. Tsui's offer. The fight might have gone different if I had been there?"

"It probably wouldn't have happened at all," groused Garrett. "They only attacked because they think he's weakened right now. And he is."

"And that's my fault, I guess, right?" I shot at him.

"Right or wrong, the truth is the truth," he answered back.

I sighed, trying not to get drawn into an argument. "Well, there's one opinion. Erin, what do you think? Is it an offer, an opportunity, or an obligation?"

She sighed as well, trying to show me some sympathy in her eyes. "Honestly, it's a bit of all three."

I laughed. "If you're gonna say 'honestly' it means there's other times you're not, right? Anyways, that's what my mom always jokes."

"Ha," she said with a smile. "Also, ha. But back to my point. It might suck, but you have been given a pretty strong responsibility here. And I won't deny we kind of have a vested interest in convincing you to say yes." She laughed and looked over at her brother. "Yes, even Wren here. We would all be safer if Dominic had more leverage against his friends."

Following her gaze over to Wren, I asked, "And you? You've helped me out here and there, and you've made it clear what you think of Mr. Tsui personally. But what about this Assecla business?"

He shrugged his shoulders. "Fifty-fifty. More time to get to know you, but you might decide you like Dom better than me."

I could see Wren was trying to play it off, but there was a twinkle in his eye that told me he wasn't nearly as cold as he was making it out to be. It made me want to get him alone and ask again.

"Did he tell you guys he offered me a ton of money, and even said I should send my mom off to be safe somewhere else?"

"Yes," said Wren. "It wouldn't be a terrible idea."

I couldn't help it. I laughed. "You guys don't live in the real world, do you? I'm fifteen! I'm in school. How the hell am I supposed to keep everything running, get food, deal with teachers, hell, keep the power on?"

The three of them looked at one another. Finally, Erin spoke up. "Jason, sweety. You need to look around. You aren't living in the real world, either. We're in Avernus, and you would be under the service and protection of one of the dominant members of the town. Hell, Dom would probably set up a runner to go grocery shopping for you and put the whole school under his Mesmir, just to have you say yes."

"You guys are that sure I should do this?" I asked. "Seriously, if Mr. Tsui and his enemies are such a problem, why not just ask them to leave? Get rid of them all?"

"Dom is caught between two sides," Garrett spoke up. "He made the Jiangshi promises before leaving China, but to bring them here, he had to make other promises to American Vampyre."

"Yeah, that 'whatever it was' mentioned part of that. And speaking of all this, what happened to getting some help with Plague threatening me? I guess I'm getting left out to hang?"

"No," said Wren. "You aren't being 'left out to hang' as you put it. Dom got your message. Or at least, Montgomery got your message, which is the same thing."

"Montgomery hates my guts."

"He doesn't." said Wren. "He's like that with everyone. I really think Dom keeps him around to dissuade people from bothering him unless they really need him for something he deems important."

"It still leaves me watching over my shoulder for Plague to come back."

"Unfortunately, that's part of what has Beishang de Wenyi on edge, supposedly," said Garrett. "Dom's brought you here in some bid to gain enough strength to renegotiate the whole bind against him and the rest of the Jiangshi. So now *you* are the one leaving us 'out to hang', as you so eloquently stated it."

I scowled at him. "I really think you're enjoying this. You really got a problem with me?"

"I know you're being greedy and selfish."

"The hell? I didn't ask for any of this. I didn't ask for anything, *including* money. I didn't even ask to *move* here!"

"Yet here you are," he shot back. "Look, kid. It's a terrible situation that you didn't ask for. But you're in the middle of it, and you have a responsibility. Fair or not, this is something everyone needs you to do. And the more promises and conditions you hold out for, the more people resent you."

"Go to hell," I muttered. I wanted to be angry, but I also believed his words. "I'm just a kid, and this is too much."

I hated letting Wren see me be so vulnerable in front of the others. It pissed me off, while at the same time made me want to go run and hide in a hole in shame. But as much as I wanted to deny it, the asshole was right. If the situation was anything like they were telling me, I really didn't have a choice. But if I was already going to be seen as a greedy punk, I would take one more thing first.

Chapter Forty-Four

Age Old Question

“Know what? Fine,” I declared. “But I want to know something first. No lies, no beating around the bush, no BS.” I looked Garrett in the eyes, daring him to deny me or dodge. “How old are you? And how old are the twins here?”

Garrett paused, frozen in apparent surprise. Then he laughed. A genuine, hearty laugh. The twins looked at one another, and I couldn’t tell what they were thinking of the question. Finally, Garrett composed himself, though he was still filled with merriment.

“I’m a fairly young Vampire. I was turned in the Roaring Twenties, during a pre-Depression garden party. But these two?” I was prepared to hear they were around for the Roman Empire or something. “The beauty twins here were born in the last bit of the last century. They aren’t even forty yet. To the Vampyre, they are as much children as you, Jason.”

“Hey!” laughed Wren. “You aren’t exactly ancient, yourself!”

“So how is it you are on this council?” I asked Wren.

“See, Wren has plans. Because Garrett here serves Si-Jing-Fu in order to represent the younger Vampire population, which is a sane reason to get into local politics," Erin interrupted with a grin, "However, despite how much he might dally around and play the Lothario, my dear brother here has political ambitions, so he got onto the council for his own grand reasons. And is good at it, much to Garrett's dismay."

"Alright, but considering you," I said to Garrett, "are the same flavor of spooky as Mr. Tsui, why is it Wren here is the one who keeps keeping me company and explaining everything to me?"

Erin laughed and said, "Because Wren got your attention first, and you haven't run him off yet."

"Is that really it?" I asked Wren.

Garrett looked me up and down. "It doesn't help that you took a pretty fast dislike to me."

"What? I haven't said anything like that!"

Tapping his temple, he smirked. "You don't have to say it out loud for me to hear it."

"Oh, well that's not my problem," I grumbled. I addressed Wren while hooking my thumb in Garrett's direction. "It's no wonder Count Dracula here disses me. I like the babies more than him, and he's jealous!"

Petty, but he earned it. I really just wanted to put my head down and make everything disappear, but I knew I couldn't. Garrett started packing up, but then Erin asked him if he wanted to play a game, since their earlier attempts had been interrupted. I paused, trying to get up the courage to take the plunge. I was usually not one to hold back, but this wasn't about maybe embarrassing myself. This was literally life and death. In the end, I just said "screw it" to myself.

"Fine," I said out loud, not looking at any one of them in particular. "Set it up. I'll do it." Then to Wren I asked, "It's late. Will you please walk me home?"

Chapter Forty-Five

Chill Acquiescence

We snuck into the house a little after eleven, and I dragged Wren up to my room. He started to reach for me, but I playfully slapped his hands away.

"Uh uh," I whispered with a grin. "It's my turn tonight, Junior!"

"Junior?" he laughed as I pushed him back onto the bed. I was getting used to the cooler temperature of his skin, and really enjoying it.

"Yeah, you're practically a baby, right? Isn't that what your best buddy said?"

I pushed Wren onto his back, and he relented, though he kept his shoulders propped up with his elbows, watching what I was doing. I took advantage of that, and hooked the sleeves of his jacket back, effectively trapping his arms. Then I started running my hands up under his shirt, lifting it as I moved north. My fingers found the edge of his wound. It didn't look a whole lot better than when he had shown me an hour before.

"Let's see if we can't get you some extra energy to take care of this, shall we?" I teased. "Can't have flaws on this pretty skin, can we now?"

I could joke all I wanted, but my hands were shaking as I undid the button on his pants and started lowering the zipper. This was going to be new. Wren had always taken care of me, but I had yet to see him naked. I was looking forward to it. I had no idea what I would find, and honestly I didn't have any real expectations. Whether shaved or something else, his chest had no hair, and he also didn't have a treasure trail. I ran my fingers up and down, trying to detect stubble. Nothing at all. He was smooth.

I was not surprised at all to find him wearing panties. After all, these were girl's cut jeans he was wearing. I was, however, surprised to find they were simple cotton, rather than silk or something fancy. They were probably some fancy brand though. His skin had not begun to warm up yet.

"I must not be doing a good enough job yet," I teased. "You're still cold."

He laughed softly. "You haven't started anything yet, silly."

"Silly, am I?" I grinned.

Having never done this before, I was pretty nervous I was going to mess it up, but I heard no complaints so far. He tasted clean, with a hint of whatever shampoo or body wash he used. I made a note to ask later, knowing full well I would forget.

Wren had already proven he didn't think my body was horrible, not that I could ever compare to his flawless appearance. But he was world-wise and experienced. I didn't want to let him down or make a fool of myself.

I must have been doing a half decent job, because his skin began to warm as he gave little whimpers and moans. I was feeling pretty good about myself, considering this was my first ever time doing anything. Although if imagination helped out I would be the world's best, since I had been dreaming of being with a guy since I was about eleven.

When we finished, he pulled me in for a kiss. "That was amazing. You must have had some great experience with this kind of thing. You'll have to tell me about them some time."

"Was it really okay?" I looked away as I admitted, "That was my first time."

"Really?" Wren looked surprised. "You mean you've only done other stuff?"

"Nope." I looked him in the eye, almost daring him to make fun. "You are my first anything more than a smooch."

"Wow, I'm honored. Sincerely." He looked up at me with a bit of a twinkle.

"Wait a minute," I said. "If you are supposed to be all about sex with guys, and you're all magic and stuff, aren't you supposed to be able to like, sniff out virgins or something?"

He laughed, then kissed me again, a quick peck on the lips. "You read too many books, babe."

"I really don't," I said, laying my head on his stomach. "I just had weird interests in middle school."

"Yes, babe," Wren said, and I could hear the smile in his voice. "Those are what we call books."

I lazily played with his skin and reached up to feel his wound. I was not surprised to find it was now nearly healed. There was the faintest feel of a ridgeline to both sides of each gash, and the darker pink area was already beginning to lighten in color.

"Absolutely amazing," I whispered in awe. "And you say I'm going to be able to heal like this, also?"

"Perhaps something like this," he said thoughtfully. "I mean, each is different. There are general expectations, but the benefits can affect each person slightly differently. For example, we can see you are already having some superior benefits in dealing with Mesmir. It looks like you managed to get some Potentia in there, as well."

"You mean strength? Yeah, but I can't control either of them, can I?"

"Once you truly are an Assecla, that control will open up to you. We will also be able to teach you." He nestled me against him, giving me a bit of a hug. "So you've decided? You are really doing this?"

"It's like you guys said, I don't have a ton of choice, do I?"

Chapter FORTY-SIX

THE WRONG DOOR

I agreed to meet Wren at the game store at sunset the next day. He wanted to personally take me to go meet Mr. Tsui. It was kind of cute, him going from standoffish and bored acting, to suddenly being all protective. It made me wonder if he really was, how did he put it, Eros or whatever he said. I got the impression that having to admit he wasn't some thousand-year-old superstud opened something up with him. Maybe it let him admit he was still human, you know? Add to that the fact that I could tell when he was using Mesmir to "fancify" himself up, and now he was starting to show his true self to me more often.

I decided it was close enough to sunset and I was too nervous to be waiting around, so I crossed the store to the door marked "Employees Only, Absolutely No Admittance" on the other side of the sales counter. The guy at the counter gave me a questioning look but didn't say anything as I opened the door. It was a long hallway, pretty wide, enough for probably three people to walk side by side comfortably. The walls were cinder block, painted with a thick, white paint. The ceiling looked concrete and felt kind of low, but that was probably because of the dimensions, not that it was actually short. Every dozen feet there was a long fluorescent light fixture attached to the ceiling.

There was nothing on the walls, no markings, no signs, no pipes or cables. Nothing to break up the monotony as I headed down the hall. And I meant down, as the hall sloped slightly. After fifty or so feet, I was able to see a change up ahead, where there was a cross hallway to the left and right, and the ceiling changed over to those ceiling tiles I remembered from before.

With no warning, the lights started flickering, lowering and flashing sporadically as if their connections were loose or all the bulbs were starting to go at once. But even with the lights that were working, everything dimmed. It was almost like the very concept of light wasn't working as well as it should. Then, like you see in all the horror movies, the furthest light I could see went black. Then the next one. On and on, one at a time, lights went out and the darkness approached. My heart was in my throat. There was movement in the darkness, fluttering, crawling, slithering. A sound accompanied it, wings, scales on concrete, hissing, and thousands of tiny running footsteps.

It wasn't a thought that went through my head, more like a sense, a concept. I closed my eyes and, I don't know, I pressed. I concentrated. I don't really have a word for it, but basically, I fought with my mind. Then I opened my eyes.

The lights were on as normal. No bad bulbs, no encroaching darkness. And ahead there was still movement, but now it was a dozen or so people walking quickly toward me. They were all, for the most part, dressed in black. One or two I thought I recognized as having seen them in the store, but I wasn't sure. They stopped a few feet away from me, all but one. He strode forward until he got right up in my face.

"You shouldn't be here, kid," he said to me.

He was trying to sound all Goth and creepy, but having fought off the Mesmir, it sounded so fake. I tried to keep a neutral face, but I couldn't manage. The best I got was to only project an amused smile. Hey, at least I didn't laugh. He looked somewhat confused.

"I suppose we'll need to correct this situation," he said, trying to recover the upper hand. "Maybe we should have a little fun with you, before we make you disappear." He flashed fangs at me. I could tell they were real. This was his first act that didn't come across like some silly cosplayer. I really had no choice but to shrink back. He grinned, and this time, he didn't need Mesmir to weird me out and appear dangerous.

"I think we have time for a bit of a snack before starting our evening."

Without warning, and too fast for me to react, he suddenly had me slammed against the wall, his mouth millimeters from my neck. Stars flashed like strobe lights as the back of my head cracked against the cinder block wall and I cried out. I could feel the raw energy coming off this guy, especially as he heard my cry of pain.

"Gregor, no!" someone cried out from the group behind my attacker.

The pressure on me relented as he pulled back and turned to look at who had spoken. When I could focus, I looked as well. I thought I vaguely recognized him, though the way my head was spinning, I couldn't be sure. He was a bit taller than most of the people here, with a medium-toned skin a shade darker than Taki. One of the girls hissed and spat at the newcomer. Then I knew I was losing it, because her ear did some weird thing where the top seemed to split then come back together like a pair of scissors. He stared her down for a second, then looked back at me and the guy holding me against the wall.

Gregor, the guy holding me, laughed and said, "He entered the Warrens without escort or permission, Montgomery. He's ours to do with as we please." He was talking like his mouth was half full, probably trying to talk around his protruded canines.

"As fun as that might be, you don't want to do that," Montgomery said. "He belongs to Dominic Tsui."

Ah, there it was. And now I recognized him. This was the guy from that stupid "apology committee" nonsense. He was such an ass the first time I met him, I half expected him to be up for a bit of bullying, maybe even join in on some feeding. But not right now. He was just recognizing someone else's power.

"Plus, Si-Jing-Fu has an interest in him, as well. So back off, already."

Gregor let me go, but maybe he let go a little too quickly. The moment he did, my vision swam and I almost fell over. I had to turn and put a hand out to the wall to keep from falling. Then there were a dozen variations on "Ugh" or "Gross" as I puked up my dinner all over the floor. Everybody jumped back, trying not to get splattered. I hit my own shoes, but I also managed to get the pants and shoes of Gregor. Okay, maybe it was a bit on purpose.

"That's your own damn fault," Montgomery said angrily when Gregor started cussing and muttering threats. As he moved forward, gingerly stepping around the worst of it, he picked me up like I weighed nothing. As he turned to go back down the hall, he turned to back and said, "Clean up this mess, since you caused it."

He carried me off in his arms, as if I was some little kid, though he wasn't as careful has he could have been. I would have been embarrassed if I wasn't ready to pass out. In fact, I think I might have, because next thing I knew, I was laying on a couch, looking up at half a dozen people, including Mr. Tsui and Wren. It might have even been the couch I woke up on last time, after the operating room. Montgomery was in the process of telling the others what had happened, when they noticed me stirring.

Montgomery stopped talking when Wren looked down at me and said, "What were you doing in the tunnels, Jason? I asked you to meet me at the store."

He sounded angry, but it may have been concern instead. I was just used to hearing anger from people, so yeah.

"I knew what was down that hall, so what's the big deal?" I muttered, a little annoyed, and a lot embarrassed. "I'm either a part of your world, or I'm not, right?"

Mr. Tsui spoke up from behind the others. He was standing back, like he was trying to keep away from me. "That may be, Jason. But not all of our community knows you. Some wayward Vampyre might react unkindly to finding a mortal traipsing through the Warren."

"Fine, I get it. I screwed up," I muttered.

"Or perhaps someone should go remind Gregor about what happened to Solomon," muttered Wren.

Whatever his actual intentions with that comment, everyone went silent. Of course, to me that bat-guy was a monster. To everyone else around here, he was one of their people. I knew it as well, sort of. I kind of felt like I needed to change the mood of the room, before I found myself facing a room full of predators pissed off at me for killing one of their own.

"So, guys, are we still doing this, or should I just go home?" I still felt nauseous and I was ready to move on.

CHAPTER FORTY-SEVEN

FOR BETTER OR FOR WORSE

Mr. Tsui cleared his throat. "Who will act as witness?"

I looked around and saw there were probably a dozen people in the dimly lit room, once I saw there were more against the walls as well. The only ones I recognized were Mr. Tsui, Montgomery, and Wren. No Garrett, fine, but sadly also no Erin. The mood of the room was somber. The air was quiet, yet charged with expectation. I realized that something "official" was happening here. Not just some handshake arrangement between me and Mr. Tsui.

Wren instantly raised his hand. "I will." He had a solemn look on his face, but when he looked my way, he winked.

It was quiet for a moment, but then a woman I didn't recognize spoke up from the back of the room. "I will stand as witness as well."

There was a collective reaction from the others. Gasps, a few groans of either disappointment or frustration, along with a lot of shuffling feet. I tried to get a better look. She was an older lady, like grandma old. Asian, probably Chinese, given Mr. Tsui and a few of the others I had seen around. She was pretty tiny, under five feet, but carried herself like she owned the place. Like, people moved away from her, giving her room. Mr. Tsui had a surprised look on his face, but quickly covered it, nodding solemnly.

"Hold on, I'm saying yes, obviously, but I have a couple of requests."

God, I felt like I was on a stage under a spotlight, when everybody turned to look at me. It made me feel childish, to be asking for stuff at this stage. I shrunk back.

"Never mind," I muttered, embarrassed. "I'll deal with it later." With more confidence, I sat up straighter and asked, "So how does all this work?"

"Fortunately, most of the work was already done," said Mr. Tsui, "with your ancestor, a man named Willem Jansen. He was a good friend, and I made him into my Assecla in 1588. All I truly need to do at this point is to reconnect with the blood of your ancestry."

"Any chance this is going to risk turning me into a Vampire as well? Or that you are going to try to drain your power back out of me?"

"No," smiled Mr. Tsui. He seemed amused by my question. "Those are both completely different processes. Both of which would involve draining your body of all its *prima vitae,* that being your blood." More seriously, he said, "No, I will only be taking a small amount of your blood."

"What about this damn headache," I asked. "Should we deal with me being slammed into a wall first?"

Wren piped up at that one. "In about ten minutes, your head will fix itself. Don't worry, you'll like this."

There was something like a time skip, and I found myself waking up yet again on the couch. Only this time, I didn't remember anything like passing out. One minute I was in the middle of talking to Mr. Tsui, and then the next, I was looking up at the ceiling.

"Woah, I think I blanked there. What happened? Are we getting started? Or did I miss the whole thing?"

He chuckled. "We are finished, young Mr. Docker. I told you, most of the work was already done, many years ago. And as promised, the process was quick and painless."

I looked at Wren, who nodded. He was already smiling. Then I startled, as the woman I had forgotten was behind me spoke up. She spoke with a heavy Chinese accent. "Yes, the connection is there."

"How do you feel?" asked Wren.

"Um," I had to think about it for a moment. "Actually, really good." I don't know why I was surprised. Wren had said I would feel good in a few minutes.

"Excellent," exclaimed Mr. Tsui. He seemed to be in a really good mood now. He was probably feeling the thrill of having all his old power back.

"Now that this is done and our power is back under control," said Mr. Tsui, "Jason, would you care to have dinner with me?"

"Uh, only if I can run home and change first. I'm a bit of a mess." I could feel that the collars of my hoodie and T-shirt were sticky with bits of blood. I guess I got fed on while I was out?

"I'll take him," volunteered Wren. And very quickly, I noticed. I smiled at that.

"Very well," said Mr. Tsui. "Shall we say, in two hours? At the hotel?"

"I'll have him there," said Wren.

He reached forward, offering me his hand, helping me to my feet. The party broke up, and Wren led me down another tunnel. I thought we were going to have a bit more of a walk, but he pulled me into an alcove, where he hopped into a small electric cart. It looked like a golf cart, but was lower to the ground, and only wide enough for a single wide seat. Fortunately it had a second seat behind the driver, facing backward. He took off down the tunnel, and I was reminded of the ride through the DC airport, riding backwards on their cart.

"How come you don't just have wider tunnels, and use a regular golf cart?" I asked as we zipped along.

"These tunnels are hundreds of years old, and only slowly get updated," he answered back. "They only got updated with blocks and cement in the fifties. Before that, they were stone and dirt. Avernus has been here quite a while."

Very quickly we were in sections where the lights appeared to be motion activated, with new lights snapping on as we approached, and going dark as we left. Riding backward, it was pretty creepy watching the lights vanish one by one. It gave the impression of what happened near the store, when the group of Vampyre were using Mesmir to make it appear the darkness was swallowing the light. I shuddered at the memory, and the reminder I was seeing over and over, as every new light winked out.

After a few turns down different tunnels, I was surprised when we ended, not at a sloping tunnel like before, but at a set of wooden stairs. They looked a bit dark and dusty, as if this area was rarely visited. The tunnel continued on, even after our stop. Wren parked the cart next to the stairs, and there was this feeling of anachronism when he plugged the cart into an outlet at the base of the stairs. I was able to see there was an industrial extension cord running down the underside of the stairs from the top.

He led me up the stairs to a short landing. The landing was barely three feet by five, concrete floor and concrete walls on three sides, the fourth side open to the tunnel a few feet below. The whole area was painted black and had almost no lighting. There was a little metal teardrop flap a bit shorter than eye level, hinged on a screw. It reminded me of the covers used on some apartment doors to shield the peephole in the front door. Then I realized that was exactly what it was. Where were we?

"Now Jason, don't get upset until I have a chance to explain," whispered Wren.

"Explain what?" I asked. "What exactly is it you think is going to upset me? Where are we?"

"Well," Wren paused, then sighed, slumping his shoulders. "Here."

He reached forward, swinging the cover to the side to reveal a peephole, just as I had guessed. It was obvious he was leaving room for me to approach the door, so I did. I was nervous as hell, with no clue what to expect. I looked through the little hole, and saw... Nothing. It was black.

"What the hell?" I said, stepping back. "I don't see anything."

"Ah, yes. Of course you wouldn't, without any lights," said Wren. "Sorry about that. Here, let me see if I can do something about that."

He reached over, and flipped three latches, spaced along a thin line on the interior wall to the right of the peephole, one just above head height, one about my belly, and other about knee level. From there, I realized on the far-left side were a set of hinges, and a thin portion of the wall swung toward us like a door. The door was really narrow, probably two and a half feet wide and six feet tall.

I couldn't see into the room yet, since the alcove we were in was not lit well at all. Wren slipped partway into the door, reaching along the inner wall. Then I heard the soft click of a wall light switch, and Wren entered all the way in. I opened the door a little wider and was able to see into the room.

CHAPTER FORTY-EIGHT

THE LOWEST BETRAYAL

"What in the absolute hell!" I yelled out. "Have you always known about this, you asshole?"

I pulled the door shut behind me, then turned around, looking for the seam in the wall. I was barely able to make it out but realized the door couldn't really be pulled fully flush from this side since there wasn't a handle or anything. So, I looked for the peephole. It took me a minute to find it, since it was hidden in the patterning of the wood grain covering the walls. Well, that was definitely getting puttied over. Assuming I didn't weld the whole damn door shut. Maybe I'd just go ahead and burn the whole place down, while I was at it.

I turned back to Wren, who had gone over and sat down on the couch. "So anyone can just waltz in here anytime they want? Not to mention peek in through this damn spyhole? You know that's not going last, if I have *any* say in things. Why are you showing me this now?"

"You needed to know," said Wren. "You're all in, now."

"No, asshole! I mean, why are you only JUST NOW telling me there's a goddamned Vampyre door into my goddamned basement!"

Wren was silent at that. Because he was, in fact, sitting on *my* couch in *my* basement. Finally, he said, "I'm sorry." He at least had the decency to look upset about it. "It's difficult, being Vampyre. You have to keep secrets from everyone who isn't like you. And sometimes even from other Vampyre. I'm not a fan of it being here, to be honest. But here it is."

"I'm going to go change clothes," I said grumpily.

Smiling, Wren said, "Yeah, probably best we take care of that. Want some help?"

"I don't know," I said as I started up the steps. "I kind of want to stay mad at you. Besides, my mom might be upstairs."

"What's that going to matter?" said Wren, hopping up and following me up the stairs. "She'll explain it away with the Mesmir. Come on. Let me make it up to you."

Mesmir. Always with the damned Mesmir. Was there some kind of balancing thing with this? I'm good at repelling Mesmir, so Mom has to be terrible at it? And this whole thing about her "choosing" to go back under the Mesmir. I think that messed me up more than I was willing to admit. Was she that messed up over losing Dad? Was she feeling overwhelmed by the responsibilities of a new house, in a new place?

Was I not worth mentally sticking around for?

No, I knew I wasn't being fair, to her or to me. And dwelling on it wasn't going to solve anything either. I had to deal with everything in my way, she was allowed any safety nets she needed. Would it be better for her to be away from Avernus? It was looking like all she could be here was "fake happy". Maybe she really would be better off back home with Aunt Susan?

And what about me? Would I be better off if she were gone? Obviously, I would be best if she were here, not just physically, but mentally. But if she was going to stay Mesmired, I had a feeling that would be nothing but stress. At best, it would be a constant reminder that I couldn't really have my own mother. Maybe Wren was right that it would be for the best.

Mom was upstairs at the worktable when we went up. "Oh, honey, I didn't know you were gonna have company over. And such a pretty little thang!" She reached out to shake hands with Wren. “Hi there, I’m Jason’s mom, Renee.”

Wren offered his hand. “Hi, Renee. I’m Wren. Wren Stormbreak.”

“My, what a fascinatin’ name! Well, what are you two getting’ up to? You need anything to drink? Should I whip up some cookies?”

She quickly started cleaning up the brush she was using and closing the pot of paint she had been using. Just as quickly, she excused herself and headed downstairs to the kitchen.

“See what I mean?” I asked as I opened the door to my bedroom. “She’s never been like that. She didn’t even notice what a mess I am.”

“Maybe she’s just as happy as you to be out from under your father?” Wren came into the bedroom behind me, shutting the door.

“I’m going to rinse off in the shower,” I said, starting to strip off my clothes, throwing them in the hamper.

“Should I join you?” asked Wren with a smile.

I sighed. “As much as I like the idea, I really want to be quick. Plus I meant it when I said I still kind of want to be mad at you.”

“Are you really mad?” Wren asked, showing a good bit of nervousness.

I looked away, stripping off the rest of my clothes and not really caring I was naked in front of Wren. I wasn’t in the mood for playfulness.

“I’m disappointed you kept it a secret from me. But I get it. I guess you needed to know how I would react, and what I would do, before you could tell me.” I turned to give him a once-over. “I’ll get over it eventually, I promise.”

I stepped into the bathroom, but before I turned on the shower, I heard him call out, “I’m not worried. I’m too pretty for you to stay mad forever.”

When I got out of the shower, Wren was sitting at my desk playing on his phone. I came into the bedroom still toweling myself off.

“So, Jason, are you still mad at me?” He was smiling as he looked me up and down. Considering I was wearing nothing but a towel, I thought about trying to be all shy and embarrassed. Hell, Wren was absolutely stunning, and I didn’t feel like I had any right to think I was anywhere in his league. But at this point, I was kind of beyond caring.

“I like you too much not to forgive you.” I was hiding a small smile under a fake pout. "Even if you did me dirty."

If I was honest with myself, I was more frustrated with the circumstances, than really being pissed at Wren. Plus, I was thinking too much about what was about to go on with Mr. Tsui. I kind of stopped at that. It had really happened. I was his Assecla. I was Vampyre now. Thinking back to just an hour or so ago, I realized I had straight up had a concussion. Maybe even damage to my skull. I had hit that wall pretty hard. After all, if you skate long enough, you are going to experience one or two concussions. A wonderful father is a good source as well. And now? Nothing. I felt great.

I was smiling by the time I finished drying off and went back in to hang up my towel. Walking back into the bedroom, I saw Wren giving me a more blatant once-over. I got the impression he liked what he saw.

"Alright, alright," I said. "I give up. You are forgiven."

He chuckled at that, setting down his phone. "I know," he said with a smirk. "I told you, I'm too pretty for you to hold a grudge."

I decided maybe I could get a few answers before going back into the lion's den. "Hey Wren. Does being an Assecla block me from being made into another form of Vampyre? Like, could I later be turned to being a Vampire or something?"

Wren got a thoughtful look on his face, then said, "Not accidentally. Someone would need to remove the bond you have to your current Vampire, before a new bond could be put over you." Laughing, Wren said, "While I enjoy the floor show of watching you put on that underwear, we've got to fix your wardrobe. Babe, those are hideous."

I laughed and flipped him off. "Does that mean another type of Vampyre could be reversed? Like, if being an Assecla could be reversed, could, say" I stalled, then continued, "a Succubus be reversed as well?"

I looked over at him out of the corner of my eye, and Wren was smiling. My heart melted, he looked so gorgeous. "No, Jason. I could not become human. And neither could you. If your bond to Dom is ever broken, it would need to be replaced immediately, or you would die. Just as Dom taking his power back would have destroyed you. Being an Assecla, being Vampyre, is now a part of you."

I stared at Wren, silent as we both processed what he had just said. Then I exploded. "Wow, that's definitely a downside somebody forgot to mention to me," I said, a bit spiteful and pissed off all over again. "You mean if someone attacks and kills Mr. Tsui, I die right then, too? Nobody thought to mention that to me, all the times I asked you, him, absolutely ANYONE, what the pros and cons of this mess were?"

Wren looked worried. "You're right. I took it as such a given, I didn't even think to mention it. I'm betting Dom took it the same way. It's the same with any deep bonds between Vampyre." He looked down at his lap. "I apologize, Jason. It wasn't something I was hiding. I honestly didn't think to mention it."

"Well let's go find out what else Mr. Tsui might have 'forgotten' to mention."

"I just got you over being mad at me," Wren murmured, pulling me to him and wrapping his arms around my waist, "and here I've upset you again."

"I'm upset at the situation. I'm upset at being forced into all this. I'm upset," I poked him in the chest, "that you keep forgetting to tell me things. I want to trust someone I'm fooling around with."

"You can trust me, babe."

"In that case, I have a question for you. What was that Greek stuff you said the other day? The part where you said you only thought I was worth banging?"

"Ah, I believe you are referring to Ludus and Eros" he said, trying to hide a smirk.

"Explain those to me again," I said. "And go slow. I'm just a dumb kid, right?" I said with a smirk to match his own.

"You're never dumb, babe. But Ludus is playful love. It's quick crushes, puppy love, the amorous play of the first few dates with someone when you are lusting after the idea of who you see, even when you don't really know them yet."

"Alright," I said. "And that's the one you said you were feeling, right? The one that makes me 'mister right now'?"

"Something like that," said Wren. "The other was Eros. Eros is passion, it's lust, it's a desire to lose all control. Eros is a desire to lose yourself in the person you are with."

"And that's not what you are feeling?" I laughed. "You aren't feeling passion and lust with me?"

Wren picked at the hem of his skirt. "Eros isn't just about the physical pleasures though. It's more about the rush of romance, the desire to take one and one, and make a whole new, larger one." He sighed. "Jason, you're hot. You are kind, and definitely interesting and intriguing. You are fun to feed with, and I love being with you. But Eros is about getting lost in the relationship you are forming with a person."

He was quiet for a minute, and I took the time to think about what he was trying to say while I finished getting dressed. Maybe it was like he said. Maybe we could fool around but shouldn't try to be a "thing". After all, he was something like forty, and I was fifteen. Sure, he looked my age. And I guess because of that, I couldn't think of him like he was an old man. But maybe he looked at me like I was a little kid. That made me sad. I perked up a bit when he spoke up, even in my frustration.

"Who knows though," Wren said. "After all, you are Vampyre now. You are young now. But in a hundred years, we will both still be young."

Chapter Forty-Nine

The Devil's Crew

If it was weird entering the house through a tunnel under the basement, it was even weirder leaving that way. You don't normally walk out of your generic suburban basement and immediately enter a tunnel that looks like you are in some science fiction movie or a government bunker. A few minutes after heading down the tunnel, Wren slowed, and we passed two women on another cart heading the other way.

"They aren't heading to my house, are they?" I asked.

"No, babe. There are plenty of other stops down that way," answered Wren. "Your school, for one."

"Where else do you have them? The town hall," I said. "What about the church on the square?"

"No, the town hall is too obvious, since there is a public shelter in the basement."

"Oh, so you can have a door in my basement, but not in the town hall's basement?"

"Look, I'm sorry—"

"I'm kidding, I'm kidding," I interrupted. "Mostly."

"Anyway," Wren continued. "We have the church on the south side of the square, and LGM on the east side. Why do you ask?"

"Just being nosy," I laughed. "Or maybe I'm gathering data on my enemies! Mwa haha!"

Yeah, it was a terrible attempt at an evil villain laugh. I loved it anyway.

Soon enough we passed through several more common areas, places that looked more like cafeterias, a few more pocket areas with couches and chairs, and lots and lots of side tunnels. Nothing was marked, labeled, or offered directions of any kind. I guess you either knew your way, you had a guide, or you gave up and got lost. It seemed as good a defense as any.

We finally got to the elevator for the hotel, and I had to ask, "Why all this security crap?"

"What do you mean?" Wren pulled out a keycard, which he swiped.

"I mean all this. You need a key card, then you are about to need a key. But before the elevator will move, someone is going to come on a speaker and say something in Chinese, I guess, that you have to answer. I guess it's a password of some kind?"

"Yeah, that's pretty much it," said Wren.

"But from every other end, there's no security at all! I mean, the entrance from the game store is guarded by a 'Do Not Enter' sign, for God's sake."

"There's—"

I cut him off. "And don't give me some BS about some kind of mystical barrier, because if normal people never wandered into your tunnels, Gregor wouldn't have attacked me like he did."

"There's a lock on that door," Wren said, a bit angrily. "It was left unlocked. There's also cameras on the door, inside and out. It's being looked into."

"Cameras on all the doors, inside and out?" I asked in alarm.

"Places like your basement, there is a camera on our side. But no, there's not a camera in your basement. Just the peephole."

"Which is getting covered ASAP," I groused. "In fact, I'm figuring out a way to lock that crap down from the inside."

"We'll see if we can get something that will fix it for you." Wren held up a finger when someone said something over the speaker in the elevator. This time I paid more attention to what was said, even if I couldn't understand the language. After the female voice spoke, Wren leaned forward and spoke into the panel, enunciating "Jing-Kok." The elevator started to rise.

"So, what did that all translate to?" I asked.

"It was Cantonese, Dom's native language," explained Wren. "She asked if I had business here, and I answered by saying 'correct'."

"So, even if there are cameras and a lock at the store, that is still pretty low grade compared to all this."

"Dom is pretty heavy handed on his security."

"Wait, what? Isn't all of this Mr. Tsui's? All this underground stuff?"

Wren laughed. "Oh, no. The hotel is his. Certain areas of the Warrens. But he is only one of the council members. He may have moved the Vampyre into Avernus, but he is a long way from owning the town."

The elevator reached the top and opened on the upstairs reception area. Ms Flannagan, the sourpuss, was sitting at the desk, and frowned when we exited the elevator. Wren quickly crossed over and led me to the hallway on the right. I still had no idea what was behind the giant steel doors to the left. Maybe later I'd ask for access.

The second the door closed behind us and we were alone in the hallway, I whispered to Wren. "Damn, every time I see that lady, she looks more and more pissed off."

"You mean Joyce?"

"Yeah. I swear, if anyone needed to get laid, it's her. Either that, or she needs to cut back on the raw lemons."

We were almost to the door where I had first met Mr. Tsui for dinner, when it opened. The goon who had given me the pat down stepped out, gesturing us inside.

"I hear you're moving up in the world," he whispered as I passed him.

I really couldn't answer without others hearing me, so I didn't bother. Stepping into the room, I saw we were definitely not the only ones here. Mr. Tsui stood to greet us as we entered. There were two empty seats to his right, then Erin. To Mr. Tsui's left sat Montgomery, and beside him was Garrett.

"Come in, come in," said Mr. Tsui, gesturing to the two empty seats. "Please, join us. Garrett, please get them drinks."

Sodas were poured for the both of us. It was pretty obvious where he wanted us to sit, so I took the furthest seat, the one by Mr. Tsui, while Wren sat between me and his sister. I decided to shake things up by testing the waters, so I looked across the table at Montgomery.

"Thanks for earlier, with Gregor. You were a complete ass the first time we met, but at least you were only half an ass tonight."

A look of complete incredulity crossed his face, before he and several at the table gave a nervous laugh. Our host smiled, but it was easy to see that he was lost.

"I'm not sure I would describe myself as being ass-like, but I suppose I could have been more gracious," smirked Montgomery. "Maybe a few more times saving your ass from people like Gregor, and I'll be back to breaking even."

"Maybe," I responded. "But I'm a scrapper, so being a jerk to me puts you in my doghouse a lot faster than assault." Then I turned to the head of the table. "Sorry, Mr. Tsui. I should have thanked you for inviting me to dinner first. So thanks."

"You are most welcome, my dear Assecla. It is I who am in your debt," he said. "Now earlier, you mentioned you had, as you said, requests. Why did you fear to ask at the time?"

"I figured there was no point in airing out our dirty laundry in front of people I didn't know."

"Very wise," he said. "Would you care to ask now?"

"Your call," I said, looking pointedly at Montgomery. "I know almost everyone in the room."

Mr. Tsui smiled. "Montgomery here is my right hand. He has surrendered his seat for the night, in honor of your new position."

It was interesting he hadn't been around, acting as a go-between to help out when his boss was having his power control issues. Why was Wren doing all the diplomatic work with me? Well, I guess that was a question for later, because I wasn't sure asking with everyone here would be worth the hurt feelings.

"Alright," I said, taking my time to make sure I worded things right. I was going to treat this like one of those "evil, literal genie" kind of situations. I wanted no misunderstandings. "First, I've thought about what you said before, about my mom. Can you please arrange for her to get back to Alabama, somewhere near my aunt? She's going to need a decent bit of money. Probably not millions, but enough to set her up for a year or two. And can anything be done to keep her away from whatever the closest Vampyre are? I'm sending her away to keep her from this whole world, not to get her involved in a whole new Warren or whatever, yeah?"

"Of course," nodded Mr. Tsui. "That will be taken care of, along with your care and cover here. Your school and other authority figures will not interfere, short of you throwing drastic parties every weekend. I shall also arrange for assistance at your house. Would you prefer a housekeeper a few times a week? Or someone more permanently there to cook daily?"

"Um, the first one's fine. And I'm not a party person, but I'll have friends over most weekends."

"As would be expected. I'm sure your house will become quite popular with your school mates. What else would you like?"

"Can I get like, some more information on who can be trusted and who are problems? Enough that I won't be accidentally stepping on anyone's toes or something?"

"That can be arranged," he said. "And I like that you are thinking ahead. Anything else?"

"Yeah, on that topic, am I actually going to have any responsibilities, any authority, anything like that?"

"Not at this time," he replied with a smile. "Let's get you through school first. Ah, here's dinner."

The door opened, and a couple of guys came in with trays of food. Erin, and Wren, and I had food laid out for us, while Mr. Tsui and the other side of the table were served goblets, along with one of those plastic coffee pitchers they use in restaurants. I guess that meant Montgomery was a Vampire like Garrett and

Mr. Tsui.

I honestly didn't give a crap about the food. I was too hyped about the day to actually be hungry. It was a burger of some kind, and I didn't care enough to dig through to see the toppings. Mr. Tsui continued with what he was saying.

"We will give you access to the Warrens, on a supervised basis. My understanding is that you already have cell numbers for Montgomery here, and for Wren? Please call one of them if you need anything. In addition, I will get Ms. Flanagan's number for you as well."

"Yeah, okay," I said. "You mentioned money at one point, when you were tryin'a get me to cuddle up with you on your side in this fight.," A few people choked in their drinks over that. Mr. Tsui merely smiled. "You even mentioned millions."

"Yes, I did," he said cautiously. "Is that what you are wanting?"

Garrett gave me a look reminiscent of what he had shot me the day before, when he called me selfish and greedy for holding out. I did my best to ignore him.

"It sounds fancy, but really, I just want some spending money, maybe get some stuff for the house, you know? I mean, I don't have to be Richie Rich. I just don't wanna have to worry if I want to treat my friends to pizza and a movie."

"Completely understandable," he said. "I'll get an account started and get you a debit card. In the meantime, once I get a housekeeper set up for you, I can ensure you have a small amount of cash each week for, as you say, spending money. Will this satisfy you?"

"Absolutely," I replied, absentmindedly picking up a french fry and nibbling on it. "You said I won't have responsibilities or a job or anything. So how am I going to be useful to you then? Does our connection have a certain range limit or something I should be aware of?"

"If you are within Avernus, I can draw what I need, when I need it," he said. "I would ask that you make arrangements if you wanted to go off on a road trip out of town."

"Understood. One last thing, and I mean this in the nicest way possible," I stated, keeping my most serious game face on.

"Proceed."

"Nobody owns me," I said earnestly. "We are agreein' on a working situation here. This doesn't mean I'm suddenly your property, to get bossed around." Mr. Tsui was getting a bit of a smirk on his face. I had no idea how the others were reacting since I was giving the boss my full attention, trying to read his reaction. "I'll do whatever is reasonable to help, like if you need to travel and need me to go. But you also don't get to tell me who my friends are, who I date, or nothin' like that." Yeah, I knew my southern accent was coming out, but right then I didn't care.

"Mr. Docker, you have my word. I think we will both be able to bend where needed, to ensure this is a smooth relationship."

I sat back and nodded, popping another fry in my mouth. I don't know why, but I was suddenly wrong footed. It felt too easy. I felt somehow like I had just been swindled, even though I had gotten everything I had asked for. I was back to that "evil genie" feeling.

The rest of the meal felt a bit awkward, as if nobody really had anything to talk to me about with other people around, and yet they didn't want to talk about their own Vampyre stuff with me there. I wrapped it up as quickly as I could without feeling rude. It was especially weird, because the three Vampires kept staring at me, though with different looks. Garrett seemed amused at me, like I was some joke. Montgomery acted like he didn't like me, like I was trash he wanted to kick out of the room. And Mr. Tsui, no matter what Wren had said before, looked like he wanted to eat me.

CHAPTER FIFTY

ACCEPTANCE

I spent the next several days trying to spend time with Mom. Sure, I was trying to get in whatever time with her that I could. But there was still some part of me, maybe the childish part that still hoped Santa Clause was out there somewhere, that insisted if I tried hard enough, if I believed strongly enough, if I said the right words, I might break Mom free and have her back. Maybe if I held my tongue at the right angle or something.

I wasn't getting her back, at least not now. But I still did what I could to be with her. I let her ramble happily about her perceived reality. I even took note of the details she currently believed, either hoping I could eventually refute them, or at the very least, I could help my aunt and uncle navigate whatever came out of all this.

I really thought about that part as well. It wasn't like Mom wasn't in touch with reality in such a way where she couldn't deal with society as a rational human being. She could hold a job, pay bills, and make normal decisions. As far as I could tell, the only area where she was irrational was with the details around Avernus and this whole situation with Mr. Tsui. So, with that being the situation, did it make sense to send her to Alabama? Considering the questions that were going to be raised by Aunt Susan, would it make better sense to set her up on her own with an apartment and a bank account somewhere on her own?

When I brought it up with Wren he thought I had a valid point. He promised to handle all the details for me.

Finally, it was time for me to say goodbye to my mom. It was such a weird situation, because while I was going to miss her and was seconds away from crying, she acted like she would have had more emotions about driving to the grocery store. It let me know I had already lost her, which just upset me more.

My dad, I didn't give a damn about. He had always been horrible to me. I don't think I was ever a real person to him. But Mom had always tried to find ways to reach out to me behind Dad's back, even if she wouldn't stand up for me in front of him. This last month or so since he died showed that, by how much she opened up. But then the Mesmir took it all away.

And that was it. She was all packed, the car's trunk and back seat filled, and she just... drove off. She was headed off to Albany, where a new apartment waited for her, along with a new life. She would only be two hours away, but considering what she believed, she might as well have been down in Alabama after all.

But even two hours away was too much. So many times, I almost tried to stop her. But Wren, Erin, even Mr. Tsui had all told me this was best. People here in Avernus settled under the Mesmir because nothing in their lives conflicted with the story their minds had. Their limited interactions with the Vampyre were easily explained away. But Mom was living with the contradictions in her story daily. Her mind was going to bounce from one excuse to the next. From cover story to cover story. For her own sanity, I had to let her go. Never mind what it might do to my own sanity.

I was left with the full intention that I was supposed to go to school, but I couldn't. I moped around the house for hours, desperate for a good cry to let it all out, but it wouldn't come. I wasn't able to settle down to any one activity. I tried painting models for a bit, then reading. I tried napping, and for the shock of it, even tried some homework. I just couldn't get my brain off the fact that I was all alone now.

My dad was dead, and my mom was now living in a fantasy rather than helping me out.

I was pulled out of my wallowing by the unexpected ringing of the doorbell. I barely got it open when I was practically shoved aside by all five of my skater friends piling in.

"Where you been, man?" asked Taki.

"Yeah," said Wheeler. "You weren't in school today. What's up with that?"

"Why'd you ditch?" added Scott.

"You've been hiding for a week, and now you cut school? You're avoiding us or something!" Liam laughed.

Boots was the only one who remained quiet as I let everyone grab drinks and then dragged the crew downstairs. Once we were all getting settled, I explained the cover story which had been arranged.

"Sorry guys, it's been a roller coaster. My mom's got some health things to take care of, so she's going to be gone for a while."

"Is she okay?"

"She's not dying or anything, right?"

"Are you okay?"

"What's wrong with her?"

"You're not moving, are you?"

"Guys! Guys!" I stood up and held my arms out with a laugh. "I appreciate it, but it's all good." They quieted, and I sat back down. "Nobody's dying, everything's fine. She's just going to be away for a while. I'm not going anywhere though."

"Yeah, but," Scott couldn't help but jump in, "what's going to happen with your house here?"

"You guys aren't getting rid of me that easily! No, my uncle is going to be making sure the lights stay on and the refrigerator has food. He even promised to sign my permission slips."

"And your detention slips, I'll bet!" laughed Liam.

"Damn!" exclaimed Taki. "You mean you are going to get to live in this huge house all by yourself? With no parents?"

Wheeler jumped in with, "Sign me up!"

That seemed to be the sentiment of the rest of the group as well. Except for Boots, who stayed kind of quiet, and kept looking at me out of the corner of his eye. We dropped the heavy conversation and fired up a couple of video games. The TV that was supposed to have been for my bedroom had never left, so we were able to keep two systems going at once. I was trying to remember a weekend where at least most of the crew hadn't stayed over here. I guess my basement had become our clubhouse.

When I said I was going to run upstairs to grab some drinks for everyone, Boots jumped up and said he would help. I was glad, because I had decided on a few things during the day, and wanted to talk to him. It turned out he wanted to talk to me, as well. We ended up grabbing drinks and sitting at the island bar to talk for a minute.

"Dude, are you alright?" he asked.

"Yeah, I guess. Things have just been so screwed up ever since we moved here." Then I scoffed, "Not that things were exactly sunshine before."

"I get what you mean," he said quietly. "And the other guys really aren't seeing the problems with what all you got going on here."

"About that," I said. "Come upstairs with me real quick. I've got something for you."

I grabbed his hand and started running up the stairs, dragging him behind me. "You said the game I started playing with Liam looked cool, right?"

"Yeah," Boots said cautiously.

We made it to the upper living area, and I pointed over to the work desk. "Mom left all these minis. I know she already started on them, but, I mean, do you want them?"

He started shaking his head, ready to object, but I cut him off. "Please? I don't want to do this army myself. And besides, this way we can play together. Please?"

I think he knew what I was really asking, because he didn't seem surprised when I pulled out a house key. "And will you come over and keep me company every once in a while? The rest of the guys only really want to come over to hang out on the weekends. I'm hoping you'll come hang out more often."

He gave me a quick hug and slipped the key out of my hand, then grabbed my hand without saying anything more than his smile told me. I'm pretty sure he knew I was asking him so he would have a safe place to crash whenever his home was problematic and was trying to help him save face. But deep down, I really did need the company.

We grabbed drinks for everybody and went back down to the basement. Through the little windows I could see that it was overcast and snowing, so it was definitely a day for staying inside and gaming, instead of being out in the streets. We all laughed and cut up. I had a bit of a thought, and pulled up my phone, looking up some ideas. Finally, I found what I thought I wanted. I just needed to check.

"Hey Liam, what are the sizes of the tables up at LGM?" I asked.

"You mean for Hammers & Hordes?" he asked. "We play on four foot by six, but the tables are four by eight, so there's extra room on each end for books and stuff."

"That's what I thought," I said with a laugh. I showed the item I had pulled up on my phone to Boots, and when he saw what I was pointing at, he laughed.

"Yeah, right. If only," he smirked.

"Bet," I said, pointing at the empty end of the basement. He looked at me confused, then suspicious.

"How?" he asked.

By this point, Liam and Scott were looking at us curiously. Taki and Wheeler were too caught up in their fighting game to realize something was going on. I smirked at Boots, then started filling out the information to place an online order. While the others watched, curious as to what was going on, I pulled my wallet out of my back pocket. I whipped out the card Mr. Tsui had given me and entered in the payment details into the website.

"There!" I announced when I was done.

"No way," laughed Boots. "That's insane." I flipped my phone to face him, showing him the confirmation page. "How the hell?!? That's like, fifteen hundred bucks!"

“What’s fifteen hundred bucks?” asked Scott. “What are you guys doing over there?”

I flipped back to the item page and then tossed him my phone.

“Wait, what!? You bought a pool table!?”

“Better,” I said. “It has a padded topper that’s a ping pong table. It will fit right over there just fine,” I said, pointing to the middle of the basement. “And the best part is they are both regulation size, which happens to be,” and I looked right at Liam, “Four feet by eight!”

“No way!” exclaimed Liam. “You’re going to have your own Hammers table down here?”

“That depends,” I shot back with a grin. “Are you going to help me get some terrain for it?”

CHAPTER FIFTY-ONE

DARK DISCUSSIONS

Boots started telling Liam about the miniatures upstairs I had just offered him. He was so excited, and I was glad I had been able to do that for him. I remembered what it was like being priced out of hobbies my friends enjoyed. With Alen and Lisa, it had been video games. That reminded me of being able to give Boots a safe place to crash when he needed it. The thought of him staying over here more often made me think about our little basement visit, though, and I turned to look at the spot at the bottom of the stairs where the secret door was. I still needed to tape over that peephole, especially before we had another sleepover down here. I couldn't believe I had forgotten to do it already.

After another hour, Scott and Wheeler said they each needed to get home. Liam took that as his cue. Before he said his goodbyes though, he had to leave me with a parting shot.

"That's great you're bringing a new victim into the game and all, but you're not much better. When are you going to break in your own army?"

"Yeah, yeah," I replied. "I've stuck my fingers in this game about as much as I've stuck my nose in your business."

Everybody laughed, and Liam said, “Name your time and place.”

“How about Saturday? We can hang out at the store, then come back here for...” I looked at the others, “Wings? Burgers? Pizza?”

“Pizza!” everyone called out.

Liam and I bumped fists, but before he turned to leave he asked, “Why a pool table? You know they make cool tables just for games like Hammers & Hordes, right?”

“I mean, I guess? But I figured this gives even more options. Come on, we’re gonna have our own pool table down here! Besides, if I only got a Hammers table, how would I get these other bums to pry their eyes away from a TV screen?”

“Fair enough! We’ll start looking at terrain next week or something.”

With that, Liam headed up. Taki and Boots ended up staying for a while longer, and I ordered a pizza for us all to share.

After we ate, we played some more games, but Taki would look around every once in a while, almost like he was waiting for a signal for something. I thought he was waiting for Boots to say he was ready to leave, because eventually Taki started talking about needing to head home, and looked at us curiously when neither of us made moves for Boots to leave with him. Finally he gave a knowing smile and headed out, leaving Boots and I to talk a bit better. Of course, he jumped right into it.

“What’s really up with the key? I think I’m missing something,” he said, keeping his eyes straight ahead at the video game screen.

I was a little surprised. I thought it was obvious. “I’ve told you a couple of times what my thoughts were. My best friend back home, Alen, always let me stay over at his place whenever I had to get away from my asshole dad. It’s not pity. I’m just showing you I meant what I told you before. I want you to be able to get away when you need to.”

He looked at me kind of skeptically. “And you also want the company, right?”

I smiled. “Yes, I also want the company.”

“How deep are you in with the Ravens?”

I was taken completely off guard and didn’t have time to hide my nervousness. "What do you mean?" I tried to ask as cover.

"I'm hoping nobody can hear us here in your house?" he asked, looking around.

"What do you mean? Why would you ask something like that?"

"Because you're surrounded by a lot of sketchy people, and I don't trust what some of them might be up to."

I had to think about that one for a second. Maybe Boots was a bit more perceptive than I had noticed before. "Let's go upstairs," I said. "We can talk and paint."

Boots was right about the Vampyre. I didn't know how domineering and controlling they might be, but they were definitely sketchy. Even Wren, the one I was closest to, I knew wasn't telling me everything. I was starting to realize how few lifelines I really had here in Avernus.

I didn't think there were cameras or mics down here in my basement. I wanted to trust Wren, but I hadn't had a chance to check, and I didn't want to risk anything. I covered it by saying I wanted to mess around with the miniatures while we talked. I got my guys out and we both started to halfass work on them.

"Why are you asking about the Ravens?" I asked once we were both seated at the work desk.

"Oh, come on," he said in quiet frustration, not looking at me. "Your dad, now your mom? You're all alone with a house, you suddenly have money, and your 'uncle' is taking care of you? Plus, that Wren guy– He *is* a guy, right? –is always hanging around lately."

He looked over at me, obviously nervous about the topic. Boots was saying out loud what I had just been thinking. Dad was dead, Mom was off her rocker and moved off for her own safety. I was not being funded, and being kept, by "Uncle Tsui". It had to look odd. Then he floored me with his next question.

"So, how deep are you with the Vampires? I'm guessing Wren is feeding on you or something?"

"What do you mean, Vampires?" I asked, trying to keep any worry out of my voice. I wanted to play it off by laughing, but I didn't want Boots to think I was making fun of him. I was glad we had the models to work with. It kept us from having to make eye contact while we talked.

"You don't have to hide it with me. I've seen them around, and I'm not going to say anything." He was keeping his voice quiet but speaking matter-of-factly. "They like this time of year, you know, winter? The sun sets so much earlier." Looking over at me, he picked up a new paint color and said, "I guess they aren't hurting you, and they aren't turning you, since you are still going to school. But is that why your mom had to go away?"

I sat there in shock. Finally, I responded quietly, "It's a bit more complicated. Do you know how dangerous what you are talking about is?"

"Hey, I keep my head down, I don't go to the hotel, and I don't talk to the zombies about it."

"Zombies?" I asked in surprise.

"Yeah, zombies," he said. "I don't mean like 'eat your brain' kind of creatures. But they don't get to think for themselves. All the people in town are all mind controlled, so zombies. Liam was free for a while, but he kept mouthing off, and they put him back under. I never said anything to him about it, but I liked knowing someone else knew."

Ouch. That hurt, considering Liam being re-Mesmired was my fault. "So why are you talking to me about it?"

"Because you're inside," he stated. "Apparently, they don't want you as a zombie, but also not as a Vampire. I just wanted you to know you had a friend on the outside who knows what's going on, in case you need to talk about it."

"But why risk it for me, when you didn't for Liam?"

"You're nice to me, and I like you," he said. "Liam's a friend, but that's all he is. Plus like I said, you're involved with them. Liam was always on the outside, and always pissed off because of... Well, he was pissed off when he remembered, and Zombie the rest of the time."

Finally, a third party I could ask. "Do you know?" I asked. "What happened to his sister? Nobody seems to want to tell me anything."

Boots was silent for a while, but finally said, "She, um, died. Everything was covered up and everybody was made to forget, but some Vampire got ahold of her," he said quietly. "I didn't see her body, but what I heard before everybody got zombified was she had her throat ripped out and drained of blood." He looked a bit pale as he said all this, and his voice stayed at barely more than a whisper.

"Damn."

"Liam was real close with his sister. She was only a year younger than him. Everybody forgot about it within a few weeks. But then a couple of months ago, right around her birthday, Liam remembered again. He held onto that memory, until a couple of weeks ago. I don't know what happened then. I guess he mouthed off to the wrong person, and a Raven heard about it."

"Maybe," I muttered. "So, um, are you gonna be mad if I keep seeing Wren?"

"Seeing him?" smiled Boots. "That almost sounds like you two are dating."

"Kind of? But I promise, I swear, man, he's not a Vampire. He doesn't drink blood." Boots looked at me skeptically. "I promise, man. He's not."

"Uh huh," he laughed. "Whatever you say, dude. As long as I don't find myself short a few quarts, I don't care. It's your neck, not mine."

"I swear, he's not like that. You're safe."

We were both silent for a minute, then he said hesitantly, "I guess that answers the other question though."

"Oh? What question is that?"

Quietly he said, "Whether you're taken."

"We-ell..." He looked at me curiously, so I added, "He doesn't think he wants to be tied down by being exclusive."

"So he's a player," Boots smirked.

"Or maybe I am!" I laughed.

"Nope!" he laughed with me. "If you were, you would have been hittin' on me already."

"Is that your way of hitting on me, now?"

"Depends on whether you would be interested," he said. "Otherwise, it's a joke, and you're a sicko for perving on me like that!"

I laughed and socked him lightly in the arm.

"Hey, man! You're going to mess up my paint job!"

We painted in silence for another couple of minutes. Eventually I said quietly, "I do think you're cute, and who knows what might happen. But right now, you're too much like a brother."

"Aww." His hands were full with a model and paintbrush, so he leaned over and tapped his head against my shoulder. "That's probably the nicest way anyone's ever told me to eff off."

We both laughed. Then my phone chirped. I set my stuff down and pulled it out of my pocket, hoping maybe it was my mom, letting me know she was stopping for the night. Instead it was a text from Wren, asking if he could come see me.

"Are you staying here tonight?" I asked Boots.

"As much as I wish I could, I really need to check in at home. Plus it's school tomorrow and everything."

"I get it. But you know you can crash here if you need it."

Obviously trying to change the subject, he asked, "Will you be in school tomorrow?"

"Yeah," I sighed. "I should have been there today, but I just couldn't deal."

"Dude, I get it. But tomorrow's Friday. Think I can come over tomorrow with you?"

"I'm hoping you'll spend the weekend."

He smiled and let himself out. I stood at the top of the stairs, watching him leave, and heard him use his new key to lock the front door after himself.

CHAPTER FIFTY-TWO

VELOS

Wren and I wasted no time getting into bed when he showed up a bit later. I mean come on. He's hot, and I'm fifteen and horny. I wasn't exactly going to say no. Still, I knew he was feeding. So it kind of tainted the whole thing. Would we be together if he wasn't feeding? Right then I wasn't sure I cared. After all, the second my lower half got involved, all the blood flowed out of my brain.

But once we were drained, laying there in our afterglow and his skin was warm, my brain started working again. Now I had to ask my questions.

"What's the real thing with you and Mr. Tsui?" I asked. "Your sister and Garrett both talk like he's a terrible person, and you kind of badmouth him. But for someone you claim not to like, you always seem to be in each other's business."

"Hmm," he mused. "I guess it does look that way, from your perspective. Mostly it's more about doing business and favors for the council. They just happen to usually be his favors, when it comes to you."

"Then why hasn't Montgomery been doing them?" I asked. "He literally said the guy was his right hand, or whatever."

"Aww," Wren grinned. "Do you like him better than me?"

"Who, Montgomery? I barely know him. The first time, he came off as arrogant, with the 'apology committee' crap. But otherwise, I haven't been around him enough to know him."

He looked at me a bit more seriously. "What's your real question, babe?"

I sighed. "I've just tied myself completely to Mr. Tsui, and I'm surrounded by people who I don't know if I can trust."

"Harsh," he said. "And I'm one of those you don't know if you can trust?"

"I mean, I totally want to." Damn. Was I ruining things here? "I mean, we're doing stuff together. You know I really like you, and I'm practically feeding you whenever you want."

"You're getting some pretty good sex out of this yourself," countered Wren. I couldn't tell his mood, exactly, but he sounded annoyed. "But for real, do you have any idea how often a Succubus has to feed?" I shook my head. Of course, I had no clue. "It's no big deal to go five or six months between feedings."

"Oh. So why are you feeding so often with me?"

"Because it's fun, and you're cute," he said. "I'm just stepping up to stake my claim. Isn't that what you wanted?"

"You know," I said, sitting up. "That seems a bit contradictory to the whole 'don't want anything serious' claims you made. You can't blame me for questioning things here. If you want to take this stuff personally, that's on you." I was starting to get pissed. "I'm drowning in the deep end here. I'm just trying to figure out if I can trust you as much as I want to."

Wren blew out his breath, as if he was trying to also blow out his frustration. He rolled over, wrapping his arms around my bare waist. "I get it, babe. Sorry if I was being judgmental. What can I do to help assuage your concerns?"

"Assuage?" I repeated with a laugh. "Being fancy."

"Fine." He smiled. "What can I do to 'lessen' your concerns? Better?"

I leaned in and hugged him. "I wish I knew."

Wren got this look, like he'd had an idea. "Grab your coat," he said, and before I could really ask anything, he had grabbed my hand and dragged me from the house.

"I want to test something," he said as we were walking down the street. "Whether you trust my motives yet or not, for this moment, I need you to trust that I'm not going to hurt you, alright?"

I was hesitant, because if he had to start with "trust me" and "this won't hurt", I had a hard time keeping my heart out of my throat. But I nodded my head. He reached out and took my hand again. "Run with me," he said. We started running down the middle of the street, the slap-slap of our sneakers the only sounds I heard in my ears. A light snow dusted over the top of previously melted slush in all the yards, but hadn't really stuck to the pavement. For a Southern boy like me, it looked like winter wasteland, with the starlight reflecting off the snow.

"Keep hold of my hand and let me guide you," Wren said as we continued running. "I want you to close your eyes and do your best to stay with me." I started to object, but he quickly interjected. "I promise, I'll keep you from falling."

Going against every instinct I had, I closed my eyes. I concentrated on keeping my feet moving, on the sound of our feet hitting the pavement, on the feel of his hand in mine. The pull became insistent, as if he was trying to slip away from me, but I gripped him harder, picking up my pace to keep up. I was starting to lose my breath, but it eased up pretty quickly. It felt like we were slowing down.

With a voice that sounded like it was being carried away in a howling wind, I heard Wren say, "Open your eyes, Jason!"

I did, and houses were blurring by. I nearly stumbled, losing my momentum for a split second. It felt like we were barely running, but we were moving at interstate speeds, like we were driving! Street signs whipped by so fast I could barely tell there was writing on them.

Wren laughed and yelled, "Let go of my hand, and see if you can keep up!"

It took all the courage I could muster, but I did it. I let go of his hand.

For a second I thought I was going to falter, but I managed to keep going. I gave a cry of delight, somewhere between a shout and a laugh. We ran for several more minutes, ending out by the hotel, but by way of the school, which was in the opposite direction. When we finally stopped, I collapsed to the ground.

"Oh my god, that was awesome!" I shouted.

"I think it's safe to say we found out one of your powers," Wren said as he smiled down at me. "That one is called Velos, effectively superspeed. But," he looked at me curiously, watching my response. "Are you really tired? Let alone tired enough you need to lay down in the snow?"

I paused, assessing how I felt. I should be out of breath, right? I should be catching a stitch in my side, my legs feeling like jelly. I should be exhausted. I mean, how many miles did we just run? But I didn't feel any of that. I sat up, a sense of wonder flooded through me.

"Wow, I guess not," I said. "So what else you got for me?"

"Well, we know you have strength in there, Potentia, but it was uncontrolled. Unconscious. Now we will have to learn how to bring that out of you. Most of it is going to involve tricking your brain to forget what it has learned are your body's restrictions. That's why I needed you to close your eyes, until we could get you up to speed."

"But how did you know I'd be able to do that?" I asked.

"Speed is a very standard ability, as is strength," he said. "Almost all Vampyre have them, including Assecla. As you grow and practice, you will likely continue discovering new powers, as well as ways to expand the abilities you already have."

"What about the bit with brushing off Mesmir and mental stuff?"

"I'm not sure exactly. Maybe one in fifty?" Then he got a curious look. "But if you can go further than simply seeing through the Mesmir, it will be interesting to see if you have any other psychic abilities."

I popped up. "You think I might be able to read minds, like Garrett?"

"Probably not that far," Wren said, smiling slyly. "But emotions, empathy, things like that, might be possible. Actual telepathy, Cor Decere, is something restricted to Vampires and a rare few other Vampyre. It's not as common as Garrett makes it look."

Are the things like Plague one of the ones that can read minds?"

"Jiangshi?" Wren paused for a moment, looking thoughtful. "I actually don't know. And you would think that would be a useful bit of information to have."

"You think? Who would have that information."

"Dom did hang out with them for a couple of centuries, so he'd be my best bet."

I gave him a skeptical look. "Then why wouldn't he have already told us."

"I don't know. But considering Beishang de Wenyi is still close by, I wouldn't put it past Dom to be holding a lot close to his chest."

We hung out for a bit longer, going for a run a few more times, until I felt more comfortable starting and stopping on my own. He also had me do some regular running as well, so my body could tell the difference.

"You are going to want to practice this occasionally. You don't want to be accidentally breaking the sound barrier in PE."

"Wait, I can do that?" I exclaimed with a laugh.

"You mean like this?" There it was again, that sound like a training clicker. Wren blinked out of existence for a split second before reappearing.

"What the hell was that?" I asked.

"You might have heard it, or felt something," he said with a grin. "Here, take out your wallet. Hold it in your hand."

I took it out of my pocket, holding it clenched in my hand.

"No, hold it flat on your open palm. I'd rather not accidentally tear off your thumb or something."

I did as he asked, while he walked twenty or so feet away. "You ready? Are you watching your wallet?"

Taking my eyes off Wren, I looked down at the wallet. There was another 'click' and I felt the tiniest pressure pushing down on my palm, as suddenly the wallet disappeared.

Looking up, Wren was standing right where he had been, but now he was holding up my wallet in his hand. We walked forward to meet in the middle, and he handed it back to me.

"That is awesome," I exclaimed. "Is that what we've been doing tonight?"

"No, sadly. We've been moving pretty fast, but not quite that fast. Moving like that is only really good for short bursts. Try doing a marathon at that speed, you'll pull your body apart. Even for short distances, it takes a lot of practice to not touch someone so hard you move into their space." He chuckled. "Trust me, that sucks."

"I'll take your word for it." Then something occurred to me, a sensory memory. "Wait! You did that at the store, the day we first met!"

"So, I did. Good catch."

CHAPTER FIFTY-THREE

A QUIET DAY OF FIRSTS

The weekend was quiet, or at least, as quiet as it can be with a houseful of friends over. Friday, when Boots was over, us hanging out in the basement reminded me I still needed to do something about that damned peephole and secret door. Unfortunately, I didn't have a chance before the rest of the guys came over. A half dozen times I caught myself looking over at the wall at the bottom of the stairs, working out the best way to cover it all over.

When I was in school Friday, someone had been in the house. The refrigerator was newly stocked with lots of snacks and simple-to-make food stuffs, and all the beds had been stripped, the sheets washed, and everything remade. There was also a note that they would contact me after the weekend for us to speak, so they could get a better feel for what groceries I wanted stocked. I had been doing my own laundry for years, so I was able to avoid having a complete stranger handle my underwear.

Sunday, Boots and I got to hang out at the store for a quiet evening. Boots was learning the basics of the game from a guy I had seen playing up there but hadn't actually talked to. I offered to get Erin to teach him, explaining how patient and nice she was, but he said he would "rather learn from someone who wasn't going to be tempted to tear his throat out if they lost". I'm mostly sure he was joking?

I hung around while the guy went over the basics of the rules with him. This also served as a refresher for me and a confidence boost, since for the first time I felt like I was "in the know". Boots seemed at first to be a bit hesitant, but I could tell he was quickly gaining confidence and asking good questions.

After a bit Erin came into the store. I stepped away to chat with her for a bit, and instead she pulled me over to the closest gaming table to give me my first ever game of Hammers & Hordes with my very own miniatures. It was a really small game, and we barely kept score since Erin was spending more opportunities showing me more of what could be done, rather than making strategic decisions.

My only "real" game to date had been when I took over her game on the night of the attack on Mr. Tsui and Wren. At that point I had been completely in over my head. This time I was playing using my miniatures and the army rules I had actually read. I was more confident, instead of feeling like I was out of my depth.

Near the end of our game, I checked to make sure nobody was close enough to eavesdrop, and said to Erin, "Can I ask you about something that's been on my mind for a while? Like, 'hotel stuff'?"

"Of course you can ask anything, and I will try to answer," she looked at me quizzically. "What do you mean by 'hotel stuff'?"

"Back when we first got here, we stayed at the Avernus Inn for a week. The whole time I was there, I kept seeing things, like spooky stuff. Menus that bled, time skipping around, feeling like someone was in my room with me, stuff like that. It was pretty freaky. And whenever I was out back of the place, I was always getting this weird feeling like someone was out in the field by the road.

"I'm asking because while I've gotten answers on most of the weird sh– stuff... that's been going on, this is one thing I haven't been able to figure out. So I just wanted to ask, do you know what was going on?"

"I can guess," Erin said, "but it would only be a theory. Your situation when you arrived was pretty rare. You were Human and therefore susceptible to the

Mesmir, yet you also had some capabilities from having the blood of an Assecla. I think Wren has explained something about your abilities in breaking through the hold of the Mesmir, yes?" I nodded. "Most likely, that ability was allowing your mind to feel the ominous presence, the danger, of the environment you were thrown into. While you were unable to fully break the Mesmir, your mind was still trying to give you something tangible to explain your fears to you. I have a feeling the visions you saw were your mind attempting to warn itself about the new locale. Have you experienced anything like that since you completed the process of becoming Dom's Assecla?"

I actually had to stop and think about that one. "Now that you mention it, I haven't, except when Plague has been screwing with me."

She put a finger to her chin, clearly something occurring to her.

"On that note, has anyone told you about Beishang de Wenyi and the hotel yet?"

I moaned at the memory of that conversation. "Yeah, that my parents' sanity was sacrificed to that bastard as a compromise for me coming to town?"

"Well, that, yes." She had the grace to look embarrassed. "But the Jiangshi regularly feed at the hotel. That is why guests are never put on the ground floor. Several of the Jiangshi will visit the hotel to feed, especially that particular.... Well anyway, it is also likely you were reacting to his presence as well. He was singularly focused on you, particularly since he was strongly opposed to you coming to Avernus. He really doesn't like you and what you represent."

"You think? I mean, considering he's threatened me to my face."

CHAPTER FIFTY-FOUR

DINING WITH THE DEVIL

MOnday, I got hit with a double whammy when I got out of school. I received another email telling me I was invited to dinner at the hotel at seven. Then I got home, with Boots in tow, to find the new housekeeper sitting in the kitchen. We introduced ourselves and she stayed long enough to hammer out details with me. She seemed nice enough but was either quite scatterbrained or under some pretty strong Mesmir. Guess where my opinion was?

"Hot damn!" exclaimed Boots the moment she was gone. "How lucky is your ass? Someone coming around and doing all your chores for you? Whatever food you want, whenever you want? And she'll come cook it if you want?"

"Only at the cost of both my parents," I muttered.

"Oh yeah. I guess there is that. But quit bragging, unless you want to trade with me."

I did a double take before realizing he was smothering a grin. "Keep it up and I'll make you move in permanently." I pulled him into a buddy side-hug. "So what are we up to today?"

We hung out, just the two of us, for a few hours. We ended up going upstairs and pulling out our miniatures to work on. I even pulled out my laptop and put on a movie for us to ignore. Eventually I told him I had to meet my uncle for dinner. He balked at that but didn't say anything about it. But I made sure he knew he could stay or go, as he wanted, and I would be back in a few hours.

When it was close to time, I made the walk over to the hotel. I decided I wanted to try to make a bit of a better impression, so I dressed up a little bit. I don't know, maybe it was something of a peace offering. I wasn't quite sure what was the best way to do this without raising a stink, so once I got there, I texted the number I had been given, saying I was downstairs in the lobby. Stepping inside, I saw that the tall, creepy guy was at the desk, August. I was glad I texted. I didn't want to talk to him if I didn't have to.

Within minutes the two goons came around the corner. Once we stepped into the elevator and one of them gave the password, I turned to the one I always seemed to get stuck with, the same one who had frisked me.

"Hey dude," I grinned, turning and sticking my ass out a bit. "My ass is right here, if you need to cop another feel."

He shook his head and smirked, trying to hide his embarrassment. His buddy grinned but didn't say anything. When the doors opened, I saw the same secretary sitting at the desk, the same sourpuss look on her face.

"Mr. Tsui is expecting you," she said, pointing to the hallway.

I entered the room hesitantly. Something felt odd. I had a completely different outlook going in to see him this time than my attempts before. Looking over it all, I tried to put my finger on what it was. It wasn't the meal. Everything was just as lavish as the other two dinners, the food brought in for me just as excellent. But it wasn't grabbing my attention.

Mr. Tsui sat smiling, watching me eat. His suit nearly glowed. It was somehow extra shiny. I felt a compulsion to compliment him. To tell him how good it looked. I wanted to tell him I was excited to be here. I wanted to boast about the gifts I had gotten. I shook my head. Something wasn't right. Normally this would not be my thing, but for some reason, this time it sounded like a great idea. This time I *had* to say something.

We discussed the powers I had already begun displaying, interspersed among other minor topics. I wanted to ask about more details on all these abilities, but he put off any talk about details. So instead, I took the opportunity to clear up the question I had asked Wren, this time from Mr. Tsui's side.

"Last time we met, you said Montgomery was your 'right hand man', I think is how you put it."

"Yes," he nodded.

"So, if that's true, why is it Wren has been doing all the talking to me, instead of him?"

"Hmm," he pondered for a minute. "The Stormbreak twins implied that you seemed, let's say, incompatible, with him. But even more, Montgomery is not what you would call a 'people person'."

"Then why let him be your assistant?" I asked.

"He's fine with other Vampyre. Just not with mortals."

"Oh," I muttered. "He came off to me like I was beneath him. And aren't I supposed to be Vampyre now?"

"You certainly are, and to be sure, he knows better, now," said Dom, suddenly stern. "He will not give you any problems going forward." He took a drink from his cup. "So, your house. Are things satisfactory?"

"Oh, yeah, thanks. I met Mrs. Sinclair today. She seems nice. Thanks for that."

"You are most welcome. Is there anything else I can do to help you settle in with the new dynamic?"

"I mean," I hesitated, afraid to say what I really wanted to ask. I definitely had a question that needed to be handled, but I also didn't want to piss him off.

"You guys forgot to tell me about a small, tiny, insignificant detail about being an Assecla," I said. "I mean, it's nothing really, so I can see how it got overlooked. I already talked to Wren about it, and he lost a few pounds of ass when I got finished chewing him out."

Dom grinned, his eyes widening in amusement. "Oh, this sounds rather more than insignificant."

"Nobody wanted to tell me that if you die, I die? Just slipped your mind, I guess?"

Dom smiled, damn near close to a laugh. “My boy, I told you how durable you would become once you became my Assecla in truth. That only compounds with age. At this point I am old enough I could likely survive sunlight for a time. So no, my dear Assecla, that is not something you should concern yourself with. It is a scenario I genuinely do not fear, and you were already so difficult to sway that I saw no need to fill your head with unfounded fears.”

“Yeah, right. ‘Hard to kill’ is not invulnerable, and ‘long lived’ is not immortal. Four hundred years isn’t so long, in the history of everything, you know.”

This time he did laugh. “My dear Assecla, it has merely been four hundred years since I lost my old Assecla and was made to leave Colonial America. I was born far earlier than that.” He chuckled. “But that is a conversation for another time.”

“What are your plans for dealing with this shared enemy you sicced on me? Plague of Sorrows?”

His face showed the tiniest look of surprise before going supernaturally blank. I forced my thoughts through his Mesmir, but his real face was as pleasantly blank as his mask.

“I will be dealing with Beishang de Wenyi soon enough. He is my problem, not yours.”

“So, no more threats?”

“Your dreams are perfectly safe, my Assecla.”

I pouted but let it go. Eventually, I needed to find out more about who Mr. Dominic Tsui really was.

CHAPTER FIFTY-FIVE

TERROR LEVEL TWO

I was still a bit grumpy when I got home. But finding Boots still there picked me up a good bit. I felt like we weren't necessarily a couple or anything, but the way I was feeling I definitely needed company. I let him know I was appreciative of his presence, even if I was reluctant to tell him why.

"Jason, the whole benefit of having me here is that I know about the spooky underbelly of this town, remember?"

"I try not to remember you know all that."

Boots looked surprised. "Why would you do that? I can help! Talk to me about what's going on. What happened at dinner with 'definitely not your uncle'?"

"Ugh. It's just a bunch of complications, is all."

"*Li-ike* what kind of complications?" Boots prompted.

"Like the complicated kind," I said. "I really like you. But there's levels of trouble here." Wow, I was sounding exactly like Wren when he dodged my questions at the beginning. It seemed like now I was the dodgeball ninja. "They see all the mind control as safety for them. It's not for keeping everyone as some kind of food supply. They're not all a bunch of Vampires, I promise. If they see you are not under, like Liam, they will just re-Mesmir you. But if they find out you actually know details about who and what they are? I don't know what the response would be. And I like you too much to want to risk finding out."

Boots grinned. "Re-Mesmir, huh?"

"Why you gotta be like that?" I grinned, even though inside I knew I had opened the floodgates.

I dodged answering questions, and while at first Boots was earnest in trying to get answers to his questions, it quickly became teasing, with him asking things like whether the moon landing had been faked by Bigfoot, and if Elvis was actually an ancient Eldritch monstrosity that just went back into hiding.

I think he could tell I was still stressing about things, because he spent the night sleeping up with me, instead of downstairs in the basement. As we were laying there, trying to let sleep take its hold, I looked at Boots' face, just barely illuminated by the window's light. He was so innocent laying there. So pure. In that moment, I really wished I could kiss him. But I didn't.

We headed to school together the next morning. I didn't ask if we needed to swing by his house. He was already starting to leave spare clothes over at my place. I liked that, because it meant he trusted my place to be a safe backup. Just thinking about what my situation had been back in Alabama with Alen and now seeing Boots with the same problem really pissed me off. It made me so glad I was able to help him out, but it also made me wish I could just fix everything. You know, kick his parents down a well and just adopt him or something.

Thursday the new pool table was delivered, and I invited Liam over to help me break it in. We threw a bed sheet over the table, and trash talked about all the cool terrain we could get for it, like hills, buildings, and all of that. Friday, Boots and I broke in the table with some pool. Both of us were crap at it, but we had fun trying to figure it out. Soon enough Wheeler and Taki took over the table, both of them showing off an insane number of trick shots. I made a note never to play either of them one on one.

We spent a few hours rotating between video games and pool. Liam spent a good bit of time having me pull up websites on my phone that sold gaming terrain for Hammers & Hordes. Meanwhile, while by no means being blatant, it seemed every time activities swapped around, Boots invariably ended up near me. I have no idea if anyone else noticed, but I noticed and appreciated the closeness and attention.

After dinner Saturday, most of the guys went home. Boots and Taki planned on staying over one more night. Taki even offered to try to show us how to play better at pool. I was playing around on my phone, looking at some websites Liam had mentioned for some cool looking terrain, half watching the other two go head-to-head at a shooter game. I became confused when the sounds changed in the room. The trash talk, the clack of the controllers, even the video game sound effects, all stopped. I looked up and saw Boots had slumped over where he was sitting on the floor with his back to the couch. Taki had been sitting on the futon across from us, but he was slumped over as well, the controller fallen from his hand.

I started freaking out, whipping around to look behind me. Sure enough, there at the foot of the stairs was a wave of fear and oppression, spreading in a cloud of pinkish red mist. It filled the space as if threatening to displace the oxygen of the room. And floating in the cloud was what I now knew to be a Jiangshi. I would put all the money I had to my name that it was the same bastard coming back for round two.

The bloody mist parted to reveal the floating head of the old man, revealed as if floating to the surface of some murky pond. Draping from the bottom of the skull was that gross spinal cord hanging down like a sick parody of a tail. In fact, it actually undulated back and forth, like a cat lazily swinging its tail in a hypnotic rhythm.

I didn't want to show him I was scared this time, so I went with pissed. Of course it was only an assumption this was the same... thing, so I wanted to be sure before I completely went off on him.

"The hell do you want this time?" I yelled at him. "What was that BS name you called yourself before?"

There was a whisper of sound, like the wind flowing through the tree branches in a forest. Not the peaceful summer afternoon forest though. No, this was the fall forest at twilight, when the setting sun was already being blocked by the leaves and branches. Then the sound became that of escaping steam, and it began to speak.

"Last time I... gave a name... but this time... I give a warning."

"Last time you gave a name. Plague, or some crap like that."

It hadn't hurt me before, and I was probably getting a bit too cocky. Still, it was that or show fear. And considering this thing was the entire reason I was in this mess, I'd be damned if I gave him the pleasure of seeing me scared.

"Heed... what I say... Jaaa-ssss-on... Tell your master... I will have... what was promised..."

"Heed this," I said, flipping it off. "Get the hell out of my house." God damn, why had I never blocked up that door?

"I see... you need... persuasion..."

The floating head drifted forward. I scrambled back, then hopped over the arm of the couch, almost kicking Boots in the head by accident. Seeing Boots there at my feet though steeled my nerves, giving me a renewed desire to fight. I rolled around, nearly losing my footing, and grabbed up one of the pool sticks. I cocked it back like a baseball bat, but it had stopped moving toward me.

The subtle but shrill sound of escaping steam reverberated around the basement as the sheer volume of red steam from Plague doubled, giving the impression of a super-weapon building up to launch. I suddenly had the weirdest thought flitting through my mind. What was his name? I remembered several people telling me his Chinese name, but all I could remember was Plague of Sorrows, the English translation. What a stupid time to think of such a stupid thing.

As it floated there, hundreds of little flickers of pink lightning flashed through the red mist surrounding Plague, for all the world like a daemonic storm front. The half-rotted head turned toward the futon and the whistling steam morphed into what was clearly a hollow, moaning scream. Taki started twitching, throwing his head side to side, and moaning, "No, no!" He started convulsing, his whole body twitching violently, then began to scream.

"I will have... my promise from... your master..." moaned Plague, "or I will feast... on your friends... until he submits..."

I have no idea how a skull can have an expression, but I felt every indication that Plague was focused on Taki. Its spinal tail was flailing around, and the amount of mist jetting out of the bottom of the head had expanded, forcibly ejected downward like a steam engine.

I felt frozen for a moment, in sheer confusion and panic as I noticed that sick flowers smell again. Then Taki's obvious cries of terror brought me to my senses and I leapt forward, whacking the head upside the, well, head, with the pool stick. I heard a muffled "crack" over the screams, and Plague was shoved a foot to the side. It stopped screaming, instead turning into a whistling sound. Taki stopped screaming as well, instead crying and whimpering. Deep, chest-wracking, sobbing-style crying.

The head floated back, away from us. I whipped the stick back again, reading to swing, as once more it spoke.

"You have had... my warning, Ja-ssss-son... I will have... what was promised... by Tsui..."

The massive volumes of mist, which had primarily stayed collected around Plague's skull, flowed out into the room and the thing faded back into the cloud. I knew it had just gone back through the door. That thing was getting fixed, asap. I tossed the cracked pool stick to the ground, kneeling down to check on Taki. He had quieted, but was still rocking in his sleep, whimpering and moaning.

"What the absolute hell happened?" I jerked up to see Boots sitting back up, rubbing his eyes and staring at Taki. "What's wrong with him?"

"Vamp garbage," I muttered, sitting down and wrapping Taki in my arms, trying to comfort his shaking. Boots came over and slid down on his other side. Together we held our friend for another fifteen minutes until whatever nightmare rushing through his head finally ran its course and his body calmed down.

Boots looked up at me after a few minutes and asked quietly, almost in a whisper, "Are we safe here?"

All I could do was shrug my shoulders and shake my head. "Are any of us really safe in Avernus?"

Chapter
FIFTY-SIX
ARGUMENTS AND GO BETWEENS

If I had been willing to storm the gates of Hell to get answers about my dad, that I hated, then, I'd be damned if I wasn't willing to do the same for my friends. So off I went to the good ol' Avernus Inn and Suites. I was a bit more cautious about how to handle things this time. Less storming and more knocking. But still, really loud knocking.

"August, yeah?" It was the creepy older guy at the desk this time. He nodded and looked at me expectantly. "Hey, man, I need to see someone upstairs." He stared at me blankly, so I added, "You know, the boss? The third floor?"

He looked at me like I was a dead fish hanging on a wall of drying paint. Then almost creepily slow, he stepped to the side and picked up the phone. After a second, he muttered something that was either not English or was him having a verbal seizure. He put the phone down, never changing his facial expression.

"So... Is someone coming down?"

"Yes, Mr. Docker." It was as if a switch had been flipped. He went from slow and bored, to the shiniest customer service person ever. "As you requested, a representative is coming to escort you upstairs. Please take advantage of our complimentary seating, should you wish to be comfortable while you wait."

I was put off a bit, but I could tell when I was being dismissed, so I went over and sat down. A few minutes later I groaned as I saw Montgomery strutting across the lobby. I stood up, and he actually stopped, beckoning me to come over to him. I just kind of internally sighed, muttered, "whatever", and walked over to him. The smile on his face was waxy, fake, and condescending. I concentrated, only to find there was no Mesmir to break through. He really was wearing this smarmy, saccharine grin.

"Good evening, Jason. It's good to see you again."

"Yeah. Same, I guess."

I was really in no mood to deal with this clown. Fortunately, I could ditch him once he got me upstairs. There was a tiny change on the security measures in the elevator, in that it was a deep male voice doing the password challenge this time. We got to the top and found a young Asian man sitting at the receptionist desk. He nodded at us and as we walked over to the side, Montgomery led me over into the glass walled conference room, instead of the door to the hallway.

"This is new," I said. "Why are we in here? Where's Mr. Tsui?"

"We are..." he paused, his look letting me know he was deciding what words to tease me with. "...where we are both allowed to be."

The implication in his words were definitely that I was the holdup. He gestured for me to a chair and we both sat down. I definitely didn't need his attitude, but results were more important at the moment. And since honey was better than vinegar, or whatever, I tried to stay levelheaded.

"Well, I need to talk to Mr. Tsui. It's pretty important."

"I am his right hand. You can tell me anything important, and I'll make sure it gets handled appropriately."

"No offense, but I tried to tell him about this before. Wren was going to fill him in so something could be done. I never heard back."

"Don't be a child. Tell me what's going on, and I can let you know what needs to be done."

"Ugh, fine. Plague of Sorrows keeps coming into my house and threatening me and my friends. He keeps saying he's going to keep doing it until he gets whatever he was promised by Mr. Tsui. I was warned I would be adopting his enemies, but I wasn't expecting to be fighting them alone. What's Mr. Tsui doing about this?"

"Dominic, Mr. Tsui that is, is doing what he is able with Beishang de Wenyi. Have faith in your master."

"My master? Is that how he refers to himself about me? Or is that what you call him? 'Cause he's not my master, or anything like that. I don't care if he's got more power than me, we're partners with a business arrangement."

Montgomery laughed. A mirthful belly laugh. And very condescending, at that.

"Please tell him that. Please? I want to see his reaction to that so bad!" He recovered from the laughter but kept the mirth. "Dominic is quite aware of what is going on with Beishang de Wenyi. I gave him Wren's message word for word. If you have a message for him now, another warning from Plague, I will pass it on as well. He'll get back with you when he is ready to do something. Until then, go back and play with your friends."

I balled up both fists. I wanted to knock him straight through the glass wall. "Play with my friends? What? Do you think this is a game?"

"Oh no, Jason." Montgomery stood up, looming over me in his best, and unfortunately successful, attempt to loom over me. "I am very aware this is not a game." He leaned forward into my face. "Are you?"

CHAPTER FIFTY-SEVEN

THE TERROR OF FORGETFULNESS

Fortunately, Boots was keeping me company when he could. He had to go make appearances at his own house occasionally, but more than half the nights in a week he was staying over with me. After what had happened with Plague's last "warning", Boots had taken to crashing in my bed with me for quite a few nights. I couldn't tell if he was afraid to sleep in the basement now, or if he was worried I needed the company. Either way, I hated to admit it did help me sleep better.

He and I hadn't actually done any fooling around yet, not that it hadn't come close a time or two. I couldn't even say why we hadn't. Hell, it might have been easier if we had. Now there was this tension between us, a barrier that made us careful. We held each other in bed but were careful we didn't do any "naughty" touches. We had not seen each other in less than our underwear. Hell, I think I'd only seen Boots without a shirt like, two or three times. Sucks for him, since I refuse to sleep with a shirt, no matter where I am. He was starting to turn into some kind of "forbidden fruit" or something.

I couldn't help wondering about things with Wren. What was going on with us? Was he part of why I hadn't made a move on Boots? I really liked Boots. But I also really liked Wren. Of course, there were completely different reasons why I liked each of them, but which one did I want? I didn't think I was selfish enough to try for both.

Even though we hadn't fooled around, that didn't mean there wasn't something growing there. We were becoming more comfortable with each other. We relaxed. I thought less about how Boots might react to something I'd say, because I was already learning his likes and his triggers. He seemed to smile more, and I think I was, as well.

I had occasional nightmares. Who doesn't? But I didn't think I was having more than a normal amount. Still, it made having company at night all the more comforting. Then one night my whole perspective changed.

I usually don't remember many details from my nightmares, more just the impressions they leave. However, since moving to Avernus they have often become more vivid. This particular time I found myself running through the house. I knew Boots was somewhere in the house with me. I knew, I *knew* he was being chased. Hunted. Every time I tried to enter a room, it would be blocked by a wall of pinkish-red smoke, and I would have to push through it. Each time it would give way, but it always had more substance than mere smoke. More like water.

I could hear Boots calling out to me in panic, and each time I heard his voice, the closest red cloud would spark with pink lightning. I began running from room to room, always getting closer to his voice, yet he remained forever out of sight. I pushed my way into one last room and ran face to face with Wren. The shock of suddenly seeing him there in my dream forced me awake.

I bolted upright, my hand feeling Boots laying there beside me, safely asleep. I sighed in relief, my heart coming down from its pounding staccato beat in my chest. That's when I caught a flicker of twinkling light in the corner of my eye. I looked to the foot of my bed and saw the last sparks of a retreating storm fading away in the red halo around the head and trailing spine floating in the air.

"We can... continue this..." it said in that hissing, airy way it had of speaking, "for as many nights... as you wish... Jasss... oon..."

"What in the hell are you doing here?"

It came out as a wheeze, as if I couldn't get any breath behind my words. I think I was even more scared than his visits in the basement. Somehow it felt worse with him invading my bedroom. Maybe it was the old childish understanding that the monsters can't touch you through the blankets, but the bedroom was supposed to feel like a safe space. Especially in your own actual bed!

"I am here... for Tsui to fulfill... his promise to us..."

I caught the change, and it made me both curious and nervous. "What do you mean us? And what are you doing in my room?" I had a stronger voice now, but I still tried to keep my volume down for Boots' sake.

"This can stop... as soon as Tsui... releases me.... Until then... I will plague... your nights.... And you cannot... stop my visits... when you cannot remember... to block the door... And I can ensure... you never remember..."

I tried formulating a way to deal with this bastard, or even another question, when I was hit with an impenetrable wave of fear. Fear that made me want to be anywhere but here. Fear that paralyzed me where I sat. And fear that blinded me to the point I could no longer see Plague.

Then just as I began feeling my mind crack, I found my anger. It allowed me to regain enough control to fight. I pushed back, and the fear didn't recede, it snapped. It was sudden, the same way I was able to break Wren's hiding of his face.

I looked up at the red cloud, when the spine began thrashing and massive amounts of new mist billowed out. Plague, it was obviously Plague, began backing into the mist, which followed him out of the bedroom. I got one last confirmation of his physicality as my door snapped shut, providing a barrier as strong as the bed sheets.

I slumped down into myself, staring at my lap, left blind after Plague's red light went with him. While I wracked my brain to think about whether he had been in any of my other dreams. I did remember one, the crazy maze in the ceiling, with his red mist flowing down the various paths.

Then I remembered the second part, where I had been in that half stage between waking and sleeping. Had that been real? Had Plague been in my room then? He hadn't introduced himself by then, but according to both Wren and Mr. Tsui, he had known who I was even before I came to Avernus. Hell, he'd fed on Mom and Dad's dreams our entire first week here. I was also now wondering about that creepy feeling at the hotel, when it felt like someone was in the room with me, watching me. And I was starting to suspect this was not the first time he had been in my bedroom here either.

In fact, I just realized the smell.

While he had left, the one thing that remained was a faint whiff of vanilla, flowers, and puke. I had been smelling that crap way too often in the last few weeks, and every time was right after either meeting Plague, or waking up from nightmares about him. Odds were, he had been physically there every time.

Odds were, I was pretty screwed.

The next day was spent quietly with Boots. He could tell something was bothering me, but he was great about blending in with me and just kind of meshing with my mood. I thought about telling him about the haunting visit, but I didn't see where it would do any good, and I could think of all manner of ways it could mess with our good vibe.

A bit after we had eaten dinner, I got a text from Wren. I was not looking forward to this. The moment I saw his message I realized it had been several days since we had really talked, not to mention actually seen each other. I didn't think I was avoiding him. I guess I had just had a lot on my plate, and two visits back to back from Plague. You'd think I would have run right to him for answers, but I had done that the first time and seen nothing for it. I got a few answers, but nothing to stop him from giving a few return visits.

Note to self. Block off the damned basement. Why haven't I done that yet? Oh yeah. Because Plague apparently won't stay out of my head. I looked up from my phone to talk to Boots about the change in plans. I expected him to get annoyed at the interruption of Wren coming over.

"I'm sorry man," I said to him. "This is something that has to be handled."

"Is it Wren?" he asked. "Or is it worse?"

"I mean, it's Wren, but I also need to talk to him about the visit that happened the other day. The one in the basement."

"How come you haven't already talked to him about that? Don't get me wrong, I've kind of liked that we've been able to hang out all quiet, but I get that you have this whole other, I don't know, existence."

"I guess," I said. "But I've been enjoying hanging out in the quiet for a bit. There's just been too much going on."

"I get it. Can I ask--- No, nevermind."

"Come on," I prompted. "You said it yourself. You're an outside observer, yet you're in the know. What is it you're thinking of?"

Boots sighed, and finally said, "Every time we're downstairs in the basement, you always glance over at the stairs. Like, obsessively. It's almost as if you are afraid to be down there. What's up with that?"

I tried to think of what he meant. Then I wanted to slap myself upside the head. It wasn't sixty seconds ago I was thinking I needed to deal with that peep-hole, and now here I was, forgetting it was a thing.

"Damn it," I muttered. "I think you're right, man." When Boots looked at me with confusion, I reluctantly explained, "It's not the stairs. It's the wall at the bottom of the stairs."

His face scrunched up in confusion, which slowly morphed into fear and concern as I went on. "There's a hidden door there that leads to their area. I always mean to block it off, but I only seem to think about it when either I'm not home, or the guys are over and I can't do anything about it."

"And now you're thinking that if we went down there right now, you would, what, forget about it?"

"Or I'd think about it, but decide it wasn't a good time to do anything about it."

Boots hopped up off his counter stool. "So let's do it now." He grabbed my hand and pulled me downstairs.

"Come on, man," I said. "Wren will be here soon. Are you really going to stick around for him to be here?"

"I thought you told him an hour?"

"Yeah, so he could be here any time. We'll need to deal with this later."

"Dude, it's been ten minutes, if that," he said with a laugh. "Man, they've got you good."

We headed down to the basement and we started looking and feeling along the wall. I took a few minutes to explain what it looked like from the other side, about having the cover that blocked it from the other side, hoping that might help find the peephole.

"I'm totally sure about blocking the peephole. I hate the idea of being spied on," I said. "But should we maybe leave access to the door, you know, for some kind of emergency thing?"

He looked over at me, in confusion. "Can you open the door from this side?"

Now it was my turn to be confused. "No? At least I don't think so. The only time I've used it, we left it ajar so we could go back down."

"Then why would it help you from this side?"

"Damn it!" I hung my head in frustration and embarrassment. "Man, they have me all twisted up."

"Do you have any ideas on who it is?"

"Yeah," I sighed. "I only know one, well, person, who has used the door without me knowing, and they hinted they were going to keep me from blocking it off."

"Wren?" Boots said with a scowl.

"No, that monstrosity, Plague. The one who keeps coming and giving nightmares."

"Is something being done about this bastard? Don't you know someone, Wren or somebody, that can help with this?"

"That's what I'm about to ask. Man, I wish I could keep you with me, and help me stay on point."

"Why can't I?" he offered.

"Because then they would know you aren't under their control."

"Oh yeah," Boots said sadly. I knew he was thinking about how dangerous we both had it here. Then he added, "But you like Wren, right? Maybe he's really on your side, and he won't give you a bunch of runaround?"

"Maybe," I said. "But I'll see what I can find out. Because you're right. Something has to be done."

I begged Boots not to leave, but instead to stay down in the basement while Wren was here. I felt like just knowing he was around might help me stay centered. He agreed, saying he could keep looking for this hidden door. When I realized I had already forgotten about our search for the door, I admitted just how screwed I really was.

CHAPTER FIFTY-EIGHT

BECAUSE OF REASONS

"Babe, I'm here," Wren called softly as he closed the front door behind himself. "Where are you?"

"Up in the loft," I called out. I had only been up here maybe fifteen minutes waiting for him. I was caught between a rock and a hard place, wanting to put as much space as possible between Wren and Boots, yet not wanting him to pull me off track with his usual ways.

I double checked, and my bedroom door was definitely, purposefully closed. I had no intention of letting him distract me with his stupid, aggravating, sexy, desirable Succubus powers. Oh god, the closer he got up the stairs, the more excited my body was getting, and the less I was thinking about things with my brain. I stared at my modeling supplies, to try not to stare at him when he got up here.

"Babe, are you okay?" Wren asked as soon as he joined me in the loft.

"Why?" I asked, trying to play it cool. "What's wrong?"

He laughed a little. "You seemed to have mangled your Phase Beetle."

"I, what?" I looked down at the model tank I was assembling. I say tank, but it was supposed to look more like a long bug soldiers could ride on, and now I saw I had glued the last few pieces completely out of position, leaving the entire tank lopsided. I muttered an expletive, setting the whole mess down.

"Here, babe," said Wren.

He sat down in the other chair, carefully setting Boots' Cosmos Emptor models back out of the way. He moved them delicately, as if trying to touch them as little as possible. The look of distaste on his face told me clearly that he knew they were Boots' models, and he didn't like that they were there. Taking my model from me and setting it in front of himself, he picked up a hobby knife and a few other tools and started performing surgery on the giant bug.

Tonight's outfit was straight out of an Anime, with thicker, tight leggings that went all the way up until they were lost under a miniskirt. Skimpy shoes fit with the tights, and a shaggy sweater gave a sexy, top-heavy feel to the whole outfit. The black outfit made his pale hands and face stand out even more. I was a bit distracted when Wren spoke.

"Now, what's going on?" He asked, concentrating on the model and not looking at me. "What has you so on edge? And why have you been avoiding me for the last few days?"

I sat in silence for a minute, watching him work at salvaging my model. I had to admit that him not looking at me seemed to take some of the pressure off. Still, I wasn't sure how to answer him. I really didn't know how much I wanted to say about the deeper stuff, so I stuck to the big elephant in the room.

"I've had another visit from Plague. Two actually, back to back."

Wren looked surprised. "And this is why you've been silent?"

"Would you believe me if I said I wasn't entirely sure?"

"Sure," he replied with a grin, still focusing on the model. "But you still might want to elaborate. Something made you decide the best course of action was to dodge me, even if you weren't sure why."

"You won't like it."

"Oh, I'm sure," Wren laughed, leaning over to bump shoulders. "If it ran you off, of course I'm not going to like it. But I still need to hear it."

The move was familiar, intimate. But bumping shoulders with me wasn't Wren's move. It was something Boots would do. It didn't make me feel comforted, instead it felt like my personal space was being intruded on.

"It's a couple of little things that all add up to one big thing," I said tentatively. When he nodded but didn't interrupt, I elaborated. "First there's the fact that when I asked you and Mr. Tsui a few questions, I got a lot of the same answers, some of them almost word for word."

"Okay," he said hesitantly. "Do you remember which questions?"

"Yeah, one was about your supposed rivalry, and yet still working together."

"I told you–"

"I know what you told me, and his answer was almost word for word the same. It was creepy. I also asked him why you were working with me, supposedly at the request of the 'Kung Fu' council, when he has his own assistant who could have been doing it for him."

"Well, I don't know what the situation is with–"

"Let me finish, please," I interrupted again, "unless you don't want to hear the rest."

Wherever that came from, I was obviously more pissed about this than I realized. This was becoming a recurring theme with me lately, and wasn't like me. And it was always with the Vampyre, particularly with Wren. I liked him, I really did. But I was living with this gut feeling that he was teasing out information. And not just information, but feelings. And just then it occurred to me. I couldn't tell what he really felt for me. All of his little sub-definitions for love were maybe a way to keep me at an emotional arm's length.

But Wren pulled me back from my realization as he nodded and gestured for me to continue.

"I very clearly remember asking you if there were any downsides I didn't know about, to becoming Mr. Tsui's Assecla. I can't believe you 'just forgot' the tiny detail of me dying if he dies. You just accidentally forgot something like my death?"

We sat in silence for a moment, I think waiting for the other to speak. After a minute, Wren said, "Is there anything else? I mean, those are legit, but did you have anything else you need to add before I say anything?"

"Yeah, there's this thing with Plague. And there's also something else, but it's a lot more personal. Let's talk about this first."

"Wow, alright," he said. "I'm guessing this has been bubbling inside you for a while. Well, first, I'm sorry I've given you a reason to distrust me. As far as Dom and I giving some of the same answers, you need to remember that we attend all the same meetings. And you also have to understand that Dom's attempts at getting you up here have been discussed for more than a year now. If the wording is the same, it's because we have been kind of limited in what we could say, especially earlier in speaking with you."

Wren reached over and set the corrected model in front of me. He was showing his talent, because it looked as if I had never screwed it up. "Here you go. Now, as for the trouble with you being an Assecla, please understand that Dom is the first time I have ever dealt with the whole idea of this. I've never met an Assecla before, so I apologize if I forgot something, even if it was something important."

"Uh huh," I deadpanned. "Interesting that it's all, 'I need to understand', and 'I need to remember'. I trusted you. You asked me to trust you and let you help me out with learning about the Vampyre."

"I know. I'm sorry."

"And learning about Vampyre, a while back when we were talking about powers I could get, we talked about whether... Jiashi?"

"Jiangshi."

"Yeah, Jiangshi. We talked about whether Jiangshi could use telepathy. Did we ever get an answer about that?"

"I have not had an opportunity to discuss the topic with Dom. But didn't you speak with him? You had dinner with him, didn't you?"

I froze and blushed. Now it was my turn to feel stupid. "I... forgot to ask. I was," I sighed, "too busy being mad and telling him off about not mentioning the whole 'dying' thing."

"It's alright. I get it." I could see Wren side-eyeing me. I fought to keep my eyes focused on the model in front of me as he said, "Why are you bringing this up? Has something happened that makes this an immediate concern?"

"Ever since you showed me the door and peephole in the basement, I have had every intention of blocking it up or at least covering the peephole. But I can only think about it when I am unable to do anything about it. And if I can do something, I immediately get distracted or forget about it completely. And Plague said something about how he was going to keep me from doing anything about the door as long as Mr. Tsui was not 'releasing him'." I even gave him the air quotes.

"So, you think it's possible Plague is mentally manipulating you in some way? Maybe even some version of the Mesmir?"

"What else could it be?"

Wren's face scrunched in thought.

"Are you saying that's not possible?" I asked.

"I'm not saying that at all! I'm very young and would never even pretend I know everything about the Vampyre. I've admitted more than once that I don't have all the answers. Have you told Dom about this?"

"Not yet. It just happened last night. Did you know he's been creeping in my bedroom when I'm asleep just so he can give me nightmares? He was actually bragging about it!"

"Well, you certainly need to fill him in on that. And when you do, he can perhaps give you more information on what Plague is capable of, and what he should be doing to protect his Assecla."

CHAPTER FIFTY-NINE

WHITE HOT ANGER

Wren picked up the last model Boots had been painting, turning it in his delicate fingers, inspecting the novice paint job. A silence hung heavy in the air, expectant and troubling.

"This is definitely something that needs to be addressed with Dom. Sooner, rather than later. But since we are here, you said you had something personal to discuss? Was that it, or is there something else?"

I couldn't get myself to face Wren, with the delicate topic I needed to bring up, so I fiddled with the brushes on my desk, rolling them around nervously. "Yeah, there's more. I've... Well, I've been realizing that I feel different about you when you are right here, than when I'm alone and can actually think. Like I'm not sure I'm capable of thinking normal when I'm alone with you. And that scares me."

"Babe." He transferred the model to his other hand so he could rest his right hand on my thigh. "You've trusted me ever since we met. You should still be able to trust me."

"And I did! I trusted you too much." I got a bit quieter when I added, "I even trusted you enough that I gave you my cherry."

"What do you mean?" asked Wren, surprised. "We haven't even done that. Yet or otherwise."

"I mean oral, you ass," I yelled in frustration, smacking his hand off my leg. "Before you, I've never done more than second base with someone before. And you barely asked! You just got me horned up and went for it."

"You were perfectly fine with it at the time," said Wren, and I could tell he was getting annoyed. "And all the other times we messed around," he added. "And now you are getting buyer's remorse?"

I finally looked over at Wren, who just sat there and looked at me like I had slapped him. Seriously, he looked like he was halfway to crying.

"So, this entire time," he said softly, "you have been worried I was taking advantage of you." He didn't seem angry. Instead, he seemed worried. "Oh, babe. I'm so sorry. I think I forgot for a time just how young you are."

"Screw you! This isn't about me being too young! This is about you using your damn powers on me."

"No, no! I didn't mean it like that." Wren seemed to be struggling to keep his voice steady, probably trying to calm my ass down. "Maybe young wasn't the right word. Inexperienced, maybe. You're getting thrown into a new high stress scene, a new situation of having to learn about the Mesmir and how to overcome it, and then your first real sexual relationship all at once. I should have known better and waited."

"Maybe," I mumbled. "After all, I was just some fun for you, someone who you just found intriguing." I couldn't look at him. "I mean to you I'm just a novelty, right?"

"That was cruel of me. I'm sure you were hoping for more."

"Yeah, but that's not my problem," I said, trying to skirt that little issue. "It's more about feeling like I can't trust myself around you."

"Can't trust yourself?" Wren grinned. "What, am I really that irresistible?"

"I don't trust that you aren't mind manipulating me."

The grin disappeared. "Is this about you being pissed I won't 'go steady' or whatever." He even made air quotes at me. "Jeez, Jason, grow up already."

"It's like you aren't even listening!" I was about to lose it, for real. "You tell me to 'grow up', and yet you don't even hear what I just said." I punctuated my words, jabbing my finger into the top of the desk with each word. "I. Am. Scared. You. Are. Using. Mesmir. On. Me!"

Silence reigned. We stared at each other as I tried to figure out what was going through his mind. Then... he laughed.

"Babe," he said, still with a bit of a laugh that was seriously pissing me off, "you've already proved you can throw off Mesmir when you want to. I couldn't use it on you, even if I wanted to."

"Again, asshole, like I just told you, Plague seems to be able to! You want to laugh, go for it. Go ahead, don't take me seriously."

His laugh was gone. "You're seriously going to keep comparing me to Beishang de Wenyi?"

"When I see something that compares, yes!"

"That's pretty harsh." Wren muttered. "And you are absolutely convinced I am doing the same thing to you? Just running with it, no doubt in your mind?"

"I didn't say, 'no doubts'. I said I worry about similarities I've noticed. I can't seem to think the same when you're around."

Wren just stared at me. "And the fact you've already admitted you have the hots for me can't account for that? Or is that the real issue? That I haven't asked you to be my 'boyfriend'." Again, he used air quotes. "Don't think I don't know about that kid you have hanging out all the time over here. Sharing your bed? Pretty much moved in? I'm betting he's down in your basement right now."

"Hey, you don't get to pull that garbage," I snapped back. "You're the one who didn't want to date. You're the one who just wanted an interesting friend-with-benefits. You don't get to play the jealous boyfriend now."

"So, you do want me to be a boyfriend."

"I never said yes or no," I countered. "You told me that wasn't an option."

"Babe, I told you that wasn't what I was looking for when we first met. But I also said that other options were possible in the future."

"How long for this potential future to come around? Should I sit around and wait? I can look forward to letting you come over a few times a week to come sex me up?"

"So, you want a boyfriend. Dates and sleepovers and all that?"

It was said so casually, so flippantly, that I thought he was making fun. But looking in his eyes, he seemed serious.

"I can try out being a boyfriend. I've never done it before, but it can't be too hard, right?"

My jaw was literally hanging open. I couldn't remember the last time I had heard *anything* that callous. "You cannot be serious right now."

"Damn, alright. Did I misunderstand what the problem is here?"

"I can't tell if you are trying to be mean, or if I just don't know you."

"Babe, I really like you. And not just to feed with. If you are telling me that this is some kind of contest between me and your human friend, then I can give you what you want, and play the dutiful boyfriend."

"Get out." I was done. I really should have walked away that first night.

"You're kicking me to the curb? Seriously?" He looked shocked.

"I need someone who's serious. And you're really giving me this vibe that you'll do whatever to keep me around to entertain you and feed you, even if it means pretending to like me."

Now he was mad. "You're really throwing away your only ally? For a human? Unbelievable."

"I've got allies, Wren. Mr. Tsui's an ally. Your sister's an ally. Hell, Montgomery's an ally. This has nothing to do with allies. Nothing to do with politics, or the Vampyre, or even the rest of Avernus. You're sexy as hell. You know that all too well."

Wren had a look on his face that was a cross between confusion and disbelief.

"But I'm trying to find someone who wants me for *me*! Not what I can do for them. You are nice, when you want to be. But sometimes I can't even tell how much you actually *like* me."

"Maybe learn to pay attention."

Wren's chair was knocked back from the desk. Before it even had time to hit the ground, I already heard the front door slam.

Sitting on the desk was a pulverized Cosmos Emptor model.

CHAPTER SIXTY

CLOSING DOORS

It took several minutes before I could even move. What the hell had just happened? The entire conversation had snowballed out of nowhere, like a car crash I could only watch happen. Did we just break up? Did we even have enough of a relationship for us to be able to break up?

I mechanically stood and righted Wren's chair. Then, shaking my head, I pulled out my phone and dialed the number I had for Mr. Tsui. It was Montgomery who answered, but I suppose that was good enough.

"I need to talk to Mr. Tsui." I said. "Tonight, if possible. Can you please find out when and where?"

Montgomery was silent for a moment. "I'll set something up and text you back in a few minutes."

"Thank you, Montgomery. Just tell him I'm having trouble with Plague, and it's important."

"Damn. Alright," he said. He didn't sound offended, more surprised. "Just hold tight, and I'll message you right back once I talk to Dom."

He hung up and I practically ran down to the basement. I thanked whatever gods might be out there, because Boots was still downstairs, safe and un-messed with. He looked up in concern when I came storming through the door and down the stairs.

"You good?" he asked as soon as he got a good look at me.

"Not particularly," I muttered. "It seems Wren doesn't like sharing his toys."

Boots' jaw dropped and he took a step back. "Really? I thought he liked you. Guess there's a longer story there? Don't worry. You don't have to tell me details if you don't want to."

"Thanks. I don't mind telling you, I guess. You've been pretty good about this stuff so far." I took a few minutes and filled him in on the overall details of what went on upstairs.

"But that's my problem to deal with," I said, plopping down on the couch. "Did you find anything down here?"

"Oh, yeah!" He hopped up and stepped over to the wall, where he started pointing out different things. "Here's the peephole you said was down here. I put this little sticker here, and found a marker to darken it up. This way it's covered, but you can always remove it if you decide to go insane and let somebody see us." He laughed, trying to lighten the mood. "I also think I found the door. Here, look."

Boots was able to show how he was able to slip a playing card into a practically invisible line in the wall. Once he slipped in the card, it was pretty apparent to me that he had found the edge of the door.

"The only thing is, I can't find a way to open it from this side," Boots said. "And without getting it open, I can't think how to seal it without either making it obvious from this side to the gang, or moving something in front of it."

"But, it's too narrow an angle to put shelves or anything. So, anything we put there would leave us tripping over whatever it was, when going up and down the stairs," I said, finishing his thought.

"Exactly," he said. "So what do you want to do about it? It looks like they did too good a job setting up this door."

"I guess this is the best we are going to get for the moment," I replied back. "Now I've got to figure out what to do about this Vampyre problem. I'm tempted to be as stupid as I was before, and get right up in their faces again." I explained about going to the hotel after my dad was killed, confronting Mr. Tsui, and the fallout from all that.

"So it was completely stupid and dangerous, you were almost killed, and then you found out everything you wanted to know?" Boots sat there, a bit stunned and in awe. "Sounds like if this was a movie, this would be the part where the hero and his plucky sidekick grab flashlights and go exploring the spooky evil tunnels."

I laughed, for real, and he joined me. "Well, we don't need flashlights. The tunnels are all lit up, most of them with motion sensor lights. They aren't exactly caves. They're fully dug tunnels, with concrete and paint. They even have these mini golf carts to ride around on."

"Damn, so less 'Dracula', and more 'Dr. Evil'."

"Exactly. All that's missing is the volcano and the frikkin sharks with frikkin lasers on their frikkin heads," I said, quoting the aforementioned movie. "Wait a minute. How would you seal the door, if we could open it? Like, how would that help?"

"Easiest way would be to caulk the whole thing in the door jamb, then shut it," he answered. "After twenty-four hours, it would be better than superglue."

Thinking about it, I mused, "I'd probably deal with it better if the door went both ways, so that it was useful for me."

"I guess," said Boots. "But why would you even want to use it? Having a door here at all is way too creepy."

"Speaking of, dude, there are three other bedrooms in this giant-ass house. Take one so you can quit crashing in the basement when you don't have to."

Boots looked a bit guilty, muttering, "I don't want to impose."

Chuckling, I said, "So you'd rather let me worry about you and this damned door?" He started to say something else, so before he could, I added, "And don't say you just won't come around as much." When he looked surprised, I explained, "Dude, I was the same way with my friend, Alen. I crashed over at his house all the time when my folks were fighting, or my dad got too drunk. I really need you to get comfortable living here, dude."

He paused, as if trying to process what I said, before saying, "Living... here?

Not just crashing here occasionally?"

"Yes, dude. Go check in with your parental units whenever you have to, but get your crap, bring it over here, and pick a bedroom to put it in."

He thought about it for a second, then with a sly smile said, "That's pretty fast, considering we haven't even had our first date."

I laughed and punched Boots in the shoulder. "Shut the hell up with that, or I'll kiss you!"

We both got a good laugh, especially when Boots started blushing. I'm pretty sure I hit a button with that one. In the most epic level of "saved by the bell", my phone went off with a text message. I pulled out my phone, and saw it was Mr. Tsui's number.

Give us two hours, then come to the hotel.
Tell the desk you need to go upstairs for a meeting.
Message me if this is a problem.

I showed Boots the message and his shoulders slumped. "I wish I could go with you."

"Oh yeah? So come."

"Yeah," he chuckled. "And how are you going to explain bringing a normie with you? I'm not supposed to know anything, right? Besides, you remember what happened to me the last time I went near the hotel." He shuddered, and I remembered that creepy feeling, like something was watching me, or more like stalking me. "Pretty much everyone from town feels it whenever they go near the place."

"That's weird," I said. "I've only felt it a couple of times. The one time with you, once alone out behind the hotel, and another time inside my hotel room. Though that one was weaker and might have been something else. I think I might know what it is, but I don't know for sure. You've been in this town longer, watching. Do you have any ideas?"

"Hey, you're the one with all the inside knowledge, my guy. I'm just a spy. So what are we doing?"

"I guess I'm going to go meet Mr. Tsui and try to get a few answers," I said with a shrug.

"Answers? Or protections?"

I matched his shrug, trying to sound braver than I felt. "More like trying to find out if Dom is holding back. So... answers?"

"How are you doing with what just happened? I still can't believe Wren went off on you like that. I thought you said he wasn't interested in being serious."

"Yeah, well, he seemed to have maybe changed his mind," I grumbled. "He seemed to really have it out about me spending time with you. Like he was mad it wasn't him."

"Jeez. Sensitive much?"

"And he teased about it at first but having you staying here in the house really set him off. So I guess we need to both stay out of his way for a minute, yeah?"

"Dude, you would think he would have thicker skin."

"I know, right?" I said with a laugh. "I mean, I am definitely not worth losing your head over." Boots muttered something quiet I couldn't catch. "What's that?" I had to ask him.

He blushed, but he raised his head and did this thing where he spoke clearly, but he kept his eyes closed, as if by not looking at me, it wouldn't be as impactful or personal or whatever.

"I said, you've got enough going on to be worth 'losing your head over'."

Even with his eyes closed, he was embarrassed enough to be turning pretty pink in the face. Meanwhile I was left torn in two directions. I mean, I wanted to dig into what he found fascinating enough to say that about me. But flip side, I wanted to skip the "whys" and just jump straight into figuring out if Boots really was saying he was interested in me. I guess in the end, I was somebody who needed answers too badly.

"You're gonna need to take a step back, my guy," I said, even as I sat back down on the couch next to him. "We are both into dudes, sure. But what's this garbage about me being worth getting upset over, or whatever? What's possibly so special about me?"

"Dude, you walked right up to Taki and Liam literally your first day in town and made yourself right at home with our crew. You're brave enough to jump straight into everything handed to you by the town spooks, even when you thought they were the Mafia."

For whatever reason, I just saw those as standard, what anyone would probably do. But then he kept on going.

"Then there's the fact you've been super nice to me, whether you had to or not. Then how you've kind of hinted a few times you might be into me but haven't made me feel weird about it at any point. Add to all that, you are all fit and well put together."

"I mean, I wasn't exactly going to be a dick to you or anything. And yeah, you're really cute. My mom even thought so."

"And," he continued, as if trying to info-dump all his points and ignore what I had just said, "speaking of your mom, you were cool about her. First, wanting her to not be controlled, then when that wasn't possible here, sending her away to be safe."

"I don't think I really had a choice about that. Not if I wasn't going to be a complete dick. She's my mom. I had to keep her safe, and if she's a zombie or whatever, she might not be able to look out for her own best interest. I'd do the same for our guys, if I could."

"See what I mean?" he asked. "And now you have this giant, amazing house all to yourself, with no parents, and nobody to boss you around. And the first thing you do is insist I come over and stay the hell out of my cesspool of a house."

Um, wow. That was a lot of opinion to take in. So what do I say? Thank you? Naw, that would be too silly. Instead, I said, "Are you trying to say you want to go out?"

CHAPTER SIXTY-ONE

POTENTIA

I let Boots off the hook and let us chat about more mundane things for a while. But I still left early for the meetup since I needed to clear my head. Normally this would mean going out and tearing up the concrete, but now I had a new skill to try out. It took me a few false starts, but all too soon, I got myself up to "superspeed" though I couldn't remember the name for it, whipping up and down the streets of Avernus. Each time I had done this it became a bit more natural, and I was able to use the exercise to kind of zone out.

It was odd, because I knew if I was running like normal, I would be breathing hard, sweating, and fighting a stitch in my side. Something about the process of this Vampyre speed was apparently more like magic than metabolism, so it didn't seem to take as much of a physical toll on me. I guessed I was using up some kind of mystical, voodoo reserve instead. If I was really lucky, it was Mr. Tsui's reserve and not mine.

I was tired of waiting around to find out about the other abilities I was supposed to get. Someone was supposed to be showing me how to use my strength, plus help me dig for any other abilities.

Obviously, that hadn't happened, so I may as well try on my own, right? No time like the present.

I stopped running when I found myself in an area with nothing but old businesses. There were some older cars, but I didn't want to risk messing up someone's day, considering anyone around here could likely be one damaged car from a lost job and homelessness. However, there was a dumpster. One of those green monstrosities with the double plastic lids. I started messing around with it, trying to push it, lift a side, anything that seemed like it would take Potentia. Nothing happened.

I took a few minutes to think back on what I remembered in Solomon's surgery-lab. I couldn't remember much, more like feelings, impressions, sensations. I remember seeing red. Like, literally red. I remember everything I had touched felt as light as cardboard. However, what I suspected was what I had been feeling. And what I remembered was being a combination of scared and pissed off.

I was tired of being at the lowest rung of the power struggle here in Avernus, and I couldn't help thinking I needed any advantage I could get. Finding some way to access my strength would certainly be an advantage. Mr. Tsui and Wren both seemed pretty scared that I could be so strong. I was feeling a bit frustrated, thinking about how I hadn't received the promised help, then I started thinking about the crap Wren had just pulled. I realized I was getting frustrated and annoyed, so I leaned into it.

At first nothing happened, but then I remembered Wren bumping shoulders just before our fight, in a mimic of that cute move Boots would pull. At this point it felt like obvious manipulation, and suddenly something snapped. My vision filled with the same red haze, but rather than dulling my limited vision, it was like slipping on a pair of night vision goggles in a shooter video game.

The world exploded into high resolution in my eyes, even while shaded in black and reds. I kicked out, and the dumpster slid away with a rending screech of metal on asphalt, crashing into the side of an abandoned auto shop across the street. The cinder block wall caved in under the impact, leaving the green metal box half embedded in the wall. I did a double take at what I had done. My foot hadn't felt a thing.

The red filter on my vision started to fade, and I tried to fight it. It faded further, but I thought about Wren again. Picturing the anger in his face as he left caused the red to return in full force. In exasperation I kicked a beer can near me, and it went flying into the night. I heard the sound of glass breaking somewhere way in the distance. Good. Now I knew how to bring it on. It was time to go find some answers.

Pulling out my phone, I got a general idea of where I was in relation to the rest of the town. I was way off west, and the hotel was south of downtown. I took off with my Vamp speed and headed east. Before I could really register what was going on, I was standing in the front parking lot of the Avernus Inn and Suites. What GPS said was a thirty-minute walk took a little over three minutes. I could get used to this!

It was only as I stood there looking at the building that I realized I had only passed two cars in the entire run. It wasn't even eight pm on a Saturday. You would think a town like this would be out doing stuff? Using restaurants, shopping. Maybe going to see a movie or something? I was really beginning to think the people in this town have no life outside of whatever serves the Vampyre.

I steeled myself and walked into the lobby. The creepy tall guy, August, was at the desk. I told him I had a meeting upstairs, as Montgomery had instructed me, and went to go have a seat. About ten minutes later, a pair of goons came down to the lobby.

They barely said hello as we took the familiar elevator ride up, where we found Ms. Flanagan sitting at her desk.

"Good evening, ma'am. Are you happy to see me?"

"Not particularly. You tend to complicate my evenings," she said dryly. "Mr. Tsui will be with you shortly."

Even with her sour attitude, I appreciated her honesty. We were taken back to the lovely office I had been locked in before. When I saw where we were going, I tensed up for a moment, recalling the frustration of that day, but I managed to keep putting one foot in front of the other.

One of the goons opened the door and motioned for me to enter. It wasn't exactly an ideal situation, because waiting to see me was Montgomery. Not exactly my favorite person. But maybe this could be an opportunity to get some sneaky, behind-the-scenes answers. We exchanged pleasantries and he motioned for me to sit down.

"Dominic will be here in a few minutes," said Montgomery. "Now fill me in on what happened with Beishang de Wenyi?"

"Wow, so where to start," I said. "I know the joke says, 'start at the beginning', but I don't think that's where the problem starts." I gave Montgomery a serious look. "Have you heard everybody saying I'm able to slip Mesmir?"

"Yeah, you did it with Gregor at LGM."

"Pretty much, yeah," I said.

"There was also Dominic's mistaken attempt with you."

I smiled at that one. "That's what we're calling that incident? Well anyway, is there another kind of Mesmir? Or any powers similar to Mesmir?"

This time it was Montgomery's turn to smile. "Oh, there are as many powers as there are species of Vampyre." I had to think about that. He waited, and when I didn't immediately comment, he asked, "Where are you going with this?"

"Everything Wren says, is that I'm able to break Mesmir on me. But you know that door from the Warrens into my basement?" He nodded. "I've been trying since I learned about it, to cover up the peephole. But every time I do, I forget about it. It's blanked from my mind."

"So this is why you are asking about other types of Mesmir... You think it is Beishang de Wenyi?"

"I mean, he pretty much said so."

"Interesting. When was this?"

"Last night," I said. "But this was the third time he has spoken to me, even though I'm now pretty sure he's been creeping in and giving me nightmares a lot more than that."

"The third? I wasn't aware there was a second."

"I told you about the second. When the first visit happened, Wren said he would tell Mr. Tsui about it."

"Why would you go to him and not me? Am I not your contact to Dominic?"

"Everybody keeps telling me that Wren is my handler, and whenever I need a go-between to Mr. Tsui, I contact him."

Montgomery's face went dark for a moment at that. He looked really jealous for a second.

"I only called this number," I went on, "Because like I said, Wren went off on me. After that, I didn't hear anything about his conversation with Mr. Tsui. So the second time I tried the direct approach. Since he was out, I had to talk to you."

"And why did Wren, as you say, go off on you?"

"It's personal," I said with a glare.

Montgomery looked at me like he couldn't believe I was being so stupid. Then he sighed. "And has Beishang de Wenyi tried to injure you, or do more than threaten?"

"Yes! If you were listening, I said he has been sneaking in and giving me nightmares. Probably to feed off me. He's also messed with my friends. In particular I have a human friend who stays at my house a lot. So, you know, Plague's messing with normal people, coming right in the same room with them."

"Staying over a lot, you say? My, my," Montgomery teased. "You do seem to get around."

"He stays at my house a lot 'cause of abusive parents, you ass! I'm not screwing my friend, no matter what Wren might think."

"Ah. There it is."

"You're pushing all my buttons. Maybe you don't remember me telling you how being an ass to me is the best way to lose brownie points with me. I don't care enough about you to stomp you down and put you in your place."

"I'd love to see that," Montgomery said with a smile.

I glared at him. "Make yourself worth it, and we'll see what happens. Are you going to be smiling as wide when I do the same to Mr. Tsui the second he gets here?"

"Absolutely," he remarked without hesitation. "I really do not care what you think of me. You are nothing more than Dominic's Assecla. Barely a puppet."

"Damn. No wonder Mr. Tsui said you weren't a people person. That makes me wonder. What are you to Dom? What is he to you?" He looked at me in confusion. "He says you're his personal assistant, his right-hand man, yet he has

Wren do all his negotiating with me?"

Montgomery's face went cold, but he didn't speak.

"So, this whole situation where you aren't allowed to handle me. I'm pretty sure you're jealous." That got a scoff from him. "No, not about me. You've made it clear a couple of times you aren't a fan of me. No, you're jealous that the responsibility was given to someone else."

He went angry, but suddenly his face went blank, neutral. I squinted, concentrating. It took a second, but his smooth perfection melted, to be replaced once again by barely controlled anger and disgust. It took a moment before he got his emotions back under control. I had no idea if he could tell I was seeing through his blank Mesmir face. Finally, he stood and addressed me.

"You can finish this conversation with Dominic when he gets here." And with that, he left the room.

I let his petty ass go. He wasn't the one I wanted to talk to anyway. Although losing my temper with him and getting under his skin wasn't a smart move and might give me a new thing to worry about.

I thought about testing if I was trapped here but decided it didn't matter. I was here for answers, so it was worth it. Besides, I wanted to assume I was trusted and liked to at least some extent and didn't want to burst my own bubble.

Chapter Sixty-Two

Unhelpful Assistance

I didn't have to wait too terribly long, maybe ten minutes, before the door opened and Mr. Tsui came in. He seemed somewhat distracted yet still presented a pleasant demeanor.

"Good evening, Jason. What can I assist with?" he asked as he sat down opposite from me. "Montgomery said you have been having some issues? Visits from Beishang de Wenyi and a disagreement with Wren?"

"Wren's more my problem, except he's probably going to take a break from being your liaison."

"Interesting. I may need to speak with him about that. See if he needs a reminder about duty and responsibilities. Now, tell me everything that has happened with our good friend, the Plague of Sorrows."

"Ugh," I huffed. "What hasn't happened? He showed back up in my basement a second time, threatened me, he says, for you not releasing him. Then he attacked my friends."

"Attacked?" he asked, calm as anything. "Can you please elaborate?"

"I had two friends over. He knocked them out with his voodoo powers, threatened me, and made them scream with nightmares."

"So, he entered your home when mortals were with you?"

I concentrated, fighting to see through whatever Mesmir he might be using to conceal any worry or anger. Sure enough, I was able to catch flashes of frustration and anger.

"Yes, there's been someone in the house, usually in the same room, pretty much every time he's come in. Uninvited and unwanted, I might add."

"Every time?" All signs of his emotions were gone again. I couldn't see anything but his "polite" face. "How many times has he been with you in your house?"

"He's confronted me three times. But I'm pretty sure he's been coming into my house, into my *room,* when I'm asleep, to mess with me and give me nightmares."

"I apologize that you have had to endure this. Is there anything else you wished to discuss?"

Endure, sure. Meanwhile he was just going to sit here, watching. He had his battery now, his safety net that made sure he was safe enough to not get attacked again. I was going to have to figure out a way to change his mind on this. But right now it looked like I wasn't going to get any immediate direct help. Maybe I could at least get something more indirect.

"Yeah, do..." I had to stop and try to remember the real word. "Do Jiangshi have telepathy?"

Mr. Tsui seemed to ponder for a moment. "I am not aware of Cor Decere being an ability available to them. Why do you ask?"

"What about any other mental powers? Anything similar to Mesmir? Mind control? Anything like that?"

"Ah." He perked up at that one. "Now that, my Assecla, is the precise opposite of Cor Decere. You have been shown more than once how the Jiangshi are able to project nightmares into the minds of those around them, the better to feed on said negative dreams. Yes?"

I nodded, but didn't say anything, prompting him to continue.

"This would be the Vampyre projecting thoughts out, rather than gathering them in, would it not?"

Again, I nodded.

"I now find myself intrigued. Why do you ask about this? Why this particular curiosity?"

"That damned door in the basement," I said. "Every time I think about trying to cover up the peephole or do something about that door, my mind goes fuzzy and the whole idea slips away. I'll either forget about it, or I'll invent some crazy reason why it's just not a good time."

"And you believe this is the work of Beishang de Wenyi."

"He said it himself. He said that until you fulfilled your promise to, as he said, 'release us', I would be able to do nothing to block up the door, and he would continue to keep coming back."

"Interesting."

"So now there is an 'us'. Why is there an 'us'? Are there more enemies than just Plague?"

"That is my business." Dom was no longer smiling.

"The hell it is. It's my business now that you roped me into this! It's my business when I've been visited and threatened three times. And that's not counting the nightmares, the feeding, and how he's messing with my friends!"

"Just as you are my business."

I froze, staring at him. "You mean your property." He just looked back at me, a blank look on his face. Coldly I said, "I told you before, nobody owns me."

"I'm afraid that time has passed," he said softly. There was something like sorrow behind his words, but mostly I just saw the arrogance. "You are mine, of my blood."

"Are you sure?" I shot back coldly. "Is that really the corner you want to back me into?"

He smiled again, but this time it was arrogant and self assured. "I will not back you into any corner, my Assecla. I will give you all the leash you want. You have given me back my power and for that I am grateful. For everything else, I can be patient."

The arrogance. The smug attitude! I was done with this conversation. I didn't know if there were more answers here right now. I was too angry to think of the questions. Figuring he was trying to piss me off so I couldn't think straight, I decided it was time to retreat and regroup. I needed to decide what to do next. I didn't think I was ever going to get any proper answers out of Mr. Tsui. And if I was really honest, maybe not out of Wren, either.

"Fine," I said. "You want to be patient? I guess now I have time to be patient as well. Good night, Mr. Tsui." I wasn't feeling the compulsion to call him that. I just figured it might put him more at ease. Let him think he won more than he really did.

"Good night, Jason. In time, I think you will come to realize everything our arrangement will bring to you."

I was pissed. I wanted to go ballistic on him, now that I knew how to do it. But I knew it was better to save that as a secret weapon for later. Instead, I made myself stay calm and walked to the door. Thankfully it was not locked, and I was able to leave. One of the goons was waiting in the hall and took me back downstairs. I wasn't really in a mood to play around, so I walked home. No superspeed, no stops anywhere else. I wanted time to think.

CHAPTER SIXTY-THREE

FAMILIAR ANSWERS

It was a bit after nine when I returned home. The house was quiet, just as eerie as the empty streets I had been walking down. The lights were just as I had left them. Fortunately, when I opened the basement door, I heard the TV on. Heading downstairs, I found Boots was still here, engrossed in a fighting game. He paused the game when I was halfway down the stairs, turning to see what I had to tell him.

"You want the good news or the bad news?" I asked him once I got to the bottom.

"Bad news first," he said with a serious face. "Then you can cheer me up with the good news."

"Well," I said, sitting down next to him, "I got pretty strong confirmation that Mr. Tsui's assistant, his *right-hand man,*" I emphasized sarcastically, "really doesn't like me, and it seems like he would rather I disappear than help me."

Boots hissed in frustration.

"Then when I talked to Mr. Tsui, he wasn't much better. He was nicer about it, sort of, but he definitely gave me a 'wait and see' attitude and was absolutely no help at all with Plague."

He cursed a little under his breath. Then he looked at me with hope in his eyes.

"Does the good news make up for that in any way?"

I laughed. "You tell me, dude. It looks like all I have to do is get pissed off, and I can kick a dumpster through a brick wall."

"Seriously?" he yelled in excitement. "No way!"

"Yup! So now it seems like I can do superspeed or superstrength at will. That should be helpful, right?"

"Absolutely," he said.

"Anything to get me killed quicker, right?" I said with a laugh.

Boots shook his head, then asked, "What's the next move?"

"Don't know. I think I need to take a few days. Think about the problem. Plus, it'll give it some time to see if one of them does something else."

"You're not worried about giving either of them too much time to stew, and start some new problems?"

I sat back into the couch, shaking my head. "It's just as likely that me jumping the gun causes more problems."

"So, no more errands tonight?" he asked.

"Nope. I'm gonna watch you play some of your video game and then probably crash early."

"Good," he said. "Because you've dropped a lot tonight, and I need some clarification. Why are you messing around with someone named Plague?"

Oops. I got carried away and forgot Boots wasn't really "in the know".

"Is there any way we can just acknowledge that there's a bunch of insane stuff going on, and ignore the details? Like I said the other day, there's a big difference between them finding out you aren't under the Mesmir, and you actually knowing details of the Vampyre."

"I thought you said they weren't all Vampires?And why are you saying Vamp*yre*? What's the difference?"

I sighed, noting that was oops number two.

"Time to throw caution to the wind, I guess. Are you *sure* you want to know all this?"

"Are you *sure* you want to keep me around, and *not* know what to avoid?"

"There are Vampires here, including Mr. Tsui and a couple of others. But only a few. The rest are other kinds of supernatural creepies. The name for all of them together are the Vampyre. So Vampires are just one type of Vampyre."

"Ah. And you said a while back that Wren wasn't a Vampire. So what kind of Vampyre is he?"

I cringed. "A Succubus."

Boots paused for a heartbeat, then busted out laughing. It took him a moment to catch his breath, then he squeaked out, "So *that's* why you said he's a player!" Then his eyes really lit up. "And did he suck-your-bus?"

"You're a doofus," I said with a grin.

"So this Plague punk. Is he another non-Vampire Vampyre?"

"Unfortunately. His name is Plague of Sorrows, or at least that is the translation of his Chinese name. And yeah, he's edgelord enough that he gave himself the name." I screwed my eyes shut, trying to concentrate. "I think the Chinese name is Beyshan de Wenyu or something like that."

Boots gave a sour look as I continued. "Anyway, he is that bastard, that... thing, that has been coming in here and causing us all our troubles. He's a thing that gets off on giving nightmares."

"Ouch. So why does everyone else put up with him?"

"I get the feeling that right now they don't have a choice. He's kind of an enemy they are locked in the same house with."

"So, we've got the big scary monster. You said something about a Mr. Tsui?"

"Yeah, he's kind of like my sponsor, I guess? He's the reason we even came to Avernus, because I had something he wanted. But now he's got it, and I can't leave."

"Wow, ouch. You make it sound like you sold your soul or something. Did you at least get something cool for it?"

"I got this house, so that's something."

"Anything else?"

"I'm pretty sure I got a boyfriend out of it."

Chapter Sixty-Four

Alone Together

I'm not sure which of us blushed more, but we moved the conversation on to safer topics. The questioning was over for the moment.

We sat around for a while, just chilling. Boots tried to get me to play his fighting game with him, but I wasn't feeling it. I told him I was going to try to get some sleep. He didn't finish his game, didn't even hesitate, just hopped off the couch and powered off the system.

"Can I get a shower?"

"Why are you asking me?" I said with a laugh. "Do what you need to do."

While Boots started up the shower, I stripped down to my boxers, tossed my clothes in the laundry hamper, and cut the lights off before climbing into bed. Tomorrow was Sunday so I didn't set an alarm before plugging in my phone. A few minutes later, the shower cut off. My eyes were still adjusting to the dimness of the bedroom, a small amount of light coming in around the window curtains on one side, and the crack at the bottom of the closed bathroom door on the other.

It occurred to me that on the other side of that door, Boots was very naked and rubbing himself down with a towel. For a moment my dirty mind pictured him twisting and contorting around, finding all the parts of his body that needed drying. I couldn't help but imagine him reaching around to dry his back, bending down to rub his legs. Then his body would be on full display as he dried his hair.

Damnit. I hadn't taken an opportunity to relieve myself tonight, and Boots was about to come climb into bed with me. Not only that, but we had finally laid everything out in the open earlier, and I knew, no more guessing but knew, he was into me.

I was worried I would be too horned up to sleep if he came in here after everything we'd talked about recently. Saying "down boy" wasn't going to be enough.

I thought about running to the bathroom as soon as he got out but realized he would see the protrusion in my boxers and know what I was up to. Then I thought about running to the hallway bathroom now, while he was still in there, but then he'd come out to an empty bedroom, it would get weird, and I'd have to do a walk of shame back in from the hall after he was in here in bed.

The bathroom door opened, spilling light into the bedroom. I glanced over and did a double take. Normal procedure when he was sleeping in here, Boots would go into the room next door, where he kept his clothes and stuff, and take fresh undies into the bathroom with him to put on after his shower. However, moments later a very naked best friend climbed under the covers with me. Up to this point we had still never seen each other in less than our underwear, so this was new territory. Needless to say, little Jason was standing at full attention. I lay there on my back, waiting to see if this was going where I thought it was.

Boots turned in the bed, and the way I could feel his breath, I knew he was on his side, facing me. I was afraid to move, scared of chasing him off, wanting him to make the first move. I felt the blankets move slightly, then felt his hand touch my upper arm before laying on my chest. It feathered off so slightly, as if he were afraid to commit to the touch.

"Is this okay?" He whispered, super close to my ear, making me shudder.

I could hear the hesitation and nervousness in his voice. I nodded, then knowing he couldn't see me in the dark, I managed to croak out a soft "Yes." But I reached up to grab his hand.

"What's wrong?" he asked nervously, as if fearful he had messed up.

"Why are you doing this?" I asked. I tried to project curiosity, not annoyance. "Why now, after all these weeks?"

He slipped his hand out of mine and went back to touching my arm. "I guess I've been waiting on you. You've had a lot going on, you can be a bit intimidating, and... you've had Wren hovering around you as long as I've known you."

"You don't need to be intimidated by anything with me, dude."

"I know that now," he said, and this time I could definitely hear the smile in his voice, "and now I also know Wren isn't in the way, either."

"Ah. Well in that case," I said with a smile of my own, "what did you have in mind?"

I wasn't trying to compare Boots' efforts to Wren's. Honest, I wasn't. For sheer "walking on cloud nine" effect, Wren had it down cold. But his perfection came across as, well, supernatural. Boots might not have as perfect a technique, but it was all heart and desire. He was doing this because he knew it was making me feel great.

I let him set his pace, even though I wanted to rush forward, guns blazing. But I was more interested in making this feel good for both of us. I didn't know if he'd ever done this before. It could have been his first time, or he could have had some friend he's been practicing with for years. I just knew he was the second guy I'd ever been with, and by far the one I liked best.

Once we finished, we lay there for a minute so we could both catch our breath. I could hear and feel him sighing contentedly. "Wow," I asked with a bit of a laugh. "You okay?"

He rubbed his face back and forth against my chest like he was settling in even more comfortably but knowing he was tickling the hell out of me. He giggled in the cutest way and mumbled, "Yup. I'm just happy."

The next thing I knew it was morning. As my mind was pulled back to consciousness, I realized the bathroom was calling to me, but I couldn't move. I couldn't even feel my legs. As I became more aware of my surroundings, I discovered my problem, as there was an entire person laying over my legs.

"Dude!" I yelled with a laugh.

"Huh?" I heard muffled under the twisted-up blankets, "What's going on? Mmm. It's so warm." Then it was followed up by the most contented sigh. The laziest cat in the biggest sunbeam could not have sounded more relaxed.

"Hey," I laughed, pushing his head back and forth as he was draped over me. "Get off me. I've gotta piss!"

Of course, he fought lazily against me trying to move his head, nuzzling sleepily into his "pillow".

"I'm warning you, Boots!"

"Alright, alright," he mumbled.

He started moving, just not very fast. I threw the covers off of us violently, and he yelped as the chilly air of the room hit his body. I threw him off me with a laugh, climbing out of the bed. Giggling, Boots raced me to the bathroom.

We messed around like a couple of six-year-olds, teasing each other while washing our hands and brushing our teeth, reveling in being naughty and being happy. Once the giggling and goofing off wound down, I really expected us to get embarrassed, but it didn't happen. Now that this invisible barrier had been broken down, Boots was even more physical with his affection than he had been before, but neither of us felt weird about it.

CHAPTER SIXTY-FIVE

STRANGERS AND FRENEMIES

Everything stayed calm for a few days. I didn't hear from Wren and wasn't sure what to think about that. I really didn't know if I wanted to see him, hoping he would be back to normal, or if I was done with him and would be better off without the complications he brought.

Wednesday I went skating with the crew, and as it was getting dark Liam asked me about playing some Hammers & Hordes. We had played a couple of times in my basement, but since he wanted to pick up a new model we decided to play at LGM. It kind of worked out for me, because it was one of those rare nights when Boots was needed at home. He didn't want to say why, and I hoped hanging out with Liam would keep me from worrying about him.

It was well after dark when I got to LGM, and the Vampyre players were already at the tables. I worried about running into Wren, but neither he nor Erin were there. However, Garrett was. He lit up when he saw me, and nodded a hello my way. I worried a little over why he would seem excited to see me, but decided to ignore him. The twins weren't there, and Montgomery wasn't there. For the moment, that's all I really cared about.

The game was fun, and exactly what I needed to take my mind off things. I still hadn't beaten Liam, but with each game I played a little better than before, and I really thought I was learning. The last turn was a nail-biter, but really was mostly about whether my Commander died or not, and whether I lost by twenty-five points, or merely twenty.

Just as we were wrapping up, Garrett came over. He gave Liam a fist bump and a smile.

"Hey there, Liam. Haven't seen you in a while. Everything good?"

"Oh yeah," Liam answered. "I'm still playing and all that. Jason's got a sweet new table in his basement, so we've been playing a lot over there."

"Oh, really?" Garrett gave me a look I couldn't quite place. Definitely some level of amusement. Still looking at me, he said, "It's good to see that Jason's resources have been put to good use."

Flipping his smile and his gaze back to Liam, he asked, "Do you mind if I borrow Jason here for a moment? I need to talk to him about something real quick."

I had been both dreading and expecting him to want to say something, but I definitely wasn't going to ruffle Liam if he still had any "anti-Raven" memories drifting through his brain. However, he didn't seem to have any reaction at all, not even a shrug, damn the Mesmir. So reluctantly I followed Garrett a little way off. I didn't say anything though, forcing him to make the first move.

"No, I'm not going to try to talk to you about Wren," he said in a serious tone. Damn. I forgot he could read minds.

"Is this going to all be one-sided? You talk, and then pluck my opinions out of my head, whether I want to share them or not?"

He sighed in frustration, looking down and away. "I'm not reading your mind, Jason. I know you only think of me in terms of me hanging out with Wren, even without reading your mind. I'm here about something else, although honestly, I think you're right and he's being an unforgiving asshole."

"Unforgiving? What does he think I need to apolo–" I stopped myself and threw up my hands. "You know what? Doesn't matter. What did you want to talk to me about?"

"I want to see if you would be willing to meet someone. Someone who wants to talk to you about Dom."

I was surprised, and I know I showed it. "I thought you weren't involved in all the politics and stuff."

"I'm not. Or at least I try not to, as much as being on the council will let me.. But really, I think this is something you need to hear."

I tried to figure out if this could be some kind of trick, or trap. After all, this was Wren's best friend. Wren, who was currently pissed off at me and didn't want to bother explaining why. Would Garrett try to do something to me, in revenge for his friend? Would that risk a problem with Dom or the Si-Jing-Fu? Was Garrett being a poopy butt-zit and reading all this in my mind?

Cool, no reaction from Garrett. So, either he was keeping a good poker face, or he wasn't reading my mind. I stared at Garrett, imagining a giant, red pimple on his forehead, then it bursting and running down his face. Still no reaction from him. I guess my thoughts were safe for the moment.

I gave him one more annoyed look, then sighed and nodded. I figured that between my political coverage from being Dom's Assecla, and my own mediocre powers, I shouldn't be in too much danger for the moment. He nodded as well, seeming relieved.

"Grab your coat. He's outside."

When we stepped out front, I wasn't thrilled to find the sidewalk empty, but he started leading me down to the end of the line of stores. It was dark, definitely spooky, and I was already distrustful. I didn't care if I sounded like a wimp by this point.

"What's going on, Garrett? This really feels sketchy, and you already know you're not my favorite person."

"I get it. He's right here."

I stepped away from the corner of the building, staying where I could see him and not give him my back. I also stepped off to the side, not turning right at the corner in case someone was lying in wait. No way was I getting jumped today.

"Are you cautious?" came a soft voice as I came around the corner, "Or paranoid? Which is more helpful, I wonder?"

I turned to be faced by an ancient Chinese "stereotype" old man with a "stereotype" long stringy mustache.

"We must talk, Jason. Will you speak with me?"

"I get why you couldn't come in the store, but it's cold as hell out here. Can't we talk underground or something?"

"It is not safe to speak of what we must, in any place where other Vampyre might overhear."

Garrett jumped in. "We could go to your house, if you think that will work better for you."

"How 'bout you give me the short version now?"

"My name is To Hong Bai. You may call me Bai. I– I should say, we," he motioned to Garrett, "have been working against Beishang de Wenyi and his machinations here in Avernus."

"You mean things that Si-Jing-Fu hasn't bothered putting a stop to? Like, oh, breaking into my house to stalk me in my bedroom?"

"Bigger even than that," said Bai. "I would prefer to save anything further until we meet at your house. The privacy of this conversation is paramount"

"Can you give me an hour? Or do we need to continue this immediately?"

They both glanced at one another, and Bai nodded. "We will see you in one hour."

"I guess you can use the door in the basement. But knock first. And I've covered over the peep hole." I looked at Garrett. "Are you coming as well?"

"Do I have an invitation?"

I laughed. "Is this the old Vampire trap about needing an invitation to enter a house?"

"No," he grinned. "Just curious if I was welcome. After all, I'm 'not your favorite person'".

Chapter Sixty-Six

Frenemies and Conspiracies

I quickly headed home, where I fixed something quick to eat while waiting. I was trying to think over all the events since I'd been in Avernus, seeing what I knew about the politics of the Vampyre here. There had to be plenty I didn't know about, especially considering Wren had said Mr. Tsui only controlled the area around the Avernus Inn and Suites. So, Mr. Tsui and his allies was one. He could be shady and definitely acted in his own self-interest, but he seemed quite confident in his power and abilities.

Garrett and this new guy, Bai, said they were working to stop Plague from something. Whatever his plans were. No idea where the twins are in all this. Wren is Garrett's friend, but he also seems to be working well with Mr. Tsui. Is he part of this anti-Plague conspiracy?

Then of course, there was Plague himself. Everyone seems to hate him. But that doesn't mean he doesn't have his own friends and cohorts.

Just as I was plating my food, Boots showed up. I didn't even hesitate but split my food onto a second plate and threw some extra chicken nuggets in the air fryer.

"Everything alright at home?"

He groaned. "Can we not talk about it?"

"Sure, but it's probably tame compared to what I've got."

"Really? Sounds like you couldn't even get through a game with Liam, without Vampyre crap getting involved?"

"You know it," I said as I started eating. "And this is one better. I got to meet a couple of people involved in some super-secret fight against Plague of Sorrows."

"Wait, fighting against? So, he's a problem for more people than just us?"

"I mean, he's been a problem for Mr. Tsui since I got here. Or really, Plague is supposed to be the reason Mr. Tsui even brought me up here. But yeah, there's other people considering him enough of a problem to fight against him."

"Like fight-fight? Or just 'beat him in the next election' kind of thing?"

"I'm not completely sure, but I don't get the impression that Plague is bothered with being political. One of them is Garrett, Wren's friend. No idea how that is tangled up. But he and this guy, Bai, claim they have been working behind the scenes against Plague. They're actually coming over in a bit to fill me in on what's going on."

"Garrett needs to decide whether he wants to be a good guy, or keep being an arrogant ass. I barely talk to him and I don't like him. So can I stay and hear this? Please?"

"Don't you think you should wait upstairs? What happened to staying low and not letting them know you aren't Mesmired or whatever?"

Boots was giving me some real sad puppy dog eyes here. I didn't think it was worth the risk, but I also didn't think it was really my call. Part of respecting someone as a real person was letting them take their own risks.

"Let's go find a good place to hide you. They should be here soon."

I swear, if Boots had a tail, he'd be wagging it! It was definitely cute. We clambered down the stairs and started looking at what we could shift around. It had to be far enough away for him to be effectively hidden, but close enough that he could hear anything being said. In the end, we threw a sheet over the pool table and stacking some boxes and stuff on it.

"You know," he said as we were finishing up, "this gives you some backup. If they start messing with your mind, I'll be here as a witness, to snap you back out of it."

"If that's the plan, hold onto this just in case."

I handed him the broken pool cue I had swung at Plague. He started to duck under the table but suddenly changed his mind and ran to the bathroom first. He was quick and came back out after washing his hands, to find me grinning.

"What?" he chuckled. "I didn't want to give them the opportunity to scare the piss out of me!"

"Goof," I said as I helped him under the table.

Now it was my turn to sit around nervously. I didn't want to strike up a conversation, in case they just walked right in, or could hear us through the door. I paced for a little bit, then sat on the couch. When I stood back up a minute later, Boots muttered, "Jeez, calm down, dude!"

I sat back down and pulled out my phone, just to try and distract myself. I don't think I would have been nearly as nervous if I didn't have Boots hiding in the basement with me. Maybe this wasn't such a good idea. Just as I was about to say as much and ask him to run upstairs, there was a tapping on the wall. It was too late now.

I hopped up and went over to the wall, knocking back. The secret door opened and Garrett poked his head in. "Quick question. Is it okay if Bai stays in his natural form? Playing human after dark tends to drain some energy."

"When you say 'natural form', do you mean the float—"

"Floating head, yeah."

I sighed in annoyance. "Look, if you are just going to sit here and read my thoughts all night, what's the point in talking? But yeah, whatever he needs. Just stay out of my head, either mind reading or magic. Hopefully Bai isn't going to start talking about feeding on my friends and family though, just 'cause he's in spooky mode."

Garrett laughed. "So no Cor Decere, no Mesmir, and no threats. Got it." In a more serious face he added, "I just ask one thing in return, that you listen, really listen, before you do anything."

I nodded, and Garrett slipped back out the door for just a moment, then came right back in. He was quickly followed by a Jiangshi. I knew it was Bai, but what did I know about one Jiangshi from the next?

"Is the human form an illusion? Or do you really have a physical body you slip in and out of?"

"It is... a form of... mental projection.... It is unknown... how we do it.. We just do it... naturally...."

Damn, I was biting my tongue, but if all of his speech was going to be this slow and wheezing, I sure hoped Garrett was going to do most of the explaining.

"Right," I said while sitting back down. "You're welcome to have a seat, assuming you do sit?" I looked between the two of them. "I'm not trying to be rude. I just don't know what's protocol with a floater."

Bai sighed. At least I think it was a sigh. He released a long, low wheeze of air while dipping his chin and shaking his head slightly. A greater volume of red mist began flowing from beneath him, then as if in reverse camera footage the mist retracted back to his center, forming the human body he had worn outside the LGM.

"I'm sorry," I said as he sat down on the futon across from me. "I wasn't trying to cause problems."

"It is understandable," he said, folding his hands in his lap. Garrett slipped off the other end of the couch and joined Bai across from me. "I forget how difficult it can be for you to interact with one of my kind."

"Well thanks for being so understanding, I guess." I slapped my hands on my knees in nervousness. "I guess we're alone now. So what's being done to fight Plague of Sorrows?"

"You were told about how Dominic was sent away from the Americas," began Bai. "But were you told why?"

I shook my head. "Just something about the Jiangshi needing to be banished."

"Two in particular. One was hunted down in his home territory in Jiangxi Province, in China, nearly two hundred years ago. He had turned feral and killed too many people, too publicly. The other..." He paused, as if he didn't want to finish.

"The other was Beishang de Wenyi, the Plague of Sorrows," finished Garrett.

Bai nodded. "He was barely tolerated by those in power while back in his home territory these last few centuries. He was in his home region and knew how to feed his appetites while barely raising enough ire from those in power for them to feel he was worth the fight. But here, before being forced back to China, he was feeding on and terrorizing whole communities, both colonial and native."

Garrett added, "Plague was the Vampyre equivalent of a serial killer."

CHAPTER SIXTY-SEVEN

NOT SO SECRETS

Well, that wasn't scary or anything. So, I have a serial killer messing with me and my friends. Great.

But I was confused about the big picture. "Is this situation with Plague somehow linked with this 'promise' everyone keeps mentioning?"

"It is," said Bai. "And it is part of why China was so willing to allow this move to occur, since Beishang de Wenyi would be leaving with us. Dominic Tsui was to provide the Jiangshi a safe base, a home, here in the Americas. A place to establish ourselves until we were, each on our own, prepared to move on. Each of us were to spread out to find our own territory to feed and survive."

"He hasn't done that? It seems like that's what Avernus is?"

"The Plague of Sorrows was to be contained here in Avernus. Instead, we have all been imprisoned here."

"Wait," I said, just catching up on another detail. "Are you saying Mr. Tsui built Avernus? Like, the whole town and everything?"

Garrett shook his head. "The town was already here, and the underground facilities were an old Cold War-era military complex. There was also a small collection of Vampyre eking out an existence here. But Dom expanded it, pouring money into the town to ensure humans would come here. He offered the Chinese Vampyre a place here and then tempted many of the younger looking Vampyre from around the country with an invitation to come to a place where they would fit in due to sheer numbers."

Giving something of a self-deprecating chuckle, Garrett said, "Most Vampyre turned early, say twenty-five and younger, have a harder time blending into society. It just takes so much less time to realize we aren't aging. Too many groups shun younger Vampyre, for their own safety. Dom opened Avernus, and many of us took up his invitation. That's why there are so many of us here who look like teenagers or college aged individuals."

I nodded. "I also wondered why the 'Kung Fu' council had a Chinese name. So, Dom really runs Avernus."

"No," said Bai. "He may have backed much of the work, but the Si-Jing-Fu is truly a community led council. He controls territory around his hotel, he owns the plant where a good chunk of the townsfolk work, and he holds a seat on the council. But Avernus is far from his alone. It is also true, however, that Dominic has enacted a barrier, a Jiéjiè, which now prevents any of the Jiangshi from leaving."

"How many of you are here?" I asked.

"Twenty-three Jiangshi," said Garrett grimly. "And since the Jiangshi feed on nightmares and mental misery, their presence in such concentration has been slowly driving the humans here mad for years."

"Damn, no wonder this place feels broken. So why won't he release you guys?"

"Ostensibly it is to keep Beishang de Wenyi from leaving, but it also comes down to power and protection," said Garrett. "With Bai and his buddies here, most Vampyre won't come near Avernus. Too many horror stories. And it does make sense, after a fashion. It was especially helpful in the early years of establishing Si-Jing-Fu and the Vampyre community."

"Seriously?" I laughed. "Sounds seriously lame!"

"And yet true," said Bai.

"So, what's with the attacks on Dom? Are those real, or just BS he was using to manipulate me?"

"No, they're real," said Garrett. "Some of the Jiangshi were desperate enough to try force in order to get away. And that's why as much as we may not agree with Dom on many things, you need to understand how much of a threat Beishang de Wenyi is. He is likely equal in raw power to Dom."

"He still is? I thought my power boost made Mr. Tsui strong enough that Plague's attacks would have to stop."

Bai nodded. "Dominic Tsui has gained enough power from you, his Assecla, to finally overshadow Plague in most respects."

"So, if he has more power now, and I'm so important to him, why isn't Mr. Tsui doing something about him?"

"Dom is old," said Garrett. "Scary levels of old, if the rumors are to be believed. While this means more power, it also means he can be annoyingly slow to act."

"In addition," added Bai, "part of his agreement to bring us to the Americas was a vow that he could not destroy a Jiangshi. So, it is entirely possible he simply does not yet have a plan that falls short of death."

Regardless of how downright terrifying the whole situation was, it was refreshing actually getting some questions answered so directly. "So, since Plague didn't like me giving Mr. Tsui that leg up, does that mean Plague or one of the other Jiangshi was trying to get me held up at the airport on the way back from my dad's funeral?"

"It was a desperate ploy," said Bai, "and one we haven't fully deduced. Beishang de Wenyi does not have the contacts or resources for such a move, and nor do any of the Jiangshi here in Avernus. But we are certain it was enacted by someone working for or with him. Fortunately, you were able to alert Wren Stormbreak, who was able to use Si-Jing-Fu resources and contacts to bring you home."

I grinned at the memory. "I gotta know. Were those guys actually Secret Service?"

"They were indeed," said Garrett. "And no, I can't tell you anything else about that."

"Damn," I said. "I suppose my second question then is, where is Wren in all this? Is he fighting against Plague? Is he pushing against Mr. Tsui because of the politics? Basically, considering whatever recently happened... is he an ally and friend?"

Bai and Garrett shared a look, then the Jiangshi said, "I do not have any information on this. You are his friend and companion."

Garrett sighed. "Look, Wren isn't exactly blameless here, but he's not going to let his personal feelings keep him from doing the right thing. He just isn't. He's been on the opposite side of most issues from Dom, yet he still works with him. And I can't see him becoming an asshole just because of a fight."

My eyebrows raised. "Do you know this? Or is this Wren's best friend talking?"

Garrett took a deep breath. "I don't–"

He stopped mid-sentence, then took a deeper, sharper inhale. With a sly grin, he looked at me. "Who's here, Jason? Where are they?"

"What?"

No, no, no, no! I fought hard to stay calm, but adrenaline shot through me and my heart leapt into my throat. This is exactly what I had been worried about. I needed to deflect. I had to.

"What do you–"

"There is a human here with us, Jason. They have heard things they shouldn't. Who is it?"

"No, no. I have friends over here all the time. One friend practically lives here in my basement most nights. That's gotta be who you're smelling, right?"

"Bai?"

The Jiangshi stood, then like a miniature explosion, his form collapsed into red mist, leaving him floating in his 'spooky head' form. That "escaping gas" sound started up, and those spots of pink sparkling electricity began flickering through the clouds around him. Interestingly, along with the lightning came that flower-and-vomit smell. So that wasn't unique to Plague. Plus it only seemed to happen when they powered up or whatever.

He turned and began drifting slowly right past me and Garrett, toward the middle of the room where the table was hiding Boots. Poorly, it would seem.

"Ah... I sense... his mind..."

"Damn," I muttered. I don't even know why I was bothering. I had forgotten I was in a conversation with a creepy creature who was psychic through and through. Oh yeah, plus Bai.

"Guys, you have your secrets, and I have mine. I have a friend who isn't under your town's Mesmir. I'm not going to out him, because you're just going to go straight to melting his brain."

Garrett shook his head. "Jason, this is dangerous."

"I don't care!" I shouted. "Have you heard of any problems being caused? Has anyone said anything? I bit my tongue when I screwed up and Liam got outed and back under Mesmir. I didn't know what was going on then, and I also know he was having an attitude about you guys. So I get it. But this other friend hasn't caused any problems. Hasn't said anything!"

"Except to you," said Garrett softly.

I deflated instantly. "Except to me. Yeah. Look, you want my help? You want me to trust you? Then this is my price. My friend is left alone."

Garrett and Bai shared another glance.

"Look," I said. "My dad's dead. Killed by Dom. My mom's gone, her brain fried with Mesmir before she even left physically. You gotta give me this." I looked from one to the other. "Please."

They exchanged another look. Bai gave a small nod, and Garrett said, "I think I know who it is anyway, but we'll leave this with you. His safety, and his mess ups, are on you. You are responsible for your friend and what he does. Just know that if he does cause any problems, Si-Jing-Fu will treat it as if you have done it. Are you good with that?"

I nodded.

"We need... you... to say it..."

"Fine," I said in frustration. "Monkey see, monkey do. If he does it, I did it. You guys are being real dicks about this, but at least you're letting it go."

"Hey, we're running real close to putting our lives on the line with this," said Garrett. "The biggest reason we are agreeing is that we are already deep enough as it is. Vampyre law charges the Vampyre for the actions of their humans."

"Wait," I said as something else occurred to me. "How much trouble would Dom be in if his hotel employees were talking about Vampyre stuff in front of random guests?"

Garrett looked stunned. I had no idea if Bai was showing any surprise. "Like what kind of business? What was the conversation?"

"My parents were complaining about having nightmares when we were staying at the hotel, and when two of the employees were talking, one of them said they were surprised my parents were in that specific room. Something about, they thought they were supposed to be being nice to my family. They acted like their room assignment was why they were having nightmares."

"And they had this conversation in front of you?"

"Well, in the hallway outside my room, before my door was closed. Wren once said Plague fed on my parents when we were staying at the hotel, right?"

"Many of... my kind... will use the rooms... below guests... to feed from strangers... passing through..."

"But Beishang de Wenyi opposed Dom bringing your family here. His compromise with Dom was that he be allowed to feed on your parents himself. The Plague of Sorrows was responsible for your parents' bad dreams. Dom's staff was certainly out of line, but if that's the extent of what they said, it likely wouldn't be enough for Dom to be censured."

"Damn. Oh well. You and Wren have both mentioned that word, 'censured'. What is that?"

"To be censured is to have a black mark. Kind of an extreme disciplinary measure. In the short term, it could mean a loss of allies of convenience, as other Vampyre scramble to not be associated with you in other Vampyre's minds. Privileges and responsibilities could be stripped for a time. Long term, others might seek you out when things go wrong, looking to see if you are to blame. It also makes future censuring more likely."

"But is it something we could use to 'convince' him to step up his help?"

"Blackmail?" said Garrett. "As amusing as that might be, hell no. That's juggling with nuclear-powered dynamite, and it's the quickest way to turn him into a real enemy."

I shook my head. "Okay, I get it. Fine. So, what's the next step? What's the plan?"

"We have... not yet decided.... We merely–"

"We just wanted to get you into the loop," said Garrett. "Can we count on you?"

I nodded hesitantly.

"By the way," said Garrett with a smirk, "that's a nice table you have over there. Is it the Hammers & Hordes table Liam mentioned? That's gotta be pretty sweet." He paused, then added, "I'll bet there's lots of storage space underneath it."

CHAPTER SIXTY-EIGHT

CLEANSING BODY AND SOUL

I winced at Garrett's remark and ushered them out the door. I didn't care if I was being rude, I needed time to think. I even remembered that I might want to do something with the door, while it was open and inspect-able.

"Guys, before you disappear, do I need to leave this door in case you need it? Or is it safer for me to close it off?"

Garrett glanced over at Bai as he floated out in the white hallway, then said, "If you're too worried, do what you need to do. But it might be better if we have an emergency way to meet with you. Particularly if we need to sneak you down here into the Warrens."

I nodded and sent them on their way, wincing as I watched the door seal, evading my best chance of blocking it off. Then I turned away and helped Boots out from under the table.

"Damn, I thought for sure they were going to jump under here and drag me out!"

"I was worried that was going to happen, too. But I think they are going to leave you alone. It seems like you are my problem now."

I grabbed him in a headlock, and he tried pulling away. We both started laughing as we fell to the couch in a heap. It was less about really being amused, and more about blowing off the tension. And deep down, I think I needed to feel that he was real. After tussling and goofing around for a few minutes, we settled down and fell back into the couch, shoulder to shoulder, catching our breaths.

"Are you worried?" asked Boots.

"Paralyzingly terrified. But one way or another, this has got to be handled. I'm stuck in this, as sure as if I were born into this messed up family." I sighed. "In a way, I guess I was."

"Hey, at least you know they are going to let me here to help you, right? You know I got your back."

"Yeah, and I appreciate it."

"And... " Boots tried to make eye contact with me but couldn't quite do it. "You know I gotta ask, right?"

There was no point in playing dumb. "Yeah. I was kind of hoping you didn't catch that."

"What happened when Liam went back to being a zombie? What did you mean when you said you screwed up?"

"I didn't know who anyone was yet, or I guess, *what* anyone was, and when Liam's name came up, I made a comment about him always being pissed off whenever I mentioned meeting the Ravens. Next thing I knew, they had mindwiped him. It wasn't until later I realized it was my fault. Whether I knew or not, I screwed up and the fallout is on me."

I sighed and stared at the far wall. "I've actually been pretty pissed off about it, mostly at myself."

"I thought it might be something like that. But I guess you didn't know what was going on yet. So I get it. It's not your fault. I can't be mad at you for their psychotic paranoia. I'm glad you stuck up for me right now. I'm sure if you ever need to, now that you know what's going on, you would stick up for Liam as well."

"I'd absolutely do my damnedest."

"Liam going back to being a zombie, this is about that Mesmir you mentioned before, right? And what they were talking about?"

"Yes, it is. So, not to change the subject too much," I said, still not able to risk eye contact. "Are you, uh, okay with everything last Saturday? I mean, that was a pretty big leap. We're not exactly 'just friends' after that."

"Yeah, it was great!" he piped up, clearly relieved for the lighter topic. "Why, are you having second thoughts or something?"

"No, not at all. I just wanted to ask. I mean, after all, I didn't do anything back."

"Yeah," he said with a giggle, as he bumped shoulders with me. "You kind of fell asleep instantly. It seemed like you needed the rest."

It was my turn to smile. "You didn't exactly seem too uncomfortable where you were."

"I didn't mind," he said softly.

Last weekend had been spontaneous, at least for me. I had no idea how premeditated it might have been for Boots. For all I know, he could have been planning for hours or even days, exactly what he wanted to do. We also hadn't done anything more or even talked about it until now. And while everything with Wren was certainly sexy, it was like he said, there was no innocence to it. Messing around with Wren was all about getting off in the hottest way possible.

This fight I had with Wren made me reevaluate the whole thing with him as well. My body loved being with him. But emotionally he was clueless. He's never had a real relationship before. He's flippant and casual, and he's never had to *care* before. And if he thought there was something I needed to apologize for? Yeah, he could go hang.

Not the same with Boots though. With Boots, I actually liked him. He's not just cute and sexy, though he is also both. I liked being with him. Not just naked stuff but just being in the same room. I trusted him, and he trusted me.

I told Boots I needed to get a shower. When he stalled about getting up off the couch, I stopped at the bottom of the basement stairs and was like, "Well? Are you coming?"

He grinned and practically launched off the couch, following me up the basement stairs at a run. I stopped to make sure the house was locked up and the lights were out, then headed upstairs. When I got to my bedroom, the light was off, but the bathroom light was streaming into the bedroom. I peeked in as I was pulling my hoodie over my head, and saw Boots leaning against the far wall, smiling shyly with his legs crossed and his hands folded across his very naked lap. He looked like a cross between excited and nervous, positively vibrating in anticipation.

By the time I was ready, Boots had stepped up and started the shower. I walked in to join him in the bathroom and he kind of stood there, his arms wrapped around his torso. I'd never seen him this shy. He definitely wasn't like this last Saturday.

"Is this really okay?" he asked.

I grinned and walked right up to him. In answer, I reached up to his face, but my hand around to the back up his head and pulled him in for a kiss.

I did my best to give him the kind of kiss you see in movies, the kind you're always embarrassed about seeing your dad give your mom. My lineup was perfect, face tilted slightly so our noses wouldn't squish, lips parted, after a moment, tongue searching forward to ask him to open his own lips.

His lips melted into mine as his body pressed against me. With one hand holding the back of his head, the other reached around his lower back, pulling our hips together. For a moment he seemed unsure what to do with his own hands, but very quickly they began sliding all around my back.

Eventually I began to pull back from the kiss and he let me, albeit reluctantly. His eyes were closed and he appeared to be in such a state that I don't think he could have fought me even if he had wanted to.

"Come on, sexy," I whispered. "Let's get cleaned up."

I turned Boots away from me and grabbed the body wash and a washcloth. I could see him tense, then visibly relax as I started scrubbing his back. When I got to his hair, I realized it was getting longer. I liked it though. It made him look soft, without being girly. His hair wasn't quite blond, more of a light brown, but it was thin, and soft, and straight. Even dry, it had almost no curl at all to it.

Washing him down allowed me to admire his body. Maybe he was hitting a little growth spurt, or maybe he was just starting to finally get regular meals or something, but he seemed to be filling out a bit more. Don't get me wrong, he was still skinny as hell, but he didn't seem as bony as I remembered.

I couldn't help myself and nuzzled his neck, which caused him to dance away, laughing. I moved forward, trapping him in the corner. Grinning like a hungry predator, I thought it would be cool to have a little fun with some of my new abilities.

Reaching for my superspeed, my Velos, I looked around in awe as the water droplets froze in place. I picked Boots up by grabbing his upper arms and moved him where he was a hair's breadth from the wall, placing my body against him. Letting time rush back, I pressed him against the wall and went in for a kiss.

He let out a gasp, letting my lips find his, and my tongue invaded his mouth. His gasp turned into a moan, but when he started shaking his head, I realized it was a moan of pain.

"What's wrong?" I asked, taking a step back. He crossed his arms over his chest, grabbing his upper arms, feeling them tenderly. I winced in sympathy as I could already see red discoloration on each arm despite the heat of the water. Discoloration clearly the size and shape of my fingers. I wanted to cry when I realized I had hurt him.

"Oh my God," I said softly. "I'm so sorry."

So much for a funny prank. Better not to touch people during Velos.

I reached out to hold him, and for the tiniest moment he flinched, but he just as quickly relaxed into my embrace.

"I'm alright," he said into my shoulder. "Learning curve and all that, right?"

I couldn't see his face in our hug, but I could hear the grin in his voice.

"Right," I said, stepping back to let him see my smile. "Let's rinse off and I can make it up to you in be—"

I hit a slick spot on the tiles and my foot slipped. The world flipped sideways, my vision going crazy as my foot flew out from under me. I reached out to catch myself, feeling Boots scrambling to grab my arm. I felt the cold tile outside the shower on my shoulder, contrasting with a warm spot centered on the back of my head. Seemingly retroactively I heard a dull 'thunk', like a watermelon being torn open. Then nothing.

CHAPTER SIXTY-NINE

TOGETHER ALONE

As I began waking, I fought to figure out what I was feeling. I was warm, but not really. It was almost like when we had a really muggy day back in Alabama. There were times when the air was so thick with humidity it didn't matter what the temperature was, even in the air conditioning you were going to sweat. It was just inevitable. It felt like that, but not quite.

That's when I realized I was all warm in bed, under the blankets, but that the bedding was damp. That was the cooler, wet discomfort I was feeling. I stirred, trying to figure out what was going on, and felt Boots shift against me. He mumbled something incoherent, pulling me against him.

We were asleep in my bed, and the room was awash with the harsh white light of the bathroom at our back. The sheets we were laying in were soaked, and as my brain started working again, I realized I couldn't remember how we got here.

Boots was laying behind me, playing the big spoon. I could tell he was just as wet, as damp, as... moist... as me. And although I realized neither of us were wearing anything, I was too out of it to care as much as I knew I should. I felt incredibly weak, almost feverish. I desperately wanted to get up and do something about the absolutely nasty discomfort I was feeling, but I literally didn't have it in me.

I woke up again to a more normal sensation, the need to pee. Boots was still cuddled up with me, and the sun was shining in through the curtains. Time to get out of this soaked bed. I pulled Boots against me, waking him up with a hug. He started to stir, then opened his eyes.

"Get up, slug-a-bug," I said. I wanted to kiss him again but felt self-conscious here in the daylight.

"Slug-a-bug?" he laughed. "What the hell?"

"I don't know," I said with a bit of embarrassment. I started climbing from under the blankets as I muttered, "It's something my mom used to say when I was a kid and being lazy."

"So now I'm being lazy?"

"Totally lazy," I said, shivering a bit.

Giggling, Boots ran around the bed, racing me to the toilet. I was laughing about how stupid we were being, when suddenly I was the only one laughing. In fact, I was the only one making noise.

"Boots? What's –"

He was frozen in place, standing in front of me and staring into the bathroom. "Boots?" I spoke softly.

I looked past him and suddenly didn't have to ask why he was upset, as there was blood in the floor of the shower. In the better areas it was diluted into a pale pink lined in the spaces between the floor tiles. In others the stark red lay in swirls that looked dainty and delicate. Almost pretty, if you didn't know it was blood.

My blood.

He didn't respond. I put my hand on his bare shoulder, and he didn't so much jump as shiver.

"What happened? One minute we were in the... in the shower, and the next we woke up in bed."

"Oh God, Jason," Boots said in barely a whisper. "I was so worried about you. You fell, and there was so much blood. And then there wasn't."

"You slipped on the soap," he continued in a voice near dead of emotion, pointing to the offending bar in the corner. "You went down so fast I couldn't catch you. I nearly fell on top of you, trying to catch you."

Boots' voice was still devoid of emotion, but began picking up in speed and volume, as if he was expelling the words forcefully. "Blood began spreading out across the ground, almost black. It looked fake, like a bad movie. And the water was still spraying down and hitting your face, and you weren't reacting and I grabbed you up and was yelling for you to answer me!"

I grabbed Boots from behind, pulling him back against my chest. We were nearly the same height, so I rested my chin on his shoulder, forcing his head to the side. His voice was breaking, beginning to show his panic, and I felt like I needed to hold him, to ground him. To remind him I was still here.

He tensed up for a split second, then relaxed back against me. After a moment he continued talking, this time more relaxed.

"At first there was so much blood. I put your head over in my lap, trying to get you to respond. The shower was so loud, I couldn't even tell if you were breathing. My hands were getting sticky and my legs were getting covered in blood. There was so much." His voice caught as he choked up for a second. When he continued, his voice was more settled.

"But then you gave this loud, deep inhale of breath. I had to turn you away so you wouldn't swallow a ton of water or something. So, then you were obviously breathing, but still unconscious. That's when I realized the water was running more pink than red. The color was weaker and weaker. I felt the back of your head and couldn't find any wound or anything.

"I did what I could to clean us both up and dragged you into the bedroom. It was all I could do to drag you into there and lift you into the bed. I think I was still out of it, because the last thing I remember was climbing in behind you. I seriously don't even remember falling asleep."

"Well, I seem to be fine now," I said, giving his body a squeeze. Of course I was absolutely *not* fine. But while I suffered the injury, Boots suffered the trauma. For his sake I could feed him the happy encouragement I could tell he needed. So, I smiled and pulled us into the bathroom.

"I guess one of the good things about what I am now is that I have super-healing. Let's rinse off real quick and go get some breakfast. We still have school."

Chapter Seventy

Romantic Runaround

Other than being hungrier than usual, I didn't seem to be suffering any lasting effects. Boots was maybe a little quieter at school but insisted he was fine. When we got home after school, I saw the upstairs was all cleaned up, the bathroom spotless and my bed stripped and remade. I shot Mrs. Sinclair a quick thank you while we started making dinner. I even managed to tease Boots about us making a "cute little domestic couple". He blushed a bit and grinned but didn't knock it.

We were just cleaning up our dishes and discussing a possible game of Hammers & Hordes when my phone sounded with a text. Checking it out, I saw it was from Montgomery's number.

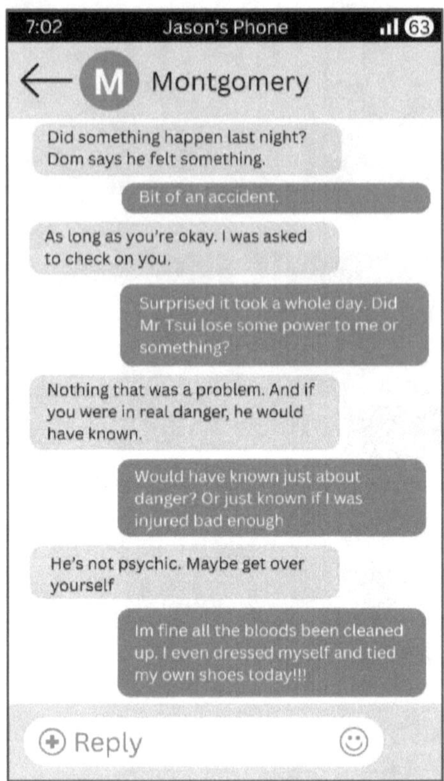

I was not surprised when I didn't get any more responses back. I hadn't intended to be snarky, but I couldn't help myself after all. So, sue me. Good to see Montgomery was his reliably terrible self. After all this, I still loved that they dodged direct questions. No real answers ever given.

Boots and I had a couple of days alone, where we were able to re-normalize ourselves from the accident. Then I got talked into everyone staying over Saturday night, as if it was hard. We were all sitting around eating pizza and playing video games, and I relaxed and goofed off with the guys. I had some concern that Boots might act different around the rest of the guys now that we had hooked up, but so far I didn't feel like he was acting any different.

As for the guys, it was really cool I was able to hook everyone up, provide tons of snacks and offer a stress-free place to hang out that wasn't lame. Even better, the crew didn't fawn over me, trying to thank me all the time or act like they owed me. They were cool, said "gracias", and let it go. Nobody made out like I was buying my way in or anything.

In between rounds of video games, Wheeler got into a big debate with Scott about who were some of the hottest girls in our school. Apparently, they varied widely on what they each considered "hot". Taki quickly joined in, even as he solidly trounced my character on the screen in front of us.

"Nobody needs to ask my boy Liam here about his opinion," said Wheeler, laughing and throwing his arm over Liam's shoulder. "We all know he's all about the freak Raven girl at the comic store!"

Liam turned fifty shades of red as I looked over at him with my jaw on the floor. Surely, they didn't mean—

"You mean the crazy white haired twin chicks?" asked Scott in confusion.

If Liam was red before, his face was positively scarlet now. Wheeler doubled over in hard laughter, which set everyone else off to laughing. It took a few minutes, but finally Wheeler calmed down enough to wave Scott off. "No, no, man. One of 'em's a dude!"

"I heard that," said Scott, "but I didn't believe it. Besides, why are we talking about Ravens, as if they're cool?"

"Hey, hot is hot, Raven or not!" Wheeler said with a laugh. "But for real, yeah. One of the white-haired chicks is a dude." He turned from Scott over to me. "You've been hanging with 'em, Jase. Tell Scott here I ain't lying!"

The whole room was looking at me now. Boots looked at me nervously. I tried to read his face. Was he worried we were getting into Raven discussions, or was it a more personal angle, touching on Wren? Everyone else was expectant, still on the edge of laughter. I didn't know how to take things yet, so I just nodded without saying anything.

"Let me guess," joked Scott. "Did you find out the 'hard' way?"

Now it was my turn to blush a bit, my body instantly remembering Wren and his magical touch. But I was also getting a bit defensive, especially with Boots in the room. We hadn't really touched on sexuality and opinions as a group too much.

Taki looked over at me, not pissed, but not really laughing anymore. "By that reaction, I'd almost think you've been stepping out on our boy Boots," he said, throwing his arm around Boots' shoulder.

"Say it ain't so," exclaimed Liam. "You're the best thing that's happened to Boots in forever! Are you cheating on him with the twin?"

"The *twin,*" I emphasized, "is someone I haven't even talked to in at least a week."

"So?" Taki shot right back at me. "You've been 'hanging out' with Boots for a lot more than 'at least a week'."

"Guys, guys!" I threw my hands up in surrender, tossing down the controller. "First, it's none of your damn business who I'm with or not with." I was trying to keep it light and not get pissed. Still, I was surprised things were so open. "If you really must know, not," I threw a smile and some southern charm into my words, "that it's any of your *damn* business, but even though I am not exclusively dating *anyone*, not naming ANY names..." I grinned at Boots, who smiled back, "I haven't been with anyone else since I've been with a certain someone else."

I ended with a smirk, and after a beat of dead silence, everyone busted out laughing, even Boots. And since his reaction was the one I was most concerned about, I relaxed.

"You dog!" yelled Taki. "So you really have hooked up with someone else besides Boots?"

"For real, did you actually hook up with Wren?" asked Liam. Then a bit softer, "Or Erin?"

I got up off the couch, saying, "A gentleman doesn't kiss and tell." Halfway across to the pool table, I added, "And neither do I!" Which got another laugh. Then I put my hand on Liam's shoulder, leaned in, and whispered, "I'm just friends with Erin. I'm no rival there." I felt his shoulder relax a bit, and he was smiling when I pulled back.

Considering the original conversations when I first met these guys, I was very surprised over how relaxed everyone was when talking about Wren and Erin. The conversation moved back to lighter topics, but I also noticed the time was slipping away and it was getting later. I kind of looked around at everyone else. Someone was missing.

"Guys, where's Boots?"

Everyone kind looked around at everyone else, shaking their heads. But Wheeler casually said, "He left just a second ago. Said something about checking in with his folks, so maybe he's upstairs on his phone?"

I headed upstairs, but looking around, he wasn't anywhere I could find. I even ran upstairs and ran through the bedrooms. He hadn't said anything, which if nothing was wrong hurt my feelings a little. I double checked my phone again, just to make sure.

Trying to hide my concern, I headed back down to the basement. "I don't see him."

Taki looked up, saying, "He's not here? I guess he had to run home instead."

"You guys know his address?"

They all laughed as I started up the stairs, shouting out catcalls and whistles as they teased me good-naturedly out of the basement. I threw on my heavy coat as I stepped out of the house, throwing up my hoodie and dreading the freezing drizzle outside.

Did I really think something was wrong? Not necessarily. Still, it seemed out of character for the Boots I had come to know, for him to not have said something to me.

Maybe something was going on with the parents he didn't want me to know about. Maybe he thought I would think less of him. I remember how messed up my head would get when keeping stuff about my parents from Alen back home. But on the flip side, I really was worried something from my problems might have happened to him. And that was something I couldn't live with.

CHAPTER SEVENTY-ONE

DUEL AT HIGH DARK

Jeez, it was cold. It wasn't raining exactly, more of a slushy mist at the moment. But the wind was swirling it around, making it impossible to keep out of my face, and making it feel ten times colder. My eyes were stinging and I was looking down at my feet as I trudged along down the street. My GPS said it was a little over twenty minutes to walk there. I thought about pulling out the Velos, but I'd never done it in the rain, and with my luck I'd slip in a puddle and get eighty yards of road rash to the face sliding to a stop. So instead, I walked.

I was a bit over halfway there when I got a text from a number I didn't recognize.

Where are you currently? Dominic Tsui has ordered that you go to ground. There are complications being addressed.

What the hell? I guess that meant trouble, but they didn't identify themselves. Was it Garrett or Bai? Someone else? I guess it should have been obvious they were trying to stay secret, since they were texting from an unknown number. Then I remembered Wren saying his number was one digit off from Montgomery's. Maybe a bunch of Vampyre had a big group of numbers, like maybe the Si-Jing-Fu had a business account or something. But I checked and no, this number wasn't even close.

I kept going, but when I turned onto the street Boots' house was on, I saw someone just standing in the middle of the street. They weren't watching any of the houses. Instead, they were watching me. I wanted to run, to save myself, to avoid whatever Vampyre crap this was going to add to my night. But I couldn't just walk away until I knew what was on the line. I needed to know Boots was okay. That he wasn't involved. That he didn't need my help.

As I approached, they raised their hand in greeting, and I recognized it was Montgomery. I would have waved back, but I didn't want to pull my hand out of my pocket. I kind of half waved my pocket at waist level as a compromise.

"Dom will be glad to see you are okay," he said as I approached within earshot.

"Why wouldn't I be? What are you doing here?" I tried to keep my tone from being accusatory and instead went for curious.

"Dominic sent me to find you. He didn't say why. I didn't ask."

His voice was pleasant enough, but I could also see he was being snide and condescending. I couldn't tell if it was him being annoyed at being sent on an errand on a miserable night like this, or if it was something more personal with me.

"Why are you looking for me here though? Seems out of both of our ways."

He smiled. It was almost like he thought I was being a moron and missing something obvious. Montgomery doesn't smile at me unless he thinks I'm the butt of some joke.

"Just following the GPS on your phone and saw you had a friend in this direction. I took a chance and guessed right." He looked around now, as if he had heard something. "Now come on. We need to go."

No way did he just "guess right". If he was here, he knew who Boots was. And he was a Vampire. He may not have Garrett's mind reading, but there are a lot of abilities in the mythology, including mind controlling a human to come outside. Could that be what happened? Could that be why Boots left without saying anything to me?

"Sure thing. I just need to check on my friend first."

"There's no time. Dominic wants you back before—"

He stopped short, his eyes narrowing as he looked at something behind me. I had already half turned when I realized I had fallen for the oldest trick in the book. I stopped my momentum of turning, whipping back around. In my mind's eye, I already saw Montgomery rushing me. To my surprise he was still standing the same distance from me. His gaze held something that was a cross between annoyance and dislike, but was directed past me, not at me.

I turned more cautiously, seeing that someone was approaching up the street toward us. I may not have recognized the designer trenchcoat, but I sure knew the long, white hair being thrown about in the wind. Wren. It may have been Erin of course, but my money was on Wren.

I'm sure my face looked similar to Montgomery's, pretty full of annoyance. This was the last thing I needed tonight. I had enough on my plate and did not need a fight with Wren to top off my evening.

It occurred to me I really didn't want my back to either of these guys right now. I didn't think Wren would physically attack me, but I wasn't taking any chances. I started backing toward the sidewalk, trying to get to a point where I could see both of them in my periphery.

"Jason," called out Wren. The way he said my name, I knew it was him and not his sister. "You need to come with me. Please."

There was caution in his voice but also fear. He was speaking like you'd talk to a person standing on the side of a bridge, or that was holding a knife at you.

"No way, pretty boy. Dominic wants him at the hotel. Jason, we need to go. Now."

"Jason, please. I'm sorry and we can talk about everything. I'll try to explain and you can rant at me all you want. But please, I really need you to come with me."

"Jason, we both have orders. Hotel. Now."

Damn. Love-hate, or hate-hate? I was tempted to turn my back and go with Montgomery just to spite this arrogant, childish punk. Wren had hurt me, had thrown me off. Hell, he'd thrown a jealous tantrum for me even being friends with Boots. But then looking at Montgomery, I was filled with a sense of self-righteous anger. I was not Dom's lapdog, to come running on command. "Screw you both," I yelled, whipping my hands out of my coat and giving them both the middle finger. "I'm going in there to check on my friend, then I'm going home."

"There's no time," growled Montgomery. "We are leaving, now."

"You keep saying that, Monty, yet we clearly aren't. Now leave me alone so I can go see my friend."

"He's not in there," said Wren from behind me.

I jumped. I'd turned my back when I ranted at Montgomery, and he'd clearly taken the opportunity to move up on me. I was no good at this. If either of these guys were here with a weapon to hurt me, they could have. I spun around to face him, but realized that was just as stupid, so I stepped back and to the side of Wren, putting them both back in front of me.

"What do you mean, he's not in there?" I said angrily at Wren.

"I'm sorry, but something has happened. Come with me and I'll explain."

"If something big has happened, maybe I should check in with Dom anyway, just in case." I started to pull out my phone.

"Garrett talked to me," Wren said quietly. "Don't go with Montgomery. You'll never make it to the hotel."

I have no idea how much Montgomery heard of that sentence, but probably all of it, considering the super hearing a lot of Vampyre seemed to have. Regardless, he burst into movement, whipping his coat open and reaching for something inside.

Then my head exploded with noise. I dropped to the ground, my ears thundering, as Montgomery jerked backward and to the side. Blood tore from his torso as he spun around. He dropped to a knee, then with a leap, he vanished in a burst of speed.

From my back I looked up to see Wren standing over me, a real-as-hell *pistol* in his hand. I thought there was smoke coming off the barrel in the cold, but it could have just been the drizzling rain. I could see Wren's mouth moving, but I couldn't make it what he was saying over the ringing in my ears. He had fired that damn gun right by my head!

Finally, he shook his head, putting the gun away inside his long coat. He reached his hand down, offering to help me up. I looked at his hand, then back up at his face. I didn't know what to make of him right now, and I didn't want to take his hand. It wasn't that I didn't trust him, although honestly, I didn't. It was more like, I didn't trust myself with him.

I scrambled away from him and pulled myself to my feet. I felt lightheaded, but my ears were quickly clearing. Natural recovery or super healing, I didn't know. I've never had a gun shot right by my ear, to know how long it should take for your hearing to return. Once I was back on my feet, Wren gave me a sad smile, dropping his offered hand.

"I was an ass. I get that. But I'll try and make it up after we save your life. Deal?"

"You're damn right you're an asshole," I said. "And what did you mean, telling Garrett that I owed you an apology?"

"Is this really the time to have this out?" Wren asked. "Lives in danger and all that?"

Was this guy for real? I sighed. Sadly, he was right, and I was just going to have to take his help and his attitude, whether I wanted to or not. Boots was too important. Besides, I could punch him through a dumpster later.

"Fine. Truce for now," I said. "But can we walk and talk?" I asked. "I feel kind of stupid standing here, when you say so much crap is happening. Now tell me what's going on."

"Garrett said he filled you in about the Jiéjiè and the other Jiangshi. One of Bai's friends was taken out about a half hour ago."

"Friend?"

"Co-conspirator. Fellow Jiangshi. And by taken out, I mean destroyed."

"How do you kill a Jiangshi?"

"For good or ill, I don't know," Wren waved me off as our walking became more of a speed walk. "The point is, Plague of Sorrows did it. But that's not all.

It's just part of him making a play against Dom."

"Oh really," I said, showing my skepticism. "And which side are you on, if you're shooting at Mr. Tsui's right hand?"

"Plague's coming at you so he can weaken Dom and bring him down. He's turned Montgomery to his side."

"How do you know that?"

"Ask Dom. He's put out a hit on Montgomery with Si-Jing-Fu."

"Damn. So, Montgomery wasn't taking me to the hotel, huh? You'd think he could've sent me a warning or something!"

Wren showed genuine surprise. "His assistant, Ms. Flanagan, was supposed to contact you."

I pulled out my phone and showed him the mystery text. "You mean this vague crap?"

He cursed under his breath, shaking his head.

"And by the way," I added, "how does all this wrap up with my friend?"

"Am I not your friend?"

God, Wren was being an insecure ass. He actually sounded hurt. We didn't have time for this.

"Grow up and answer the question. Where's Boots in all this?"

Wren sighed, obviously wanting to pout, but at least answering. "Plague took him. Earlier, before he killed Bai's friend. He used his abilities to summon him outside, away from your friends. He wanted to get you out of your house, since you had so many witnesses hanging out at your place. Good call on that, by the way. Accidental or not."

"Thanks, I guess," I answered distractedly. "But if he could mindwarp Boots into leaving the house, why didn't he just use his voodoo on me?"

"You're an Assecla," Wren answered, as if it should be obvious. "You're Vampyre. Your friend is human."

"Ugh, fine. Is Boots the only one that was taken?"

"Only a few other hostages were taken. Allies or followers of a few Vampyre with resources here in Avernus. I highly doubt they are dead yet. Even with a power play like this, Plague is going to be looking for cooperation with escape, so he's going to keep casualties light. He'll want to try not to piss off Si-Jing-Fu any more than he has to."

"So they took my friend... why? They hoped to put me on the sidelines? If so, why was Montgomery going to take me off to the 'not-hotel'?"

"I don't know," Wren answered. "It does seem like a strange bout of overkill. But I also know for a fact Dom's hit on Montgomery was because he discovered Montgomery was planning on killing you. So maybe he was just planning on taking Plague's plan one step further."

Wren grabbed my arm, pulling both of us to a stop. I thought he'd spotted something dangerous, but instead he was looking at me with a soft, concerned expression.

"Look, Jason, I'm really sorry I was such an ass."

I looked him up and down. He looked hot as always, but I was ignoring all that right now, instead trying to figure out his angle. This was definitely one of those times I wish I had my own mind reading powers.

"Save it. Get me to wherever Boots is at. When he's not being threatened with death, then I'll better believe whatever you wanna say."

CHAPTER SEVENTY-TWO

MAKEUP SMACKS

We reached the church and Wren led me in a side door. It had been a minute since I'd been in a church, other than my dad's memorial, and I'd never been in one like this. It felt old, made all of stone and heavy dark wood, with lots of cubbies and gargoyles and crap. I was used to white siding or bricks, pale wood, and bright stained glass. Southern Baptist churches, not these northern Methodist or Catholic churches, or whatever this was. Hell, this place was so creepy, between its design and nighttime lack of lighting, that it absolutely put me in the mood for the Vampyre we were about to be screwing with.

It also made me question all the old stories. Vampires in a church? Was that just a fake myth? Or were Vampires barred, but other Vampyre could enter a church with no problem? I distracted myself with all this while we made our way to the church's basement.

What about other supposed weaknesses? Could Wren go outside in the sunlight?

And while I knew I had seen that Mr. Tsui didn't have a reflection, I thought

I had caught Wren without a reflection that one time. Or had that been what I thought at the time at LGM, and it was just a bad angle with him moving away?

When we were at a dead end down in a corner of the basement, I just had to ask something. “Before we go down, what are we looking at? Who’s with us? Who’s against us?”

Wren looked back at me, and in the near darkness, I couldn’t make out his mood. Was he annoyed at my questions? Scared at the situation? Pissed I wasn’t fawning over him? Hopefully he was at least glad I wasn’t fighting him or acting pissed, myself.

“We know Plague is the real problem, and we know he’s somehow convinced Montgomery to betray Dom.” He sighed. “Other than that, we don’t know how many of the Jiangshi he has turned against Si-Jing-Fu. We think he has convinced a few other Vampyre somehow, because he appears to have a number of soldiers working for him. There are always a few Vampyre that think Si-Jing-Fu has too much power.

“As for our side? I know Bai and Garrett. I don’t even know Dom’s take on what’s happened. Hell, I don’t even know how much he even knows yet. It could be that he is incommunicado and doesn’t know anything yet, or he could have already suffered his own attack.”

“Well, he obviously knows about Montgomery,” I snapped. “So there is that.”

“Yes,” said Wren, looking away. “There is that.”

“Do you know where the hostages are? Where’s Boots?”

He wouldn’t look at me. “No.”

There was a reluctance in that word. A hesitancy. “Would you tell me if you did know?” I shot back.

“Yes,” he responded. There was something like surprise, or maybe offense, in his reply. “I’m not a monster, Jason, whatever you might think of me right now.”

“Ri-ight,” I drawled out. I was being petty and I knew it. I was hurt and pissed, and Wren was available. That made him my victim for the time being. “So what do you know then? Where are we going?”

“I know that if I hadn’t shown up, Montgomery would have killed you by now."

"He would have tried."

I guess both of us were being catty. I guess it comes naturally when my life is threatened. No idea what Wren's problem was.

"Anyway," Wren continued. "I'm taking you to Garrett. He begged me to come find you. He would have come himself, but he's with Bai, trying to save others."

"Damn. Sounds like a civil war or something."

"It might be."

He grabbed my sleeve and pulled me to the end of the walkway we were in. One side was cinder block wall, the other was pipes and machinery, at the end was a series of gym lockers stacked against the back wall.

"We have to be quiet once we're through here. Move quick, stay down low, and don't lose me. If I say run, it means I'm about to use my Vampyre speed, and you really need to try and keep up."

I think he could see the nervousness in my face, because he softened up and added, "I want to save that for immediate danger though. I want a chance to make up with you, so let's keep you unhurt."

"Got it," I shot back. I wasn't a hundred percent about us getting back together, but I'd rather have Wren as a friend than an enemy.

He opened one of the lockers and pulled down on the coat hook in the back, and a passage opened into the Warrens. Reminded me perfectly of the "pull on a book" lever in a library. After the creepy darkness of the church basement, it was nice to have some light again. Almost immediately we were in the well-lit main tunnel I remembered from our little golf cart ride to my basement. Once we started down the main tunnel, however, I was hit with a different level of paranoia. Being brightly lit and stretching on indefinitely both front and back, there was no place to hide, should we be discovered.

Wren seemed to pick up on my fear, because he reached back and took my hand in his. I felt somewhat comforted in his icy grip as he pulled me up to walk level with him."What are we going to say if someone tries to stop us?" I asked nervously.

"Just try to stay relaxed. What I say will depend on who it is. Just remember that technically I outrank a lot of people down here."

"That reminds me. Not that this is the best time to talk politics, but exactly how many people are on the Kung Fu Council?"

It's funny how someone can sound both annoyed and amused at the same time. "Si-Jing-Fu, babe. Again, it's Si-Jing-Fu. And there are seven. Always an odd number."

"Wow. And you're so young but you're on there? There must be some people who hate that."

"Not my fault, babe. Not my problem."

Chapter Seventy-Three

The Warrens

We moved off down the tunnel, doing our best to move quickly but quietly. I was kind of wondering why we weren't using our Velos, but then realized if we did, we would have no time to react if we ran into a problem. And no room, either. So far we had not run into anyone, but if we did, especially if it was in one of those mini carts, there wouldn't be a lot of room for maneuvering.

We rushed down the tunnels for several minutes before Wren stopped our running just outside an open room. I recognized it at once as the same rec area where I had been finalized as Dom's Assecla. It was surreal seeing it filled with such a relaxed atmosphere, compared to the somber mood everyone had at my change.

There were several people in here, none of whom I recognized. I quickly followed Wren's lead as he casually walked into the room. In addition to a lounging area, it also seemed to be a hub of some sort, as multiple tunnels led off in various directions from this room.

My heart was in my throat as I kept expecting any second for one of them to show surprise or raise an alarm. But they seemed more interested in chatting with one another and tracking me. I'm guessing they either knew who I was and were curious about the new Assecla in their midst, or they didn't and were curious about the new face. Either way, I tried to play it cool and not shake too much, nodding at a few of the ones staring at me, but doing my best to hide my nervousness.

Once we skirted the edge of the room, we took off down a side tunnel the open rec room offered. Minutes later, we heard a yell of alarm from up ahead, followed by the sound of boots echoing down the tunnel. Wren spun around, grabbing my arm and sprinting us back the way we had come. When we emptied back into the rec room, the half dozen Vampyre had all stood up, reacting in surprise and confusion to all the yelling, and all showing concern as we ran into their midst.

"What's going on, Wren?" called out a girl on the far side of the room.

Wren ignored her, frantically scanning the room as if looking for exits. Two of the closest Vampyre stepped forward, but Wren grabbed my hand and maneuvered us to keep one of the couches between us. Then making a decision, he led us into another tunnel. I guess at that point he decided subtlety was out, because he started running faster, quickly using Velos to pull us into superspeed.

We ran for several minutes, and I know I would have pancaked into several walls if I didn't have Wren's icy hand whipping me around random corners. Of course, that didn't help when we ran headlong into a throng of men in the middle of the corridor. A few shots ricocheted off the walls before we ended up in a heap of arms and legs, and probably a good bit of road burn as well.

Climbing to our feet, Wren shook his head and said, "I don't know if that was lucky or unhelpful. I don't recognize these men, so I don't know if we just knocked down some allies."

And indeed, looking at the four men sprawled out on the floor, they were all FBI-looking, suit-wearing soldiers. All of them were armed, and two of them even had those compact machine guns on slings under their jackets. Wren knelt down and quickly unhooked one of them, pushing something and tossing it to me. I juggled it for a moment, panicked it was going to go off in my hands. By the time I got it under control and turned around the right way, Wren was already standing back up, cradling the other one.

"Seriously?" I said, not bothering to keep the panic out of my voice. "Are we really going to start mowing people down with actual machine guns?"

"Try to relax, babe. This is just a precaution." He reached over, twisting my gun to its side, peering at it, and flipping a little switch. "Think of it as a scare tactic. It'll get someone's attention. But I just clicked the safety on, so you can point, but it won't fire."

Before I could formulate a response, Wren was already walking off in a half crouch, carrying the gun two handed, like he was stalking through the jungle in some war movie.

I followed along, trying to make sense of what I was feeling. Before, I had been nervous, anxious to find Boots and figure out what was going on. But now carrying, not some dinky little pistol, but a whole ass machine gun? All of this suddenly felt so much more real. Deadly, even.

"Where are we going?" My words were sucked up by the carpeting and the whisper of the air vents pumping heat into the room, making them sound hollow, even in the large room.

"We're trying to get to the living quarters." He gestured to the left. "This way will get us there."

"Wren, I–"

"I'm really not trying to start something here, babe. Save the bodies now, we'll worry about the heart later."

"Fine," I muttered under my breath. "You're obviously so over this."

Chapter Seventy-Four

Alliances

In no time, we came to a more sedate section, with an atmosphere I hadn't experienced down here. The lighting was more subdued, all table lamps and wall sconces, no garish overhead fluorescents. It was a large room that seemed half rec hall, half library. Pools of light centered around leather couches and overstuffed armchairs. The ceiling here was tall and dark, while the floor was a tan carpet so deep, it looked like you could roll around in it like grass.

Perhaps a dozen people, Vampyre, I'm sure, lounged around the room, singly or in pairs. Heads poked around chair backs, or swiveled on stiff necks, from all corners of the room. As Wren glanced around, seemingly taking in the scene, all of the room's occupants stood at once.

I was reminded of the first time I had seen the Vampyre teens enter the game store, how they had seemed to move in sync, like a flock of birds in flight. The way everyone stood at once, staring at us, as if following some unheard cue, I was reminded distinctly of their inhumanity. They were a mix of ages and genders, yet their clothing was identical, as was the intensity of their gazes.

I looked over at Wren, trying to get a cue as to how much trouble we were in. But he was scanning the room, almost casually. In the back, a middle-aged woman stood, and like a bird folding its wings, all the remaining Vampyre disappeared back into their chairs as one, leaving her standing alone. Creepy.

Wren started walking forward and to the side, and I followed, still keeping an eye on the people in the room. None of them spoke, and they all kept their heads down as we passed through their midst.

All except one. Or at least, one at a time. One of the strangers was staring unblinkingly at me, but never the same one. Every few seconds, a new person would look up to lock me in their gaze, and the first would lower their head. The best I could figure was it tended to be whoever had the closest view. Again, very creepy.

As Wren crossed the room, it appeared the far wall was mirrored, because his double matched his movements over on the other side. I guess I was getting my answer about Succubi having a reflection, and I must have been wrong about what I thought I had seen him in the game store that time.

Then I had a "duh" moment and realized it was Erin walking towards us. There was no mirror, just Wren's twin. It didn't really lower the creep factor though, as once the twins met, all the strangers in the room turned to look at us, leaving a dozen sets of eyes staring unblinking at us, like we were a fascinating TV program.

The twins hugged as soon as we reached one another. Wren looked around questioningly and Erin answered his unspoken question.

"Ezekiel has declared their intent to stay out of any fight," Erin said. "They are concerned that since their priest is one of the hostages, they don't want to exacerbate the risk to one of their own. But they have enthusiastically agreed to act as lookout, at least."

The standing woman nodded in acknowledgment, and both twins returned the respectful nod. As one, all the Vampyre in the room stood, and without looking at one another, walked out of various exits from the room.

"Come on, Garrett's this way." Then Erin turned, acknowledging me with a smile. "Glad to see you're still alive. Good on you."

Erin let go of Wren long enough to give me a quick, loose hug, then used the closeness of the hug to snatch the gun out of my hand. Before I could object, or even figure out whether I should, she had already turned and was threading her way through the room. I followed, trying to both keep up.

Just ahead, we were met by two teenage-looking Vampyre with guns pointed in our faces. As soon as they saw the twins, the guns were lowered and we were ushered past them down the hall. A door midway down opened, and Garrett stuck his head out.

"Oh, thank God. You made it."

"Less problems than I expected," said Wren. "Everybody seems to be watching what's going on, but not many seem to be taking sides."

Garrett ushered us through the door, closing it behind him. We were standing in a well-furnished living room with sofa and chairs, an open kitchen, small dining set, and who I was pretty sure was Bai, in all his floating-head glory. Accompanying him was another Jiangshi, another head trailing a spinal column. But the dessicated face was a woman, also ancient beyond belief, her lack of beard made up for by her long, stringy ashy grey hair. Behind them stood two Asian men of indeterminate age, their hulking shoulders hidden by matching black suits. These two screamed "bodyguards", and I couldn't help but wonder if they were humans or Vampyre.

"What do we know?" asked Wren.

He seemed to direct the question at Garrett, but I caught his eyes flicking to the two Jainshi as well. Garrett leaned forward and grabbed Wren in a hug. As he pulled back, he answered.

"We know where the hostages are being kept. They were dumb enough to take one of Ezekiel's hosts, and even though they blindfolded him, he can still hear. And of course, the remaining hive mind has been hearing all of it as well. It seems Beishang de Wenyi has pretty much committed to using hostages to get what he wants."

"Where's Dom in all this?" asked Wren.

"Holed up in his goddamned ivory tower." Garrett shook his head in frustration. "Sixty seconds of his time, and this wouldn't even be a thing. Instead, he's putting all of Avernus in danger."

"Sixty seconds?" I asked. "What do you mean? You mean this could all be avoided?"

Erin leaned her head in my direction. "If Dominic would just let the Jiangshi go like he promised, we wouldn't be in this mess. He's the one holding them here with this barrier."

I nodded over across the room while leaning back in toward Erin. "Speaking of, who's the other Jiangshi? That first one is Bai, right?"

"Yes," she whispered back while the other two continued their discussion. "The woman is Zhou Hua. She is on Si-Jing-Fu, and she was the woman who stood witness back when you became Dom's Assecla."

"Oh, cool. And since she's here, I guess she's on our side?"

"Most of the Jiangshi are, actually. They agree Dom needs to drop the Jiéjiè, but they don't like being lumped in with Plague."

"Wren said something about one of Bai's friends getting killed. Was it a Jiangshi? Or was it some other kind of Vampyre?"

A look of sadness crossed her face for a moment, before being replaced with a look of grim determination. "He was Jiangshi, yes. Cheng Wei was a good man."

"Sorry. So same question I asked your bro. How do you kill a Jiangshi? Or if we don't kill Plague, how do we stop him, or lock him up, or whatever we end up trying?"

"No better people to ask," said Erin.

I gathered my courage and stepped forward, addressing Bai and his companion. "I'm, uh, really sorry for the loss of your friend. And I know the timing of this question sucks, but since we have to deal with Plague, how do you kill a Jiangshi? Or at least stop him? Contain him? Something?"

Bai moved forward. Floated forward? The trickle of red mist coming from his spine poured out thicker momentarily, like a locomotive building up a head of steam, as he moved closer. I watched in morbid fascination as the tail of his spinal cord ran into the arm of a chair, draping up and over, unnoticed by Bai.

"The courtesy... of your sympathy... is appreciated." The hissing, water-pipe wheezing of his breath barely carried his emotional state. "A stake... made of the peach tree... will cause a form... of suspended animation. However... a strong force of will... can sometimes break through. Otherwise, fire will destroy... or sunlight... but only if you separate... the head from the tail... and destroy each... on opposite sides... of moving water. Last, the head... may be pierced... with a sword made... of melted coins."

"Well damn," I said before I could catch myself. "I don't suppose we can just throw him in jail?"

"Beishang de Wenyi has tormented... killed... and kidnapped. A prison... would not hold... one of our kind."

"Speaking of kidnapping," I said, looking between Bai and Garrett, "Erin said you know where Boots is being kept?"

Bai nodded to Garrett, who spoke. "Yeah, we got it. He and a few of his allies are holed up in the basement of a warehouse south of here."

"The Tombs?" asked Wren.

Garrett nodded. "Afraid so."

"So right in Dom's back yard, and he is doing nothing." Wren's frustration seemed to be felt by everyone else in the room.

"Dom got what he wanted," scoffed Garrett. "Now that he has Jason here, he has his protection." Running his fingers through his hair, he conceded, "There is that one other pesky problem Bai mentioned a while back. Dom swore an oath never to kill a Jiangshi."

I had to ask, although I thought I knew the answer already. "Can we do this without Mr. Tsui?"

Everyone looked around, seeming to be debating the answer in their head. Then Erin said, "We might, but people will die. We can let Si-Jing-Fu vote this away, but there's no telling what it will cost, or how long it will take."

"And she means months," interjected Garrett, "not hours."

I winced, then asked, "And if Mr. Tsui got involved?"

Erin said, "Setting aside Dominic simply dropping the barrier, he also has the power and resources to handle any opposition Plague's allies can put up."

I didn't like where this was looking. Every person in this room has had the opportunity, and probably already has made the attempt, to ask Mr. Tsui, to beg him, to do his damn job and intervene. Well, everybody except me. I didn't want to do it. I was a little bit in awe of Mr. Tsui, and a lot-bit intimidated by him. But I didn't put up with bullies very well, and watching someone have the power to deal with something and not use it, usually pissed me off just as bad. So screw it, I'd do what I always did.

"Fine," I said to the group at large. "Somebody get me to Mr. Tsui's hotel without getting killed by some hidden ally of Plague, and I'll talk to the bastard."

Chapter Seventy-Five

A Meeting of the Minds

Wren and Erin escorted me, looking impressively badass with their matching outfits, matching attitudes, and matching machine guns. Of course, if I was being honest, I also felt like we looked a little ridiculous, being a bunch of teenagers stalking down a bunch of underground tunnels with guns. Yes, I had one, too. Garrett had given me a pistol before we left. While not as heavy as the machine gun I had earlier, Xbox still doesn't prepare you for how heavy one of these things are.

We got to the elevator at the bottom of the hotel, and Erin swiped a card to open it up. When they gave the passphrase to the voice inside, we were met with Ms. Flanagan's harsh voice spouting off something in Cantonese.

"We don't have time for Dominic's games," yelled Wren into the open elevator. "We have his Assecla here to see him, and it needs to be NOW!"

There was a pause. Silence. Then in answer, the elevator door closed, and it began moving up. We didn't talk as it rose up to the third floor that had made me so curious in the first week, so long ago. The doors slid open, and sitting at her desk with the one and only, lemon-sucking Ms. Flanagan. I'm pretty sure she had been the voice on the other end of the password check in the elevator. She was flanked by four of Mr. Tsui's armed goons. All of them were carrying the same kind of machine guns the twins had. It made sense for everyone to be on high alert.

"Mr. Tsui will see you now," she said in the most sickeningly sweet voice she could manage without an actual smile to go with it. We started toward the door that led down the usual hallway, when she called out, "No, not you two. Just the Assecla."

We all stopped and looked at each other. Erin shook her head no. She clearly wasn't having me going in alone. Wren sighed in frustration, but locked eyes with me. He was putting this in my court.

"Did he say why?" I asked.

"Only that he wished to meet with his Assecla alone."

I gave a grunt of frustration, then sighed. "I gotta do this, guys. It sucks if you can't come in, but I've gotta talk to him."

There really wasn't anything else to be said. Erin looked pissed. Wren looked worried. But there were really no other options short of shooting the place up, which would be stupid, considering we were here to get help. I nodded to them, then squared my shoulders and headed toward the door alone. One of the goons coughed, and when I looked over, he nodded down at the pistol I'd honestly forgotten was in my hand. I shrugged and handed it over to Wren.

"Geez. Now can I go?" I muttered to the room in general. Wren gave a chuckle, and Erin even managed a wry smile.

Another goon inside the hallway escorted me down to the sitting room I had once been locked in the day I confronted Mr. Tsui about my father's death. And here I was, throwing my life to the wolves to confront him again. Before I was allowed in, the guy motioned for me to lean against the wall and frisked me. At least this time he didn't take my phone or anything.

Shaking my head, I opened the door and was shown that disconcerting image from that same day. There sat Mr. Tsui in one of the armchairs, but in the wall-to-wall window reflecting back the room against the darkness of night, his image was conspicuously absent.

"Come in, my Assecla. Come and join me," he said in a pleasant voice. He was so relaxed I half expected to be served refreshments.

I sat across from him, but I couldn't match his mood. "Respectfully, we need to talk about Plague and the Jiangshi. Why aren't you doing anything?"

"Good evening, Jason. How are you?" Mr. Tsui asked with a smug, mocking air. "Are you well? How is school?"

"Huh?"

"It is called manners, Mr. Docker. I'm sure you are familiar with conversation. Politeness, and all that."

"Do you really think we have time for all this?" I slammed my fists against my legs, trying to keep from shaking in frustration. "People have been kidnapped and held hostage, including my best friend! More have been killed! And you are sitting up here doing nothing?"

"You forget yourself, young Mr. Docker. You are my Assecla. I tolerate a limited amount of brashness from you because of the usefulness of your bloodline. Do not mistake me for someone who tolerates disrespect."

"Look, I'm more than just a battery, Mr. Tsui."

"I do understand that," he said. "What is the point you are attempting to make?"

"You're stuck with me." I kept my voice flat, doing my best not to vent my frustration. "What I'm trying to say is I've been getting used to this place and what we have together. But I'm a person. I've got feelings, and opinions. And you've seen how stubborn I am when people try to treat me like an idiot and keep secrets from me. I've worked with you. I've done anything you've asked. But for real, you're being stubborn and for no other reason I can see except your own pride."

"I see." Mr. Tsui paused. "Just so I understand, it is your belief that I am jeopardizing my own and others' safety... for my pride."

"Dude! Plague's attacked you at least once that I know of. He's threatened me, trying to get to you."

"Explain to me how he threatened you?"

"Are you being serious right now? You were told over and over that Plague kept showing up at my house, giving me and everyone else nightmares, and threatening me if you didn't let him go! Montgomery promised... Damn. He blocked all my messages, didn't he?"

"It would seem there is quite a lot to lay at his feet," Dom said.

"And now he's got Boots!" I yelled, firing right back up. "He's a damned serial killer version of people who feed on people! And he's obviously turned your current second in command away from you. Not to mention that four hundred years ago he got you kicked out of America so that you lost your Assecla. Do you really want to risk it happening again?"

"What would you have me do?" Mr. Tsui asked. "I can't release the Jiangshi without releasing Beishang de Wenyi. And as much as I hate him, what would you have me do? Kill him? You believe he should die?"

The question made me pause. Did I want him dead? Really, I wanted him gone. But thinking he could just disappear out of our lives was wishful thinking. Still, I had to be realistic and admit it wasn't in me.

"Send him back to China," I said. "The original ban happened because of him, right? So put him back in time out. Let him be someone else's problem."

"Interesting," Dom mused. "It is possible that plan might have merit. It would involve numerous political strings."

"But the point is, you need to act. This 'sitting on the side lines' crap is getting people hurt, even killed."

"There is a time to act, and a time to think. The skills of a long-lived Vampyre come from patience, planning, and subtlety. You have given me the power to take a much-needed step back in order to plan."

"How does patience and planning help the people who are in danger right now?"

Mr. Tsui smiled. "My dear Mr. Docker. Are you familiar with the Trolley Car Problem? A delightful scenario I learned of recently, which may fit our current situation. We have a few individuals who may or may not be in danger at the moment, but we have historical proof of the damage Beishang de Wenyi can unleash upon this new land."

"Again, China!" I yelled. "Everyone keeps saying he behaved himself back there because he was kept under control by whatever Vampyre were in charge or whatever."

He looked at me, surprised. "Behaved himself? Who told you that? Beishang de Wenyi was just as destructive there as he would be here in the Americas. He went unnoticed simply because we controlled the media, and his antics were not allowed to be known. The same would not be true here."

"And I was told that attempting some kind of imprisonment is not an option."

"That is exactly what the Jiéjiè is, Mr. Docker. It is very much a prison, as narrowly designed as I could manage."

"But you said it yourself when you were trying to convince me to tie myself to you as your Assecla, that all this could be too many years too late. You've been planning. You've been subtle. Now you need to shut this down." Dismissively I added, "Or not. The hell do I know? I'm just curious how much more insult and damage you are willing to put up with, while you are planning and being patient and everything. But what would it cost you to look at me as a partner, instead of just a tool? How much longer are you going to let the inmate run your prison and hurt everyone around you?"

"I... see."

Dom paused, as if momentarily lost in thought. I studied him, trying to figure out what he was thinking. Trying to figure out what might motivate him to act. I wanted to get angry, but that definitely wouldn't help.

"Well then!" Dom's voice rang out in apparent excitement, causing me to jump as his palms slapped down on the arms of his chair. "It seems you will not rest until I have defended my honor in your eyes!"

He stood just as suddenly as he had spoken, and I leaped to my feet to join him. As he opened the door, one of his goons was already holding out Dom's shiny black trench coat and a sheathed honest-to-God sword! Dom took the sword and strapped it across his back, then took the coat to put on over it. He popped the collar and straightened out his hair around the hood, before looking back at me.

"Come along, Assecla. Don't hold us up." For all the world as if I was the one stalling.

CHAPTER SEVENTY-SIX

THE TOMBS

We headed down the hallway and as we approached the door to the foyer, Dom turned with a bit of a mock bow, gesturing for me to go out first. I opened the door and froze in my tracks. Six of the black-suited guys were standing there flanking Wren and Erin, wearing bulletproof vests instead of suit jackets and upgraded to military assault rifles. M-16s or AR-15s or something like that. The spacious room felt a lot smaller with all the men and guns.

I didn't even have time to react before I felt Mr. Tsui's hand in the small of my back, pushing me out into the lobby.

"Looks like we had enough to gather an army after all?" I managed to get out.

Both twins seemed relieved I was back, though clearly frustrated they had been left sitting in the lobby. I tensed as Mr. Tsui's hand clamped down hard on my shoulder.

"Well, friends," said Mr. Tsui, his voice almost playful. "It seems my Assecla has declared that my honor is at stake, and that my fellow Vampyre will no longer respect me if I do not act to bring Beishang de Wenyi to an end. It seems I have no choice in the matter."

The elevator door opened and the six goons all squeezed inside. Once the door closed, Mr. Tsui squeezed my shoulder even harder, practically pressing me down with the pressure and pain. Then addressing the twins, he said, "Young Jason has declared himself to me to be my equal. By his words, my partner. Therefore, we will handle Beishang de Wenyi together."

Ms. Flanagan stepped forward, roughly thrusting a pistol into my hand in such a way that I reflexively grabbed it. Then she handed Mr. Tsui a long black tube before stepping back. He slung it over his shoulder by an attached strap, before turning and gesturing just as the elevator dinged open.

I'm sure we made quite a sight as we exited through the lobby of the Avernus Inn & Suites. Fortunately, or planned, there weren't any customers around, but Mina was at the desk with her jaw dropped, and August's creepy ass was standing at the front door, literally bowing us out.

I had quite a bit of deja vu as we walked across the parking lot, then turning and walking down the road. It was like I had come full circle, coming back to the area behind the hotel where I had been skating those first few nights when we first arrived in Avernus. Mr. Tsui walked ahead of us, his fine black coat billowing in the cold air.

"There it is," he said.

As we approached, I began to better see what he was looking at, a seemingly abandoned warehouse across an unkempt stretch of grass, separated from us by a beat-up chain link fence. It didn't look like anything more than an old-ass building to me. But this was Avernus, so I wouldn't be surprised if it was a nuclear launch facility.

"When we get inside, what do you want us to do?" asked Wren.

"Your contribution will be unnecessary."

"Then you don't need us," Wren replied.

"I need one of you two to witness what happens here, and report their observations back independently to Si-Jing-Fu. I do not necessarily need both of you." Mr. Tsui cocked his head back in our direction. "However, I would enjoy your company regardless. It is unfortunate your compatriot, Garrett, is not here as well. It would seem I will have an opening for a Vampiric lieutenant quite soon."

Neither of the twins commented, choosing to keep quiet for now. Instead, we all followed Mr. Tsui as he started walking toward a driveway entrance. There was a chain link gate, held shut with a chain and padlock. One of the goons started forward, pulling a ring of keys from his pocket, but Mr. Tsui didn't wait, instead reaching forward, grabbing the chain and lock with one hand, and ripping it apart as if it was paper.

"Shall we?" he said, casual as anything.

There was a loading bay with three roll up doors for semi-trucks, and a regular door beside them. That was what we were heading for. I had no idea what to expect, so I just followed along and tried not to show how tense I was. I expected the door to meet the same fate as the padlock, but it was unlocked. The place was pitch black inside, and four of the goons attached flashlights to the barrels of their guns. The other guy handed out tiny pen lights to me and my other friends, which I appreciated, even if they were pretty weak. I flashed back to Boots joking about us using flashlights to explore the Warrens, and I was momentarily filled with a deep sadness, which quickly morphed into a grim determination.

The massive space was half filled with defunct machinery. It felt like a graveyard for old steel monsters. Mr. Tsui led us through the building, a space that simultaneously felt claustrophobic by the massive machines, yet threateningly open due to the expansive ceiling. Soon we approached a set of wide, concrete stairs leading down into unknown darkness. There was a thick metal industrial floor cover that had been thrown back, massive enough to seal the entire staircase entrance.

Of course we had to go down. Garrett and the others had said they were in the basement of a warehouse. And looking down those stairs, which felt ominous and claustrophobic despite their width, I knew this wasn't going to be some small, simply organized, open basement. A happy, shiny basement doesn't get a nickname like "the Tombs".

Just as we prepared to descend, I was overcome by a wave of paralyzing fear. In that moment, I wanted nothing more than to be somewhere brightly lit, somewhere I could see a mile in every direction, three-hundred-sixty degrees, and yet know there weren't any doors into where I was. Nothing down there below was worth dying for, not even Boots or Wren. The best thing, the smartest thing, the *only* thing, was to run!

But that didn't make sense, and some tiny part of my brain knew it. Probably the part that was moronic enough to fight bullies, to question Mr. Tsui, and to push away someone as hot as Wren. I grabbed onto that little corner of my brain and pushed. I fought against the fear, and my little corner became a touch bigger. I used the extra room to remember the smile on Boots' face when he was relaxed in my house. Then I remembered the look of unease he wore the first night he walked me back to the hotel. The look of dread which made me see him as prey, as a target. He had to be feeling a hundred times worse right now. And I knew he was below. Just down those steps.

Frustration and anger and concern boiled out of me, exploding the cage that the fear held on my mind. Now I was pissed. Mesmir, fear, whatever this rotting bastard, Plague, wanted to throw at us, I'd fought it before and I'd fight it again. I looked around at the others as my mind was suddenly clear.

Erin and Wren were both struggling to fight off the fear, not yet running, but not aware of their surroundings. Even Dom seemed to be affected, though even as I watched, he shrugged off the effects of the fear. The difference was, he was grinning as he came back to himself. I actually felt a wave of satisfaction from him, but whether it was pride at shutting it down, or being impressed at a worthy adversary, I had no clue. Nor did I care.

While four of Dom's guys were still standing there struggling with the Mesmir, two of them were bolting in blind panic for the door. I moved to Wren and was about to shake his shoulder when he and Erin both slipped themselves free of Plague's power. Soon after, the other men with us did, as well.

"It seems your powers as my Assecla are serving you well," Mr. Tsui said with a grin.

"Maybe I just know what to do with them," I said while half ignoring him.

"Indeed," Mr. Tsui chuckled. "Shall we continue?"

Wren and Erin got the four goons back in their right headspace and moving, and we followed Mr. Tsui into the basement. When I asked, he confirmed my suspicions that these four were Vampyre, while the two who ran were human. That certainly explained things.

Now I felt microscopically better. We were surrounded by tough as nails Vampyre, and I had a feeling that was probably the hardest Plague could hit us with his Mesmir. It sucked he could hit us all at once, even Mr. Tsui, but I was glad to see that the most he could do to us Vampyre was distract us.

Wow, wait. Did I just think of myself as Vampyre? I mean, I guess technically I am? But until now, I've never thought of myself that way. Interesting.

We made it down to the bottom of the stairs where they opened up into... a small, tidy basement. What?

Chapter Seventy-Seven

Unrequited Hatred

It was a decent sized room, don't get me wrong. Maybe the size of my home basement, but not the cavernous expanse I was expecting. It was all concrete, a bare ceiling, with walls painted an industrial pale blue. There were a bunch of metal racks breaking up the space, and one wall was filled with tiny lockers, each maybe a foot square. One of the goons found some light switches and flicked with them, but nothing happened. I had a feeling the building didn't have power. Hooray for flashlights.

Mr. Tsui led the way into the room, acting for sure like he knew the place. Hell, for all I knew, Wren and Erin knew their way around down here as well. After all, they knew enough about the place to know its nickname.

Following Mr. Tsui around the corner of a particular pile of tetanus, I saw what I'd envisioned the whole time, a service tunnel leading off down into the darkness. I was immediately reminded of the Warrens, except this place was painted a darker blue-grey instead of white, and the ceiling was dotted with regularly spaced bulbs in cages, rather than fluorescent light panels. Oh yeah, and the lights here didn't work.

I wanted to take a step back and let somebody who could spit out a hundred bullets a second take point. But I think it was safe to say that Mr. Tsui expected me up here with him, so I couldn't do that. Me and my big mouth. Why did I have to be the one who talked him into moving his ass?

We stepped into the tunnel and out of nowhere, the world exploded. Thunderous roars surrounded me as gunfire erupted both from in front of me and behind, the echoes off the concrete walks blurring it into a solid wall of sound. I felt like my ears had burst, a fraction of a second before my right shoulder screamed in pain.

My ears were ringing as I collapsed to the ground, dazed and probably in shock. I put my hand up to my right shoulder and my fingers found a wet, ragged hole in my hoodie, and when I flinched at a stinging pain, my fingers came away bloody. I had just been shot!

"Get up, 'partner'," Mr. Tsui said as he grabbed me by my hoodie and lifted me to my feet. I was still trying to figure out how I could hear him so soon, when he spun me around to face him. "You're fine. It was only a standard bullet."

"Standard, my ass!" I screamed at him. "I've been shot!"

But even as I said this, I poked back at the injury in my shoulder and realized it already didn't sting as bad. Sure, it hurt like hell, but the blood was already stopping, and the skin was closing. What the hell?

Looking around, I saw that one of our goons was picking himself up off the floor, and ahead, two of their people were down. But their people were down-down, because the twins were already up ahead, standing over the bad guys and scanning for more.

I half walked and was half dragged by Mr. Tsui as we caught up with Wren and his sister. He didn't seem too fussed about his goons keeping up, so I tried not to, either.

"Babe, are you okay?" asked Wren.

"I guess it's good I'm wearing a black hoodie," I chuckled wryly, then winced as Wren poked at the wound. Looking down at the two baddies, I asked, "Are they dead?"

"No," said Erin. "Just incapacitated. The council can deal with them later, assuming we win."

"Then by all means," Mr. Tsui smirked, "Let's go win."

After another twenty minutes of twists and turns that totally lost me, we found ourselves in the basement of another building, this one well-lit and filled with boilers and other machinery. The noise was loud but not so deafening that I wished I had earplugs. It was also dirtier, instead of dusty. More "in use", I guess.

Poking around a corner, we were treated to a scene out of a bad Batman movie. One of those neon-colored ones where the Terminator plays Mr. Freeze, and the Batsuit has nipples.

A half dozen teenagers, Vampyre I'm sure, stood around nervously with various guns all pointed at us, while three support girders had people tied to them with ropes. It was almost comical. Well, except for all the guns. For real, what was their plan here, and why couldn't Bai, Garrett, and a few others have dealt with this?

Then I realized what was probably happening. Nobody was shooting, because the big bad Mr. Tsui was here. Even if a "Kung Fu" Council member like Wren had slowed them down and made them hesitate, I'm guessing that if the boss weren't here, there would be a gun fight. Instead, everyone knows that Mr. Tsui is the biggest dog around, council be damned.

"Well go on, 'partner'. Ask them where we might find Beishang de Wenyi. You took a bullet for the information. Go get it."

I looked over at him. He was being a real dick about this, and absolutely making me earn his involvement. Damnit. Fine, I guess.

I stepped forward, looking around to see if I recognized any of the people down here. I thought I recognized one of the girls from the game store, but that was it. I told myself I was looking around to gauge the threat, but I was lying to myself.

I looked over where I was avoiding, at the people tied up. I didn't see Boots, and my throat knotted up in fear. Was all this for nothing? Was he not here?

Was he dead?

But then I saw him half hidden around one of the poles. He was bound with a pair of adults. I know it didn't matter how cool I might try to play it, seeing him alive and squirming in his bonds sent a rush of adrenaline through me. I stepped forward, rushing to get to him, but before I could even take a step, Montgomery stepped out from behind the pillar, a pistol aimed at me.

"This would have been cleaner if you had just come with me in the first place, Jason."

I could see he was trying to act arrogant, but I also noticed the twitching in his stance. He was nervous, scared, regardless of how he tried to cover it with Mesmir. And those twitchy fingers made me all too aware of the dark barrel I was staring down. I may have survived a bullet to the shoulder, but if his finger slipped, the next one would probably be to the face. And who's to say he had "standard" bullets in this gun.

The gun I was holding, half forgotten, didn't mean much when everyone else had bigger guns and one was already pointed at me. The whole situation was pissing me off, so I did what I always do. Something stupid.

I held out my empty left hand while keeping my eyes locked on Montgomery. Over my shoulder I said, "Mr. Tsui, would you happen to have a blade I could borrow?"

I was praying he might have a knife, or worst case, maybe he would not be too insulted by giving me his sword for a minute. Instead, he tapped my shoulder. When I looked, he had slid the black tube off his shoulder, unzipped the end, and pulled out an entire second sword. Even in my distracted state, I recognized it as being the one hanging on the wall in his hotel office. When he placed it in my outstretched hand, I looked up at him in surprise. But with a grin I swapped him for the pistol.

"Whatever beef you have with me, Monty, I don't care. I'm here for Boots, and then I'm here for Plague. Now I'm going to go over there and cut down my friend, and then you can tell me where I can find Plague."

"Don't worry about him," snarled Montgomery. "You can deal with me."

"I'd love to say I was interested in knowing what he promised you, to make you turn on Mr. Tsui, but I'm really not. The way you act sometimes, I wouldn't be surprised if you were somehow jealous of me."

"Don't think so high of yourself," Montgomery yelled at me. "I've been at

Dominic's right hand for *decades*! You are *nothing*! Yet you come in, a complete pissant, and he gives you anything at all, no matter how rude you are..." He shook his head in disbelief. "It was like, the more disrespectful you acted, the more he gave in! Pathetic!" he spat. "And then he had the balls to give you MY seat!?"

"You really think I wanted any of this?" I asked incredulously.

"That's my damn point! Dom's over there handing you everything that should be MINE, and you don't even WANT it!?"

Now it was my turn to shake my head in disbelief. "And you somehow think this is going to get you what you want with him?"

"You'd be surprised," said Montgomery. "I've had decades to watch the most innocuous things impress him and grab his attention. Even rugrats from Alabama."

"Hope it works out for you—"

But before I could say more, Montgomery began to levitate, rising up higher than his already impressive height. I looked around, trying to figure out what was happening, and how everyone else was responding. Everyone was staring, with mixed looks of awe and fear, but nobody seemed to be making even the smallest move to intervene. Then I noticed the sword blade protruding inch by inch from his chest.

"You disappoint me, Montgomery," came Mr. Tsui's voice from the blackness behind him. Then the darkness shifted, fluttering back like the wings of a thousand bats, yet pulling back as smoothly as curtains being drawn. Mr. Tsui stepped forward, effortlessly holding his sword one handed, his former right hand man pinned and held aloft like nothing more than a skewer of meat.

"I have missed your heart by an inch, child," he said, voice laced with playfulness. It was clear he was enjoying himself. "Please do not make me regret my strike. Help me end this. Where is Beishang de Wenyi?"

Montgomery twitched as he reached up, slicing his hands deep as he tried to grasp the sword blade and lift himself off. His struggle was useless, and his mouth flapped open and closed, unable to draw breath enough to speak. I winced and stepped back in sympathetic pain, watching him destroy the flesh of his hands, grasping at the blade suspending him above the floor.

"No? A pity." mocked Mr. Tsui. "My Assecla, draw your sword and finish him."

I took a step even further back. "What? No! Why?"

"Assecla, you declared yourself my partner. My equal. Now, when it comes to honest work, you would become complacent, leaving it all in my hands?" He stepped forward, closing the gap between us and holding Montgomery aloft as if nothing more than a grotesque flag. "Very well. I shall be kind once more, and remove this responsibility from your young shoulders."

I flinched at his sudden movement, and before I could register what was happening, I was showered in hot fluids, overwhelmed by the scent of coppery blood. I stepped back as several people started screaming. As I wiped the thick fluid from my eyes, I saw Mr. Tsui holding halves of Montgomery in each hand above his head, blood and viscera pouring over himself, his face looking up to accept the offering in ecstasy as he swallowed over and over from the flood literally raining down on him.

I was stunned. I may as well have been shot again. This was the monster I was bound to? I don't think I could have asked for more proof he wasn't human if I had a century to think of ideas. From a corner behind Mr. Tsui, barely audible over the machinery around us, came a breathy, echo-y voice.

"Was that... necessary?"

Chapter Seventy-Eight

Of Mist and Blade

"My apologies for having crashed your party, Wenyi," said Mr. Tsui. His coat was slick and wet, his face a crimson mask. "You have overstepped, and it is time to collect."

Plague's voice, hollow as it was, still carried out into the vast room. "You would... break your oath?"

"Oh, bié dòu le! Heavens, no," laughed Mr. Tsui. "I could never destroy you. I vowed never to destroy one of your kind."

A wall of red mist preceded Plague as he floated out of the shadows. "You will... release us? You will release... the Jiéjiè?"

"I swear to all the Gods who no longer exist, that this night I will see you dismissed from Avernus. You will no longer stand behind the barrier which stops you from making your way to the four corners of this land."

"It is good... you have finally... come to your senses." Plague looked down at the wreckage that had been Montgomery. "It is sad... the young one... needed to be destroyed."

His voice was such a weak passage of air, that it was difficult to make out all his words, even as close as I stood. Still, I was glad to hear how agreeable he was being. It was actually surreal, like there wasn't blood and gore all over the place.

Looking at the signs of slaughter surrounding him as if he were the center of a bullseye, Mr. Tsui remarked, "There are others who may ever serve me better."

He reached up and flicked a bit of remains off his shoulder, as if that did absolutely anything about the complete mess that was his outfit.

"Now," he said to Plague. "To our business, perhaps? As this is between you and I, and our business is soon to be concluded, are the hostage theatrics truly necessary?"

Plague turned his attention to the other Vampyre around the pillars. "Release... the hostages."

But before anyone could react to Plague's order, Mr. Tsui struck out lightning-fast. I jumped, and suddenly Plague's head was on the concrete floor, pinned under his boot, while the tail of his spinal cord was held in his hand, pulled tight. The heavy red mist surrounded them both like a swirling backdrop.

"Jason, it is time for you to act," said Mr. Tsui. His voice was calm, but there was power and authority behind his words. "Draw the sword I gave you. Draw it now."

"Your word..." whined Plague, at the same time I shouted, "What the hell?"

"Jason! I understand. You didn't want to punish Montgomery, and so I took his life as was needed." He twisted to look at me. His eyes flashed a radiant orange glint. "But you heard this monster. I have vowed not to destroy a Jiangshi, upon pain of final death. Nevertheless, he has earned his destruction." He pointed at me with his sword, still wet with the innards of his former assistant. "I cannot do this. But you can do this. You will do this, Jason. My Assecla. Draw that blade. You merely need to pierce his eye."

I looked down at the scabbard I held, now feeling like it weighed a thousand pounds. Could I do it? I knew he had to be stopped, but was this really the way? And could I be the one to do it? Mr. Tsui locked me with his eyes. I felt him asserting his will, not with Mesmir, just with the sheer strength of his righteousness, and the power of a being who had lived centuries.

"It is one simple thrust, Assecla," said Dom, more softly.

I jumped when someone brushed my elbow. It was one of the twins. I searched their eyes, and they gave me a soft, encouraging smile. From the look, I knew it was Erin.

"This is going to have the backing of Si-Jing-Fu, Jason," she said. "It sucks, but Dominic is right. You have to do this."

I looked back to gauge Wren's reaction. He nodded sadly. I turned back to Mr. Tsui, carefully drawing the sword from its scabbard. Looking past him, I saw Boots, twisted around in his bindings to keep track of what was happening. His eyes were white with fear, but I could tell it wasn't me he was afraid of. I did my best to ask for his opinion without using words. One shake of his head, and I would refuse, Mr. Tsui and the whole Si-Jing-Fu be damned. Instead, he closed his eyes, took a deep breath, and nodded. I felt like my heart was breaking when I saw the look of hurt in his eyes.

I handed the scabbard behind me, and Erin took it from me. Then I took the sword in both hands, blade down. I knew I had to pierce the eye, but I was tempted to drive it through Mr. Tsui's foot to get there. Instead, I drove it downward as intended. I didn't strike hard, or fast. But I struck deliberately.

There was almost no resistance. For a brief moment, I was worried Mr. Tsui had set me up, that nothing was going to happen. Didn't Bai say it would take a sword made of melted down coins? Who keeps one of those laying around?

Suddenly, blue-white flames shot up the length of the blade, licking the metal as if a liquid. The head began flashing with cracks of pinkish red energy. Great gouts of blood red mist vented from the length of the spine, which Mr. Tsui let drop to the floor. There was a scream from our feet, but it was soft, as if an echo of an echo. Within moments, the rotten head crumbled into a creamy pink powder. The air was filled with a puff of a flowery smell, but for once no sickness with it, and I knew Beishang de Wenyi was no more.

Chapter Seventy-Nine

The Wrap Party

A week later, things had calmed down to whatever passed as normal for Avernus. All the humans held in the Tombs had been mind-wiped under a pretty harsh dose of the Mesmir, bullying their brains into forgetting what they witnessed that night. Unfortunately, this included Boots. I tried. I really did. Mr. Tsui wouldn't bend on this. Neither would Wren, though I couldn't help but wonder how much he really wanted to fight for it.

Wren gave it a whole day before showing up on my doorstep.

"Babe, where do we stand? Didn't we say after the bodies were saved, we'd figure out the hearts?"

"I've got a lot to sort out here, dude. My mind's all over the place. I need time to process and crap. Besides, I really don't know how I feel about you insisting Boots needed to be Mesmired. I don't know if that was Si-Jing-Fu, or you trying to keep me all to yourself."

"You really do have a low opinion of me right now, don't you?"

So yeah, we were kind of chilly at the moment. So much for him treating me like a casual fling. I'm pretty positive his feelings were hurt.

As for Boots, he remembers us being friendly, and he still stays over at my house more than he does at his parents'. He doesn't remember us being an item, so we are back to that "forbidden tension" we had before. I'm afraid to push too hard, too fast. I'm afraid of what memories I might open in his head. So, for now, I am trying to live with us just staying friends.

Si-Jing-Fu acted like this was business as usual. The other Jiangshi tried to get Mr. Tsui to drop the barrier, the Jiéjiè. But now that Plague was gone, it looked like they lost one of their big bargaining chips to get him to change his mind. The fact that he had originally claimed the barrier was there because of Plague didn't seem to matter.

To Hong Bai also sought me out. In his human form, no less.

"I regret how much responsibility was thrust upon you. Nevertheless, I am both thankful and proud that you were able to follow through with what Dominic was unable to accomplish."

"Well, I'm thankful you brought me into the loop. I get the feeling Mr. Tsui might have left things 'business as usual' if you hadn't."

Bai nodded at my words. "In gratitude for your assistance, I swear to you an oath that I now owe you a favor, should I find a time and place to repay this debt."

He bowed and left, leaving me feeling like I didn't understand what had just happened, but hoping I might have made a bit of an ally. Of course, that did not stop him from attempting to steal the sword I had used on Plague, before slipping away to some secret corner of Avernus emptyhanded.

It turned out Mr. Tsui had commissioned a contact to make that sword for him a century and a half ago. It had been forged from more than a hundred old silver dollars, and it had been waiting for him once he returned from China. Having an impressively high silver content and made from coins which had actually been in circulation, it was a powerful weapon against many species of Vampyre. I don't think Bai liked the idea of it staying in Mr. Tsui's hands.

As for Mr. Tsui, I had to satisfy a curiosity.

"Something's been bugging me since we first rolled into this town. What's with all the goons you keep around? And why did my dad think he was getting a job working for the Mob?"

He grinned. One of those cocky, "I know something you don't know" grins. "But my young Assecla. I am Mafia."

"Bull," I said with a laugh. "You've already said you've only been in the US for a few decades. Besides, you're not Italian!"

"My boy, the true Mafia is bigger than Hollywood imagines. You must promise me you will never enter Albany or New York City without me there with you."

Wait, Dad was right? Was he saying Dad really did work for the Mob, even if only for a few days? Wait. Did I work for the Mob? That was definitely way too much to think about.

So that was it. My first few months in Avernus, and I had two maybe-boyfriends, though fortunately they weren't currently fighting. I'd become a Vampyre savior. Plus I had a house all to myself at the age of fifteen. Things seemed to be settling down, with a few less problems. Besides, it was almost April, it was warming up, and the snow was melting off.

It was going to be spring break in a week.

SAINAN SOCIALS

@greyson_black_author

@greyson_black_author

www.sainanbooks.com

CHAPTER II

What was this madness?

Dad was right that he moved to Avernus to work for the Mob?!?

Alen was right that I was going to get mugged in New York City?!?

What was next?

Boots was going to go from boyfriend to enemy?
Wren was going to start stalking me?
I was going to get attacked by giant spiders?

April showers bring May flowers... showers of blood and terror!

Chapter II, coming soon!

Greyson Black grew up in a restrictive church, so he was never allowed his own coming out. This has led to a lifelong interest in exploring stories with teens who were allowed the privilege.

An intense love of the Gothic world led to an interest in Vampires and similar Cryptids. Now he gets to combine the two.

As one half of Sainan Books, he is able to write epic fantasy with his friend and co-author, E. Scott Clevenger, while also enjoying the luxury of exploring YA and other tales in his solo works.

www.ingramcontent.com/pod-product-compliance
Lightning Source LLC
Chambersburg PA
CBHW020543130726
48054CB00019B/40

* 9 7 8 1 9 7 2 8 3 2 0 0 4 *